CYPRUS RAGE

BOOK 3 OF THE SAUWA CATCHER SERIES

J. E. HIGGINS

MERCENARY PUBLISHING

ALSO BY J. E. HIGGINS

The Dublin Hit: Book 1 of the Sauwa Catcher Series

The Bosnian Experience: Book 2 of the Sauwa Catcher Series

The Montevideo Game

The Ilyushin cargo plane whined and jittered angrily throughout its big steel body, a constant reminder of both the aircraft's age and poor workmanship. The plane was a flying death trap by almost any assessment, a fact not lost on Sauwa Catcher as she pressed against the bulkhead, bracing herself. It didn't help that they had run smack into a series of thunderstorms over the Turkish-Iranian border, adding to the possibility of a fatal crash.

Only a few hours earlier they had landed at a remote and forgotten military base somewhere in Azerbaijan, where Sauwa and her colleague, Ivan Gorev, were met by a frizzle-haired officer Sauwa presumed was the post commandant. The introductions were brief.

A couple of large trucks rolled up to the plane's ramp. A forklift removed large wooden crates and slide them into the hull of the aircraft while a fueling tanker made its way toward the aircraft's wings to fill the aircraft with petrol.

Sauwa asked no questions as Gorev dealt with the

commandant. There was no point. She had been briefed only on what she needed to know: what she was picking up and who she was delivering it to.

Gorev, a former diplomat with the Russian foreign ministry acted as liaison. Similarly, the flight crew only knew the coordinates to their destinations and the passwords that would grant them access to a restricted military base.

Using a crowbar, Sauwa cracked open the side of one of the larger crates and then a smaller one. When she was confident the material was acceptable, and the inventory count was what she was told to expect, she made a call on her satellite phone.

Andre Valikov answered instantly in English. Sauwa gave him the code they had worked out before her departure from Turkey that let her boss know all was good, then she hung up. Gorev, who was not privy to the code, stood by nervously.

It would have been foolhardy for Valikov to allow money to physically change hands, and Andre Valikov was no fool. As usual, Sauwa's boss had made all the arrangements directly with the base leadership, part of his meticulous planning and compartmentalization. No money on site meant it couldn't be stolen in an old-fashioned double-cross. Robbing Sauwa would be pointless. And she couldn't steal it herself. A few minutes later the commandant received a call on his own sat phone confirming his payment.

The cargo loaded and the plane refueled, they were back in the air and on their way to the next destination.

Sauwa grumbled over Gorev's unsuccessful, half-hearted attempts to get a maintenance check done prior to the take-off. The commandant had little interest in them staying after

Gorev had been paid and, by the decrepit look of the base, it was doubtful that they would have been able to do much anyway.

Now, back in the air in a plane that was already in questionable condition, the cargo bounced wildly. Aside from herself and Gorev, the only other people on the flight were the two Russian pilots, whom she had just met Turkey prior to take off. Valikov had briefly explained that the pilots were formerly in the Russian air force and had flown in Afghanistan for the Soviet Union and in Chechnya. Otherwise, she and the aircrew were complete strangers.

This was a practice Valikov promoted in his organization. When the people he had working together were strangers, they were less inclined to conspire. His business had been growing rapidly and, as a result, he was hiring new people all the time to keep up with the ever-growing list of customers and their continuous appetite for weapons. The only exceptions he made to this rule were those in his most trusted inner circle—who needed full disclosure to help him run his operation—and those such as Sauwa, on whom he maintained other forms of leverage.

Sauwa didn't like working under such conditions. Carrying out dangerous operations, it was helpful to have a good relationship with the people you counted on. Moving illicit weapons over the borders of several volatile countries to deal with even more suspicious and volatile clients was not a good time to find out how different people responded in an emergency. As a professional, she would have preferred to spend time war-gaming the mission with the team involved and developing operating procedures for everyone to fall back on in the event of a disaster. Even if she were working with a questionable sort, external threats often made for strong loyalties among strangers in desperate times.

The plane continued to shake. Gorev sat across from her, extremely pale, his eyes tightly closed, shivering nervously. Apparently, such forms of air travel did not suit him. He clutched a set of bars as if they were a means of divine protection, and Sauwa wondered what drove a man obviously unaccustomed to rugged living to work in this business.

A man in his early fifties, Gorev had a large, round stomach indicating a history of too little exercise and far too much self-indulgence. He was bald except for a sprinkle of salt and pepper hair lining the edges around his skull. He wore an ill-fitting white collared shirt and tan slacks. An old green military field jacket was the only garment that did not fit tightly over his obese frame. Even from a distance, Sauwa could see the brownish sweat stains on the upper portion of his white shirt.

She had only known the plump diplomat for a short time. Though she tired of his reminiscing about his supposed illustrious diplomatic career, she found him at other times to be a kind man. He was a perfect gentleman around her, never neglecting to rise from his seat when she entered a room and provide a chair for her when she went to sit down. His command of the English language was excellent which made it easy to talk to him. His favorite topics of art and western literature were a welcome departure from the usual subjects of weapons, operations, and tactics or the tiresome topics her colleagues favored — sex, liquor, and petty side-wagers.

And he was enthralled with Africa where he had spent several years posted to various diplomatic missions. When he met her a few months ago, he instantly recognized her accent as South African. His interest piqued. he tried to strike up conversations with her when they found themselves together. Normally, she didn't mind engaging the older man's interest in the Dark Continent. She was sure that if it weren't for Gorev's current shattered nerves, they would have been deeply engaged in some topic about African tribal cultures. In this case, though, she needed to be alert and keep her wits about her and that meant resting.

Leaning back against a rubber mat she had found, she attempted to get some sleep before their next meeting, but it was difficult to relax. Throwing her field jacket over herself she tried to find a comfortable position, all attempts thwarted by wild jerks as the plane dipped and bounced in the turbulence.

The time was 1837 hours when the intercom began to squelch. She retrieved the mike from its cradle.

"What is it?" Sauwa groaned into the device.

"We've just crossed into Iraqi airspace," the heavily accented voice of the pilot replied. "We were instructed to inform you the minute we did so."

Valikov had instructed the pilots accordingly. Now in Iraq the pilots would be taking their orders from her until the job was completed. It would make things a lot easier when dealing with the next portion of the trip.

Somehow, she was having trouble forming a coherent thought. "Thanks," she finally spat out. "How far out are we to the landing zone?"

"Roughly twenty minutes."

5

Rubbing the mike gently against her forehead she looked around at the stacked piles of wooden crates filling the plane's giant hull. With a deep sigh, she spoke into the mike. "Stay airborne for now. Don't try to land until I tell you. Wait for my instructions."

"Roger, out."

Reaching inside the brown canvas bag sitting at her feet, she pulled out a satellite phone, dialed, then waited as the system connected. A few seconds later, she heard a click, followed by a man with a deep, forceful voice. "This is Red Wolf, send it," the voice instructed.

"Red Wolf, this is Ghost. We're twenty mikes out," Sauwa replied with a cold, direct voice of her own. "What's your status?"

It was a few seconds before the man replied. "We've got your contact in sight. They're at the rendezvous point and have been there for about an hour. They have a standard operation force, five small vehicles being used for tactical purposes carrying between six to eight armed personnel per vehicle and dispersed to cover the flanks of five larger trucks intended to carry the equipment. All small arms are in the vicinity of the meeting spot with some RPGs and a machine-gun mounted on two of the smaller trucks. They look to be 7.62 caliber systems. I have no movement in any of the surrounding buildings and no activity along the hillside. You're good to land. What do you want us to do?" Red Wolf spoke English with natural ease. It was evidently his primary language.

"Hold your position," Sauwa said, thinking out her next move. "Maintain security until contacts have vacated the area. We're coming in. We'll maintain contact and adjust our plan based on the situation."

"Roger, out," Red Wolf hung up.

Valikov had a diverse array of clients, some more volatile than others. Sauwa's job, as she quickly found out when she was pressed into his service, was to be his right-hand, managing deals with the more combustive clients, and there were many of them. In situations like this, meeting with a radical group whose politics tilted heavily in the Marxist direction who had numerous enemies in their own right, she found it wise to take steps putting the odds in her favor.

On her recommendation, the Red Wolf team was set up to be involved in such deals and provide advanced recce intelligence. They would stage a few days ahead of time in the location where the deal was to take place. They would recce the area to ensure nothing was afoot. When the deal was conducted, they would move to a location where they could provide the best security in the event anything went wrong. If that happened they would become a quick reaction force and, hopefully, neutralize the threat.

This was only her second job with the Red Wolf team. Aside from the contact over the sat phone, she had never actually met any of them in person. Another measure engineered by Valikov. A measure she found difficult to work around.

When it came to preparing for such operations, a routine was followed. Valikov and she went over the details of the transaction — what was being delivered, to whom, and where. After that, they planned the operation in his office. When they worked out some plausible course of action, he would brief the plan to the Red Wolf team separately. Presumably, they would have no issue with it. Sauwa was not present for that briefing nor was the Red Wolf team present for her briefing. this left open the possibility complications were discovered by the team and rectified without her. Unsettling, to say the least.

Tucking the phone into her coat pocket, Sauwa reached for the radio mike that linked her to the cockpit and the pilots again. "Go ahead and take us down," she ordered.

The mike squelched,"Copy, we're beginning our descent."

"Roger," she replied. "When we land, keep the engines running and be prepared to move quickly. We don't know how we'll be received. If you hear shooting don't wait to hear from me. Just close the ramp and takeoff."

Though the pilots were supposedly experienced military flyers with combat experience, this was their first time working for Valikov's operation. It was doubtful they had ever done a similar job. She didn't want to assume the pilots would know what to do in the event of hostilities.

"Copy that, will do," the pilot's voice held a twinge of concern, which only confirmed her suspicions.

"We'll be landing soon!" she shouted to Gorev, who was shiny with persperation. He opened his eyes and managed to turn his head in her direction. She shouted again. "We're landing!"

His face soften with a look of relief. He seemed to consider cut-throat guerrillas a safer option than the junker plane.

Though he had been in service to Valikov for several months, this was the diplomat's first excursion into the field. Normally he was in Turkey at the mansion advising Valikov on international issues. For some unexplained reason, Gorev was accompanying her on this operation. All she knew was that he was to take the lead in the transaction, and she was provide security to the best of her abilities and make sure nothing bad happened. But something bad could always happen.

Gorev gripped the seat, his knuckles white, as the plane began its descent.

2

The descent was as rocky as the rest of the flight.

Sauwa picked up her tactical webbing that was tucked behind the rubber matting. Throwing it over her shoulder, she placed the padded shoulder straps over her thin grey T-shirt, added the tactical vest, and finally clipped the web-belt snuggly around her waist. The magazine pouches, fully loaded with banana magazines, were cumbersome. She adjusted them, but between their weight and stiffness, it still proved to be an uncomfortable garment.

Running her hand across the top of the pouches she felt each snap to ensure the magazines were properly secured. She reached to the center-right pouch and unsnapped the cover. If it came down to a gunfight, she didn't want to have to fight to get her pouches open. Keeping one unsnapped ensured ready access. She had practiced grabbing from the center several times until it was muscle memory, so she wouldn't have to think about it when it was needed. She also chose a center pouch because it provided easier access in the event she was wearing a coat over her vest.

As she started to dress, she caught Gorev out of the corner of her eye. She saw him watching her intently with a blank look on his face. She presumed that seeing her get into her tactical gear made him finally realize the danger they were about to face. This sudden revelation now superseded the fear of being in the flying death trap as he relinquished his grip on the bars and sunk down into his seat. His attention was now entirely fixed on her.

She continued dressing, throwing on the green camouflage army coat she had picked up at one of the Russian army bases. She preferred to wear her tactical gear under the coat so that it would be less conspicuous and therefore invite less unwanted attention from the wrong people. Reaching down she grabbed an object wrapped in plastic sheeting. Carefully unwrapping the sheeting, she retrieved an AKSM assault rifle with a magazine taped to one side and the skeletal shoulder stock collapsed into the upper receiver. With the knife she carried in her coat pocket, she slashed the tape and removed the magazine. Depressing the locking mechanism, she extended the shoulder stock to its full out position. She proceeded to insert the magazine into the weapon's magazine weld as Gorev continued to watch her prepare for battle.

She laid the weapon over the rubber matting and went behind a pile of sandbags she had brought on board. Kneeling she unwrapped more plastic sheeting and, when finished, she was looking at a Soviet-built PKM 7.62 mm general purpose machine-gun and a box containing a belt of ammo for it. It was the Soviet variant of the M-60 machine-gun used primarily by the U.S. military. Aside from the Soviet trademark, wooden shoulder stock, and trigger grip, the two weapons were virtually identical. The weapon had gained some popularity with several of the old Soviet Bloc and client states, particularly among the Polish Naval Assault Force.

Sauwa opened the ammunition tray and fed the ammo belt into the weapon's chamber. If Gorev had been nervous by the sight her AKSM, she wondered what was going through his mind as she lifted the massive weapon against the sandbags where the muzzle protruded well above the stack. In a city such as Ismar, such a monster would have been excessive, however, in the middle of a lawless backwater in the third world, hostilities often turned into full-blown combat. It was just good sense to have a more powerful backup weapon if things took a bad turn.

The final piece of her preparation was tying her hair up into a loose pile and slipping a black knit balaclava over her head. She did not wish to be recognized by anyone, especially the clients they were about to meet. Kurdish guerrillas, even those who belonged to fringe splinter factions, tended to be well connected throughout the region. This included various intelligence services from the surrounding countries, not to mention the state of Israel who shared a deep alliance with the Kurdish world against their mutual enemy, the dominating Arabs. Besides, the mask, along with the field jacket, combat trousers, and military boots fit this part for the region and the people they were dealing with — something that would help them be taken seriously. Guerrillas tended to work better with people who looked like their own as opposed to those that were obvious aliens.

She stood up and quickly surveyed her area to see if there was anything else she could do to improve her position. She caught Gorev's shocked look as he gazed at her.

She was a completely different person than the one he had been flying with. Decked out in her black combat boots and tactical trousers, Russian field jacket, tactical webbing, and mask, she probably looked every bit like the Chechen guerrillas he had seen on the news when he was in Moscow.

THE PLANE LANDED ROUGHLY on the weathered stretch of dirt that served as a runway. The experience was especially taxing for the travelers in the back who were balanced awkwardly and trying not to fall over. Thankfully, the crates of weapons and ammo remained in place despite not being properly strapped down. The plane taxied to its final destination. Sauwa turned to face Gorev who was leaning over and breathing hard.

"Let's clarify some things. Listen carefully to everything I'm about to tell you because we don't have much time," Sauwa said. The diplomat perked up a little and focused on her as if he was a child being spoken to by his mother. "When this hatch opens, we'll be face to face with our buyers. If you've never done this before, let me tell you how this will go. These guerrillas are unpredictable. They will either play fair or if they turn out not to have the money, they may decide to try and rob us. So, don't go far from the plane. Stay on the ramp. If they want you to come down and meet them, assume something is wrong. There is absolutely no need for you to leave this plane. If I say drop, you fall to the ground and try to crawl back inside the plane or wait for my instructions, because at that point, a gunfight is about to happen. Do you understand?"

Gorev started to sweat. The reality of what was about to happen and the dangers were becoming too real for the former diplomat. The plane came to a full stop. Sauwa moved from behind the sandbags and retrieved her rifle. She didn't like the awkwardness of the long shoulder stock and would have preferred not to use it in such close quarters, but the AKSM fired 7.62 rounds and, being a woman with a smaller frame, she would have found it hard to control without the stability of it at her shoulder.

She took up a position at the far corner next to the plane's back hatch. Gorev rose slowly to his feet and began smoothing his clothes trying to look more dignified and professional. The ramp began to descend slowly. Sauwa dialed her sat phone.

Seconds later the voice of Red Wolf answered. "We have a visual on you," he said instantly.

"This is Ghost, remain on standby with your phone," Sauwa responded. "I'll have my phone in my ear, so report if you see anything."

"Copy. Will do," Red Wolf replied curtly.

"Are you ready?" Sauwa shouted to Gorev who was holding his stomach and breathing hard.

He looked up and caught her glare through the slit in her balaclava. She asked again, "Are you ready!" He nodded hesitantly as he made one last effort to straighten his clothes. The ramp lowered to the ground revealing a picture of rocky, barren terrain surrounded by jagged hills and mountains. The image seemed more like the Mojave Desert in the American Southwest than the wastelands of the Middle-East.

Outside they were confronted with exactly what Red Wolf had described — four Toyota Hiluxes parked several meters from the rear of the plane. They were loaded with armed men dressed in olive green military fatigues. Positioned in a rough semi-circle just outside of the plane, they faced outward overseeing the surrounding hills.

Sauwa thought this was a good sign. In her experience, a party intent on a double-cross usually took steps ahead of time to put the situation in their favor like placing their gunmen with more emphasis on the other party than the external perimeter ready for alien threats. Another concern would be having their people close the distance as quickly as possible to more easily take control. In this case, none of the guerrillas had moved or seemed eager to get on board the plane — this was also a good sign.

Of the four Toyotas, two of them had machine-guns mounted over the hood of the cabs. Similar to her own, they were Soviet model, general purpose machine-guns, 7.62 caliber just as she had anticipated. The weapons were poorly rigged with wires and a few poles for stabilizers. But they would be no less effective in a fight.

Looking at the guerrillas posted at the trucks, they were an assorted collection of men and women. By their behavior, they appeared to be a mixture of seasoned professionals who manned their positions properly plus some fresh novices who seemed aloof and were only half-heartedly attending to their responsibilities.

Racking back the bolt on her rifle, Sauwa chambered a round as she slid up to the door of the plane where she had a full view of everything. She tucked the shoulder stock snuggly into the pit under her arm and took a firm grasp of the hand grip and upper receiver. The muzzle of the weapon remained pointed toward the ramp of the plane ready to be brought into action at the first sign of trouble. She had set the sat phone on a bar just inches from her head where she could hear it easily and shout into it if needed.

Directly behind the pickups was a line of about ten large military hauling trucks — no doubt spoils lifted from incursions with the Iraqi army. They were in relatively good condition, which was a rarity for that part of the world. They remained about two hundred meters away. Her understanding was the whole place had been an airstrip at one point and had been used decades ago when Iraq was a British colony. Since then, it was nothing more than a ghost town and only used by people conducting business such as theirs.

Gorev started down the ramp. Still slightly shaken, he tried to maintain a professional demeanor. As he descended, he was met by a woman who appeared to be in command of the guerrilla force. She was a stunning woman in her late thirties and carried herself in a confident and commanding manner as she marched up to the plane. She had the body of a toned athlete and fit nicely into her olive fatigues. Her focus was on the Russian, but she was watching Sauwa out of the corner of her eye as she scanned the area. Clearly, she was no amateur.

Gorev met the woman and extended a hand in a respectful greeting. Remaining statuesque the woman extended her own arm. She spoke first not giving Gorev the chance to voice his usual diplomatic spiel. Surprisingly, she spoke in Russian, and it was nearly flawless. Though Sauwa could only make out a few words and phrases, she could tell the woman was educated and in command of the language. She sounded just like the Russian businessmen who constantly visited her employer. They were men who had come from the echelons of the Soviet's elite society and were the products of the old empire's finest academic institutions.

After a few minutes of dialogue, the woman made motions that suggested she wished to come aboard. To Sauwa's dismay, Gorev obliged and motioned for the guerrilla leader to come inside. The ordeal was made worse when the woman turned and waved back to her troops. At that point, two men wearing headscarves wrapped around their faces started toward her. By their movements, Sauwa could tell both men were professionals. They carried their weapons, AKM assault rifles, at the tactical ready. As they moved, they separated themselves making it difficult for Sauwa to take them both if hostilities should arise. Catching sight of the masked figure inside the plane, the man walking closest to her transitioned his rifle so that it was now pointing in her direction.

The woman came aboard and immediately turned to face Sauwa eyeing her masked figure with a glance that felt like it took an eternity. She then turned her attention back to Gorev who was waving his hand toward the stacks of crates as if she couldn't see them. She looked the crates over sliding her hand gently over the closest stack. She seemed to be carefully studying the writing. At the same time, Gorev continued to speak as if he were trying to close some unsettled deal.

The two guards stepped to the foot of the ramp. They stopped and eyed Sauwa trying to figure out who they were dealing with. She raised her rifle slightly indicating they were not to come aboard. They held their positions at both sides of the ramp. Seeing the tension, the Kurdish woman raised her hand signaling her men to remain where they were. Sauwa was not oblivious to the fact that the guerrilla leader carried a sidearm and that the flap on her holster had been unsecured to make for easy access to her own weapon. This made three different potential hostiles in three different areas who were a potential threat. The situation had already become ungovernable.

Gorev was trying to play the diplomat and be accommodating to a potential ally. His training and experience had taught him to do this. And, it was normal that clients would want to inspect the merchandise before buying it. However, the safe procedure would have been to keep the Kurds off the plane. The Kurds would point to a random crate, and it would be brought down to them for inspection outside. Now they had a Kurd on the plane, and she was too close for Sauwa to react. With the two men near the base of the ramp, the Kurds could overwhelm them easily, if that was their intentions.

The Kurd commander settled on a crate from the second stack. Obligingly, Gorev moved to bring it down. Unprepared for the weight and completely out of shape, he embarrassingly strained himself trying to move it. After the first attempt, he gave what Sauwa guessed was an apology to the Kurdish woman, who dismissed the Russian. His next move was to beckon Sauwa to come and assist him. Not wanting to leave her post or argue with him in front of the client, she ignored him and kept her attention on the two Kurds standing below.

After a few failed attempts to get her attention, Gorev made another attempt to get the crate down. This time he began a slow and laborious exercise and gradually pulled the chosen crate off the stack setting it carefully on the floor. He was aided by the guerrilla commander, who took one side of the box and helped steady it.

When Sauwa had to do these jobs herself, she used a ladder that was kept in the back of the plane. She would have also had the aid of Mikael, a former Russian paratrooper. Valikov had hired him at the same time he hired Sauwa and for the same reason. Sadly, Mikael had been killed when the last operation took a bad turn. The result was a hellacious gunfight with some anti-government Shia rebels operating in Yemen who tried to hijack the cargo. The decision was made then to employ the Red Wolf team.

Gorev was tired and sweaty after bringing down the crate. He gave the impression he was about to have a heart attack. Taking a crowbar, he slipped between the crate and the guerrilla commander and proceeded to work the top open. Seconds later he cracked the front half open revealing a row of pristine Kalashnikov rifles. The Kurd commander stayed stoic and gave Gorev no more than a slight nod as she eyed the weapons.

Pointing to another smaller box in one of the first stacks, she and Gorev went back to the rear of the plane and came close to Sauwa. The Kurd commander caught sight of the PKM resting against the bags, ready to deploy if a fight should occur. At that moment the Kurd woman showed the first hint of emotion when she looked at the weapon and turned to face Sauwa cracking a slight smile. At that moment it seemed as if the sight of the fortified position and the machine gun had brought the gun runners up in the guerrilla's respect. She certainly hadn't been impressed with the clumsy display from Gorev. The more prepared and professional manner displayed by the security agent was a different picture altogether.

Gorev slipped the chosen crate off the stack, this time with more ease. He laid it on the ground and cracked it open with the crowbar. The top came off revealing several bundles of 7.62 caliber gleaming metal ammunition. The guerrilla knelt down to have a closer look. Again, she gave only a slight nod displaying her approval. The exercise continued with two more random boxes. This was a common practice among the more experienced gun buyers. They understood the tricks of more dubious black-market merchants. One such trick was for a merchant to line the top of all their stacks with top-notch merchandise to give assurance to the buyer. The crates below contained either second-rate junk or were filled with sand or garbage. This was a ploy the Kurdish commander seemed familiar with as she chose the next two crates from the third row down in the stacks. A demand the out-of-shape diplomat loathed immensely.

Satisfied with her inspection, the guerrilla commander exited the plane in a parade-like march. Her two guards remained at their posts keeping watch on the weapons as she exited the plane. The two recognized the strategic advantage of limiting the distance and keeping close to a potential threat. They wouldn't have wanted to charge back across open ground knowing a machine-gun was inside ready to mow them down if it came to a gun battle. Sauwa recognized the strategy. It was another reminder that she was not dealing with amateurs. The woman walked back to one of the pickups. Pushing away one of the men, who was standing lazily against the door, the commander reached through the open window. She came back out holding her own satellite phone. She was soon speaking into it.

After several minutes Sauwa's phone was ringing from her coat pocket. Releasing her hand from the front grip, she reached into her pocket for her phone.

"Send it," she said.

"The customer is satisfied; the money has been paid. Go ahead with the delivery." It was the polished, accented voice of Andre Valikov.

"Roger, we'll begin the transfer," she replied."

"Good, operate at your discretion," he responded. With that, Sauwa heard a click on the other end, and he was gone. When it came to business, her employer wasted few words.

3

U nlike what was seen in movies, illicit deals were never done in a fashion where money was passed in some black suitcase at the same site where the merchandise was delivered. While the weapons transfer was being carried out at some remote site in Northern Iraq, the money transfer was taking place half a world away at a casino in Macau, China. There, Valikov sat across from the Kurdish representatives in some high-end casino waiting for confirmation that the guns had been approved. When a call was received from their side, the Kurdish reps casually walked across a large room, shook hands with the weapons merchant who was sitting leisurely at the bar. After a quick drink and some exchanged pleasantries, the Kurdish reps would allow the merchant to make his own call to his people telling them to transfer the merchandise. When that happened, the Kurds would excuse themselves from the table leaving behind a case of casino chips equaling the agreed upon payment. The chips were color-coded to indicate their value. The merchant could see the chips being bought from the casino and could keep his eyes on them the entire time. He would only need to casually count the number of chips in each stack to ensure full payment.

This practice was done to allow for protection on all sides. Casinos offered the perfect place to conduct criminal business. They were heavily guarded by top security that had loyalty to neither side. Because the casinos had to honor the chips and money circulating their floors, they had a vested interest in purging counterfeit currency and did it better than most governments. This meant the chips being used for business transactions were more reliable than actual money. It also raised fewer questions because winning large at a casino happened frequently and would be the answer given to anyone showing up at the cashier cage with a large pile of chips.

This procedure protected the parties involved with the weapons exchange. Buyers carrying bags of money to a meeting with dubious characters stood a good chance of being robbed and murdered by the sellers. Likewise, merchants went into such deals concerned they would have their goods hijacked from buyers who turned out not to have the money and never had any intention of paying. The priority was on ensuring the protection of the cargo until payment was assured.

Criminal deals were not so simple as to pass over a satchel full of money with both sides thanking each other and walking away observing some honor system. Receiving cash in such a fashion meant having to count it and study the bills at the site to ensure they weren't counterfeit. Having to take these steps in some remote location with threats all around you caused serious problems. This issue was compounded by the fact that such business was not always conducted using U.S. dollars as the currency of choice. Sometimes the payment was in the form of diamonds, gold, silver, or occasionally platinum — the preferred methods of payment for guerrillas and warlords operating in remote parts of the world.

In the illicit world, criminals and their clients tended to have limited options for accessible currency. This meant black-market business moguls had to be flexible with what they'd accept as payment. It also meant that the agents they sent to manage such transactions were forced to work with money and currency they knew nothing about or how to ensure its authenticity or how to count it.

SAUWA LOOKED AT GOREV. The diplomat had his fingers pressed to his lips in nervous anticipation. He shuddered to think what would happen if the message came back that the deal was off.

She raised her fist with her thumb extended indicating all was well. He nearly fell over, sighing in relief, but walked out onto the ramp and shouted to the woman commander in Russian. The woman raised her hand in acknowledgment. Gorev wiped the thick beads of sweat from his forehead and started moving down the ramp.

Sauwa became concerned when he stopped on the ramp placing himself in her line of fire. Despite things going well so far she remained vigilant knowing that bad things could still happen with the right spark. Dealing with guerrillas was always a shifty business, especially when it came to the Kurdish separatists. Kurds were the largest displaced ethnic group in the world. They claimed an ancestral home known as Kurdistan, but their traditional lands were in part of southeastern Turkey, northern Syria, northern Iraq, and a portion in northwestern Iran.

Unlike the displaced Palestinians who unified under the government in exile known as the Palestine Liberation Organization, the Kurds developed their separatist insurgencies independent of one another. Instead of a unified effort, each country spawned its own indigenous group aimed at liberating their particular area from the host country. This created a terribly convoluted political labyrinth. A labyrinth that was exploited by the intelligence services of the countries who used the Kurds as their own proxies against each other. Iran frequently supported the Kurds of northern Iraq against their mutual enemy, the Saddam Hussein regime in Bagdad, while the Turkish government backed Kurdish groups in Iran waging war against the regime in Tehran.

It was a likely assumption that the guerrillas they were currently dealing with were part of the Iranian resistance. This would mean that far from a financial gain, Valikov was doing this at the behest of the Turkish government. It was a way of gaining political favor from the government that was hosting him and his business.

Gorev's diplomatic instincts had him acting as if he were attending some garden party. He started moving further down the ramp for reasons lost on Sauwa. He was just a step away from exiting the ramp completely when Sauwa called out to him.

"Sir!" she shouted trying to get his attention in a way that didn't seem suspicious. Gorev turned to face her with a bewildered look on his face. "I have some documents you need to review." She hoped none of the Kurds spoke

English. But just in case she wanted to sound as if her need for him was entirely innocent.

"Paperwork? What paperwork?" the diplomat questioned as he still stood at the edge of the ramp utterly oblivious to the two Kurdish guards standing on either side of him.

Trying not to lose her temper, Sauwa tried again. "It's instructions the boss wrote down. I'm not sure I understand them. Could you look them over?"

"Can't you see we have more pressing matters?" Gorev was being more obtuse than arrogant. It was another reminder of how new he was to this business. An even greater question was why Valikov would send him on such an exchange.

"No!" she hollered back curtly surprising the diplomat. "Do your job and review these papers, so we don't have a problem." Her course manner caught his attention. He was between shock at her sudden display and irritation that this young lady would speak to him in such a manner. He was about to stand his ground and protest, however, his diplomatic instincts reminded him it was never acceptable to argue in front of a foreign host. He began marching back up to the plane.

Back inside he started over to his young cohort. "Sauwa!" he snapped as if about to discipline an unruly daughter, "this is most unprofessional..."

"Get in the back!" She interrupted as she growled through her teeth in a stern whisper. "I told you not to get off the plane. This isn't some diplomatic luncheon in the president's mansion. These guys are dangerous. This whole fucking thing is dangerous. Stay right here. There is nothing you have to say that they care about. They want their guns, and they want to leave. In cases like this, the less interaction the better. No one trusts anyone else, so don't try to make friends with people who don't give a shit."

Gorev was taken aback. She had never spoken to him in such a manner, but her words struck a powerful blow in reality. He looked at her suited up ready for a war. He looked outside at the equally clad guerrillas moving around outside. It was then that her words hit home. Defeated, he slipped past her and made his way to the back of the plane.

At that moment a voice called over the sat phone wedged on the bar. "Ghost, Ghost, do you read, over?" It was Red Wolf.

Reaching for the phone, Sauwa placed it to her ear. "This is Ghost, send it."

"We have movement. A large force. It looks like the size of a battalion moving in a column in your direction. Judging by the markings on the vehicles, they look to be Iranian military. Most likely they are the Revolutionary Guards Corps. They have several troop carriers and armor support. The force is moving toward you rapidly and should be on you in about ten mikes. What do you want us to do?"

"Shit!" she responded. "Roger! We don't have time to unload the merchandise. We're going to have to make a run for it. Concentrate your fire on our clients and prepare to give us fire support. The Kurds are gonna get hostile when we make a break for it with their property."

"Roger. If they're smart they'll make a run for it themselves," Red Wolf stated.

"Just be ready for a serious firefight," Sauwa replied as she stuffed the phone into her pocket.

Even though Iraq was firmly under the control of the Iraqi dictator, Saddam Hussein, northern Iraq had long been a no-man's land left largely to the Kurds. It was the closest thing they had to an actual Kurdistan. Because the Iraqi government was only marginally involved in the area, it had become the prime haven for almost all Kurdish separatist groups. They set up training camps, headquartered their operations, and ultimately launched attacks over the border into neighboring Turkey, Syria, and Iran. For that reason, the Iraqi government tended to ignore military actions taken by neighboring countries into the northern region of their country. As a result, artillery and aerial bombings from over the border were common. Iraq seldom intervened when Iran or Turkey briefly deployed ground forces over the border to engage Kurdish guerrillas in their camps.

Turning to Gorev, who was standing behind her, she said, "Gorev, shit's about to get bad. I need you to shout out to the Kurds that the Iranians are coming and will be here any minute."

The color drained from the diplomat's face right before her eyes. And his jaw began to waver. He seemed frozen in his tracks.

"Gorev, do it!" she growled. She took up her weapon preparing for what was inevitably about to happen. Gorev inched slowly closer to Sauwa who was near the ramp, wedged against the side of the opening. Taking a deep breath, Gorev worked up the courage to shout out to the guerrilla commander what Sauwa had told him. Over the loud roar of the plane's turbines, he could barely be heard. One of the guards, positioned at the ramp, perked up when he heard the diplomat. He, too, must have spoken Russian. He quickly turned and began shouting back to his comrades.

The Kurds turned and looked on in shock. The guerrilla commander quickly reasserted order among her troops. She waved and shouted toward one of the Toyotas which promptly started off down the road. Not inclined to take the word of shady arms traffickers, she was likely sending her own people to confirm the story. She then turned back to the two men she had posted at the ramp of the plane.

This was the moment Sauwa had anticipated. "Get to the back!" she shouted to Gorev. The Kurdish guards began their ascent onto the plane. Gorev whimpered something in Russian as he made for the rear of the plane. Her rifle already lifted to eye level, she fired a burst. The bullet tore into the upper torso of the guard who had made it onto the ramp. Instantly, his weapon dropped to the ground as he fell back. Sauwa had no time to assess anything as the other guard began firing wildly in her direction. She dropped her rifle as bullets whistled inches past her. She barely caught sight of the guerrilla as he leaped up onto the ramp using his legs and free hand while firmly maintaining his rifle at his shoulder and a finger on the trigger mechanism. He continued firing in her direction as he ascended, keeping a barrage of fire on her that kept her from being able to fire back. The tactic was known in the military world as cover by fire.

He continued firing while racing onto the ramp. This maneuver served to keep Sauwa from being able to retaliate as he made his way inside the plane. Crawling on the floor, it was pure chance when her hand fell on the barrel of her weapon. Grabbing it, she managed to slide behind a pile of sandbags.

The shooting had stopped, and she heard a metallic clicking sound — it was a magazine being ejected from a weapon. Rolling onto her back she looked up to see the Kurd guerrilla approaching rapidly. She assumed his magazine weld was empty, and he was reaching into the pocket of his tactical webbing to retrieve a spare. Seizing the opportunity, she thrust her foot hard into a couple of the top bags of her stack. Weighing fifty pounds apiece, she didn't expect the bags to launch far. As close as the gunman was, they managed to fall at his knee forcing him to jump back. Scrambling to get her rifle into her hands, she lined it up on the Kurd, hastily sighted in, and took her shots. One bullet grazed his head and another cut across the top of his shoulder. It was enough to get his attention. He lifted his head to see her aiming at him again. Tilting the rifle a little more to the right she fired another burst. This time the round tore through his skull. The lifeless corpse fell back plopping onto the floor.

Not wasting time, Sauwa jumped to her feet as she grabbed for the PKM. The bipods had been retracted to make it easier to navigate the wall of sandbags. Unlike the M-60, the PKM bipods retracted forward when not deployed for stability. She knelt down as she raised the weapon up. She looked out to see a group of guerrillas racing toward the plane. They had obviously heard the shots and were in route to support their comrades.

Racking back the bolt of the weapon, she let loose a powerful barrage of gunfire in the direction of the oncoming force. The rounds tore through the group of men as if they were tissue paper. Several of them dropped to the ground instantly — lifeless corpses. The remainder retreated back to their pickups screaming at their comrades to alert them to the machine gun. On the truck, one of the men was grabbing the gun mounted at the cab to turn it into action. Sauwa started to aim in on him. She was about to fire when the mounted gunman suddenly exploded into a splotchy, bloody mess. More guerrillas manning the other gun or driving were being hit. It didn't take long for Sauwa to figure out it was Red Wolf and his team taking sniper shots from their positions and neutralizing key elements of the Kurdish threat.

Seizing the opportunity, Sauwa launched her gunfire into the Toyotas and their occupants. By now the plane had started to move. The pilots had apparently heard the gunfire and, true to her orders, had started the plane on a course to take off. The gun battle was interrupted by a powerful blast that seemingly came from nowhere. It exploded a short distance from where the Kurd's hauling trucks were parked. It was followed by another and then another. The truck that had been dispatched to check out the report about the Iranians was speeding back at a breakneck pace with its wheels kicking up huge clouds of sand as they slid across the ground. In the back, the men where flaying their hands wildly in the direction in which they came. It was easy to read the message. And it had come too late.

Sauwa had hoped that this new development would cause the guerrillas to retreat. Instead, the woman commander had her arm extended in the direction of the plane as she barked out orders. Her cool demeanor had switched to an angry, screaming ball of fury. Her troops moved to give chase.

The Kalashnikov assault rifle was the most popular weapon of the modern guerrilla. The Toyota Hilux was perhaps their most popular mode of travel. It was cheap, simple to use, easy to maintain, and virtually indestructible. A fact she was coming to realize as the guerrillas moved to give chase in a pickup that was still operable even after she had put four bullets through the engine block.

The plane was picking up speed as it prepared to go airborne. At the same time, the Iranian tanks had moved closer and come into view. Behind them, a swarm of soldiers was laying down massive small arms fire in support as they raced into battle with the guerrillas. Sauwa continued firing in the direction of the two pickups that were in pursuit. The rough ground, loaded with berms and dips, caused her shots to be wild and sporadic instead of aimed and disciplined. She wondered how many of her shots were even getting close to their pursuers. Her hope was that the gunmen on the pickups were in a similar situation.

The plane was now at full speed only seconds from liftoff, but the ramp was just starting to close. The barrel on the PKM was glowing reddish-orange from all the rounds fired through it. It was hot enough that it started to burn into the burlap bag it rested on. It was fortunate they were in an Ilyushin aircraft. Though it was a virtual death trap in the air, on the ground, it was a perfect contraption for operating in hostile environments. Its fuel line was protected by a thick lead casing that guarded against small arms fire and incendiaries such as RPGs. Its structure was designed and constructed to land on almost any kind of rough terrain. The plane started to rise into the air, and the ramp lifted into the closed position. The feel of the plane as it rushed into the air was orgasmic as Sauwa lowered her gun and fell onto her back. Her mind rejoiced that they had survived.

Her thoughts were soon interrupted by a strange noise behind her. She rose up on her elbow and looked back to see Gorev curled into a fetal ball. He was sobbing so loudly she could hear him over the powerful growl of the plane's engines. Rising to her feet she walked over to him and knelt down. He was shaking, and the odor of urine was unmistakable.

"It's alright," she said softly placing a hand gently on his shoulder. "We're done, it's all over, and we're going home."

"I hate this!" he screamed as he began to unravel. "I miss my days in the diplomatic service! I miss the parties and the luncheons. I miss having cocktails with government ministers while discussing important international issues. I was meant to live a life circulating in important circles of the political hierarchy, accompanying state ambassadors on private jets. I was not meant to do these damnable black operations while flying around in squalid cargo planes conducting criminal business with criminal ruffians. This is the work for Spetsnaz commandos, not men of the better classes."

"It's not an easy life, Ivan." Sauwa tried to calm him even when she understood he was referring to her with his last comment.

"I'm not like you, Sauwa! I'm not some mercenary psychopath who enjoys this — the killing, the violence!" Ivan Gorev's eyes welled up with tears. He was shaking all over.

Sauwa ignored his comments as she sat down beside him and continued to offer what comfort she could. She tore off her balaclava feeling the sweat pour from her face. She rested her head against the crates behind her and continued to rub her hand over the diplomat's shoulder. "We're going home now, Ivan. Hopefully, you won't have to do this again."

4

S ergei Tarkov felt strangely out of place walking along the streets of the brightly lit Arab city of Dubai. The city was a stark contrast to the world he had come from, and he took to it as if he were a man from some ancient time arriving in a future he never thought could exist. The city gleamed at night with beautiful glowing lights outlining majestic buildings of varying designs. Electric signs painted words in neon colors advertising the path to all sorts of pleasures only allowed in a capitalistic city. Modern artistry and architecture hung all about him from glistening water fountains that dazzled in coral with manicured trees in blue lighting lining the sidewalks.

This was the capitalism he had only heard about but had never actually seen. The reality of this world was impossible for him to comprehend. He continued looking around the streets marveling at the spectacular beauty. As he walked, he wondered how he came across to those he passed — a frowning man acting like a teenage peasant seeing his first city.

Such an assessment would not have been far from the truth. He was a man who had spent his entire life in the people's state of the Soviet Union. As a child, his world had been long bread lines, planned systems designed by logistical pragmatism with no thought for comfort or personal taste. His grey concrete apartment building was an identical replica of all the other industrial buildings designed to house the country's populace.

At fourteen, he was accepted into the prestigious Nakhimov Naval School. His father, a decorated officer and war hero of the Great Patriotic War — better known as World War II — had aided the young Tarkov to achieve entry into the elite boarding schools that prepared him for a commission in the Soviet military. However, where his father had been a proud career officer in the army, Ivan Tarkov's love of the sea had caused him to take a different route. Tarkov applied for and gained entry into the Nakhimov academy in St. Petersburg for pre-commissioning training. His family was dismayed by his choice but ultimately understood. The next four years he spent immersing himself in his studies. He constantly went far beyond the requirements spending many long nights in the academy library. He devoured every book and periodical he could find covering naval operations, mathematics, geometry, science, and navigation. He became particularly interested in the role of the naval infantry and amphibious operations.

He graduated at the top of his class and since he was not a conscript, he continued his studies at the esteemed M.V. Frunze Higher Naval School. Like his previous school, he delved into his studies and excelled at his coursework. During this time, he continued his strong interest in the naval infantry. He began to hear rumors of a secret commando unit in the naval arsenal. A mysterious unit of operatives that carried out missions similar to the missions of the army's Spetsnaz. The only difference was these commandos were highly trained frogmen who could sneak into enemy territory and conduct complex raids and operations.

His interests were peaked by this ghostly, mysterious group. He spent the next few years making quiet inquiries among the more connected members of the faculty. After graduation, he was dispatched to a post at the naval base of Ocharkov in Ukraine as part of the Black Sea Fleet. After a few months on a battleship, he was asked by his superiors to attend a meeting at port headquarters. There he, along with two other men, sat in a dark room with small windows and virtually no lighting facing a man who gave them no name but clearly possessed considerable authority. After a lengthy question and answer period, he was led out of the room. A week later he was given orders to report to another place at the far end of the base. It was an area hardly anyone knew anything about other than it was well guarded and off limits to even some of the highest-ranking officials. Rarely did they see anyone go in or leave.

Sergei was subjected to a selection course along with a large group of men — mostly conscripts. The courses contained a grueling period of harsh physical tests and exercises followed by a battery of skills tests and psychological exams. Afterward, he and a small portion of the original group graduated into what he found to be the elite naval Spetsnaz.

From that point onward, Tarkov was given extensive training in all types of commando disciplines from specialized scuba training to demolitions focusing on the means of destroying anchored ships, bridges, and docks as well as carrying out on-land attacks. They learned tactics for raiding and destroying coastal installations. They also learned how to neutralize objectives, eliminate sentries, clear beaches, and execute other operations to prepare the ground for impending military advances. He trained to conduct covert reconnaissance along enemy coastlines targeting defenses and high-level installations for strategic intelligence. The training also delved into learning the art of high-level assassinations. Tarkov was surprised to find out that in the event of serious hostilities, the role of the naval Spetsnaz was to act as a behind the lines terror and saboteur force with the task of eliminating senior military figures and other key people.

His next few years were spent on an assortment of covert missions that took him to Turkey, the Soviet Union's long-time enemy, and other recce missions along the coast of the Scandinavian countries. Like most elements of the Soviet military, the Spetsnaz was largely comprised of conscripts serving their required term of service and then returning to civilian life. Tarkov, a man set on a military career since his childhood, was positive he had found his calling and decided to stay with the force.

He participated in a few brief missions in the long-running war in Afghanistan where he gained experience working with the army Spetsnaz against the Mujahidin guerrillas. However, it was in Africa where he truly gained most of his combat stripes. Angola and other African states, newly freed from their European colonial masters, had developed an infatuation with communism and had, in the previous decades, developed close ties with either China or the Soviet Union. The thought of helping oppressed people fight a war of liberation appealed to Tarkov who saw this as the prime purpose of his military duty.

Volunteering for service on the Dark Continent, he spent most of the 1980s running missions along the Angolan coast. Angola was involved in a bitter three-way civil war. They were staving off a threat from South Africa, then under the control of the racist and capitalist Apartheid regime. At the time, the South Africans were running their own covert war in the country. It was a war he romantically identified with his country's own Bolshevik revolution and eagerly took to it with great enthusiasm.

During this time, he ran several missions to assassinate key figures of the UNITA and Renamo groups. They were fiercely anti-communists and aligned with the South Africans. Carrying out an assortment of daring commando raids, he worked to hone his skills and experience. This mission allowed him to see a world beyond the borders of his homeland and fight the enemies of the people as his father and grandfather had done in their day.

When the Soviet Union collapsed almost overnight, it left Tarkov in virtual limbo. He had spent his life preparing and fighting for the crusade of the people's revolution. Now, the revolution was over, the country he had devoted himself to no longer existed. He was left coming home to a place in a state of degradation and chaos. It was a world he no longer recognized.

Tarkov tried to make a fresh start in the service of the now independent Russian government during a time when a new war was erupting and spreading through the Muslim dominated Caucasus. Seeing his new role as bringing order from anarchy, he spent the next few years running cover missions, first in the former Soviet country of Chechnya where he saw the horrors of Islamic terrorism in its worst form. Later he was tasked to carry out clandestine missions in Dagestan against foreign militants coming out of Taliban-controlled Afghanistan and seeking to establish a continued Islamic insurgency from Chechnya.

When the war ended, so did Tarkov's love for duty. He had seen the bumbling incompetence of the Russian military commanders too steeped in antiquated strategies aimed at fighting the Western powers of the North Atlantic Treaty Organization. A war that had never come and now was irrelevant in light of the greater menace threating the country. Such a mindset and the inability to accept and adapt to present circumstances had resulted in the loss of countless lives and too many military disasters that ended in humiliation and a costly defeat of the Russian army to yet another insurgent group from a tiny country.

Fed up and seeing no future he wished to be a part of, Tarkov resigned his commission and set out to find something else to do. With the whole former Soviet Union in a state of depression, he found work non-existent. His education, his skills, all his experience had been aimed toward war. The appetite for fighting and soldiering still lived within him.

Shortly after he ended his military service, he ran into an old friend from his academy days. It was rumored he was working for the Glavnoye razvedyvatel'noye upravieniye or Main Intelligence Directorate better known as the GRU. It was formerly the intelligence organization for the Soviet military and then later for just Russia. Agreeing to meet his old friend for drinks, the two found themselves in a small bar in Moscow discussing old times. When the conversation turned to employment, Tarkov admitted he was without any prospects. His friend then divulged he had a little side business as a broker of military services for private interests. Being a GRU operative provided his friend with all sorts of potential clients looking for services they could not obtain organically in their own countries. With all the experienced, out of work Soviet soldiers and intelligence operatives having nothing to look forward to at home left Russia, it became a buyer's market for professional military types. And being GRU meant that his friend had access to all sorts of classified dossiers that allowed him to research and seek out the best candidates to recruit.

Tarkov quickly figured out his previous 'chance' encounter with his old academy friend had not been chance at all. This meeting had been carefully crafted to make a recruitment pitch. Miraculously, the friend just happened to have a job that fit Tarkov's skills perfectly. Details were vague for obvious security reasons — some parties from a country in the South Pacific needed someone to run a covert operation against a certain threat.

Only a year ago, the once committed idealist to the Marxist cause would have heard enough, gulped down the last of his drink, and walked away with no more said. Now, without a job and certainly without a cause, ignoring his drink, he found himself staying to hear more. The prospect sounded interesting.

A week later he stood on the streets of Dubai admiring the sights as he made his way toward his rendezvous with his new employers. The meeting was set for 2030 hours at a small upscale bar in one of the city's finest hotels. It was 1930 hours when he arrived. Tarkov had intentionally come early. His skills in the clandestine world had taught him that a prior recce of a place could mean the difference between life and death. He was dealing with someone who wanted to play a dangerous game, and he wanted to give himself every advantage.

The bar was a cozy establishment hosting all the necessary luxuries that catered to VIP-level customers. Polished mahogany tables were neatly arranged throughout the room, and soft jazz played over a speaker to keep the mood light. All the waiters, waitresses, and bartenders were wearing crisp white collared shirts and black slacks or snug fitting skirts. Leather cushioned seats on wood framed chairs provided a nice place for someone to unwind after a day of business.

It was also the worst place to conduct this sort of business. The outside windows were large and, with the aid of the inside lighting, anyone could be watching the entire establishment and its patrons from outside. Across the street, the lights were hung high to attract attention to the different businesses. This practice left the streets and sidewalks in utter darkness or lit with murky low lights that did nothing to help Tarkov, who was inside the bar, spot anyone who might be watching him from across the street. Since the street was lined with eateries, shops, and other bars, it would be easy for someone to justify hanging around for long periods of time.

He grimaced as he thought how much he would have preferred to have this meeting in one of the hotel lounges. He could have been shielded from people outside and the lounging areas adjacent to the bar would have been easier to monitor and conduct counter-surveillance. He was concerned about the type of amateurs who would choose such an exposed location. Then it dawned on him. Maybe that was the intention all along — have him where they could watch him and assess who they were dealing with before making contact.

Operating on that theory, he walked across the street. When he got to the other side, he casually looked around at the places that gave him the best view of the bar. It wasn't long before he sighted a pudgy man smoking a cigarette and leaning against a parked car trying to look like he was reading a newspaper. Somehow the man didn't fit the location. His features were not Arab, more Asiatic. And though he pretended to read the newspaper, the man's eyes lifted every few seconds to glance at the bar — the bar where he was to meet his contact.

Tarkov spotted another man in a small eatery a few buildings away. He was sitting at a long table with several high chairs around it. Like the man leaning against the car, he was pretending to read a newspaper. Every few seconds he lifted his head to observe what was going on outside. Unlike the man at the car, this one seemed more concerned with what was going on along his side of the road. Both men shared similar ethnic features. It was a safe assumption they were working the same surveillance mission, one watching the bar and the other watching the streets for any possible threats.

They both demonstrated a decent ability as a surveillance team. Their clothes were casual and fit in nicely with the general populace frequenting the area allowing them to go relatively unnoticed. They chose their observation posts well. They both had reasonable views of their target and their own areas while not being conspicuous or unexplainable. Their only problem was they were a little too obvious in the way they conducted their scans. Any halfway decent operative would have noticed them after a short time.

The clothes the two men wore were light, short-sleeved, collared shirts and slacks. It worked for the weather but not for concealing any types of weapons or communication equipment. From this observation, Tarkov concluded neither man was armed. This was a very sensible thing to do considering the types of weapons laws many Arab states had and the paranoid attitude the local authorities had, especially regarding foreigners.

Tarkov was not sure these men were the contacts he was meeting or whether they were with the opposition. He wasn't hired yet and that made him a tourist, not a combatant. If he was dealing with a halfway decent group with some experience and streets smarts, hostiles wouldn't make a move on him until they were absolutely sure he was in their enemy's employ. Black operations to abduct or assassinate someone was never an easy endeavor for a group working in a foreign country. Resources were limited, and a police response could be too hard to handle. It would be a fool's errand to go to the trouble of such an act against someone who had turned down working for the opposition and was on their way home and would be no more trouble.

Sergei Tarkov made the decision to let the scene play out. Crossing the street he went back to the bar. Slipping in through one of the double glass doors, he stepped over to the bar. Finding a seat, he ordered a vodka from the middle-aged bartender. A small shot glass of clear liquid was soon placed before the Russian. The bottle from which it was poured was alien to him. He didn't recognize the markings; it was not likely a Russian blend. Taking a small sip, he encountered a strong fruity sensation. It was far different than the vodka made from grain or potatoes that he was used to.

He tried the libation a few more times then ordered another drink requesting a specific brand. Thankfully, he had learned passable Arabic from his time in Syria when helping to train Force 17, a unit of Palestinian guerrillas. The PLO was trying to build their own elite commando unit to rival the Israeli Seyret Matkal and Sheyetet 13. To his dismay, he discovered Russian brands were unknown in the capitalist world. After some negotiation, the bartender was able to entice the Russian customer with a Polish brand the establishment sold. Tarkov found this brand more to his liking.

At 2030 hours, a woman entered the premises right on schedule. She looked like she was in her early thirties. She carried herself as one who was used to the life of the upper class of whatever society she came from and accustomed to being in a position of authority. She wore an expensive, tailor-made, dark grey pantsuit. In the Middle-East she may have been out of place for not wearing more modest attire or a hijab. In the more cosmopolitan world of the United Arab Emirates, the style was a common sight. She moved across the room with a confident, powerful stride and took a seat at one of the tables in the corner.

What caught Tarkov's attention was less her beauty or assertive demeanor, but the fact she was not an Arab. Her physical appearance closely resembled the two men he had seen outside. She had a clear, East-Asian ethnicity. She also caught his attention because the instructions he had been given in Moscow stated he was to meet a woman, not of Arabic extraction, wearing business attire, who would signal him by taking a seat at a table, and he was to take a seat at the bar.

He remained seated and focusing on his drink while waiting to make a move. What he did do was turn in his chair so he could scan the room from end to end in a disinterested manner. He assessed the few other patrons sitting at the different tables. None of them appeared to have the slightest interest in anything but their drinks or their own company. Satisfied that there were no other interested parties, he returned his attention to the foreign woman in the corner. She presented the appearance of someone just looking for a quiet place to have a drink. However, he could not help noticing she had angled herself in such a way that she had a full view of the bar.

From a leather carrying case, she pulled out some magazines and placed them on the table. They appeared to be business periodicals written in Arabic abjad. He kept his head facing the wall while shifting his eyes in the direction of the woman. She began scrutinizing one of her magazines acting completely indifferent. He thought he had made a mistake when he caught her looking in his direction.

She was subtle, raising her magazine to justify lifting her eyes in his direction — she was looking at him though. After determining she was his contact, Tarkov proceeded as he had been instructed. Waving the bartender to him, he purchased a bottle of Dewar's Blended Scotch Whiskey. It was expensive, but luckily he had been given plenty of expense money for the journey.

The door opened and in walked a man wearing a business suit and a dark trench coat. Though small in stature, he had a burly, muscular frame and looked like the type of man who could handle himself in a fight. He made his way to the bar and took a seat at the far end. His features were rough, so he looked out of place in the suit he wore. His neatly groomed hair was filled with gel to give him a professional appearance, but he looked like he was wearing a cheap toupee. The Russian knew he was looking at another experienced soldier. Not only that, the man was of the same Asian lineage as the woman and the men across the street.

The bottle arrived with an unbroken seal. He turned it around so the label was visible to all. Following protocol, he cracked the bottle and poured some of its contents into the fresh shot glass given to him. Taking a sip of his new drink, he extended his arm and tapped the glass three times on the counter in a nonchalant way. Several minutes passed when the woman summoned a young waitress to her. The waitress departed and returned carrying a tray with a bottle containing a reddish-brown liquid and a small glass. Setting it on the woman's table, the girl gave her a respectful bow as she cracked the seal and poured some of the liquid into the glass. The girl then scurried off to attend another customer.

The woman repeated Tarkov's motions and rotated the bottle until the label was visible to him. It was an expensive Burgundy, the type of drink he was expecting. The woman sipped her drink then slid the glass gently across the table a few times while keeping her attention on her magazine. It was the signal he had been waiting for.

Grabbing both the bottle and his glass, Tarkov moved toward the woman's table. His movements were slow and casual. If he joined her or was dismissed no one at the bar would have cared. Reaching her, he placed the bottle on the table. "Might I join you?" he asked in English. It was the language he was told to use for conducting business.

The woman put down her magazine and looked up at him. She eyed the tall, lean figure before her. Even under his black leather coat and white collared shirt, she could see the muscular frame of an athlete. His thickly lined face hosted some facial growth and a crop of salt and pepper hair cut in a military fashion that added to his rugged appearance. "Please do. It looks like it would be interesting to talk to you." Her English was excellent, but she had a highly noticeable accent that told him it was not her primary language.

Sinking into the chair across from her he took a deep breath. "I hope this brings these little games to an end."

The woman pressed her index finger to her temple as she gave him a sly grin. "Please forgive us for taking these precautions. We can't afford to be wrong, nor can we be too indiscrete about what we're trying to do. Though I am surprised. I would think a man of your occupation and experience would be quite used to such meetings."

Tarkov shook his head as he leaned back in his seat. "Contrary to what you may think, commandos are not secret agents. We don't play in this sort of field. We fight on battlefields and operate as shadows. This espionage thing is not what we do or what we are necessarily trained for. And, to be honest, I don't much like it."

"As I said, surprising," the woman replied, keeping her poise.

"So, what do I call you?" Tarkov asked, noticing the burly man in the suit had moved from the bar to a neighboring table.

"You may call me Rita," she replied.

"Before we go any further, Rita, I would like to ask you about the two guys keeping an eye on us from across the street. Are they with you, or are you having problems with them?" Tarkov's look was serious and demanding of an answer.

"I'm sure I don't know what you mean." Rita gave a slightly condescending chuckle as if she were amused by the Russian's childish paranoia.

"If you don't," Tarkov started to rise to his feet, "then I guess we have nothing more to say."

"Wait, please," Rita's expression broke from arrogant amusement to a twinge of concern. "Please sit."

He lowered himself back into his chair and looked at her with an irritated expression. "I saw those two men, and they are very interested in this place. They look like they come from the same place you and your friend next to us do. So, either I'm a fool who sees what is not there and am not the man you need for your job, or they are there. If they are not with you, and you didn't notice them, you picked the perfect place for us to be observed. In that case, whatever you are doing, you are in over your head, and I have no interest in having anything to do with you."

Rita folded her hands in front of her as she took a lengthy pause. Her eyes darted to the next table and met the gaze of the burly man, who nodded back at her. Tarkov watched the action play out unsure what to make of it. Finally, lowering her hands to the table, Rita returned her attention to him. "Those men outside do work for us. We weren't sure who we were getting, and we wanted to make certain what we were getting into before we made contact. The men outside are keeping watch to make sure no one is watching us, or we are not walking into a trap. I'm sure you can appreciate these precautions."

"And the man sitting next to us?" Tarkov shifted his eyes in the direction of the burly man at the neighboring table. "He's with you. Is he in command, or are you?"

"It is too early in our relationship to disclose that much," Rita said quietly but in a firm tone.

Not wanting to press the issue further, Tarkov nodded.

"Then what is this, an interview? Are we going to discuss my history and your situation here?"

"Not quite," Rita folded her hands once more. "This is an initial meeting to feel you out. Those whom I work for are not going to expose themselves or discuss a highly sensitive matter with a stranger. Especially one whose reasons for being here are purely monetary. Consider this a discussion to see if you are the man we want for the job."

"And, if I'm not?" Tarkov shifted his eyes again to the burly man. "Then what?"

"Not what you're thinking," Rita cracked another condescending smirk. "The whole point of this meeting is so we can decide if you are the right fit. If not, we don't have to worry about you. We simply say goodbye and depart."

Tarkov shrugged. "What do you need to know?"

"You were a former communist, were you not?" Her gaze grew cold and serious.

"I may still be one. Honestly, I don't know what I am anymore." He returned her gaze with a look of indifference. He understood now that this meeting could end either way. The games being played made him less enthusiastic by the minute.

"A reasonable answer," Rita ran her teeth over her lower lip. "My concern is why a long-serving Russian officer suddenly puts himself on the market."

"I didn't wash out if that's why you are concerned." He folded his arms and maintained his look of indifference. "My reasons are like many others. My career was over, and I saw no future where I was headed."

She took another sip of her drink. As she did her eyes looked over to the burly man. "And you are now a freelancer in the private market, why?"

"I'm a soldier," Tarkov replied sharply. "It's the skills I have, and what I do. My country is in ruins, people are living on scraps, and the Russian army can't even feed its own troops. I consider this the only paying job available right now."

"The man who recommended you gave you high accolades as a skilled operator." Not wanting to arouse attention, she chose her words carefully. "Are you comfortable using your skills outside of a state military?"

"If I have to, but it depends on what I would be doing, and what resources are available." He kept his eyes fixed on her. "Until I know exactly what the mission is and review it, I would not want to give you a finite answer. No professional would."

Rita darted her eyes over to the burly man once more. She returned her focus to the Russian and tilted her head slightly. "I believe we have what we need." She slid one of her magazines over to him. "Wait until you are someplace else then read the article on page ten. You'll know by tonight if we wish to retain your services." With that, she packed the remaining magazines into her bag and rose to her feet. "It was nice meeting you." She got up and started in the direction of the door. As she passed the burly man's table, he too rose and started to follow her.

Tarkov waited until they left then snatched up the magazine. Leaving the bottles of liquor on the table he headed out of the bar. He half expected to be stopped by one of the staff anxious to inform him that he was leaving two expensive bottles behind. No one did, and the few staff tending to some demanding costumers hardly noticed him leaving.

5

The meeting had been short, vague, and not what Tarkov expected. Being honest with himself, he didn't really know what to expect. He was unfamiliar with the world of espionage. The protocols of such a culture were unknown to a man whose experience was engaging the enemy in battle or watching him from a concealed position.

Dubai was a city transitioning quickly from the ancient to the modern. The changes were moving so rapidly it was not uncommon to find an uneven social order honeycombed within the same neighborhoods. Tarkov found a small cafe a few blocks from the bar. It was wedged along one of the less trendy streets of the city.

He liked the location. There was nothing across the street that could provide decent concealment, and the windows were covered with posters or colored paper preventing anyone from seeing inside. Walking through the door Tarkov looked around. The patrons had no interest in a new face entering the premise. This was a place generally attended by regulars where everyone knew everyone intimately which made it easier to spot a possible tail. The clientele was not the upscale business types he had just left. Older local men enjoying small glasses of coffee were watching a soccer game on the television. If a man entered and didn't immediately get received as an old friend, it would alert Tarkov to be leery.

Most of the tables were empty on the right side. He took a seat at the one furthest from the window. Anyone wanting to see what he was doing would have to get close or come inside. He had a full view of the room and the doorway. He didn't expect any serious danger. Nothing he had seen so far had given him any indication he was being followed or that he might be targeted by the enemies of his potential new employer.

Besides, the city had spent a fortune overhauling their police force — providing all the equipment and training one would find in a Western European or North American city. This made the city far above the third rate forces commonly found in the third world. It was a factor that would likely deter any enemy from attempting a violent act.

No sooner had he sat down at a chair against the wall, when an elderly woman in a traditional Muslim dress approached him. "Might I offer you some coffee, sir?" The Russian was guessing at what she said. Her language was crude, riddled with a drawl, and she used certain slang words that suggested she was a Bedouin who had come from the country to the city.

"Yes please, ma'am," Tarkov replied politely. The woman smiled and bowed slightly as she turned and quietly walked away. Taking a casual look around to ensure there were no prying eyes, he opened the magazine. Turning to page 10 as Rita directed, he found writing scribbled in black ink over one of the clearer pages. The writing was in English which he figured was another test. The message directed him to be at the pay phone center at the Dubai bus terminal at 0030 hours and wait for one of the phones to ring.

Flipping the magazine closed just in time for the old woman to return with his coffee, Tarkov leaned back in his chair thinking how theatrical this seemed. These people had seen too many spy movies or read too many spy novels and wanted to make the process as intriguing as possible. The woman smiled as she lowered a small glass containing a milky brown liquid onto the table in front of him. She acted particularly proud of the drink she was serving him — as if it were her own special recipe. She eagerly accepted the few small bills he handed her. The foreigner was not interested in either the menu or watching the game. She asked no further questions and left to tend to other customers who were working up an appetite from all the excitement fostered by the game.

Tarkov stared at the clock posted high on the wall. It read 2116 hours. Finishing his coffee, he rose and left taking the magazine with him. On the main street, he found a nearby establishment with a lavatory. Ripping the page with the instructions from the magazine into pieces, he sprinkled them into a vacant toilet then promptly flushed it. He left the establishment and hailed a cab. Thankfully, there were several cabs on the street that night eager to find new fares.

THE BUS TERMINAL WAS A NEW, modern structure with tile flooring and a concrete walkway. It took him some time to find the phone center in the maze-like structure — it was

2345 hours. He had expected the ride to take a considerable amount of time navigating the congested roadways. He arrived early and occupied himself by walking around. He frequently checked to see if anyone was trying to keep tabs on him, but he wasn't that concerned at this point. It would have been tough to trace him after everything he had done this evening.

At 0022 hours, aside from a few individuals, the call center at the bus station was a virtual graveyard. It would have been easier for him to make contact at a busier time. However, the phone chosen might have been occupied by someone else. Perhaps that was why they chose the hour they did. At precisely 0030hours, the phone at station nine began to ring. Walking over he picked up the phone.

"Yes?" was all he said.

"Mr. Tarkov?" He recognized the voice at once.

"Rita?" He responded with calm confidence.

"We've decided to retain your services," Rita responded. "Please take a cab to the Kasha Inn and go to room 31."

He heard a click on the other end signaling the conversation was over. Hailing another cab, he rode to the far end of town. The Kasha Inn was a modest, upscale establishment. It wasn't the type of place VIPs and dignitaries would necessarily choose, however for newlyweds or people just enjoying a quiet vacation, it was perfect. It was wedged between clusters of high, full-grown palm trees and thick shrubbery. While it was unsuitable for someone to move through undetected, it was perfect for deterring any outside surveillance. The closest buildings were placed at angles making it difficult for anyone to see in.

Stepping inside, he walked past the counter, which was manned by a nerdy, skeletal teenager who was more interested in the gorgeous young foreign women hanging out in the lounge than him. Avoiding the elevator, Tarkov opted to take the stairs. He didn't like the thought of being trapped in a confined box with people he didn't know.

Arriving on the third floor he walked into the hallway and was instantly noticed by two men standing at the far end of the hallway. They were the same two men he had seen watching the bar. They were wearing suits with jackets that were far larger than their frames. The Spetsnaz commando assumed that this time they were armed. They must have thought he would arrive using the elevator and were standing next to the elevator doors.

Entering the hallway from the stairs, the two men spotted him immediately. Keeping his hands raised Tarkov opened his jacket to reveal he was not carrying any weapons. The two men didn't move nor did they make the slightest gesture responding to his courtesy. He saw one of the men speak into a small walkie-talkie as he walked to room 31 and knocked on the door. The door flew open after his second knock revealing a tall, slender man with a pencil mustache, neatly groomed hair, and finely tailored suit.

"Please comrade come in. We've been expecting you," the man greeted him with a grin that was more sinister than pleasant and stepped aside to allow the Russian to enter.

Tarkov watched the man's hands ensuring they remained away from his jacket. If they hadn't, it would have meant one deadly beating. He entered a room that had been organized for a meeting. There was a group of about a half-dozen people sitting in chairs that had been arranged in a semicircle. It looked like the introduction to some weird cult initiation. Rita was seated at the far left next to the burly man he had seen earlier. The other four men were unknown to him.

Judging by their expensive looking, grey suits they were men of both means and position.

Tarkov heard the door shut behind him. He turned slightly to keep the tall man in his sight. "Please don't stand behind me," he told the man in a low and cold, serious voice. The slender man's smile turned to an awkward, nervous look as he eyed the Russian. With a shrug, the tall man slid past him and moved over to the others.

With everyone where he could see them, Tarkov entered the room slowly. "Well, you have me here," he said in English. "Now, what is this about?" His eyes carefully scanned everyone seated in the semi-circle as he tried to determine the rank structure.

"Mr. Tarkov," Rita began. While she was the one talking, it was evident that she was not the one in charge. "We represent the Filipino government in an informal way. Currently, our president is working to make great changes in our country. Changes that are meant to help liberalize the means by which more of our society can partake in the wealth in our country. A few very powerful families control the majority of the arable land leaving the rest of the population in abject poverty. There are those in power who do not wish to see these reforms come to fruition.

We have been fighting a serious political battle at home against these powerful forces, which we will refer to as the *System*. It has come to our attention that there is a plan to bring down the government by means of an insurrection. We have ascertained from our intelligence that they plan to arm several Islamic and communist rebel groups with supplies and weapons in the hopes of igniting an uprising that will be beyond the control of local authorities. Through this burst of violence, the government will be destabilized. To counter this action, the military will step in to assume control of the country. If the violence is widespread, the military will be forced to call upon the help of these powerful interests who control their own well equipped, private armies to augment the military forces. This will give the System the position they need to end the reforms entirely."

Tarkov pursed his lips as he shook his head. "If you are looking at me to be your savior in combating these guerrillas and subverting this inevitable coup, then I'm sorry. This would be far beyond my abilities as a commando. Besides, if you have all this information, why not expose this System publicly and have them arrested? That would be my advice."

"I'm afraid the political situation in our country is too sensitive and volatile to make that an option," the burly man suddenly responded. His accent was rough but clear. "The information we have is too limited to actually act upon through legal means and, even if we could, it could have a negative backlash."

"This still doesn't explain what you think I can do for you," Tarkov said. "I mean I would like to be employed. I make no secret of the fact that I currently am in need of a job, but I still don't wish to be hired based on a false pretense or lead you into something I know I wouldn't be able to handle."

"I thank you for that," the burly man answered, "but what we need you for is something else."

"Forgive me," Tarkov interrupted. "As you seem to be the man who I believe I owe for this meeting, what exactly do I call you?"

"Oh, before we go any further Mr. Tarkov," Rita spoke up, "I wish to introduce you to Colonial Carzona."

"That's not his real name, is it? Just as I'm sure Rita isn't your real name." the Russian stated.

"No, it is not," Carzona retook the conversation. "I am advising this panel on military matters. That is all you need to know."

"I agree," Tarkov replied. "Again, I apologize."

Carzona waved politely assuring he was not offended. "You see, what we have learned is that members of the System have been reaching outside of the South Pacific region in search of an arms trafficker who can fill their sizable demand. They are looking for a Muslim broker who can be the middle-man for dealing with the Islamic rebels. Apparently, they have made inroads in this endeavor through a party in Cyprus. The plan is to organize this operation outside the region where our intelligence assets have the means to monitor this, and our military has the means to conduct necessary actions to neutralize the threat. Through this contact, the insurgents, both communist and Islamic, will think they have a sympathetic benefactor aiding their cause. No one will ever be able to prove that this whole thing was being orchestrated and directed by the very group that these insurgents are fighting."

"We are a small, poor country with limited resources to operate globally," Rita added. "We're not the United States or Russia. We don't have the political clout to survive any scandal if our people were discovered and caught operating an illegal military operation on a foreign shore — especially when that country is in Europe. Which brings us to you," she turned and looked back at Carzona who resumed talking.

"We need an independent operator who can plan and direct a mission to neutralize this problem while it is still being organized in Cyprus. So long as the weapons don't make it to our country, the System will not be able to set off this chaotic insurgency, then we will be alright."

"You are asking a great deal." Tarkov scanned the people sitting before him. "You are asking me to go to a foreign land and conduct what exactly — a black operation, an assassination, an all-out terrorist act? And, you are not asking this to be done in some remote location where the interference from police is minute. No, you are asking this to be done in a European country. A country where the security forces have far better training and resources. In my opinion, you'd be better off applying whatever political pressure you can on the Cyprus government. It would stand you in better stead than what you're proposing."

"The risks you speak of have been discussed in previous meetings," Carzona explained. "The conclusion, after a great deal of deliberation, was that the mission we are employing you to undertake is necessary and worth the risk."

"Cyprus is known to play host to the black market," Rita was speaking again. "It is also known to have a somewhat volatile political situation. Even if we did apply pressure, there is no guarantee it would do much, if anything. And, it would all be pointless if a heavy influx of weapons should arrive in the country."

Tarkov took several deep breaths as he digested what was being told to him. He pondered the situation as he chose his next words carefully. The panel remained silent allowing him to think. Finally, he spoke. "If I do this, I imagine that I will be working with someone from your organization. I don't assume that you will simply trust me to run free half a world away on your tab."

"You are correct," Rita answered. "Though you will be in

command, all decisions regarding money will go through Colonel Carzona. He will accompany you and have oversight of all funds."

The Russian studied the burly figure. He had evaluated him once already as a man who was no stranger to combat. But not all soldiers are suited to all forms of war. Carzona looked the part of a man who had seen action. It was more than likely his conflicts had been entirely in the jungles of the tropics not the big cities of Europe. "I assume you're an experienced hand in military matters."

"I've fired some shots in my life," Carzona replied dismissively.

"I imagine you've fired more than a few shots in anger in your time Colonel. I just want to make sure who I'm reporting to knows what we're up against." Tarkov stared the burly man straight in the eye to get his point across. "The odds are we'll be operating in large cities and urban environments not in the countryside. As I've stated, we'll be operating in a sophisticated country, not a war zone. I can handle oversight, but only if that oversight understands what they're doing."

"I can assure you that the Col..." Rita had started to answer but was cut off immediately by Carzona.

"Your concern is well taken. I, too, have witnessed 'military professionals' who arrogantly overestimate their abilities and assume too much on their previous experiences. I have seen the dangers that it brings. I also understand that my experience in this type of situation is limited which is why you are here, and I'm not leading. However, much like you, I have fought in silent wars and know the complications that go with conducting secret wars."

Tarkov liked the answer. "Well then, I guess I will assume

the risk. However, we are going to need some people. We're going to have to assemble a team."

"We can work through your broker," Rita began to offer.

"No," Tarkov said curtly. "The elaborate interview and testing you put me through tonight are for you to make your own assessment of my abilities. You clearly had your doubts about him — as do I. If we go to him, he will more than likely be interested in hastily filling the order rather than carefully assessing the recruits. The market is awash with Russian soldiers right now. Due to the state of affairs back home, we come a lot cheaper than our western counterparts. That is why you're hiring me and not the more notable American Navy Seal or British Special Air Service soldier whose exploits and abilities have been more extensively publicized. The problem is the average Russian soldier who can be hired is most likely going to be a conscript. Army Spetsnaz is recruited straight from the ranks of fresh conscripts. Their only military experience is with the units. They serve a two-year commitment just like any other conscript. This means that most are hastily trained so they can be of some use before their commitment is up. That also means that though they boast impressive credentials as Special Forces soldiers, their training and experience is not as good. It is the same with the naval Spetsnaz. Most of our people serve a three-year commitment and, though they receive far more in-depth training than most, they have little actual experience. The few who stay and make a career of the army receive more thorough training and experience, but they are hard to sort out from the short-termers. And, all of them will try to sell themselves as seasoned experts."

The panel grimaced. The briefing they had just received was not taken well. Carzona pressed his finger to his lips as he maintained his focus on the Russian. "So, what would you recommend, if your broker is not an option?"

Tarkov sighed as he began to pace across the room. "At least to start with, we need people who know this kind of war. They have experience not only conducting clandestine missions in European cities but in working outside of the support and protection of government service. This is the lynchpin of the operation. There are operators who have worked for some of the best, most sophisticated intelligence agencies in the world and know the dark world of black operations but have never worked outside of the support network of their respected agency. We need to be careful about recruiting these people, too. What we have to do is to go through the world of illicit trade to recruit the next members of the force. I happen to have an old friend who works out of the Middle-East as an arms trafficker. He's headquartered in Turkey. He could be a good source to aid us."

"How do you know you can trust him?" Rita asked softly.

"I don't," the Russian replied. "Since he's not in the business of brokering mercenaries, and he has no personal interest in it, it should make his advice objective."

6

Sauwa savored the warm water of the shower that ran over her aching body. She had just completed her morning workout, a rough formula of weights and cardio, and wanted nothing more than to enjoy the downtime. Her adventurous return trip had been very physical. With no new jobs lined up, she was looking forward to a few months of relaxation.

Shutting off the water, she stepped through the sliding glass door, her feet touching the soft rug she had placed over the tile floor. She dried herself off. Dressed in a pair of tan cargo pants and a grey T-shirt, she made her way to her room.

Valikov maintained his palatial mansion in the upscale Cesme area of the city of Izmir, one of Turkey's largest cities. He assigned her to one of his several guest rooms. He did this to control her whereabouts. She didn't mind too much. After all, it was a nice room with a comfortable bed and nice furniture. It was a pleasant improvement over her previous living accommodations.

Padding across the plush, red Oriental rug, she made her way to the window. It had become part of her ritual to take time to view the fabulous gardens and stately homes surrounding Valikov's mansion. It wasn't just the view that guided this practice, it was her discipline. Conducting regular, informal security checks looking for anything out of the ordinary or any signs that someone was watching the house was part of her job. Valikov had not chosen her room for its comfort and confinement. It was so his skilled operative could serve as part of his security system. Satisfied that all looked well, she went to a nearby chair where she slipped on outdoor clothes, a pair of socks, and black military boots. Then she headed out the door.

In the hallway, high-grade, hidden cameras were placed at both ends. She couldn't believe it had taken her two days after moving in to notice them. She was told that they were there to protect against intruders. Judging by where they were positioned, she believed they were there as another means by which her employer could keep an eye on her. She walked down the hall then headed down a flight of stairs.

Rounding a corner she proceeded down a short hallway and stepped outside. Walking past the long swimming pool, she passed a grey building housing a gymnasium containing all sorts of modern exercise equipment. Valikov, being a former special operations man himself, respected the need to maintain physical fitness. Moving past the gym, she entered the garden. It was a majestic Eden with an extensive array of rose bushes neatly arranged and guarded on either side by tall shrubs, providing for moments of tranquility.

Her primary function was serving as Valikov's right hand managing his arms shipments. However, when back at the house, she acted as his security chief. It was here she started her rounds. Making daily random patrols around the estate daily helped ensure no one was attempting to breach it. The garden, though beautiful, was a great place for someone to enter the grounds if they intended to raid the house. Any professional team, knowing who they were going after, would notice this in their first recce to gain intelligence. Her concern, when going through the garden in daylight, was less about encountering an assailant than finding signs that someone had been traipsing around.

Walking along the narrow concrete pathway, she acted as if she were just out for a walk enjoying the plants. She didn't want to give the neighbors any reason to be suspicious about who was living next door. It was a good way to have people take an unneeded interest in what went on at the house. She proceeded to look for broken limbs or footprints in the dirt that was different from the treads she identified as those belonging to the gardening staff. She inspected the foliage for unexplainable breaks that suggested someone had tried to hide in the bushes. Though not the best tactic to sneak into the yard of a target simply to observe, it was not out of the question with less trained and inexperienced operatives.

Nothing caught her attention as she completed her rounds. However, a few times she had noticed several telltale signs suggesting intruders had slipped into the garden in the past to observe the owner and his dealings.

After the garden, she checked the remainder of the yard and found nothing to spark her concern. Completing her stroll, she went back into the house retrieving her brown leather jacket and some fighting knives that she tucked in the front and back of her belt — the jacket hiding any bulges the knives might create. Checking herself in the large, full-sized mirror, there was no indication of any weapons, her boots did not look too tactical, and there were no signs of protruding laces.

A young athletic man in his mid-twenties emerged from the kitchen and walked up to Sauwa. Wearing a devilish smile he spoke, "Ah, women can never pass up a mirror. They are always admiring or judging themselves."

Mustafa, the only name she knew him by, had been a member of the Turkish Jandarma, the militarized police force responsible for protecting and enforcing the law in Turkey's rural countryside and smaller towns. She was never clear why he left there. He never spoke about it nor did their employer, but he was hired to assist in providing physical security for the house during times Sauwa was away on business. He was a good asset — he spoke fluent English, had strong tactical skills and a good working knowledge of police operations and Turkish law. All of which came in handy when operating inside the country.

"Are you ready for our little walk?" She asked, ignoring his previous comment.

"Always. You're great arm candy," he replied jokingly. "It helps make the ladies around here jealous."

"Glad I can be of service." She adjusted her front knife a bit and checked it in the mirror.

Satisfied that she was inconspicuously prepared for a fight, she stepped out the front door and began her walk. Mustafa followed on her heels. As with her security checks around the yard and house, she made it a practice of taking an occasional walk a couple of times a week just to recce the immediate neighborhood. She would stroll about leisurely, waving to all the neighbors. Typically, Mustafa would accompany her on these patrols to act as interpreter and provide backup should they have any trouble. Since his expertise was more physical security, he found walking with a trained espionage operative quite informative. Sauwa spent time as she educated him on the arts of surveillance and counter-surveillance. She also taught him the finer points of carrying out abductions and assassinations.

Their walk began in an arbitrary fashion. They were as unpredictable about which routes they took as when they chose to conduct a recce. Routines bred a familiarity that an observant enemy could use to plan an operation, better conceal themselves, or deceive the security team. It was something Sauwa had learned when she was planning missions against her own targets.

Like Sauwa, Mustafa was dressed in a loose-fitting jacket that hid the weapons he was carrying. Neither one carried a firearm. For a country like Turkey, that had a long history of political violence and military coups, firearms were discouraged by the police. Getting caught with one would have serious consequences or lead to a lot of unwanted attention. In a neighborhood where they were both well known to the locals meant that witnesses would be able to lead the police right to their door.

Besides, it had been her own experience that if they were to encounter a threat, it would happen when they were too close to an enemy to be able to pull a gun. In a close fight, it was much easier to grab for a double-bladed knife and cut into an abductor's soft tissue or hit lethal areas up close. She could easily reach her knives whether she was being charged or grabbed by surprise. Having them positioned in front, back, and at her sides gave her multiple places to draw from no matter what her situation.

Abduction teams generally had limited windows to make their snatch, so the best strategy for their target was to buy time. Once an abduction team began suffering casualties and the target was proving intent on putting up a fight, it usually boiled down to holding on long enough for the abductors to decide the window was closed and the risk too great.

Sauwa and Mustafa began their walk taking a right and proceeding down a small hill. They viewed the streets, checking for any vehicles that looked out of place. It was a wealthy neighborhood filled with people who were like their employer — emerging entrepreneurs who were part of the country's newly rich. And, like all the new nouveau-riche, they had a desire to flaunt it. Their driveways were littered with flashy, expensive cars imported from Italy and the United States; certainly, not the type of vehicles a government employee or guerrilla group would use. Any modest, everyday car was suspect, especially if it looked like a vehicle that could be used to house surveillance equipment or accommodate a team of people.

Professional surveillance teams looked for cars that could blend into everyday society and not attract attention. They were usually devoid of any personalizing touches such as ornaments on the dash or around the car and were a neutral color such as black, grey, or white — something easily ignored and forgotten by most people. If needing to follow someone through a city or town, bright colored Porches and Lamborghinis were neither practical nor easily hidden. The usual surveillance team consisted of a driver, an observer in the front passenger seat, and one to two additional agents who worked as the foot team if needed to pursue the target. For this reason, vehicles used for such missions would also be four-door rigs capable of carrying at least three to four people.

She didn't really expect to see much. The neighborhood was tight. Most of the families had lived in their homes for five to ten years. Any surveillance vehicle would catch more than just her eye after a while. A likely call to the police from a concerned citizen would have gotten rid of them. She was more concerned with teams using disguises such as fake work vehicles. Most people would dismiss a maintenance van, or someone working on telephone wires, even if that same team was working in the same location for several weeks.

The mid-afternoon was pleasant with the sun out and a light cool breeze keeping the temperature perfect to make the day enjoyable. As a handsome, athletic couple, they gave the impression to most anyone watching that they were lovers out for their usual walk. Their façade made it easy for locals to dismiss them. Mustafa played his role, keeping a smile on his face, staying close to her as if they were sharing intimate secrets.

Nothing seemed out of the ordinary — no unusual people were hanging about, no houses were empty with the owners off on a lengthy vacation, and everyone seemed to be acting in the routine Sauwa had come to expect from her previous observations. The street appeared safe as the couple pressed on.

They turned down a side street leading to another row of houses, neither of them expecting anything unusual. Valikov's house was completely out of viewing distance by anyone staging along this route. It was more a way to get out of the house for a while and enjoy some tranquil time. As they walked past the columns of modern-day palaces, Mustafa took in the view. "Can you ever imagine us owning a house like these in a place like this?" He wore a devilish smile on his face as he asked.

"No," Sauwa shook her head. "This is all too civilized and cozy for people like us. We need to live rougher. I'd settle for a small place in one of the fishing villages on the outside of town. Or better yet, a small ranch house in the countryside."

"You know, I pegged you for a small-town type," Mustafa chuckled.

"Perhaps, I am," Sauwa replied, taking a deep breath as she began to consider what her life might actually look like when she was no longer living by her wits and forced to work for dangerous men such as Andre Valikov. It had been a long time since she had given any thought to a different lifestyle. She didn't really like to contemplate it. Deep down, she feared that such a time might never come.

Valikov had destroyed all the documents she had obtained in Ireland that would have given her a new identity. He had burned them right in front of her making him her sole means of protection. The identities that she operated under in his service were done through forgers he employed, and he always had duplicates made. In the event she tried to run, it wouldn't be of any use. All the identities she had would be useless once he forwarded the duplicates to the embassies in Ankara of all the countries that sought her arrest or assassination. She had been recruited for the purpose of handling Valikov's most hazardous business dealings. This meant being sent to the most lawless and dangerous regions of the world where she would have little hope for survival without his protection.

She lived in a dangerous world that allowed few to retire and, even if she did get released from Valikov, she would always have the British and South African governments and God knows who else chasing after her. She let the matter recede to the back of her mind as she changed her thoughts to something else. The light-hearted ex-Jandarma had a plethora of fun stories, and she could listen to him for a long time and not get bored. They circled around and came back to the original street having covered a kilometer and a half. Satisfied that they weren't being watched by anyone, they made their way back home.

Sauwa was relieved to find nothing. Her precautions might have seemed excessive, if not slightly paranoid. But only a few months earlier, she had caught sight of an out of place vehicle in the area. When she investigated further, she found a couple of cheap cars parked in strategic locations. It didn't take her long to figure out they were not local security forces. Using a decoy to convince the pursuers that they were chasing their quarry, she arranged to lead them into a run-down part of the city where she and several of Valikov's security team ambushed them. From the survivors, she discovered they were members of a Palestinian group that was looking to kidnap her employer in hopes of bargaining for weapons they could not afford to buy. It was a stark reminder that despite all his efforts to appear as a prominent businessman, she was still working for a man involved in a very dangerous business.

Returning to the house, Sauwa and Mustafa walked through the front door where Sauwa heard the low commanding voice of her employer, "Sauwa, come to my office now."

Waving to Mustafa, Sauwa headed toward the office. She walked down the hallway and entered the half-open set of wood-framed glass doors of his office. The office was designed to project power. The large mahogany desk was an antique that had once belonged to one of the Sultan's most important ministers. Its edges ended with carvings of intimidating, roaring lion's heads that faced toward visiting guests. Two identical mahogany bookcases from the same collection were set behind the desk. They were both filled with old-style, hard covered books in leather bindings. Expensive artifacts lined the tops of the bookcases and along the sides of the desk. Oil paintings depicting religious themes of the Eastern Orthodox Church covered the office walls.

The office had a semi-circle of dark brown leather chairs neatly arranged around the front of Valikov's desk with four identical chairs lined up against the wall, two on each side of the door. A tall man wearing a conservative navy-blue suit sat in one of the chairs sitting closest to the desk. His pitch-black hair was neatly cut into a short crop that framed his round head perfectly. He was a black man who looked as if he hailed from a deep part of Africa, possibly her homeland of Rhodesia — or Zimbabwe, as it was now called.

Andre Valikov stood directly behind his leather chair looking like a commander overseeing his soldiers. It was the position he most preferred when he was intending to give orders. This led Sauwa to believe that the black man was an employee rather than a potential customer. Not knowing quite what to do, she remained standing with her hands tucked slightly into her pants pockets.

"What happened in Northern Iraq?" Valikov asked. He spoke in English and it sounded clean and educated. His face was stone as he stared intently in Sauwa's direction. "The Kurds were angered by what they saw as a complete betrayal by me."

Not knowing what else to say, Sauwa said nothing more. Valikov eyed her up and down for a short time then continued. "Fortunately, while things did not go well for the Kurds — I understand most of them perished in the Iranian onslaught. Things did turn out well for us. My plane was saved, I received full payment, and the inventory came in handy to accommodate another buyer. The Grey Wolves have been hungering for weapons to send to their brethren Uighurs in China. I needed to lose the inventory so it wasn't lingering in Turkey waiting for the police to find it. That would make for some very uncomfortable phone calls. All is well from that aspect."

Sauwa still said nothing. She looked toward the other man. He was looking casually at the Russian but remained silent. Valikov grabbed the back of his chair and slowly eyed the two people. "While this all came out well for us, I feel it was more luck than proper preparation. In the future, such deals could easily fall apart. That said, I've decided to heed the advice of both of you. Normally, I like to keep my operations and organization compartmentalized for security reasons, but I will make this exception. Ghost and Red Wolf, it's time you met each other. As you have both pointed out, with the particularly dangerous nature of your jobs, you need to be able to interact. In the future, we need to mitigate the possibility of what happened to the Kurds, and that will only happen if you two are talking and planning together."

Coming out from behind his desk, Valikov moved to the center of the room. The black man rose from his chair and walked over to where Sauwa and the Russian were standing. The black man projected a powerful image. He was tall with an athletic frame that filled out his suit nicely. He could have been a prominent businessman or banker.

Observing one another, they listened as Valikov continued. Looking first at Sauwa, he said, "May I present Tyrone
Maxwell, the man you know as Red Wolf. He was in a
former American Army Ranger regiment where he served
with distinction for several years."

"How do you do?" Sauwa said softly, a slight smile on
her lips.

Valikov continued, "I also think it important that I point
out that both Mr. Maxwell's father and his two uncles were
members of the Black Liberation Army. It was a Black
Nationalist group in the United States that operated during
the tumultuous period of the 1970s into the early eighties. I
believe your father acquired quite a reputation for the
violent shootouts he had with the police. He was a staunch
supporter of the American Marxist revolutionary, Eldridge
Cleaver. It was his oldest brother, your uncle, who was
convicted of killing two policemen in a pitched gunfight in
New Jersey. He later was found dead in his cell — suspected
police retaliation."

Sauwa's eyes widened at the news. Suddenly all the
memories of the guerrilla strikes and the black militants
burning her family's farm in Rhodesia went flashing through
her mind. No doubt this was the intended result of Valikov's
introduction. She quickly regained her composure and
looked at Tyrone Maxwell trying to keep a pleasant look on
her face. Reading the discomforting look in the man's own
facial expressions made her realize she had failed.

"Mr. Maxwell," Valikov's voice broke the tension, "may I
present the one you know as Ghost? Ms. Sauwa Catcher was
formerly of the South African Intelligence service where she
served in covert operations. I believe she was considered one
of the Apartheid's more vicious and lethal assassins."

It was now time to exchange awkward glares as Sauwa was uncomfortable being in the room and could see Tyrone Maxwell's eyes light up and assumed his mind was racing with similar memories to the ones she had. "I saved some white racist!" He tried hard not to shout. Instead, his words came out in a low, animalistic growl.

"No, you saved my property." Valikov chimed in. "Kindly remember that is what I employ you both to do."

There was a deafening silence in the room. Sauwa could only imagine the pleasure Valikov was getting out of this. He had gotten the intended results. Red Wolf and Ghost had gotten their wish and finally met each other. Now to ensure some tension remained between the two, he had made sure to share such information.

"I feel I should leave you to get acquainted." The Russian smiled sinisterly as he started past them. "Oh, and remember, you both work for me, both serve at my pleasure, and are subject to my wrath. So, keep it civil, if you don't want to feel the repercussions of any blind rage that may be festering." With that, he led the two out of his office and ushered them through the house until he could leave them alone on the patio outside. He casually walked away, explaining he had some business to attend to as if he were leaving neglected guests.

When the door shut behind them, Sauwa and Tyrone found themselves staring in any direction but at each other. From Maxwell's look, she didn't know what to say or what to make of him. He wasn't some MK fighter from the ANC or one of their communist allies from Zambia or Angola; this was an American. However, she knew next to nothing about him and his initial reaction left her concerned. She decided it was probably best to let him open the dialogue.

"He didn't tell me who you were or what you were," Maxwell finally spoke up. "It was probably better that he didn't. I don't know that I care for the idea of protecting some white racist." He turned and, for the first time since they came outside, looked her straight in the eye. His gaze was cold and serious. "I heard about what went on in South Africa. Never thought I'd meet one of you Apartheid types face to face. One of their most elite killers, isn't that what the boss said?" His gaze hardened. He wanted an answer to his question.

"I really don't know," she replied coldly. "It's not something I really care to keep track of."

Maxwell continued. "I have to say, you impressed me the way you handled yourself in Northern Iraq. Killing certainly seems to come easily for you."

"I get by when I have to," Sauwa replied, not knowing what to say to his comment.

"You do more than get by," he said. "You were doing serious damage to those guerrillas from what I saw. Now that I know who you are, I have to wonder how much of that is pure instinct?"

"I was a soldier, and the war is over at least for me," she stated with curt finality. She stared back at him with indifference. Despite his towering over her, she was not intimidated.

"You can say that," he countered, "but I'm still a black man working with a white supremacist who seems at home killing people. To be frank, it is hard for me to get past that knowing what I've dealt with my whole life. My dad and uncles fought people like you on the streets of New York when I was growing up. You fought for a regime that would have people like me as second-class citizens."

"I don't see the point of debating the finer points of a

government that no longer exists." Her voice was stark and cold. "We have a job to do. So, I suggest we focus on that."

"You'd like it to be that easy," he said as he stepped a few paces in her direction. "Just have the whole thing go away."

"Actually, I would," she replied. "If we don't, all that will happen is tempers will get heated, and we will lose sight of our goal. Neither of us is here fighting for a cause. Both of us are here because we're paid by a man who has no political interests other than what makes him money. Our whole reason for talking right now is because our job for comrade Valikov is to take care of his more contentious deals. Those deals call for us to go to the most dangerous places and handle the transactions with his most violent and unpredictable clients. You could betray me out there and let me get killed horribly and tell yourself it would be justice. I just have to trust that you won't. But then you'd have to answer to our employer, who would not appreciate you losing his merchandise. As observant and crafty as he is, he would assume personal feelings led to your failure and would take it out on you in the most vicious way. Otherwise, he doesn't care about either of us."

"You do have a point," Maxwell nodded. "But you talk about trusting me. I also have to trust you. I'm a black man working with a professional killer who was trained to hunt and kill people like me. That definitely puts me a little on edge."

Sighing, Sauwa looked back at him. "I would love to tell you that what I did, I did because I was fighting a war and for no other reason — that I bear no malice against your people. It still won't change what I did. And it won't do anything to put your mind at ease. Our histories are something we have to get past because our futures are going to be dangerous and uncertain enough without distrust between us."

Maxwell ruminated for a time, his eyes fixed on Sauwa as if he couldn't tell whether he wanted to accept her rationale or kill her right here. "You heard what he said about my family."

"I hate radicals, I won't lie." Sauwa stood looking at the view. "And, yes, I've fought groups no different than your Black Liberation Army. But, he fought his war, and I fought mine. We both thought we were fighting for the better side. And, perhaps we were both fools who fed the legitimacy and fanaticism of the other's twisted causes."

Tyrone Maxwell nodded his head slightly. It was the best answer he was going to get from the South African — neither apologetic, which he would have felt disingenuous nor glorifying, which he would have loathed and resented. Accepting the answer, he started back to the house. "I need this job. I'm staying. I'm a professional, and I'll work with you because I have to. But, I don't like you, and I want you to know that."

"I need this job as well. So, on that, we can agree. Your personal opinion of me is inconsequential. I would have thought you dishonest if you had expressed any other feeling." Sauwa was still looking at the view of the garden. She wasn't quite sure where they stood. But for the time being, she liked to think they had reached some sort of détente.

7

S ergei Tarkov looked over the glistening coastal waters of the Aegean Sea as he entered the deck at the restaurant. Colonel Carzona followed him maintaining a more humble appearance. To anyone observing them, the small Filipino would have been dismissed as a simple manservant to the larger Russian he was following. Having seen the little man in a far more domineering role, Tarkov assumed the humbler demeanor was intentional.

An affable Andre Valikov promptly rose from his table to meet them as they joined him on the deck. With his arms extended in greeting and his face beaming, he behaved as a man meeting a long-lost brother in arms. The two Russians were locked in a tight embrace as they smiled and laughed with pleasure at the sight of one another. Carzona stepped unobtrusively to the side to allow the men their space. He said nothing and made no attempt to draw attention to himself. Casually, he observed the area around him assessing the location and its practicality for the business they intended to discuss.

The outside dining area was perched above the buildings and trees to allow for an uninterrupted view of the bright sandy beaches and light blue waters beyond. It was also the perfect location for an observation post or a sniper's perch. The table on the deck was far from the main building and away from other guests. The sunshades on both sides of the table masked them from anyone attempting to take pictures from inside or from another table. Someone wanting to listen to their conversation would need to go to great lengths to do so or risk exposing themselves.

Carzona thought that Mr. Tarkov's friend had chosen the place for this meeting well. The two Russians had broken their embrace and moved to the table. They took their seats next to each other while Carzona sat across from them. He started to be a little more assertive only when he was sure the hanging curtains covering their flanks had shielded him from anyone's view. This did not go unnoticed by Valikov who was watching the Asian out of the corner of his eye. He sensed Carzona was more than just a mere tag along.

"This is a most beautiful city," Tarkov began as he admired the view.

Valikov smiled as he lit a light-colored Toro cigar, exhaling the first puff of bluish-grey smoke, sending a sweet-smelling aroma into the atmosphere. "It's one of the reasons I chose this city after I left Russia." He shifted his eyes to Carzona. "For the benefit of your friend, I imagine we should speak English for the business portion of this meeting," he said in English.

"Thank you, Andre, it would be preferable." Tarkov also spoke in English.

A pair of servers in white jackets arrived with glasses and a bottle of wine. Though a Muslim country, Turkey vacillated between embracing modern practices and yielding to religious conservatism. Foreigners treaded lightly making sure they did not flaunt western sinfulness. The servers poured the wine and disappeared.

Taking another pull on his cigar, Valikov glanced over at Carzona then back to Tarkov. "I take it you and I will be discussing the particulars of your business, but it will be your friend who will be making the final decisions."

"That is correct. I'm working for the people whom he represents," Tarkov replied not wishing to waste time posturing.

"Then let us get to the purpose of this luncheon," Valikov drew again on his cigar.

Tarkov began. "I'm working for some people who are trying to thwart the efforts of a rival party in their home country. This rival group is trying to procure arms for their military wing. They have made contact with an arms dealer in Cyprus who can meet their needs. I have been retained by my colleague and his people to counter this effort."

"I see," Valikov mused. "So, you're needing what?"

"The scope of the mission is quite complex and dangerous. I'm being hired to carry out a campaign of covert operations against this rival party both outside of the law and in a wealthy European country without the aid of my government. This requires resources I can't just get anywhere. Right now, what I need badly is people. I need to recruit a team. I need people who have experience and extensive training dealing in this type of operation. I was hoping you know people who fit our requirements and could put us in touch with them."

"I'm curious," Valikov said. "These people you are working for, they're not Russian? They did not pick you up by chance. I would wager they found you through a broker. Russia is full of mercenaries these days. There are all types of people in the military and intelligence service who have side jobs brokering people for your type of client. Why not go through the broker who found you?"

"True," Tarkov agreed. "The market is awash with soldiers coming out of Russia or some other former Soviet country. I've seen what's being offered — a bunch of phonies and action junkies fresh out of Chechnya. Most of them putting themselves on the market claiming to be 'Spetsnaz operators' are typically former conscripts with only two years of service under their belt. As elite as they claim to be, most of their training is entry-level commando tactics. Their experience consists of a single combat tour lasting a few months and done in a war-torn country. They would not have the skill set I need. I don't have time to sift through all the undesirables. I need people who have operated in Western European cities and have experience working outside the support of government intelligence agencies.

"That said, I am not a fool. I know such people in this murky business can easily take your money and betray you. That means I need people who can be trusted to earn their money. If anybody knows those kinds of people, it's you. I need the type of people you would recruit for your own business."

Rolling his cigar between his fingers, Valikov sat studying it for a time. He acted as if he were alone at the table. Then looking up, he laid his elbows on the table and gazed into the eyes of his old friend. "You and I have a lot of history. We go back a long time serving our former master. Now we are the capitalists when we spent our lives fighting them." The reminiscing was cut short by a cough generated from the other side of the table where Carzona sat watching them both. Though subtle in its nature, it had its intended effect.

"I know a few people who might meet your requirements. How many do you think you'll need?"

Tarkov folded his arms as he considered the question. "For now, I need a small team, four at the most. The less recognizable faces for this mission the better. I need skilled people who can think on their feet and be flexible with mission requirements."

Scratching his chin gently with his thumb, Valikov scrutinized the short Asian still sitting expressionless. It was clear Tarkov was his voice at this meeting. "Perhaps I know a few people who meet these requirements." Valikov's eyes shifted back to his old friend. "It will take a certain commission for brokering this transaction."

"I expected it would," Tarkov replied. "How much?"

"Fifty thousand dollars, American." Valikov diverted his eyes once again to Carzona, knowing he would be the one to decide.

Tarkov also glanced in the Filipino's direction.

With all the attention focused on him, Carzona bowed his head slightly to acknowledge the price was acceptable.

Valikov didn't wait for Tarkov to confirm the obvious. "Good, then I can set you up with some people who have worked for me in the past. I know them and what they can do. I can assure you they will earn their pay."

"Thank you, my friend," Tarkov cracked a smile. "I trust that you will choose these people wisely. However, my colleague and I would like to make our own assessments."

"Naturally," Valikov smiled as he waved his hand in the air trying not to imply any offense. "I would fully expect you to make your own evaluations. I will set up a meeting at a small place I have where you can assess your recruits discretely."

"That won't be necessary," Carzona spoke for the first time. "We will establish the meeting location. We need you to arrange for your people to meet us in a designated place and ensure we have the means to identify each other worked out ahead of time. Then, the rest will be our responsibility once we have all the recruits."

Valikov slipped his cigar into his mouth as he studied the Filipino. Carzona's face was like stone as he looked back at the Russian. It was the expression of someone that was not going to negotiate this point. Conceding to the demand, Valikov nodded. "Of course, perfectly understandable. I will do as you wish."

"How long will it take for you to arrange this?" Tarkov asked.

Valikov sighed. "Most of these people are in the country. A few others are in places just over the border. I should have the people ready to meet you within four days."

Tarkov looked over at Carzona who nodded.

"Good," Valikov said, rubbing his hands together. "I will begin making arrangements today. Will you be needing anything else?"

"We will need resources for this operation — weapons and other equipment. We were hoping to retain your services for providing these materials as well," Tarkov added.

Valikov's eyes widened, "Of course, I can handle that."

"We may need to be clients of yours for a considerable amount of time," Carzona interjected. "Can you furnish a steady supply for such things? We can afford to pay quite handsomely."

"Oh, definitely," Valikov grinned, sensing a lucrative business opportunity. The Russians exchanged a few more comments about the old days, and the two guests departed.

After the two men left, the servers entered with Valikov's lunch. He leaned back in his chair, hands folded behind his head as he puffed on his cigar. The waiters served his meal and were leaving when Sauwa emerged through the doors of the main building and came to join her employer.

She sat down in the chair Tarkov had occupied. Valikov stared off thoughtfully, not paying her the slightest notice. "Report," he said suddenly.

"I observed them coming into the lobby and waited a few more minutes to see who would follow them. The only other people who came in were some businessmen who requested one of the staterooms and a young couple who didn't try to change their seating when they were sent to a table at the far end of the club. I passed by the area where someone could look out, but no one was interested in you at all. When your friends left, I followed them to the parking lot and watched them leave. No cars followed them out either. It doesn't look like they're being tailed by anyone."

"What type of car were they driving?" he asked.

"A navy blue Audi," she answered. "They chose their vehicle well. It was a common model for the city and did not attract attention."

"Then they're not idiots. They know what they're doing," Valikov said. "I guess I can assist them." It was his strict policy to vet clients before working with anyone. He had stayed successful and alive by ensuring that the people he did business with were seasoned professionals who knew how to protect their operation from scrutiny and not draw attention to themselves.

Radical groups and criminal gangs were forming all the time with young hotheads who acted foolishly. They were not long for the business or for this world. Unfortunately, those greedy enough to supply such people often incurred the same enemies and wound up following them to prison or the morgue. If his old friend and his Asian employer had brought a tail with them, it would mean they were either too hot, had too much attention from all the wrong people, or they were amateurs who didn't know enough to take the proper precautions before coming to such an important and sensitive meeting. In either case, it would have been too risky to get involved with them.

"I was able to make peace with the Kurds," he continued. "They paid for weapons that they never received. I hate betraying clients. I intend to make good on the deal and get them what they paid for. Right now though, things are hot in Northern Iraq. Saddam has been aggressive in his war with Kurdish insurgents there. The Iranians have been just as bad; they have been conducting regular artillery fire in areas of Kurdish training camps. They've also been flying regular patrols. This means for the next few months my Kurdish business will be off the table." He suddenly shifted his head to where he was looking at her in a haphazard way. "I had forgotten to ask how everything went with my old friend Ivan. Did he enjoy his little outing with you?" He was referring to Ivan Gorev, the former Russian diplomat he sent with her on the last trip to Northern Iraq. Sauwa looked at the toothy grin that was emerging on the Valikov's face.

"Terrible," Sauwa replied, almost angrily. "That guy's not

made for fieldwork. Why did you have him come on such a trip?"

"I wanted to give him a reality check," Valikov replied with a feigned look of innocence. "He was having a hard time understanding that he wasn't working in an embassy hosting formal dinners. I felt a trip with you to gain some first-hand experience with our operation would be good for him."

"More like it shot the poor man's nerves to hell," she countered, glaring at her boss. Ivan Gorev had been employed by the Russian Foreign Service. He had been brought on to work with Turkish officials and politicians to help maintain a decent working relationship and develop much-needed allies in high government positions. Sauwa was aware that her boss hated the little diplomat. Gorev was neither a soldier nor an intelligence operative. He was a diplomat. A member of the old Soviet elite, who lived a priv-ileged life while never getting his hands dirty with more dangerous or arduous work. For Andre Valikov, sending Gorev on such a dangerous mission was nothing more than some deeply seeded revenge.

"Really Sauwa, you can't tell me you feel for that little pissant. He's not a soldier like you who carried out the orders handed to you by men sitting comfortably in the safety of their offices back in South Africa while you were on the front lines risking yourself in a dirty war with no rules." She didn't answer. She didn't know what to say and kept her hard gaze on him though she could feel it slip as his words began to sink in.

Valikov decided to press the issue. "Have you ever wondered, my dear, how many times you were out on some cold night on a dark London street corner freezing as you waited to execute a risky and dangerous mission and could easily have gotten captured or killed? And, all the while, the ones who sent you on the missions were back in your homeland enjoying cocktails at some fancy party bragging about how they were the ones keeping their country safe, speaking endlessly of their jobs as if they were freezing in some horrible spot carrying out the same mission with the same risks." He looked at Sauwa and could see from her cold glance that he had struck a nerve. Taking a strange pleasure in stoking her anger, he continued. "Gorev is from the same circle of elite society as those who happily sent you to do their bidding and then just denounced you when it was convenient."

She lowered her eyes. What he had said did stoke some deep-rooted anger she had hoped to suppress. Gorev had been part of the Soviet upper class. He was from the same world as those who led the security services of the Apartheid. Those who directed her efforts and missions — the Dark Chamber and the Civil Cooperation Bureau. Then they just denounced her and her comrades for the actions they had carried out pretending they had had nothing to do with the very monsters they had created and presided over.

"Will there be anything further?" she asked, in a low, bitter tone.

"My old friend has some business, and he's asked for my assistance." He snuffed out the remainder of his cigar and turned to address his meal. "I don't have the particulars, but it involves a lot of activity that falls along the lines of covert operations. They need people who know this kind of business and are good at it. He's a good friend, and I want to help him with his first freelance job.

What's more, the man he was working for knew what he

was doing. He knows this business better than he lets on. I have the impression that what they're involved in could materialize into a long, continuous affair and last for years. I like to give good service to those who can potentially be long-term clients. I happen to have a few good people who would be perfect for their needs close at hand. And you, my dear, are at the top of that list. I figured I didn't have a need for you in the next few months, but I'm cutting your vacation short and loaning you to him for this mission."

Sauwa's eyes widened in disbelief. She opened her mouth to say something, but she was promptly cut off by her employer. He continued talking, paying not the slightest attention to her obvious anger.

"It's your world, your environment. I figure they can get some use out of you, and I can show them my ability to deliver quality merchandise." His use of the word merchandise when referring to her only added to her growing rage. It was bad enough he was renting her out like a pimp touting a prostitute. Worse, he was hiring her out to some shady group of strangers to go God knows where, and do God knows what! She wanted to protest but it was pointless to argue, she had no options.

8

When they left the meeting, Tarkov and Carzona headed straight for their car. It was a nice looking German model that didn't attract attention. Tarkov drove and Carzona sat in the front passenger seat, silent and stoic.

"I was under the impression I was to be handling the negotiations at this meeting," Tarkov said as he looked over at the Filipino. He was concerned that Carzona's reason for interjecting himself into the conversation was a sign of disapproval at how he was handling the negotiations.

"You were," Carzona replied in a low and serious tone. "Your friend was offering too much hospitality. That concerns me. I appreciate that he may be able to find us viable recruits if he can deliver the quality of people he promised. However, I do not want your friend, who we know nothing about his own dealings, to be any more involved in our affairs than necessary. This is our operation and one that is challenging. I do not wish to entrust our security to this man by allowing him to arrange the meeting where we intend to discuss sensitive business. We will meet

90

these people in a place we choose and do so in a manner that suits our security needs. And, I think you realized that."

Tarkov felt both relieved and shocked. Relieved that the Colonel had not lost faith in him to run the operation and had spared him some possible unpleasantness. What shocked him was that the Colonel was far more adept at the business of intrigue than he was letting on. He was entirely too comfortable and professional. He had been involved in this business before.

"What if the people he gets us are not up for the task? What is our next option?" Tarkov looked over at the Filipino.

"I believe they will be," the Colonel replied. "Inevitably, we will work with the best of what we can get. That is the nature of these types of operations."

"If we are not taking his offer to provide a location for the meeting, we need to set up our own safe house. It would be best if we chose a location in a more transient area. It will make it easier to move about without drawing attention," Tarkov said.

Carzona shook his head. "We've already rented a small house for this meeting. What we need to find is a place we can gather the recruits beforehand. Then we'll move them to the meeting."

"You've already done this?" Tarkov asked, feeling usurped as he looked at the Colonel.

"Of course," the Colonel replied indifferently. "I don't know what relationship you have with your friend Valikov. By the way, you two acted at the meeting, I was worried about what you feel you owe him if he should start pressing you for information. So, forgive me if I choose to act cautiously while we are here in Turkey dealing with your friend."

Tarkov couldn't argue with Carzona's logic. As a Special Forces operator himself, he understood all too well the importance of keeping information protected and being very selective to whom it was given. He had operated the same way when working in Africa with local contacts whose loyalties were dubious. Tarkov had seen how quickly information could get back to the enemy in Chechnya and Dagestan when you trusted people who had family loyalties in the enemy camp. He remembered he was a hired gun to these Asians and one who was putting them in contact with a shadowy black-market merchant who would most likely want to insert himself into their client's business. "You don't trust me right now, and I can understand that. But, if you hired me to run this operation, I need to stop being treated as some hired gun who only gets small pieces of the picture."

"I understand your concerns," the Colonel replied "and, I can understand why you have them. Make no mistake comrade Tarkov. You will be running this operation just as soon as we are in Cyprus and your expertise as a commando becomes essential. While we're here in Turkey dealing with your friend, I wish to retain operational control. Kindly understand, if your friend indicates he knows more about our operation than he should, I can only assume it was because you told him and that you are a security risk."

The Russian nodded. As insulted as he felt, he agreed with everything Carzona said and would have done the same if the roles had been reversed. "So, you said we will establish a rendezvous location where our recruits can gather. What then?"

Carzona replied, "We will give each of them a code that allows us to identify them when they enter. We won't make contact until everybody has a chance to arrive. Then we discretely take them to an awaiting vehicle and drive them to the safe house."

The plan made sense to Tarkov. "How do we vet a bunch of strangers under these circumstances?"

"While we're at the rendezvous point, we take our time assessing the recruits to get an initial feel." Carzona remained watching his side view mirror. "People hanging out in a public place not knowing what to expect can elicit several tells about what type of person they are and what we should expect, especially if they don't know they're being watched or who's watching them.

"Are they braggarts who love to talk and pay little attention to what comes out of their mouths? Do they draw needless attention to themselves in other ways that a professional would not do? Do they have a taste for alcohol and consume too much right before heading out to a job? None of these people are going to come with a resume or any means to verify their background. We have to make our own assessments based on our own expertise in this business. If we don't like what we see, we call off the meeting and leave without making contact. Then, we try a different approach. But, I don't think it will come to that."

Dropping Tarkov at his hotel, Colonel Carzona drove toward a district filled with small shops and eateries. The streets were filled with tourists representing ethnicities from all around the world. It was easy for him to be lost in a sea of foreigners. Parking the car in a crowded parkway, he walked across the street. The whole time he had been with the Russian, he was carefully watching to see if they had been followed. Confident no one had tailed them, he continued on. Dressed in dark slacks and a blue collared shirt, he looked like most of the populace scoping out a place for souvenirs or a place to eat.

It wasn't long before he arrived at a small coffee shop playing traditional Arab music. The place housed a dozen small wooden tables and chairs with a half dozen patrons scattered around. A single waitress, a young girl in her early twenties, was traversing her way through the room with a tray in her hands. Aside from a young Japanese or Korean couple that was jabbering away excitedly, no one was paying attention to anything but their drinks and their reading materials. He saw Rita sitting at a table reading a newspaper, sipping something from a small cup.

He slipped into the chair across from her. "How was the meeting?" she asked.

Carzona sighed before responding. "It went well. I think he will be eager to give us satisfactory service and find good recruits."

"You're sure he won't try to cheat us?"

"Mr. Valikov is a businessman who is always looking for new customers. I mentioned our future need to obtain weapons and equipment. He wants to make money," the Colonel replied.

"What money?" Rita looked confused. "We're running a small covert operation. Whatever arms we buy will be minute compared to the massive orders he gets from warlords and guerrilla groups."

The Colonel snorted. "Throughout the 1970s and '80s, the Israelis and the Arabs waged a vicious covert war that went all across Western Europe. British intelligence and their Special Forces conducted a similar campaign in pursuit of the Irish Republican Army. Such covert conflicts continue to this day. In every case, the conflict went from a single operation to a long-term shadow war. Wars, in any form, require resources and means of movement. Eventually, everybody in these types of conflicts turns to people like Mr. Valikov to support them with safe houses, documents, and medical assistance when their own governments cannot. This is in addition to everything else we need to operate. When you add it all up, it amounts to a pretty sizeable profit."

"You think it will come to that?" Rita asked, her voice betraying a hint of concern.

"No," Carzona's face and tone remained expressionless. "I doubt our enemies will have reason to finance further activities this far away from home once their business is disrupted, but it will help keep him accommodating our needs."

"If we stop them, won't they just try again?" Rita was still having trouble masking her nervousness. Her real name was Esmeralda Morayo. She was an attorney by education who specialized in international trade and worked for a prestigious law firm in Manilla. The firm, which was largely overseen by her father, was a powerful ally to the current Filipino president, former army general Fidel Valdez Ramos. When the conspiracy was initially discovered, it was being orchestrated by a shadowy organization known as the System. She was immediately approached by members of the president's inner circle to assist in the operation. Being world traveled, she had worked with legal firms and major businesses all across Europe. From her travels, she had a good working knowledge of the legal infrastructure of the recently created European Union and the countries comprising the old Soviet Eastern Block.

She had been the one who found the broker that led them to Tarkov and other private agencies that performed needed services for this operation. Though she had been instrumental in helping to this point, clandestine operations and intrigue were certainly not her forte and her inexperience was readily apparent.

The Colonel shook his head. "This is an incredibly risky undertaking for them as well as expensive and complex. If it is thwarted in a way that compromises the secrecy of their existence, it is likely they will decide not to pursue any further endeavors of this nature. Mr. Valikov doesn't know that and, for right now, we need to let him keep thinking that we are here for a long campaign. If I'm wrong and this does expand into a long-term conflict, then he will be a good connection to have."

Rita nodded. Her demeanor became slightly more relaxed after hearing the explanation. She knew little about Colonel Carzona, only that he was a military officer in the Filipino Marine Corps, Hukbong Kawal Pandagat ng Pilipinas, where he served for years in the Special Forces reconnaissance unit. He had spent considerable time operating in the southern islands of Mindanao and the Sulu Archipelago running military intelligence and covert operations against Islamic separatist groups, most notably the Moro National Liberation Front. He had run up against intelligence services and military advisors from countries such as Libya and Malaysia, allowing him the opportunity to hone his skills as an intelligence operative.

Carzona had been brought in at the behest of some of the president's inner circle to advise them on clandestine and operational security. The lawyers and businessmen who agreed to front the operation to spare the government any long-term diplomatic and legal exposure had no background in these affairs. They didn't have the slightest notion of how to operate, what to look for in the people they recruited, or how to manage such operations. Colonel Carzona was brought in as an advisor and operational supervisor to alleviate these issues.

Rita took another sip from her cup. "What was your assessment of Tarkov?" She looked up to meet the Colonel's eye. "He and Valikov are friends. What was your impression at the meeting? Can we trust Tarkov to work for us or will he have dual loyalties?"

"They certainly go back a long way," Carzona said breathing deeply as he slid back in his chair. "Tarkov isn't the type who goes to the highest bidder, nor do I think he would be unprofessional and put old friendships ahead of his professional duties to us. That said, I still would be leery about what we divulged to either man, and I will retain key control of the mission until we reach Cyprus."

"That would probably be best," Rita replied.

Carzona nodded, "We should expect an update on the recruits in the next three to four days. I told the Russians we will make our own arrangements for holding the meeting. Is the safe house I asked you to acquire ready?"

"I found a small house that meets your specifications. It took a few casual inquiries, but I was able to find a local businessman who was hard up for cash to put his name on the lease. Once you have approved it, he can have the papers signed and the place will be ours with no connection to us at all."

"I'll swing by it today and check it out. If it suits our purposes, I'll move my team in and set up the necessary security at once. Can we trust the man you are using not to ask too many questions or get suspicious?"

"I told him I have clients who were working on a business deal with some foreign investors, and they need some-place where they can hold discreet meetings and retain sensitive paperwork. He seemed content with that explanation. Such business and practices are not uncommon in the corporate world, so it wasn't at all out of the ordinary. He was more interested in the twenty-five thousand dollars I had sitting on the table, but I really don't understand the need for a house. Wouldn't it be more advisable to have this meeting at a hotel or other establishment?"

"For the initial meeting, we'll need a public place like a bar where we can assess our recruits. When we have reasonable candidates, we'll need somewhere more private to interview them. Once we have our team, we will still have a few days to wait for necessary preparations before moving to our destination. When that happens, we need the team to move on our schedule and not have to worry about rounding them up when we have to go. We also don't need our mercenaries talking to anyone. Some of them might be sent by Valikov with instructions to keep him apprised of our activities. We need to control this part of the operation, which is why we need a safe house. If we have true professionals, they will appreciate the necessity. We'll also need to have supplies — cots, sleeping bags, and hygiene necessities in addition to a plan for a food supply."

"I'll see what I can arrange, but logistics is not my forte," Rita said. "Though I have to tell you, I won't be able to obtain firearms for them."

"That's alright. They won't need any, and I don't want them," he said in a low tone.

Rita regarded him questioningly. "I don't understand. You're having them brought in for security. Shouldn't they be armed?"

He shook his head. "My men are trained reconnaissance operatives. Their job is to recon the area of the safe house, make sure we don't have anyone watching us, and safeguard against anyone trying to sneak in. They'll also help guarantee none of our mercenaries try to sneak out or make contact with anyone. We do not need firearms for that. In a country like Turkey, the risk involved with carrying firearms far outweighs the benefits. In reality, if we are threatened, it will most likely be by the police. In that case, guns would be the worst possible thing to have in our possession. We'll save the use of guns and other lethal items until we need them for our mission."

Putting her drink down, she rested her arms on the table putting her hands together. "I don't feel comfortable with this at all Colonel. This isn't like movies. I don't feel adventurous. I only feel concern about what can happen if we get caught. We are placing ourselves in danger."

The Colonel wasn't looking at her, but he had shifted his head focusing on the table as if he were deep in thought. "This is a clandestine operation. This is what they are like."

"I see," she replied, taking another sip from her cup.

"Is there anything else?" Carzona asked as he looked straight at her.

"No," she answered. "I'll inform the committee on what we've discussed. If they have any concerns, I'll bring them up at our next briefing."

"That will suffice," the Colonel sighed. "The next meeting will be right here at the same time." He rose from his chair and started out of the coffee house leaving Rita alone to finish her drink.

9

S auwa felt Rena shivering in her arms. The little girl was in a state of abject terror. The sound of bushes was crackling under the weight of combat boots as soldiers stepped through the thickets only a short distance away. Sauwa could feel her own heart thumping wildly in her chest as the soldiers drew closer. She hid her sister's face, pressing it tightly into her shirt, as she tried to protect the little girl from the ghastly sight directly in front of them.

Not more than a few feet away was the remains of a half-dozen or so corpses. Some white soldiers, the rest black civilians, all sprawled out with their clothes ripped to shreds and their bodies mutilated with stomachs sliced and their intestine flung about on the ground in a disgusting display. She didn't know what had happened, only that the deaths had occurred a short time before she and her group found them.

One of the bodies, a white soldier, who looked to be no more than nineteen years old, was staring right at her. His face was contorted with the terrible fear he must have felt just before his death. His eyes were begging for help she couldn't give, and he could no longer receive. She tried to take her eyes off of him, but the desperate stare seemed to bore into her. She found she was constantly looking up to meet his gaze and wanted badly to scream. But the sound of the guerrilla soldiers reminded her to keep silent.

Sauwa awoke suddenly and found she was no longer in the jungle but in her bed in her room in Valikov's home. As usual with these nightmares, she woke with her T-shirt soaked with sweat and her heart racing. As her nerves calmed and she started to relax, she glanced around the dark room. The only illumination came from the one window she kept uncovered so she could look out at the grounds below in case she heard anything strange.

The small amount of light formed ghostly images across her walls reminding her of the faces she had seen in her nightmare. No longer able to sleep she slipped out of her bed. She felt cold as the air touched her damp shirt. Peeling it off, she reached for a fresh one that was sitting on a nearby chair. The soft warm feeling of dry clothes improved her mood a little.

Stepping toward the small window she peered out at the grounds. The garden was illuminated garden lights stuck into the ground. They lit the pathway that led around the vegetation. Supposedly, it was a means of enhancing the mysterious beauty of the garden at night. In reality, it illumi-nated all the pockets intruders would need to come through if they were attempting to breach the house from that direction.

She pressed close to the wall as she peered out at the garden. She watched for a few minutes looking for any strange movements or signs of something out of the ordi-nary. Satisfied nothing was out there she went to the larger window. Drawing back the curtain, she opened the window to let in a gentle breeze. The fresh air was nearly intoxicating as she felt it caress her body. She took several slow, deep breaths allowing the air to fill her lungs feeling the calming effect as she exhaled. This was a routine she had perfected to quell her demons since coming to Turkey. Ever since she had left the battlefields of Bosnia, her nightmares had started to come back as the old ghosts of her past returned to haunt her.

With a calmer demeanor, she again gazed out at the view. In the distance, the lines of orange-red light began to crack the skyline signaling dawn was approaching. It was a hauntingly majestic sight and for a short time, she became lost in its splendor. She soaked it up wondering when she would be able to enjoy such a tranquil moment given what she was about to do.

———

THE SAKTAR BAR was a few blocks from the coast and had a relaxed atmosphere. It was nothing too fancy nor was it a dive. It provided the perfect environment for average people looking to have a good time. It catered to an assorted clientele which made it easy for one to go unnoticed. Colonel Carzona had selected it after touring multiple locations and determining it was the most suitable for his requirements.

Entering the bar at 1900hours, Sergei Tarkov and Colonel Carzona made their way to a corner table that gave them a full view of the place and the ability to observe everyone who entered. Accompanying them was a young Turkish fellow in his early twenties. He was a law clerk who worked for a firm Rita knew. He spoke fluent English and had been hired to act as an interpreter if needed. It was a Wednesday night so the crowd should be minimal. It had a large enough gathering to prevent them from sticking out but would be easy to keep an eye on the potential recruits.

Carzona had instructed Valikov to have the recruits come to the bar between 2000 to 2300 hours. It was a random enough timeframe that they all wouldn't come pouring in at once. Valikov had lined up twelve potential recruits and gave them four candidates to review the first night. The same routine would be used for the next two days. Seeing only four candidates at a time made it easier to evaluate them. If Valikov remained true to his word, the recruits should all be experienced professionals with in-depth training that should be suitable recruits for their team.

Carzona had given Valikov four distinct objects with instructions to give one to each of the recruits for identification. In his experience, the Colonel found that everyday people could be remarkably observant at the most inconvenient times when there was too much uniformity in a routine.

Someone approaching them had been given a code phrase to use and expected a carefully scripted response in reply. This would happen when it was time to make contact. The three men sat down at their table. The interpreter wasn't sure quite what was going on. He was only told to keep his mouth shut and leave the other two alone unless his services were required. By the hard, rough look of the two men, the young law clerk felt it wise not be involved any more than necessary.

Sauwa walked into the Saktar bar at 2000 hours dressed in a pair of black cargo pants, a grey T-shirt, and a black leather jacket. She didn't look too much different than many of the young professional women out that night. Even the black tactical combat boots she wore weren't too far out of the norm. The small, black knapsack she carried over her shoulder was also common among the more modern set. Her hair was tied up loosely behind her head with her bangs hanging down, adding to her casual appearance.

By the time she got there, the bar had gained a modest-sized crowd that occupied some of the seats and the dance floor. However, it was still relatively easy to walk about and see everyone clearly. Out of the corner of her eye, she spotted three men sitting at a table in the far corner. She recognized the two men Valikov had met with a few days earlier. They were drinking beer and pretending to look around the room. She assumed they were watching for their recruits.

Taking a seat that put her against the wall close to an exit, she placed her knapsack next to her. Once settled, she reached into her jacket pocket and produced a small crème colored envelope that she placed on the table. When Valikov gave it to her, he told her to place the envelope where it could be seen. A petite waitress dressed in a pair of black slacks and a white collared shirt came over to her with a smile on her face. She spoke in Turkish, but Sauwa understood enough to know the woman was asking if she wanted to order anything. Giving her the word for juice, Sauwa dismissed her as she sat back watching the room. She kept her head motionless while shifting her eyes in the direction of the three men. The lights were low enough that it was doubtful they would notice her peering in their direction.

With the help of their interpreter, Tarkov and Carzona had ordered a couple of beers and had been nursing them for the last hour. The time was 2030 hours, and they had identified two recruits by the envelopes displayed: a young woman in her early to mid-twenties sitting in the back of the room against the wall enjoying a drink and some pita chips and a man of medium build with a muscular physic that suggested he was quite the athlete. From his dark features, he was possibly Greek or maybe Italian. Like the young woman, he had chosen his seating logically. He had taken the last seat at the end of the bar and, like the women, his back was against the wall and he was close to an exit. He sat in such a way that he could catch the activities of most of the establishment with one quick turn of his head.

A short time later he was joined by another man who bore similar ethnic features and had a similar athletic build. The two men clasped each other's hands as if longtime friends. Another arrival slipped into a chair next to the first two, leaned up against the counter, and glanced around looking over the entire room. Carzona noted the new arrival, and like the other two, he had one of the envelopes identifying him as a recruit.

The newest arrival ordered a glass of beer and took a swig the second it was delivered. Carzona and Tarkov looked on with concern. Heavy alcohol consumption was common in the ranks of most any military organization. While they could respect a modest beverage nursed slowly, what they didn't need for this mission was a hell-raiser who acted recklessly and had no understanding of second and third order effects. Drinking excessively on a night they were being recruited was a sure indication he was not a man they needed. They continued to watch him carefully.

At 2240 hours, a man with a bushy crop of sandy blond hair and pencil mustache entered the establishment. Stopping at the doorway, he stepped to the side, leaned against the edge of the door, and took a few minutes to look slowly around at the crowd already engaged in their drinks, food, and socializing. Then he ventured further into the place choosing a table toward the center of the near side wall beside two tables full of nerdy looking college types. The only thing he ordered from the waitress was a small glass of whiskey. When it arrived, he let it sit there in front of him touching it occasionally.

Carzona and Tarkov took their time scrutinizing the recruits. They discussed their observations and personal assessments. The interpreter said nothing — he kept his head down and sipped his drink. Every so often he looked up to see if anyone needed his services.

For the most part, they had been impressed with what they had seen. The individuals identified had made all the right moves that showed they knew what they were doing for this kind of business. Even the man at the bar, who they had been initially been concerned with, had proven far more conscious of controlling his drinking and keeping a low profile. There was some concern about the young woman at the back of the room. Outside of the guerrillas and terrorists, they had engaged previously, neither man had ever worked with a woman in such a direct combat capacity. They questioned whether she would be a distraction or a hindrance. At first, they thought it best to leave her. Then Tarkov reminded him that some countries like Israel had used female operatives with great success in the field. To some extent, he had heard about how the South Africans had used them in their own covert intelligence missions with good results. Observing how she had done well dressing and behaving to blend in with the crowd to be easily forgotten and had made good tactical moves in how she chose her seating and positioned herself, they decided having a woman on the team would possibly give them more flexibility than if they had an all-male unit.

When the hour approached, a young man in his late twenties joined Carzona and Tarkov. He had somewhat scraggly and unkempt hair and a short beard that looked as if it had only recently been grown out. Tarkov had never seen the man before and was surprised when he simply walked up to their table. His dark skin and Asian features matched those of Carzona. When the Colonel reached out and clasped the younger man's hand, the Russian concluded the two were more than just passing acquaintances.

Despite the pleasantries, the younger man appeared hesitant to sit down. Carzona motioned for the young man to do so. He slid into the chair closest to the Colonel. Dressed in an Adidas black leather sports jacket and slightly baggy jeans, he fit in quite nicely with the younger crowd. Tarkov noticed the arrival of the handsome young man had gained some attention from a few of the young female patrons who were eyeing him avidly.

The two Filipinos spoke in a language the Russian didn't recognize. Though what he gathered from the commanding way the Colonel spoke was that orders were being given. Carzona pointed toward the various people in the room displaying the identifying envelopes. The young man nodded obediently as the older man spoke then walked out of the bar.

Not sure what was happening, Tarkov leaned over. "What's going on?"

Carzona leaned back in his seat. "That is one of my people. He has a van outside being driven by another one of my people. I told him to make sure it is ready to pick us and the team up."

A few minutes later the young man returned. He walked casually back to the table attracting no attention. This time he didn't wait for permission before slipping into his seat, talking to the Colonel in the same language used before. Carzona turned to the Russian and asked in English, "Do you have any issue with any of the recruits? This is going to be your mission to command when we get to our destination. Your decision is the final one."

This came as a bit of a surprise to Tarkov. Until now Carzona had controlled almost every aspect of the operation. That he just suddenly turned and told him he had the final approval had taken him off guard. Scrambling to collect his thoughts, Tarkov cleared his throat as he glanced around the room scrutinizing the recruits again. He looked over the candidates carefully using his most experienced eye to make his assessments.

His attention went first to the young lady. Women were an anomaly in this business, and he hesitated thinking about what problems she might cause. Still, she looked fit and seemed to act with experience. He next focused on the sandy-haired man in the center of the bar. The man was still fingering his drink which had not diminished at all. Like the others, he looked physically fit, though it was hard to tell from the large, tan military coat he wore. His clothing was not the most suited for this establishment — the green military trousers bloused into a pair of tan combat boots. He looked like a drifter or a man trying to imitate a mercenary.

The two darker skinned men sitting at the bar had impressed him. They carried on a conversation with each other while not drawing attention to themselves or overindulging. The one at the far edge shifted his eyes and his head every so often to check his immediate surroundings. The other one didn't seem concerned though he did seem to take notice every time someone new sat down at the bar. He had finished only half of his beer in the time he had been at the bar.

Tarkov wanted to discuss the recruits with Carzona and explain his rationale, but he feared in doing so he would shake his employer's confidence in his abilities. He still felt he had mishandled the meeting with his old friend Valikov and lost some credibility. He had spent the last hour expressing his views and listening to the Colonel. Yet, for such an important operation as they were about to embark on, he didn't like the idea of hedging his conclusions made from watching people he had never seen before as they sat socializing in a bar. Even though this was only the first stage, those chosen tonight would be more thoroughly vetted when they got to the safe house. Still, he didn't want to miss anything and bring an undesirable into their business.

For the most part, he liked what he had seen, and Carzona had not made any negative comment about anyone. Turning back to the Colonel, Tarkov said, "Based on first impressions, I'm good with them all. I still want to spend more time with them before I give you my final opinion."

Carzona cracked a slight smile. "I agree. We've seen a general view of their professional behavior, now we must assess their abilities in-depth." Turning to the young man next to him, Carzona whispered in his ear. The young man slowly rose out of his chair and walked away. He slipped through the tables and headed toward the young woman.

Sauwa had finished the last of her chips and was sipping her drink when a young man with a beard and wearing a leather sports coat approached her. At first glance, it was clear he wasn't Turkish — his features were obviously Asian, possibly Polynesian.

"Hey, how are things, young lady?" He asked in accented English.

"Fine," she replied indifferently.

He picked up the small white envelope and eyed it for a brief second. It was the first piece of the recognition code; her contact would instantly take notice of the identifying object. He continued speaking, "Man, I wish they had a good Polynesian beer in this place." His manner was casual — just a young foreign tourist looking to make conversation. In reality, it was the second part of the code.

As she had been instructed, Sauwa replied with the proper response. Gently snatching the envelope from his fingers, she said, "I usually only drink vodka or German Pilsners. I only enjoy a Polynesian beer when I'm in Bali."

It was the correct response. The young man's face became serious as he sat down next to her. "You are one of the recruits. Are you ready?" His hand was placed over his lips to shield his facial expressions from curious onlookers. His tone had gone from pleasant to serious.

"Of course," she responded with a feigned smile as if he were whispering something amusing into her ear. "Are you the one I was sent here to meet?"

The young man held his pose. "Go outside, turn right, and start walking down the street. You will see a blue van with a small white strip of tape on the bumper. Knock four times on the sliding door. The door will open, you will slide in, take a seat, and wait. Say nothing to anyone."

Sauwa continued her feigned smile as she reached over, grabbed her knapsack, and started to rise. As she stood, she grabbed the check and shook her head at him. He lowered his hand revealing a big grin as he shrugged while watching her leave. To anyone watching them, it would have appeared that the young man was attempting to make a pass at an attractive young woman and struck out.

Walking to the counter, she summoned the barkeep. Showing him the bill, she laid money on the counter to pay for her meal and exited the bar, turning right as instructed. She slipped past the few people on the street until she came to a blue van. Checking the bumper, there was the white strip of tape just below the tail light. She knocked four times slowly, and the door slid open revealing another Asian-looking man.

No words were exchanged as he waved her in. Sauwa set her foot on the bumper and slipped inside. The door slammed shut behind her as soon as she was in the van where a small light revealed a large barren hull. A plastic tarp covered the opening to the driver's cab masking the light and everyone inside.

Taking a seat in the far back corner, Sauwa said nothing as she observed the man who was now her companion. He bore the same ethnic features as the young man who had approached her in the bar. This man, however, was much older. He was in his mid-thirties with a pockmarked face and a rail-thin frame, and the clothes he wore seemed to hang on him. In like fashion, he eyed her as he crouched down next to the door in a position that suggested he might attack her if she tried to leave. He didn't look like much but for some reason, she got the feeling he would be formidable in a fight. So far these people, whoever she was now working for, had proven serious and were far from being amateurs.

Settling in she waited quietly. A few minutes later another four raps were heard. The little man dutifully slid the door open, and another figure quickly slipped inside. This time it was a larger man in a military jacket. Sauwa watched as this new addition slid in across from her and sank into a sitting position with one leg extended, the other bent against his chest. His bushy crop of sandy hair and mustache gave him a dismal appearance.

Another few minutes passed when knocking was heard again. The Asian man slid the door open again, and two mocha skinned men climbed inside. They appeared to know one another as they looked at the other two occupants, choosing to sit next to the sandy-haired man. The atmosphere in the van was like a funeral — no one spoke. After shifting eye glances, everyone fell into a monastic state with no one acknowledging anyone else. The small Asian vigilantly watched his charges. Like Sauwa, the other men also carried knapsacks — a sign none of them expected to be going home for a while.

There was another series of knocks at the van door. The young man who had earlier approached Sauwa in the bar entered. She looked up to see a similar expression of acknowledgment from the other three people in the van. The young man regarded the four people sitting in the back and turned to the older Asian man and said a few words in a language she didn't recognize. The older man nodded obediently, then slid out through the side door closing it behind him. Seconds later the van started, and everyone swayed as it pulled away from the curb.

The drive took close to half an hour making numerous turns in the process. It was difficult to tell if that was by design or just part of the natural route. The light in the roof was out leaving everyone in the dark. No one said anything or complained as there was nothing to see anyway.

The van turned and slowed down. Sauwa judged the distance to be a hundred meters or so before the van turned onto a ramp of some sort. It continued a gradual ascent for a few more seconds before coming to a complete halt. Wherever they were, they had reached their destination. The door didn't open immediately. Instead, they were kept waiting in the dark wondering what was going to happen next.

Outside they heard voices speaking in the same strange language as their two warders. Then the side door opened. The young Asian man waved his arm energetically gesturing them to exit. First, the dark-skinned men, then the sandy-haired fellow, and finally Sauwa stepped out to find themselves standing in some sort of garage. The young Asian waved the group toward the garage opening. Obeying the command, everyone walked out to a small driveway and patio that was in the back of a two-story house. The driveway wrapped around the house from the street leading to a backyard that was entirely concealed. A high wooden fence and some bushy trees protected the backyard, cutting it off from the rest of the neighborhood.

At the bend in the driveway, they saw two more men walking by clearly providing security. Following behind them were the young Asian and the older one. "Go into the house," the younger man said.

The back door of the house slid open and another man was standing inside waving everyone in his direction. Like a band of Muslim pilgrims, they snaked across the patio and up the stairs into the house. There were neatly arranged piles of rolled up sleeping bags, cots, and some bags that appeared to contain hygienic supplies but no furniture. It looked more like a campsite or a military training facility. An enticing aroma was coming from the kitchen catching everyone's attention.

The young man from the bar walked into the house and quickly moved past them until he was standing in what was presumably the living room. "Everyone, we will have meals ready for you shortly. I imagine none of you have had a chance to eat a decent dinner yet. In the meantime, will you follow me to the briefing room?" He led the foursome past the piles of gear through a door that led into a room that had no windows in the center of the house. For Sauwa it felt like an interrogation room with its dreary, blank, cream-colored walls. Except for a desk and a row of folding chairs, there was no furniture. As ordered, everyone moved to sit in one of the chairs. The young man gave an order to another man in their alien language then stepped toward the door. "You wait here. My commander will be in shortly to brief you."

Tarkov and Carzona pulled into the driveway following it past the two men standing guard and into the backyard directly behind the van. Concerned that the arms trafficker might be playing some sort of angle, they waited for the van to leave and followed in their own separate car. Since they were the more visible figures, it was easier to assume they would likely have the attention of anyone tailing them. If they were being followed, they would shake the tail before heading to the house.

"Well, how will this go down?" Tarkov asked looking at the Colonel. "I mean we can't just ask them their histories."

Carzona sniffed and then tilted his head to one side. "I imagine this is new for you."

"Yes, it is," Tarkov answered. "In the Spetsnaz, I had the benefit of military service records that I could review. I also had the luxury of interviewing some of these people and even having a small enough world to know their reputations. Now, I have four strangers inside who I know nothing about and have to make an assessment for a very risky operation."

"However, now we're working with mercenaries — mercenaries we're hiring in the black market. We know only what they tell us and what we observe and assess with our own professional experience in this field. In this case what we will be looking for are signs of military and mercenary experience," Carzona responded

Tarkov just looked at the Colonel. Sensing the need to explain further, Carzona continued. "We speak to them individually in a room, ask them questions, and let them choose how they answer. You'll find that your own professional experience and instincts will make it easy to distinguish the phonies who are clearly lying about who they claim to be.

You'll also find it easier than you think to distinguish the competent professionals from the idiots amongst those who are truthful about their backgrounds. We don't need braggarts or blowhards who talk too much and need to impress everyone with their exploits. Nor do we need people who think that pointless or reckless behavior is a sign of a good soldier.

Tarkov thought the Colonel was a man more used to this intrigue and covert activity than he led him to believe. The Russian felt he had been given a great opportunity his first time as a private freelancer to have such a mentor enabling him to learn about this odd world of private sector military operations.

I t wasn't the most comfortable environment, Sauwa
thought to herself.

The dead silence and the three strange men sitting next to
her made for an unpleasant situation. Still, when she
thought about the several times she had been in far worst
circumstances, she felt she should be counting herself lucky.
She had looked about the room casually once or twice. It was
a conditioned action from her training and experience.
Never waste a chance to collect intelligence and learn about
who you're dealing with. She had noticed that one of the
darker skinned gentlemen had casually done the same,
while the other two men only glanced at the man guarding
the doorway and then settled in keeping their eyes forward.

She didn't like to make quick judgments — it was a reckless way of operating. She decided that these men were all
former soldiers, perhaps from some sort of commando regiment or counter-guerrilla force. She couldn't imagine
Valikov, a man obsessed with his professional reputation and

eager to please potential long-term customers, providing anything less.

She recognized the two men coming through the entryway instantly. They were the two men Valikov had spoken to a week ago, and she had seen them again this evening at the bar. The larger man was the Russian who was followed by the shorter, large-framed Asian fellow. They said nothing as they entered the room and circled around the four seated mercenaries.

The two men scrutinized each person and the mercenaries displaying an assortment of unspoken responses. The sandy-haired man gave them both a quick up and down glance and then lowered his eyes to focus on his twiddling thumbs; the two dark-skinned men leaned back in their chairs, one shooting the two men a somewhat cocky stare while the other was deadpan serious. Sauwa rested her hands on her stomach as she looked directly at both men with the appearance of a student awaiting a lecture from her professor.

Tarkov gave a signal to Carzona who slipped to the back of the room. Regarding the assorted group, Tarkov started. "For the purposes of this operation, all discussions and orders will be carried out in English. This is a language you should all be able to speak."

The room rumbled with English responses acknowledging they understood him, and they met that criteria. "Good, then we will conduct this presentation in an orderly way. We are recruiting for a special mission that will be carried out abroad and will be dangerous. The pay for your services will be eighty-thousand U.S. dollars upon completion of the mission with the promise of a twenty-thousand-dollar additional bonus if the mission goes over two months. If you are not interested, please make this known now."

No one moved from their seat. None of the men made any gesture that indicated reluctance. Sauwa was less than enthusiastic. She would have happily raised her hand and opted out of this whole ordeal, except for the fact that Valikov would not stand for her backing out. She sat quietly allowing her face and body to express the sheer disinterest she had in this operation. She could feel the Russian looking down on her intently. She waited for him to say something. Instead, he pressed on.

"Very well, we will interview you one at a time in a room down the hall. When we are finished, you will be driven back to the location where we picked up and paid for your time this evening along with some cab or bus fare to get you back to your domiciles. If you are chosen, we will be contacting you in four days." His comments were met with nods from everyone.

The interviews began with the sandy-haired man. He was waved out the door and led down the hall followed by the Russian and his Asian associate. Sauwa waited along with the other two men. They both looked at each other as if they wanted to strike up a conversation but demurred when they looked around and saw eyes watching them. It sent the message that whoever was hiring them was serious in what they were doing and idle chit-chat might not go over very well.

Twenty minutes later, they heard a door open at the end of the hall. A second later, the sandy-haired man walked in. His demeanor was that of a statue, his face expressionless. He sat down and turned his attention to twiddling his thumbs and acting as if he were alone in the room. Sauwa watched the man play with his fingers. The two other men looked as if they were eager to ask him about what had happened but resisted.

"Next!" Came the curt command from the man guarding the door as he pointed at Sauwa. Rising to her feet she started walking to the door. The man, a near twin to the younger man who had picked her up from the bar this evening, twisted his hand waving her to a room at the end of the hallway. As instructed, she walked the short distance down the hall. She was tense, and the walk felt like miles.

The door was ajar. She peeked in not knowing precisely what to do. Inside she saw the Russian and the other man sitting behind a plastic folding table. Catching sight of her, the Russian waved her in. Sauwa walked through the door and sat down in a folding chair across from them. Her hands slid into her lap as she interlaced her fingers.

"What is your name?" The Russian opened the discussion.

"Marisa Ramsey," she replied.

He looked up at her. "That is not your real identity, is it?" His tone was sharp, and he gazed at her as if he was about to read her biography if she tried to deny it.

"No, it isn't," she replied.

"Give us your real name," the Russian commanded.

She hesitated. She looked over to see the Asian man, who had been directing his attention elsewhere but was now looking at her and letting her know he wanted an answer as well. "You have the name I gave you," she eventually replied. "I don't see any reason to press the matter. It's the one I go by right now. If you're not comfortable with it, then I guess I'm not what you need." She started to get up.

"Remain where you are," the Russian commanded in a

low growl. He glared at her intently as if deciding his next move. Not wanting to push the issue, she sank back into her seat.

"I assume you have some document to verify your identity?" He acted like he wanted to jump across the table and attack her if she gave him another rebellious answer. Tipping her head slightly, she reached into her coat and produced a leather-bound booklet. She slid the booklet across the table toward them. Picking it up, he began to examine it. It was a British passport with a picture of her likeness on it and bearing the name of Marisa Ramsey. He handed the document to his cohort and looked back at her. "You're not British though," he stated.

"For this purpose, I am," she replied, not wanting to divulge her identity to these strangers. If they dismissed her over this issue, she would at least have a valid excuse for Valikov.

"You're used to dealing with non-English speaking foreigners." The Russian cracked the beginnings of a smile. "You've posed as a Brit, but I've spent years in southern Africa. I know a Rhodesian accent when I hear it. Since the country doesn't exist anymore, I can only assume you are South African either by birth or by immigration from Rhodesia."

It was no use keeping up the deception. The Russian looked at her with certainty — she was not going to be able to deceive him. To try and continue insisting she was British was futile. But, it was utterly insane to tell a group of strangers who she really was. She thought again of walking out but realized one phone call to Valikov and she would be right back here with them knowing her actual name and history.

"You're right," she began. "I'm technically South African."

"I can assume that you have given us a fake name and nationality because you are a fugitive from someplace," the Asian man interjected. "There is no point in trying to hide. If we can't get the truth out of you, I'm certain Mr. Andre Valikov would oblige us in unmasking your identity. So, there is really no point in hiding who you are." The Asian man had come to the same conclusion she had and seemed ready and interested enough to continue this inquiry as such.

Giving a deep sigh she began. "My name is Sauwa Catcher." She waited to see the reaction of her interviewers. Their faces were expressionless.

"What is your background Ms. Catcher?" The Russian had settled back in his chair apparently content he was hearing the truth. "What is your professional experience?"

Running her tongue over her upper lip, she prepared herself. "I was for years in the employ of South African military intelligence as an operative for their direct-action arm known as the Civil Cooperation Bureau."

"I have heard of this organization," the Russian stated, half talking to her, half apprising his cohort. "My dealings with them in Africa were rare. What I do know is they were most ruthless in the way they engaged the enemy. They were also quite effective in many regards."

"We were," Sauwa said nothing more. She didn't feel the comment warranted any elaborate response either in her defense or adulation. Her opinion must have been evident in her attitude. The Russian pressed the matter further. "Then I can only imagine your work was deeply involved in covert missions and the execution of clandestine war against your enemy abroad."

"I guess you could say that." Her reply was again brief and undetailed.

The Russian scowled at her. "I do not appreciate your evasive responses," he growled. "You are not being questioned by the authorities or a prosecutor. You are here because we wish to hire a skilled operative for an important job! If you are truly interested in getting it, I suggest your replies be more detailed and open."

Her mood remained unchanged. The threatening words and tone of the burly Russian had not yielded the slightest hint of intimidation.

"Perhaps it is not a job I'm suited for," she suddenly replied. "I've then wasted your time and should leave right now." She moved to get up.

"Not so fast," the alien voice of the Asian chimed in once more. "If you walk out that door my next phone call will be to Mr. Valikov, and the topic will be about you. What will he say if I recounted the details of this interview and your behavior to him?"

She paused mid-way out of her chair. Sauwa looked at the Asian man, who was gazing back at her with determination.

"Sit down," he commanded, his voice low and curt.

Sauwa sank back into her chair and remained silent. For the first time, her demeanor had gone from quiet indifference to a mixture of anger and nervousness. The Asian nodded to his colleague yielding the interview back to him. The Russian resumed his questioning. "You gave us a false name and identity. I can only assume you are a fugitive from some government."

"Yes, I am."

"Here in Turkey?" The Russian shot her a hard, inquisitive look demanding further elaboration with this answer.

"No, not in Turkey," she sighed. "My previous missions for the Apartheid left me a branded war criminal. I'm currently wanted in South Africa. I'm also wanted by the British government and also heavily sought in Ireland."

The Russian frowned. "I don't know that I like the idea of having wanted criminals for our operation."

"If I may," Sauwa interjected. "You're interviewing for a job that is highly dangerous. I can only assume it is illegal since you're not using any of your own people. You have two highly trained and competent people for this line of work. Don't expect to be interviewing a bunch of professional soldiers and intelligence operatives sitting here with distinguished service histories and an endless list of medals and commendations. Those types hire out to fight in legitimate wars in Africa and the Middle-East.

"You've brought in a bunch of us who haven't shown the slightest hesitation to being brought to an empty house in a remote section of town by dubious means. None of us questioned it or were the least bit concerned because for us this is part of the normal routine. The person who put you in touch with us is an arms broker who is recommending us based upon the work we've done for him in the process of his criminal enterprises. We're here because we are criminals and work in the criminal world. Expect that most of us have records with the police or are known to various law enforcement and intelligence agencies."

The two men sat quietly for a long period of time. The silence reminded them of a monastery. The Russian looked over at his Asian colleague who only looked back with an expressionless face. "You've been doing this sort of work a long time?" The Russian finally broke the silence. "Your legal status is of concern, I will not lie. But you are still capable of travel and your time with the CCB has given you extensive overseas operational experience?"

"I'm wanted in Great Britain for the missions I carried out, and the operations I participated in." Sauwa had reverted back to her more comfortable rebellious posture.

"Explain further what you did in your service for the South Africans," the Russian said, his glance was one of suspicion.

"I was part of a special infiltration team, code-named Dark Chamber," she began. "It was comprised of Rhodesian born whites and South Africans of British lineage. Our mission was to blend into British society and conduct intelligence gathering against left-wing, anti-Apartheid political groups and Black Nationalist organizations operating out of European safe havens. We were to also carry out a covert campaign against these organizations and disrupt their activities and destroy any means they created to support terrorist efforts back in Africa."

"You worked clandestine operations then?" the Russian asked.

"Yes, I did," she replied.

"And since then?" he continued.

"What I'm doing now," she replied. "You could say I work as a mercenary. I've had a few masters since leaving the services of South Africa. I have worked for whoever has been inclined to employ me and for what purpose — spy, assassin, mercenary. In my current circumstances, I can't afford to be choosy about who I work for. Right now, it is our mutual acquaintance."

"This operation promises to be risky and arduous," the Russian explained. "I'm very much concerned about how a woman will handle such a mission."

Giving a shrug, Sauwa cocked her head to one side. "If you're not sure, then don't hire me. Nothing is worse than being in the field with leadership that is always worried about you and constantly inhibits your ability to do your job. If you can't have me because you think a woman needs extra supervision and protection, then it's just as well you don't hire me. Otherwise, in my experience, nothing is more dangerous than an operational leader thinking with his paternal instincts. He inevitably jeopardizes the mission and everyone because he's no longer giving sound direction or making logical judgment calls. If you can't see me as a soldier like everyone else, then you're going to get us all killed. And, that is the truth."

"Thank you for your time," the Russian said as he raised his hand off the table and waved her to leave.

Sauwa did so, nodding slightly as she rose from her chair and left the room. She returned to the main room and to the other three candidates. They were as she had left them — still sitting quietly not paying her the slightest attention. The call came for the next candidate and one of the mocha skinned men came to his feet and walked out the door.

Sinking into the chair next to the sandy-haired man, she leaned back feeling a tad exhausted from the night's events. If she didn't get picked for the job, she could at least be assured that Valikov wouldn't hear anything that would suggest she deliberately sabotaged it.

The mocha skinned man returned thirty minutes later. The next mocha skinned man left for his interview. He returned in less than ten minutes. A few minutes later the

Russian and the Asian entered the room and thanked everyone for their time. Reminding them that their process would take a few days and, it would be the end of the week before they heard anything. They were all led out of the room by the same route they had entered. They exited the house and were led back to the van where they were met by the young man who had gathered them from the bar. As they were loaded into the back of the van, the young man handed them each a thick white envelope, supposedly the pay they had earned for their time.

The ride back was as full of turns as it had been getting to the house. When they reached the bar, they were released from the van. As they exited the vehicle, the young Asian man reminded them that they needed to leave a means of contact if they wished employment. Hands were raised offering him bits of paper with their contact information. Sauwa handed him the number Valikov had given her for this occasion. The young man quickly examined it before stuffing it into his pocket. Turning around, she quietly proceeded down the street.

12

S auwa's interview had not gone well. They didn't seem interested in having a female on this mission and were not happy she was an international fugitive. She was confident she had heard the last from the Russian mercenary and his mysterious compatriots from the South Pacific.

However, at the end of the week, as promised, a call came through to Valikov, who delightedly informed her she had been accepted as one of their hires. She was shocked and bitter. This was a feather in Valikov's cap, an expansion of the client base for his business. That his friend, Tarkov, and his employers found suitable candidates from his referrals could only work in his favor.

Hearing she was now to take part in some high-risk operation with a bunch of dubious mercenary types did not sit well with her. Some small part of her wanted to argue. She knew, however, it would be a futile endeavor. Everyone was to meet the following night at 1900 hours near a small café along the shoreline. She would be met by the same man who had initially approached her and taken her to the house.

Oddly, the plan was remarkably less complex and security conscious than what she had gone through the first time. She presumed the first meeting was not just for interviews but to see if they had become of interest to a third party. The reduction of precautions told her they were confident they had not.

She spent her day completing her usual security checks with Mustafa then spent the rest of her time exercising in her boss's household gym — she was one of the very few to enjoy this perk. A solid routine of cardio and weight lifting kept her fit for her duties. Afterword, she enjoyed a warm shower and then packed lightly for her trip using her small knapsack. She had to balance personal needs with the need to travel light and be mobile. Once she left for the meeting, she would be entirely on their schedule. Judging by the camping gear and logistics, it was easy to assume she would not be leaving their safe house until they moved to their destination.

For passports, she would carry her British one bearing the name Marisa Ramsey. It was the name they already knew, and one Valikov had given her. Like the rest of her false identities, he kept them locked up in a safe at some unknown location. In a separate location, he kept duplicates that he would turn over to both the British and South African embassies in Ankara if she should ever try to run out on him. It was his way of ensuring control.

THOUGH IT HAD BEEN ONLY three days interviewing a total of twelve candidates, it still proved to be a long and arduous process. Sauwa had been right in her predictions. The men who had been found for them may have been former soldiers with extensive military experience and training under their belts, but they were also an assortment of criminals with police records in more than one country. Many, like Sauwa, were fugitives from the authorities.

The men were incredibly tight-lipped about their professional and criminal histories. It took extensive work to get them to finally open up. Others tended to be intent on reliving their heydays and talking themselves up as if they single-handedly built their respective military or intelligence services before they were dismissed. A few of them didn't even make it through the initial stage of the screening. They were left at the bar without even being approached because of excessive drinking or loud behavior that drew too much attention or threatened a bar fight.

When the process was over, Carzona and Tarkov had settled on the four candidates they felt would work for the initial part of the operation.

Sauwa Catcher, going under the name Marisa Ramsey, had a background in intelligence and covert operations that was rare. Their other candidates predominantly hailed from military backgrounds, not intelligence. Tarkov had reservations about her legal circumstances and the unwanted attention an Apartheid war criminal might expose them to. However, Valikov personally recommended her and her skill set was greatly needed. As it would be his operation to run once they got to Cyprus, Carzona had given him full discretion for determining the hires. It still helped that the Colonel had voiced the same concerns and the same interest when it came to her.

The next choice was the Italian, Gino Sacchini. He had served for a number of years with the Commando Raggrupamento Subacquei ed Incursori or COMSUBIN, Italy's elite naval commando forces. Though not as well-known as the more world-renowned US Navy Seals or the Israeli Sheytet 13, the COMSUBIN had a long history of producing excellent and highly trained commando units. While he had never been up against them personally, Tarkov had heard reports and stories from Naval Spetsnaz who had experience against them while trying to infiltrate Italian waters and facilities. The universal conclusion was they were a force to be reckoned with. In the case of Sacchini, he had insisted that while in the unit he had been part of the Incursori, the offensive arm of the unit, responsible for infiltration of enemy ships and ports and mastering techniques of demolition on commando operations behind the lines.

The next candidate was Jacques De'vor, a Frenchman who had cut his teeth with the Fusiliers Commandos de 1'Air, the French Air Commandos. Though generally, the Air Commandos have the responsibility of protecting French air bases, not necessarily the most suitable training and experience for this mission, De'vor had been with the Escadron de Protection et d'Intervention (EPI), a crack unit of commandos with the mission of attacking airfields. Like most other commando units, the EPI trains to operate behind enemy lines entirely on its own without any support. They also specialize in small raid tactics.

After De'vor, Tarkov chose another Italian Vincenzo Gorzo, formerly with the San Marco Marines and now, like the others a gun for hire. Like the COMSUBIN, the San Marco Marines train extensively in coastal assaults, reconnaissance, and sabotage. The Marines also trained extensively with the COMSUBIN at many of their schools, thus offering some degree of training integrity in the team. Being a naval commando himself, Tarkov preferred working with men of similar combat backgrounds which would make planning operations easier knowing he could work with such men.

They only had what the men told them for work histories, and it might have seemed as if they were bragging to puff up their resumes to get a job. However, enough of what they said coincided with the Russian's own knowledge and experience of western commando operations and tactics that he was relatively sure of their qualifications. For the most part, Valikov had chosen the candidates well. Only a few of them greatly exaggerated their backgrounds and experience. What it boiled down to was finding men who were familiar with commando operations. It was important to get people who had enough knowledge of the underworld to know how to move about without the support of a government, how to keep a low profile, and how to bypass the authorities. Both Tarkov and Carzona knew their team would need all these skills as they developed plans for their mission.

Aside from Sauwa, the other men all introduced themselves under their actual names and assured their potential employers that the countries where they had issues with the police were in Africa or the Middle-East. Tarkov and the Colonel hoped they would have no trouble operating in Europe.

The van cruised around the winding driveway and pulled into the garage behind the house as it had done the first time. All lights were out when they arrived but, a few minutes later, a line of silhouettes came marching up the patio toward the house. One of the Filipinos slid the door opened and stepped back. The young man, Tarkov had come to know as Miguel, who had initially approached the candidates at the bar, came walking in followed by the sandy-haired Frenchman, then the two Italians and finally the young South African female. This time, Miguel led them into the main room where they were lined up as if preparing to enter a military basic training course.

Miguel stepped aside giving Tarkov the floor as he entered the room and deliberately assessed the group. This was done less to evaluate what he had already determined but to solidify in everyone's mind that he was unquestionably in command. He was pleased that despite being out of the military for a period of time, all the mercenaries looked remarkably fit.

"We have all met before; it is time I introduced myself. I am Sergei Tarkov. Like you, I am a mercenary who has been employed to lead this mission." He looked around at the group. They all remained still with their eyes focused on him. "You have all been picked for this mission out of several other candidates. We have already discussed the basics of the mission — how long it should last and how much you will be paid for your services. We will discuss the operation on a need to know basis. For security reasons, you will be briefed on what you will be doing and who the target is when we have reached our destination." He studied the faces of his new team. They all exhibited expressions of interest and sincerity as they watched him. "Also, for security purposes, you will remain here at this house until we leave — no phone calls, no outside contact. In one hour you will be briefed on where we will be going when we will be leaving, and how we will be getting there. After tonight you will know too much for us to let you out of our sight. So, if any of you have any reservations, now is the time to leave."

He stood quietly for a time watching the mannerisms of

everyone in the line. No one moved or showed any signs of wavering. Sauwa wanted to, but she knew what the consequences would be if she did. When he was satisfied everyone was resolved to go through with the mission, Tarkov continued. "Now you will be shown to your lodgings and where you can stow your gear, then you can get something to eat. Are there any questions?" No one spoke. "That's all."

Tarkov turned his attention to Miguel. "Go ahead and get them stowed away. They can take their meals in the kitchen." With that, the Russian turned smartly on his heels, as if he were back in the military, and marched off.

Miguel took charge as he began directing the four mercenaries to grab their gear and follow him. All were traveling light and proceeded to follow him down the hall and eventually up a flight of stairs. Arriving at the first room, Miguel dispatched the two Italian men. "You gentlemen will find cots, bedding, and materials for hygiene."

Nodding their heads, the Italians slipped into their room and disappeared. Waving the other two to follow, Miguel walked a few steps further and came to a second room. He turned to Sauwa, "I must apologize miss. Our lodgings are limited, so I'm afraid you'll have to share with this man here." He motioned toward the sandy-haired Frenchman. "Hopefully, you're not modest."

Accepting that she had no choice, she shrugged and walked inside a small room with no windows and bare cream-colored walls. There were two steel framed cots with rolled up sleeping bags and some white plastic bags. At the foot of the cots were two metal footlockers each with a lock and a pair of keys resting on top.

"This is home then," a soft voice interrupted her

thoughts and caught her by surprise. She turned and, for the first time, realized she was alone with the sandy-haired man. His accent was clearly English, but it was not his first language. From the way he sounded, she assumed he was either French or from a country where French was the predominant language. Since he had spoken in English, she presumed he was speaking to her.

"For now," she replied as she walked over to the footlocker. She took the lock and keys and checked to make sure they worked. Opening the white plastic bag, she found it full of basic hygienic items — toothbrush, toothpaste, dental string, a few bars of anti-bacterial soap, some razors, and shaving cream.

Opening the footlocker, she dropped her knapsack into it. It fit perfectly with some room to spare. Throwing the plastic bag in with all the hygiene supplies, she locked it with the padlock and pocketed the keys. She turned to see the Frenchman busily storing his own equipment in his assigned locker. He was intensely focused on this activity, paying not the slightest interest in anything else.

She recognized the Frenchman but, if he recognized her, he certainly wasn't displaying any sign of it. In fact, he wasn't giving her any type of recognition at all. He was utterly indifferent to her existence. His initial behavior left her with mixed feelings. He wasn't exhibiting the obvious crude displays of sexual perversion that she constantly encountered with most black market mercenary types. Yet, he had the stone-cold demeanor she commonly associated with closet psychopaths. They were the type that was one step up from serial killers and was in this business because they loved the chaos and death. Neither one was a person she could sleep soundly around.

Sauwa rose and began examining her sleeping bag. It was a black nylon model that looked like one of the tactical pieces being introduced into the modern militaries of the world. It wasn't too cold outside and the house seemed to have ample heating. Still, she appreciated that they provided decent sleeping gear.

Finished examining her equipment and stowing it away, Sauwa stepped out of the room and started down the hallway. The Frenchman followed her, staying on her heels. They came down the stairs and made their way through the main room into the kitchen. An older man, another Asian-looking fellow, was standing over a stove managing an assortment of metal pots filled with boiling water and sauces. The counter was covered with bowls filled with vegetables and cutting boards heaped with the meat pieces and juices that had just been carved up. Whatever was being made smelled delicious. It also smelled different from the usual aromas associated with Turkish or Middle-East cuisine.

One of the other Filipinos ushered them both to the table stacked with plates and cutlery. They had just started to grab their dining utensils when they were joined by the other two mercenaries. The two mocha-skinned men greeted their new comrades with smiles and gracious pleasantries that were warm yet guarded. From their accents, Sauwa deduced they were both Italians. The two men slipped behind Sauwa and the Frenchman and quickly retrieved their plates and cutlery.

The cook, noticing them waiting, beckoned them over with his hand. As instructed, they walked to the counter. The Frenchman led and was handed his meal. He returned to the table and began devouring his supper. Sauwa filled her plate and followed suit. She was starving and in no mood for social graces. Plopping into her seat she immediately commenced eating. They were soon joined by the two Italians who were both jabbering to each other in their native tongue. The familiarity with which the Italians engaged one another suggested this was not the first time they had worked together. By the way they eyed both her and the Frenchman, Sauwa figured they were both leery of her and her roommate. She noticed all three shot her an occasional suspicious look. Apparently, she was the one everybody was most concerned about — the lone female on the team amidst these hardened mercenaries. She imagined they were all viewing her as the inevitable weak link.

Tarkov entered the kitchen and quickly glanced over at his team before turning his attention to the main room. Sauwa and the other mercenaries concentrated on their meals. None of them knew quite what to make of their employers and were inclined not to say too much.

When supper was over, the four disposed of their trash in a bag designated for garbage. Miguel escorted them down the hall to the same room where Sauwa and the Frenchman had waited to be interviewed. Folding chairs were still set up in a neat line. A table with some documents on it had been added. Sergei Tarkov was standing behind the table. The man who had assisted in the interviews was taking a position in the far back corner. It was as if Sauwa was reliving the interview night all over.

"Please, take a seat," Miguel instructed as he waved them toward a row of chairs.

Everyone slid into one of the seats. Sauwa found herself sitting next to one of the Italians who eyed her as if she had snuck into the meeting. She ignored him as she concentrated her attention on Tarkov. With everyone settled, Tarkov began.

"You have all been recruited to carry out an operation that will take place on the island nation of Cyprus." The Russian paused to wait for their reaction. He figured these mercenaries had worked heavily in Africa and the Middle-East. He wanted to test their initial response after finding out they would operate outside their familiar stomping grounds. He saw a few eyes widen and exhibit some other gestures that denoted surprise at this revelation. For the most part, everyone kept calm and maintained a professional demeanor.

Confident he had a solid team, he continued. "We will depart at 1300 hours and drive to a port where a seafaring craft will be waiting for us. We are going by water to avoid the confinement of the airport and the strict security we would encounter. When we arrive, we will stop just short of entering Cyrus water space. At this point, we will be met by a trusted friend who will take us the rest of the way into the country via his fishing boat and end our journey at a tourist marina used by the local boatmen where security will be light. After we arrive, we will be taken to what will be our headquarters location for the duration of the operation."

"If I may," Sauwa interrupted, "What type of boat are we taking from here to Cyprus?"

Tarkov replied, "Why do you ask?"

"If we are going to Cyprus, we will be going into treacherous waters. It is only a few hundred miles away from the turmoil with Lebanon, Syria, and Israel. Cyprus has a history of terrorist groups headquartering themselves there and all sorts of illegal contraband are being moved around those sea lanes. Cargo ships get stopped all the time by naval ships from those countries looking for illegal cargo or wanted terrorists. If we get stopped and boarded, I assume we don't have papers identifying us as merchant marines or commercials sailors. That will send red flags to any halfway competent naval inspector. If we're going to travel, we need to be on something that won't arouse suspicion in the event we are boarded and don't have merchant papers."

The other mercenaries nodded in agreement. They had moved out in other criminal activities and were aware of what they might encounter from patrolling naval vessels in international waters.

"We will be using a cargo retrieval boat," the Russian answered, thinking it interesting that Carzona had raised similar concerns.

Sauwa and the rest of the team nodded agreeably.

Tarkov continued, "Just before crossing into Cyprus waters, we will be met by a contact and a local boatman. We will change ships and sail in under a locally registered ship that will dock at a marina as opposed to a shipping port. The security and other bureaucratic concerns will be greatly reduced. Once there, arrangements have been made to get a false entry stamp placed on your passports. This will mitigate any situation where you will have to show your papers."

The mercenaries were all listening as he looked around the room. He was relieved to see that no one was jotting anything down. It would have been a security risk if any notes were carelessly left behind or lost in transit reinforcing his perception that this hand-picked team was professional. "Once there, we will set up our base of operation. We will live and work out of this base, manage our resources, and maintain our physical fitness in this place. I don't want to give away more details until we get there. Are there any questions?"

"Yes," one of the Italians responded. "We're all packing light for a mission you expect to take two months. What arrangements will be made for additional clothing and washing?"

Tarkov nodded, "You will be provided a modest budget for additional clothing both for your person and as the mission requires. It will not come out of your pay so long as you do not exceed your budget. We have also made note of laundry facilities in the vicinity that you will be able to use. Again, this will be part of your clothing budget so factor that in as well."

"I don't want to be presumptuous," the Italian cut in, "but I want to discuss an issue before we leave on this mission. If things go badly, what will be the escape protocol?"

Tarkov was expecting this question. "I know you're all concerned about what happens if our operation is in danger, and we need to escape quickly. If we get compromised, we have established an exfiltration plan to get everyone out. We will initiate it in any case where I deem our situation tenuous--"

"No!" Sauwa interjected, this time with an authoritative vehemence. "Don't tell us about exfiltration plans. It's a waste of time." She hadn't intended to say much, and she certainly was not speaking with the intent of impressing her new team. But hearing an emergency escape plan made her cringe. All eyes were on her, and she was extremely concerned about this outburst getting back to Valikov. Still, she had to raise the issue. She could even feel the man standing in the back scrutinizing her.

"I would think an exfiltration plan would be one of the most important things to discuss in this situation," Tarkov said looking at her indignantly.

"I agree," she spoke up. "However, an escape plan should be on the individual."

All eyes were watching her, and it was apparent an explanation was required. If she created too much of stir, Valikov's wrath would be awaiting her return. However, she was aware of how easily such missions could go badly leaving everyone in a compromised state. Her boss's anger seemed less concerning than being stuck on an island as a highly sought fugitive. "I'm just looking around this house. All the guys you have here who have been running security and handling the operation of getting us here easily show the necessary capability and intelligence to execute whatever mission you need to have carried out in Cyprus. From the look of them, I'm guessing they're a personal guard not hired guns. This makes them a lot more trustworthy for your employer to use over mercenaries you hired from the back alleys, through an arms merchant you hardly know."

"As I see it, there's only one logical reason why you would use us over them and that is we're entirely dispensable. This job, whatever it is, is going to get dangerous. I'm also guessing that whatever the blowback, it can't be traced back to whoever is bankrolling this operation. I'm also guessing they can't handle the exposure. We're just mercenaries, making it easy for you to wash your hands of us, and leave us to our own fate. This is exactly what I expect to happen if things don't go well, and the operation gets aborted. Especially if it spares the backers from having to pay us for services rendered."

The room was as silent as a mortuary. Tarkov looked at

her with a blank stare that she couldn't interpret. He was either angry that she was causing so much trouble or realizing this unconsidered revelation. She watched as he looked past her to the man standing in the back of the room. She couldn't tell what the Asian was relaying to the Russian as they carried on a dialogue communicated through facial expressions and head nods. The Russian cleared his throat as he prepared to speak. "Perhaps you are right. You have no reason to trust us in this situation or to have any concern for your lives."

"Exactly!" One of the Italians snarled as he nearly came out of his seat. "The English girl is right. If this shit goes bad, there is nothing that guarantees we will not be left on an island to fend for ourselves. Those hiring us will be too busy looking after their own arses. They'd easily cut us loose to protect themselves."

Tarkov was beginning to understand the reality of the situation. Carzona decided it was necessary to intervene. Walking to the head of the room, he relieved a somewhat flustered Tarkov. "Quiet please!" He snapped instantly asserting dominance over the conversation. "If you feel uncomfortable about the situation, we can discuss something more amenable."

"The only amenable plan," Sauwa stated, "is if we are able to affect our own means of escape. No plan that calls for your people and resources is going to be trustworthy if things go bad. If the mission gets compromised, I definitely reserve the right to make a run for it. That said, I would want three thousand U.S. dollars before we depart. If things go badly, not only do I fully believe you would abandon us, I also believe we would never see that eighty thousand or any other payment as our paymasters would have just disappeared. An initial three grand will ensure we at least get something and guarantees that if we have to run, we have money in hand and are not completely lacking resources."

The rest of the mercenaries were grumbling and unanimously nodding their heads in agreement with the young woman. It was apparent this was not going to be negotiable. "I will get back to you on this matter," Carzona said rubbing his forehead and lowering his shoulders in a sign of capitulation. Carzona returned the floor to the Russian as he stepped out of the room to contact his superiors.

Assuming control of the meeting, Tarkov was at a loss for words. He looked down at the young South African with a mixture of irritation at the near mutiny she had caused and respect for making him aware of this new revelation. "During this lull in the meeting, I want to take time to introduce everyone, so you know who you'll be working with." He shifted his body until he was facing the Italian at the far end of the row of seats. "Mr. Vincenzo Gorzo." He waved to the first Italian, a lanky, slender man with long hair and a pencil mustache — he looked more like a playboy than a mercenary. Gorzo smiled and waved to the other mercenaries.

"I would next like to introduce Mr. Gino Sacchini," Tarkov said pointing to the other Italian. Sacchini rose to his feet. A man of medium build with a slightly protruding gut, he looked quite average with his unkempt, curly hair and a day and a half of facial growth. "How do you do." He smiled politely showing off his tobacco stained teeth as he waved and bowed like he was entertaining an audience.

After he returned to his seat, Tarkov turned his focus to the sandy-haired Frenchman. "I would like to introduce you to Masseur Jacques De'vor." The Frenchman folded his arms and gave only a slight dip of his head, his eyes focused on Tarkov.

The Russian turned his attention toward Sauwa. "And finally, I would like you to meet Miss Sauwa Catcher. Who, for purposes of this operation, will be operating under the name Marisa Ramsey."

Sauwa didn't appreciate being outed this way. She suspected it was cheap revenge for the near mutiny she had just caused. She stared coldly back at the Russian, but he merely brushed it off and continued his briefing. "I wish to explain that you were all chosen because of your particular backgrounds. You men all have extensive military histories with commando units, primarily naval commando operations. You have all served for a lengthy period of time in elite units that specialized in high-level raids and assaults. This experience will be essential for our mission as we will likely have to conduct such operations. I understand that you have all continued plying your trade and maintaining your experience in addition to getting used to operating without government support."

"That's us," interrupted Vincenzo Gorzo as he scowled at Sauwa suspiciously. "If this is an important and dangerous mission, we shouldn't have a woman with us. They create unneeded risk."

Tarkov went on with his briefing as if he hadn't heard the Italian's protest. "In the case of Miss Catcher, her expertise is in intelligence — particularly clandestine operations and ground reconnaissance. She will be helping us accumulate the needed strategic intelligence on our targets and assist in the operational planning for the execution. She has worked in western European cities and has a better feel for what we should expect."

The attitude exhibited by the men was still one of suspicion and distrust. They were professional combat soldiers and women didn't figure into their world outside of being secretaries and nurses. Sliding back in her seat, Sauwa knew it would be a difficult mission trying to sell herself to these guys. It wasn't the first time, and she would make do however she had to.

Carzona entered the room and worked his way to the front of the meeting. Eye contact with Tarkov sent him to the corner, giving the Filipino the floor. "It is settled. On the day of departure, you will each receive an initial payment of three-thousand dollars upon setting foot on the ship. This payment will be in addition to your eighty thousand dollars. Will that suffice?"

The mercenaries all nodded with satisfaction. The meeting ended with everyone filing out the door. As Sauwa was about to leave, Tarkov asked her to stay. When the room emptied leaving the two of them and the Filipino, Tarkov began. "I wish to begin by expressing my apologies for disclosing your true identity to the men. I felt it was better to give full disclosure now than have it come out or be an issue later."

Sauwa studied the Russian for a good minute before responding. "I'm sure that's not the only reason you detained me for this private chat."

"It is one of the reasons," Tarkov explained as she dropped into the seat next to him. "I also understand you didn't want to do this assignment. My friend subsequently loaned you to me for this operation. And, I am grateful. With all the candidates we were given no one else really matched your background and qualifications. I want to make it clear that you were recruited because of your background. Most of the candidates we reviewed are soldiers whose experience has been in war zones. As I said in the meeting, they will serve us well when we have to initiate action against our targets, but they won't have the expertise to operate in a sophisticated urban environment such as where we will be going when we have to perform more complex operations. This is why we took you despite your legal situation."

"You are expecting this thing to get nasty, aren't you," she responded with a twinge of uncertainty in her voice.

"We aren't sure how messy it might get," the Filipino suddenly interjected. "We know we can expect to have a fair amount of gunplay. What we hope is that we can minimize it and rely on more discrete methods as much as possible to achieve our goals."

Tarkov took back control of the conversation. "We are soldiers, we fight wars in war zones. You are an operative who lives in this kind of place, and I will be looking to you for advice when planning our course."

"You're putting an awful lot of trust and responsibility on a mercenary fugitive you hardly know and wants no part of this affair," Sauwa pointed out as she rose to her feet and started pacing.

"I am," Tarkov explained. "You were the one who came highly recommended by your employer," Tarkov explained. "Which either means you are a spy who he figures will somehow keep him posted on our movements, or you are someone who does a great deal of important work and has an impressive record doing it. I'm guessing it is the latter, since Mr. Valikov was insistent I alert him the minute you disappear. He seemed very determined to have you back when this operation was finished."

"Well, maybe I'm that good in his bed," she started toward the door.

"More like you're better in the field," the Filipino said following after her. "Your questions tonight were quite astute. You know your business well, and I imagine Valikov thinks so too." He walked up until his face was close to her ear. "Playing innocent and ignorant doesn't seem to suit you, and I don't much care for it."

"This is your mission," she replied. "And, let us be clear." She turned her head enough to have her face meet his. "I'm not the only schooled operative in this room, am I?" Their eyes met in a cold glare. "I imagine you're no stranger to this business either."

"Just do the job we're paying you for," Carzona said in a low stern voice. "And, in the future, save the issues that could lead to a mutiny for private discussions, not group meetings."

The conversation ended with the two breaking from their stares, and Sauwa exiting the room.

13

I t had been years since Thorten Ridgeway had been with Her Majesty's Secret Service commonly referred to as MI-6. Then, he was considered one of the organization's most gifted operatives. He had been a successful spy master heading up the SIS's office in Italy, then later Greece, where he had matched wits with the likes of the Soviet KGB and GRU as well as the efficient East German Hauptverwaltung (Main Directorate A). He had organized an elaborate intelligence network throughout the Mediter-ranean that had effectively penetrated the echelons of the Italian and Greek governments, including their military staffs. He had also developed several contacts within the Southern European business community. As a pioneer, he had cultivated a network that gained deep inroads into the criminal organizations dominating the underworld in the region. The black market was heavily indulged by the governing elites of the communist states of Yugoslavia, Romania, and Bulgaria. It was interesting what information the leaders of the Mafia, Union Corse and Camorra had access to about these enemy nations that sophisticated western intelligence did not.

Sadly, the end of the cold war, the fall of the communist empire, and the inevitable budget cutbacks had left such gifted intelligence masters without employment. Pensioned off and having nothing to go back to in his native homeland, Thorten Ridgeway went into business for himself. Capitalizing on the vast business contacts he had acquired in his intelligence career, he established a private organization comprised of old network people and some of his old adversaries. He found a bold new market for intelligence in the world of corporate espionage. Companies were willing to pay handsomely to know about their competitors. They also paid generously to be kept apprised of the activities of the socialist parties and political leaders who sought to curb the free market. Radical leftists and communist groups were often engaged in troublesome or violent behavior. Companies sometimes paid even more to have such organizations disrupted to erode their overall effectiveness.

When Ridgeway took a private table in one of the reserved rooms in the restaurant of the illustrious Prince Ferdinand Hotel in Rome, Italy, he was intrigued by the young female lawyer from the Philippines. He had met her a few times before when her firm had wanted to make inquiries for clients looking to invest in some East European companies. A few months ago she had offered a great deal of money to retain his agency's services for a rather strange request — to monitor some businessmen from her homeland while they were in Cyprus and gather intelligence on their business contacts and dealings. At first, he considered that this was just another story of a competitive business interest. The head of his Cyprus office contacted him directly to inform him that the man the Filipinos were meeting with was Theo Kalopolis. Kalopolis was a major arms trafficker who supplied large orders of all kinds of weapons.

Hearing this news, Ridgeway decided to take charge of the matter personally. Over the next few weeks, his people continued their investigations. The more he learned the more he wondered exactly what this young lady had gotten him into. When she contacted his offices to check on his agency's progress, he took the call himself and demanded they have a private meeting. With everything he had discovered, he felt it better to have a friendly lunch at a nice restaurant where they would not attract any attention. He did not want her to come to his office and risk his agency any further.

Esmeralda Morayo entered the big double doors of the Prince Ferdinand hotel. She was met by a well-groomed, middle-aged maître d dressed in a tuxedo. She told him she was meeting Mr. Thorten Ridgeway and immediately found herself being led past the dining area through a couple of hallways that led to big oak doors. "These are the private reserved rooms," the maître d explained. Arriving at room 28, he knocked gently.

"Yes?" A gruff voice called out from behind the door.

The waiter responded in Italian, and Morayo understood he was announcing her. She heard a command to enter in the same gruff voice.

Pushing the door open, the maître d led her inside a majestic room with polished oak furniture and tasteful replicas of classic paintings lining the walls. The room was akin to what one would find at an aristocratic estate that was designed to evoke power and wealth. Accustomed to such extravagance, Morayo was not at all intimidated. She was sure the room had been chosen for exactly that purpose.

Brushing past the maître d, she thanked the man in Italian and walked over to the table where Ridgeway was seated.

"Mr. Ridgeway, it is good to see you again." Her pleasant dignified manner confirmed she was not at all unnerved by the palatial settings. The expression on his face portrayed his irritation at her calmness.

"Senora Morayo, would you please have a seat?" He rose in a gentlemanly fashion to pull a chair out for her.

"Thank you," she replied as she slid into the plush leather chair.

He waved away the maître d, who bowed humbly shutting the door behind him as he exited. Ridgeway sank into the chair next to hers. He marveled at the young woman, who was dressed in an expensive grey pantsuit and a white silk blouse. She looked like a woman who could be an innocent girl or an intimidating power player based on the setting.

"I understand you have found information for me," she said, resting her hands in her lap and crossing her legs, making it clear she intended to be the power player today. "Though I must confess, I was surprised when I learned that you wanted to speak to me directly. I expected to be dealing with one of your executives on this matter."

"I'm afraid these are exigent circumstances, my dear." His manner was the epitome of a calm professional, but his reddening face indicated the growing anger he was trying to hold back. She was not oblivious to his anger. "When my agency agreed to this mission, it was with the understanding we were gaining information on a corporate business deal. I'm not ignorant to the fact that corporations at times wet their beaks in the illicit world when it is necessary and when we come across such things, we act according to the agenda of our clients. In this case, however, you have asked for too much."

"I see," Morayo replied. Her calm, professional manner remaining unchanged. "I do apologize. When I retained your services, I knew some illegalities were at play, but I imagined your organization had come across such things before. I take it you have discovered some dangerous information about our client's enemies?"

"I have, madam," he said acidly. "Normally, illegalities are part of the business of corporate warfare. Especially in quasi-socialist countries where free enterprise is disdained, and such things are at times necessary. Yet, there are limits to the amount of exposure I will accept."

"I take it you have reached those limits?" She raised her arms interlocking her fingers in front of her face.

"In this case, yes. I feel we have exceeded those limits." Ridgeway began tapping his fingers on the table.

"Why don't you tell me what you have found, then we can settle up and go our separate ways," she said coolly.

Leaning over, Ridgeway grabbed a leather satchel sitting on the adjacent seat. Dropping it on the table and throwing back the fold, he produced a set of thick manila folders that he placed on top of the satchel. "This is what we have found for you. Your delegation of businessmen has apparently reached out to one Theo Kalopolis, a serious trafficker in illegal arms. They have been meeting with him regularly. What we were able to ascertain is that they are trying to buy up a large consignment of weapons and munitions. We don't know much — Kalopolis is a very dangerous man to run afoul of, so I limited the scope of how far we would go to obtain your information. I have told my people to keep their energies focused on your businessmen and stay clear of

Kalopolis. What you now have is what we have collected on them."

She reached for the top folder and slid it onto her lap. Opening it, she began reading the first document. It was a well-compiled dossier aided by a collection of photographs organized chronologically. The dossier centered on a five-man delegation. She wasted little time on the individual biographies. She already knew who they were. Though she had to admit Ridgeway's firm had been quite thorough in their research. They had captured academic records, business dealings, and family connections. She was impressed.

They were equally meticulous collecting and documenting intelligence on the men's stay in Europe. The men hadn't come directly to Cyprus. They had gone first to Rome, Italy where they laid low in some penthouse suites they reserved at an expensive hotel. They had sent a few of their people to Cyprus — a lawyer plus three men described as personal security types. This lawyer met with Kalopolis' representative on a few occasions over the course of three weeks. The dossier notes described the meetings as a feeling out between the two parties.

According to the report, after a series of meetings in which the few involved were taken to some private locations controlled by the Kalopolis group, the lawyer had given a satisfactory report to his employers in Rome. A week later the delegation was in Cyprus in the tourist city of Limassol. They had taken up residence in suites at one of the city's top hotels.

Morayo continued flipping through the stack of folders while Ridgeway sat quietly. The files contained further reports detailing the day-to-day activities of the delegation and the key people they kept around them. Ridgeway's people had wiretapped telephone conversations and provided surveillance photos of people coming to the hotel to meet them. The final folder surprised Morayo. It was an overview of Kalopolis, his biography, and a list of the people he used in his business dealings. It wasn't much, but it was far more than she had expected after Ridgeway's apprehension at the start of the meeting. She looked up at him questioningly.

"I did some basic research for you," he explained before she could ask the question. "I felt it was only professional to let you know something about who you were going up against. So long as it didn't endanger my people or threaten my organization, I wanted to provide quality service."

Morayo continued looking over the files. "I appreciate what you have given us. This will do nicely. The quality of your research is impeccable." She reached into her briefcase and removed a bank draft. "This should compensate you for your services."

Ridgeway smoothly took the check from the woman's hand and examined it carefully. "Will you require my services in the near future?"

"No, I don't believe so," she replied. "But, that may change. If it does, I promise I will not involve you beyond your customary sphere." She gathered the folders and returned them to the satchel. Just as gracefully as when she arrived, she picked up the satchel, said her goodbyes, and left.

14

It was early morning when the van pulled up to the Izmir
docks. The mercenaries filed out the side door, and
Tarkov led them toward the harbor. The move had been
timed to coincide with the swarms of fisherman moving
quickly to catch their quarry during feeding time. It was
easy for the mercenaries to blend in to give the appearance
of being just a few sailors on their way out to sea. To aid this
facade, the mercenaries had been provided P-coats, old
sweatshirts, and rubber boots allowing them to blend in
with the fishermen. This gear was also practical for facing
the cold waters of the Mediterranean.

Tarkov and the Filipino, who everyone now knew as
Carzona, led the mercenaries down the docks to a large boat
surrounded by thick rubber bumpers. They reached the
ladder well and were met by a man with a thick grizzled
beard covering his face and a matching head of salt and
pepper hair that made him look more beast than human. The
woolly sweater concealing his neck looked like it had never
seen the inside of a washing machine. The Filipino ascended

the thin metal staircase and extended his arm for an introduction. The grizzled man regarded the motley group standing below him with suspicion as he reluctantly grabbed the Filipino's hand. He paid particular attention to Sauwa. His expression stated that it was bad enough to have a bunch of mercenaries bringing him trouble, but now he had a woman and all the problems that was sure to bring.

The boat set out with a sizable fleet of fishing vessels and tugboats. It looked like any other craft going about its usual routine. The mercenaries were relegated to hold up in the sleeping quarters squeezed in among the tightly placed rows of bunk beds below deck, out of sight, and out of the way of the actual crew. To pass the time, the mercenaries threw their gear into a pile in the walkway of the bunk room to use it as a table. Inevitably, someone had a deck of cards — money was produced, and the poker game was on.

Tarkov, De'vor, and the two Italians needed no convincing before they were at the makeshift table. Carzona took one of the empty bunks and engrossed himself in a book he had brought. Sauwa stripped down to her tank top and trousers and began some makeshift exercises.

The men remained ensconced in their game. Money was an added factor that kept their attention focused. She could feel the occasional wandering eye directed at her. The older men, Tarkov and Sacchini, tended to give her an occasional glance expressing a warm, affectionate interest in a fit and pretty young woman that they both knew was far too young for them. De'vor continued his role as an emotionless statue, indifferent to everything except the cards. But even he had been noticed glimpsing her as she exercised. It was Gorzo, the image of an Italian stud, who didn't try to mask his interest in her. He brazenly took his time in between games to gawk at her and examine every inch of her body. It was an easy guess that he would be the one causing her problems.

The journey from Izmir to Cyprus was a long winding trip around the coast of Western Turkey and out into open waters, and the ice between the mercenaries gradually thawed. They all had time to assess one another. After two days of being cooped up in the house and then crammed together on a grimy vessel, the need for interaction gradually took hold. Everyone began opening up to those they felt comfortable with. In Sauwa's case, it was oddly enough Sacchini.

Despite his appearance that would have one thinking he spent his days hanging around bars and picking up prostitutes, he turned out to be a remarkably warm and thoughtful man. He had been with the Italian naval commandos until he retired out. Unable to shake the need for adventure, he hired on with a mercenary group working for the Sultan of Oman fighting communist guerrillas. After that, he moved between the Gulf States working a lot of short-term operations. He was the head of a small group of privately hired operators conducting covert actions against Iranian backed Shia groups trying to subvert the government. He managed some of the more dangerous transactions working on jobs for businessmen whose dealings involved the black market. These days he freelanced which was how he got recruited for this operation. Sauwa liked him. He may have enjoyed the action and adventure soldiering offered, but he wasn't a psychopath, an action junky, or a complete degenerate when not fighting on some battlefield. She had known enough of those types to recognize the traits when she saw them.

Her interaction with others was more or less hit and run conversations. Tarkov kept a warm but distant relationship with the troops while maintaining the bearing of the ever-professional soldier. De'vor kept to himself speaking very little and only to Tarkov or Sacchini. He was cold to Sauwa, speaking to her only when necessary and then he came straight to the point. He made it clear in the first days of the journey that he wanted nothing to do with her outside of business. At first, she assumed it was because he was naturally cold and was trying to give the appearance of a sophisticated professional soldier. Guy talk being what it was, he was possibly concerned that too much interaction with the young female of the team would have everyone talking and getting the wrong impression. It was when Sacchini informed her that De'vor had expressed a seething disdain for the Apartheid regime, she realized his behavior was over dealing with a white South African who had served in such a vial institution. After Sacchini's warning, she thought it best to keep her distance from the Frenchman.

It wasn't long before Gorzo proved to be the most outlandish of the group. As he grew more comfortable in the company of his new comrades, he became slightly obnoxious with some of his playful antics and his need to be outspoken with his opinions. He also began to drop not so subtle hints about having an interest in the young South African woman. Seeing himself as a world-class lady's man, he had explained to a couple of the guys how he would be sharing her bed shortly. He made a few passes around Sauwa as if he were a shark circling prey. When he did try to talk to her, he strutted up with the cool confident manner of some playboy approaching a target. Her rebukes were equally not so subtle with either cutting him off in mid-sentence by walking away or shutting him down with some cold words about her honest disgust of his behavior. He then thought of her as a tough conquest — one he was determined to claim.

Carzona kept his distance from the mercenaries and spoke only with Tarkov. Very little was known of the man. Sauwa assumed the distance he maintained was intentional to keep the hired help from having any potentially dangerous information. With the way he carried himself and the knowledge he possessed, she couldn't help but respect him. He was the kind of military commander that she could see soldiers following naturally into action.

The voyage, for the most part, was uneventful. Out on the open seas, they were alone except for the occasional sighting of another vessel. As Sauwa had predicted, naval ships from nearby countries patrolled the waters fervently. They had seen a couple of battlecruisers in the distance. A few times the captain was brought onto the radio to explain who he was and what he was doing. Thankfully, it took only a few chosen words to satisfy whoever he was talking to. The ocean was vast, and ships were in abundance. Naval patrols had far more important things to be concerned with than a cargo retrieval vessel that they figured was just randomly scavenging the waters. However, it was clear the waters were being watched and the navies in the area were looking for weapons and terrorists going to nearby volatile conflicts.

It was late afternoon when the mercenaries found themselves on the main deck with their gear watching an old fishing trawler sail in their direction. They were in international waters on the edge of entering Cyprus water space. The salvage ship had gone the long way around the island to its southern region. It then cruised about in international waters for the next several hours until it was much later in the day.

It was then that Tarkov had explained that they would be transferring to another ship. The trawler was going to be their means to get into the country. As a local ship, the trawler would be more inconspicuous coming into port. The very transfer of personnel from ships had been timed to coincide with the normal route patterns of the local fishing craft to ensure that nothing would seem out of the ordinary. In the distance, they could see other boats miles away going about their usual business.

Halting gradually, the trawler angled itself until it was parallel to the retrieval ship. A smaller boat ferried the mercenaries to their new mode of transportation. The captain and crew looked extremely relieved at the departure of the mercenaries. The new ship was not a great deal different from their previous transportation. It was a rusty old sea craft that had certainly seen better days. Upon arrival, the combat soldiers were overwhelmed by the smell of the recently caught fish. The reception from the new crew was no different than what they had incurred for the last several days from the salvage crew. They were cold and guarded, and the captain made no secret of his reluctance to have them on board.

Soon the ship was moving at a rapid speed toward shore. It was sundown when the trawler made it into port. As planned, it arrived along with all the other fishing craft, drawing no attention and looking no different from all the other ships coming in for the night. Aside from the remaining sunlight, there was little illumination making Limassol look rather sinister for those entering it. The buildings behind the port were a disorganized pattern of warehouses, local businesses, and small apartment houses.

The ship was steered slowly toward the harbor until it was parked against the docks. In the light of the diminishing sun, it was easy for the mercenaries to disembark and blend in with the crowds of sailors and dockworkers out on the pier. Two men came aboard. The first man was a pale fellow with wire-rimmed glasses and a white suit. He walked straight up to Carzona and shook the Filipino by the hand enthusiastically. It was clear they were well acquainted. The second man was short and dumpy with a thick bald head surrounded by a forest of remaining hair. He wore a cheap brown suit that was crumpled, probably from a long day of sitting.

Carzona turned from his colleagues to the mercenaries. "If you will all follow me into the captain's office." The mercenaries followed the pale figure and the dumpy man through a small circular door on the highest floor of the ship. Inside, they were squeezed into what looked like a makeshift office. After a few words with Carzona, Tarkov took over. "Everyone, because we are here for business that we can't divulge, it is necessary that we don't go through any customs office to be checked through legally. So, our employers have arranged the means for us to mitigate this complication." He turned his attention toward the dumpy man. "This gentleman's services have been retained to compensate for the difficulty of not having a stamp on our passports should they need to be checked."

Carzona's mysterious pale comrade spoke in a language the dumpy man apparently seemed to understand. The dumpy man immediately placed his briefcase on the folding table that functioned as the captain's desk. Opening it, he produced a small plastic stamp and an ink pad. One by one the mercenaries stepped up, held out their passports, and received a stamp that officially brought them into Cyprus.

The captain led the way off the ship with Carzona, the mercenaries, and Carzona's two friends following him. Once on land, the captain nodded a hasty goodbye to the people he obviously hoped never to see again and slipped back onto his vessel. Carzona's friend took the lead and directed the group through the maze-like walkways of the pier.

It wasn't long until they were on concrete heading for a blue Volkswagen van housed in a parking lot. Another man was standing by guarding over it, a brawny fellow with a glazed shin. The Dumpy man bid his goodbyes and departed with the same haste as the captain had. Led by the two men, the mercenaries continued toward the van where they were hastily piled tightly into the back seats. Carzona's acquaintance and the vehicle guard slipped comfortably into the front seats and soon they were on their way down the street.

The drive lasted for a time as it slithered through a series of streets until coming to a small warehouse in a remote part of the neighborhood. Pulling through the opening of a weakening chain link fence the van drove around a large concrete area until it arrived at the far side of the building near a small exit door. Carzona threw open the side door of the van. No one waited for his order to start getting out. They had been squeezed tightly together and were anxious for some breathing room.

After a brief time to stretch out and take some deep breaths, they were led inside. The lights flashed on creating a gloomy interior that made Sauwa feel like she was in a horror movie. As her eyes adjusted, she was able to get a better look.

The warehouse was a large open cavity that had been stocked with equipment and some basic living accommodations. Narrow military style cots supplied with small thin pillows and rolled up sleeping bags were set up. It wasn't much, but it was what one could expect in the field. Metal and wood folding tables with a series of folding chairs placed around them formed a half circle a little further down the room. Across from the tables was a long, white plastic sheet draped over one of the large garage doors. It was easy to deduce that she was looking at the operations and briefing area.

In the back corner, something resembling a workout area complete with assorted dumbbells, some weight stations for various forms of bench presses, and a few medicine balls had been put together. She was happy to see that her employers were aware of the importance of keeping athletically fit. Sauwa had learned early in her commando operations career how quickly even the fittest athletes could see their bodies atrophy with no physical exercise. The South African Naval Recce forces had discovered this problem in the late seventies. Commandos crammed on a small submarine for less than a week with no means to keep fit were too out of shape to carry out their mission. Sauwa had seen similar problems happen to operatives in her own unit who neglected their exercise and couldn't operate in the field.

Brought to a set of double doors in the back, they were led down a hall lined with closed steel doors. At the far end, they were shown the lavatory facility complete with two shower stations and five toilet areas. They were told that hygiene supplies and exercise equipment would be accessible as needed. They were next led to an empty storage area where the weapons and equipment they received would be stored to keep them out of sight.

The tour ended. Everyone was turned loose to find a cot and store their gear. Tarkov announced the initial briefing would take place in twenty minutes in the operations area. Carzona and Tarkov took the two cots furthest from everyone else to keep distance between commanders and subordinates.

Sauwa dropped her pack on the cot on the end. Gorzo went to drop his gear on the one next to her but was stopped short by Sacchini who slipped onto it first. Gorzo muttered something in Italian to the older man as he dropped his on the next cot over. De'vor marched past the group without a single word and took the final cot at the other end. Gorzo eyed Sauwa then Sacchini and shook his head. Sauwa didn't bother asking what had been said between the two. She could make an educated guess.

She sat down on her cot and took a deep breath. This had not turned out how she wanted it. What was even more frustrating was that when it was all over, if she survived, she had another near suicide mission to look forward to when she returned to Valikov. Then she would be depending on a former black militant to watch her back.

Twenty minutes later the group met at the operations area and sat around the table that was being used by Tarkov. The other Filipino men were gone leaving the original group alone in their new temporary home. Tarkov took the lead while Carzona remained quietly in the corner to prevent any question as to who was in charge.

The briefing was short — no more than a general plan for how tomorrow was going to be organized — breakfast at

0800, followed by a briefing, then a discussion on what they will actually be doing and, finally, an afternoon to do some shopping for clothes and other needs. The meeting concluded with little fanfare and few questions. Everyone was tired and in no mood for anything but a bath and some sleep.

Much like the safe house in Izmir, a natural order emerged — Tarkov and Carzona showering and doing an evening hygienic ritual, followed by De'vor and the two Italians, then when all others had finished, Sauwa took her turn. She had resisted Tarkov's and Sacchini's demand that ladies go first. She didn't need a bunch of men waiting outside while she walked about naked or half clothed. Nor did she want to provide Gorzo an excuse to 'accidentally' walk in on her when she was in a state of undress. With such a long day, they had no trouble laying out their bedding and falling asleep.

15

K ennson Rhys wasn't quite sure what to expect, but Azio Lorenza's mansion was a monument to classical tastes. The estate was located on the outskirts of Manila, the capital of the Philippines. On the outside, it was evidence of the country's European roots — a multistory, grey brick structure with a tower-like roof that looked like a French chateau or a Spanish hacienda. A long cobblestone, circular driveway led from a tall iron gate of spear-shaped bars up to and around the house. Every visitor had a chance to gape at the exotic jungle-like garden featuring all sorts of large trees and flowing indigenous plants surrounding the estate.

As he drove past it, Rhys, an experienced soldier who had cut his teeth in the New Zealand Special Air Service, could not help wondering why a man, such as Lorenza, with so many dangerous enemies, would create a terrain that would make it easy for someone to infiltrate. The veteran soldier thought it had to do with just how rich he was. As soon as he arrived, Rhys was met by a very prim looking butler dressed in a dark suit and black necktie who gave the

New Zealander the proper greeting of his station. The butler sized up the foreigner trying to discern how best to receive him. After a few seconds, the butler led the man up the stone stairs toward the large entryway.

Inside, the mansion was a museum, the halls lined with expensive classic statues from various Asian countries and ancient weapons from the medieval times of Europe and Asia. Walking past a range of rooms, he saw polished wood bookshelves filled with hardback and leather-bound books. Rhys knew many were early editions of fine classics. Elegant furniture dating from the Victorian period filled the rooms that they passed, reminding him of the comfortable times he had enjoyed cigars and whiskey in this very house.

At the next floor, the butler directed Rhys through another set of large, polished wood doors into a room that served as Lorenza's personal art collection. The four walls of the vast room were covered with priceless artwork. In the center of the room, sitting comfortably in a brown leather armchair, was a small, brown-skinned Asian man. The butler presented Rhys to the man who was enjoying a Montecristo cigar in between sips of vodka.

"Your guest has arrived Mr. Lorenza," the butler announced. He was stopped by Lorenza raising his arm slightly to silence him.

"Thank you," Lorenza said gently, his attention directed toward the paintings on the wall in front of him. "You may go now. Mr. Rhys and I have some things to discuss. The butler bowed and quietly left the room. Rhys stood fast. He figured it was best to let Azio Lorenza start the discussion. He studied the small man in the chair. For someone in his mid-sixties, Lorenza was in remarkably good shape. His body was lean, a sign of someone who still exercised consistently. His grey hair was neatly trimmed, and his thin mustache manicured, giving him a distinguished look. His khaki slacks, brown leather shoes, and tan sweater imparted the image of an academic more than a serious business mogul and one of the richest and most influential men not only in the country, but in all Southeast Asia.

"Tolstoy," Lorenza uttered.

Rhys waited a second before responding, "I'm sorry."

"You look different out of your camouflage uniform," Lorenza suddenly uttered, referring to the navy blue suit the New Zealander had chosen to wear for the occasion.

"I try to look presentable when I can," Rhys replied.

Lorenza went on. "I have never understood the fixation the wealthy western world has for the impoverished masses in countries like mine." He set down his drink and, clenching his cigar in his teeth, he rose to his feet. He only came to the New Zealander's chest, yet stood as if he were a bigger man as he sized him up. "My family, along with thirty others, controls virtually all of the arable land in the Philippines." He started to walk with Rhys following closely behind. "We control the land and in doing so we make valuable use of it. Yet, smug humanitarians protest this and despise us for this situation claiming that we deprive the peasant farmers of their right to own land."

They continued moving slowly around the room, as Lorenza balanced his attention between the New Zealander and viewing his art collection. "You know Leo Tolstoy may have written about the nobility of the poor. In fact, when he took over as the inheritor of a massive estate, he tried to bring the peasants on his land into the modern realms of thinking. He built a school for their children to learn, he introduced all sorts of state of the art farming equipment to make their work easier, and he even tried to provide medical aid. Within a year, it had all proven disastrous. The farmers dismissed their modern equipment favoring their primitive tools, none of the children showed up for school, and the space became storage rooms. The attempts to bring modern thinking about medicine and sanitation landed on deaf ears. The farmers continued to choose to reside in abject squalor rather than adopting sanitation practices that could have staved off disease."

Rhys said nothing as he waited to see where the Filipino was going with this storyline. Lorenza continued, "I say this because I find such noble gestures toward the poor foolish and naïve. My great-great-grandfather built the family fortune during the time of American colonialism in my country. During the Second World War, my grandfather negotiated skillfully with the Japanese making himself indispensable to them during their occupation and then turned around and did the same when the Americans returned. He preserved the family estates and the fortune because he was brilliant. That is what people don't understand. Our family, like other powerful families, didn't have this fortune handed to us. We work to preserve it, build on it, and have the intellect to see the future in order to adapt accordingly. That is what separates us from the small-minded peasant who knows only what they know and nothing more. I attended the London School of Economics and, for the time I was there, I tended to my studies, devoured every lesson and read every book voraciously to expand my knowledge. I studied the models of Europe's great businesses to see how I could better develop my own. I did all this because I knew what my role would be coming home."

"My western classmates would decry endlessly the

plight of impoverished countries like mine. They blamed the problems on families like mine. I had to wonder if they ever met the kind of people they seemed so concerned with — people who had never seen electricity or flushing toilets, people who believed in foolish superstitions and knew nothing outside of a few miles of their own community. They decried my family and my wealth, yet I had to wonder how these peasants would live if men like me weren't running the economy and managing the resources. If I'm gone and the land becomes theirs, they will be as Tolstoy's peasants. They will do nothing with it. The world changes, but they cannot change with it, and valuable land would become like Tolstoy's schoolhouse — a wasteland of noth-ingness. I can see this just by how easily the great unwashed of my country cling to extremist rebel armies that embrace imbecilic political ideas that only tell the fools what they want to hear and would be a disaster if they came to fruition."

This was not anything that Rhys had not heard before. It was rhetoric often espoused by many of his clients. Since leaving the service of the New Zealand army, he had made his living in the employ of Lorenza and several of the coun-try's established, wealthy families training and leading their private armies to combat the reckless bands of communist and Islamic guerrillas that plagued the country. He had made pretty good money doing so and, in all honesty, seeing the war zone of the country first hand, he was convinced that the private armies, though brutal in the execution of their mission, tended to be more effective in curtailing the guerrilla threat in the countryside than the state military.

Lorenza stopped to admire an oil painting depicting some battle from a nineteenth-century war that looked to have taken place in Russia. "The reason I have summoned you is that I and my associates need to retain your services for an important mission."

"That is normally why you call me," Rhys responded.

Lorenza turned from the painting and, for the first time since the meeting began, he looked the New Zealander directly in the eye. "As you know, I and my colleagues have been at odds with the current president. He has been pushing heavily for land reforms. He is one of the progressives who entertains foolish notions about peasants. In response, we have decided it is necessary to take action to ensure the president is properly marginalized. This action comes in the form of making us indispensable just like my grandfather did."

"I've been briefed on 'The System' organization and on Operation Chaos," Rhys said.

"Then I won't waste your time on what you already know," Lorenza smiled. "What you don't know is that we are obtaining three large consignments of weapons from an arms dealer in Cyprus. The weapons will be delivered to different regions of the country to supply various rebel groups we can quickly arm, who have the size and organization to create the necessary havoc. It has come to our attention through sympathetic sources that allies to the president and supporters to his agenda may now indeed be working to thwart this plan. If that is the case, we need to take steps to protect ourselves. We need you to assemble a team and go to Cyprus in order to neutralize this group if they attempt any such act to hinder our efforts."

"Are you sure they can even do it?" Rhys inquired as he observed the little Asian man. "I mean just because this group is onto you doesn't automatically mean they know anything. Nor does it mean that the actions you suggest I take is an advisable course of action."

"A professional soldier not recommending military action." Lorenza feigned shock as he looked back at the New Zealander.

"Military action is a tool sir," Rhys replied, "and, like any tool, one must assess the situation with a skilled eye to ensure it is the right tool to use in the situation."

"I quite agree." Lorenza raised his hand and shook his cigar toward Rhys. "I have seen military action serve with great success in addressing certain political difficulties. I, much like you, have also witnessed the folly when it has been used incorrectly."

"Which is why I think you might be acting hastily dispatching me now," Rhys explained. "Cyprus is not an island in the Philippines or the South Pacific where armed insurrections are common and someone like me could operate unnoticed. This is a country where such actions could create complications you may not want to deal with."

Lorenza twisted his cigar between his lips as he pondered the Rhys' words. "This is why I prefer you to so many of your colleagues Kennson Rhys. You are not addicted to war nor do you exploit every chance to promote it as men in your profession often strive to do. You are quite cerebral and strategic in your calculations."

"I value fighting logically sir," Rhys responded.

"I agree, which is why I want you there," Lorenza explained taking a puff from his cigar. "You're right in that we only know that the President has allies who know about our intentions. We know little other than that. This means we need to be prepared for different scenarios. If they come to Cyprus and find nothing, then we do nothing and carry on with our operation. If they go to the police, then the arms broker we are working with is quite well connected and can mitigate such complications for high paying customers. You are in position in the event we are dealing with a hostile threat that will use force to thwart our plans. The people we have there aren't skilled operators like yourself. They're lawyers, businessmen, and some trained bodyguards. Not the kind of people I would entrust to deal with trained and experienced mercenaries or terrorists."

Rhys shook his head. "What would you have me do if it should come down to that? At some level, we'd still have to find these people and figure out their network. This wouldn't be something done simply or cheaply. At some level, we'd have to worry about the police. Make enough noise in any respectable country and even a corrupt police force will have enough of you."

"That's true, that's true." Lorenza nodded as he enjoyed another puff on his cigar. "Another possibility I have considered. Which is why I want you there. Such conflict must be waged logically and discretely. You don't act in rage or believe in taking action simply for payback. A mission either adds value to the cause, or it is not done when it comes to you. I do realize the risk. But what is at stake is of great importance to our cause. I need to ensure that any military attempt to thwart these people is done skillfully and intelligently."

"I'll do what I can," Rhys replied. "But not knowing much about this enemy, I'm working in the dark. In my line of work that's incredibly dangerous."

The Filipino puffed some more on his cigar. "I understand the position I'm putting you in. You will be compensated for your troubles. You will also be given considerable resources to carry out this mission. I assume you have some men in mind for this mission."

"No," Rhys replied curtly. "Going to a European country with a bunch of Filipino guerrillas would unquestionably bring unwanted attention. I have a few local boys I know and trust. But the bulk of our force will have to be recruited locally over there. I'll need to find some European mercenaries for this job who can blend in better with the local population. In a situation like this, remaining inconspicuous is more essential than using people you're familiar with in the field."

"I understand," Lorenza said as he began moving on to admire another painting. "As I said, you will be given ample resources for your mission and, should it come to needing your services, you will be given full command of the project to carry out the fight as you see necessary."

"No matter what happens, kindly understand this won't be something like Mindanao or some other remote jungle island where we do what we have to, to win — where anything goes and repercussions are inconsequential. Mistakes in Cyprus can have repercussions and in combat, I will only have limited control over what happens."

"Again, I understand." Lorenza paused to observe another painting. This time it was a chalk sketching that looked like a Picasso. "I appreciate your concern for the political ramifications and delicacy of the matter. Still, the risk is necessary. A great deal of risk and capital has been expended already. The success of the operation is absolutely vital."

"Then I shall begin planning and making arrangements accordingly," Rhys said. "I can reach out to some contacts I have in Europe to recruit my team. Not knowing exactly what I'm up against, I'll have to keep my requirements flexible. This brings me to the next consideration. I'm in an alien environment dealing with shadows. I'll need a good intelligence source to help me figure out who I'm up against, where I can find them, and help me navigate the cultural and political waters of the country and its security forces."

Lorenza puffed his cigar. "My people and I can be flexible with funding if your recruited talent should turn out to be rather expensive. As to an intelligence source, I already have my people trying to ascertain such information and are in the process of finding someone who can acquire the needed information. They have told me they may possibly have someone you can work with as soon as you get there. And, before you ask about weapons, the trafficker we have can provide anything you will reasonably need."

"That will work," Rhys said. "I'll need a few days to make preparations here. As I said, I have a couple of guys here I want to recruit for the nucleus of my team. I have some guys I have worked with that I know will work for this operation that I can trust. I'll contact you in about four days when I'm ready to move."

The Filipino nodded as he resumed the tour of his art room dismissing the New Zealander he no longer considered of interest. Rhys turned and showed himself out the door.

16

The man wailed in a loud, high-pitched, blood-curdling scream that echoed around the room. It was cut short by a plastic bag, which was slipped over his head and pressed tightly against his face.

Dove Baker, a bear of a man, held the bag tightly at the nape of the man's neck while pulling it back behind his head ensuring no air reached the victim. Soon the wailing was replaced by violent contortions as the man struggled against the thick duct tape binding his arms and legs to the wooden chair. The man's animalistic survival instincts had taken over.

The torment lasted for several seconds before Dove slipped the bag off the man's head. The jolting stopped. The man fell defeated in the chair taking deep breaths of much-needed air. The recent trauma of suffocation had caused him to almost forget the pain from his recently severed middle finger.

The room was lit by the single bulb of an old lamp that was directly over the door, making the other people in the room appear to be shadows, ghosts surrounding the soon to be dead man bound in his chair.

"Shall we begin again?" Devon Williams said to the bound figure in a refined upper-class British accent.

The bound man had broken down into a sobbing mess. He was covered in the dark red blood from his severed finger, and he could hardly answer. "You people are monsters! This is not South Africa, you can't do this here!"

Williams moved directly in front of the man. Partially hidden in shadows, he towered over the prisoner, a horrifying demonic figure. "In this room, you are in South Africa, and you are an enemy terrorist who aids other terrorists. So, we respond to your actions accordingly." He nodded his head to Dove who slipped the bag back over the man's head. The contortions began again. After another few seconds, the bag came off leaving the man gasping for air again. "Are you ready to answer my questions?" Williams asked.

Leaning against the wall with arms folded, Sauwa watched in disgust. Her stomach churned as the interrogation proceeded. She hated the tactics they used. Despite Williams' explanation, she found the practice barbaric. James Musamba was an agent for the Southwest African People's Organization (SWAPO). He was part of a team that had been trained in the Soviet Union and sent to Western Europe to assassinate prominent South African diplomats. Sauwa and Dove had lifted Musamba from a safe house he had been staying at in London's South End.

Musamba took a deep breath in between the gulping snivels and his tears. With a quick clearing of his throat, he drew back a breath and launched a large wad of saliva and blood from his mouth in the direction of his interrogator. The spit missed Williams by a good margin and splattered the wall. "That is my answer!" Musamba replied with defiance as he glared at his captor with hatred.

Keeping his reserved demeanor, Williams stepped over to get closer to his captive. "They all talk tough at first. You all want to prove you are warriors and brave men. In the end, you all crack. It's just a question of when." Looking over at Dove, he nodded. The bear-like man moved out from behind the chair until he was alongside the captive. Grabbing Musamba's hand, Dove forced one of the clenched fingers to straighten out as Musamba was pleading and crying while he fought to resist.

Dove slid a loop of thin metal wire over the captive's extended finger. Musamba's jaw began to quiver and his hatred quickly turned to fear. The wire came from a cheese grater and worked as a cheap and effective torture device. He began to twist it tightly against the man's skin. Musamba went from terrified whimpers to cries of pain.

Not able to take any more, Sauwa cracked open the door and slid outside. She slammed the thick metal door behind her, but she could still hear the blood-curdling screams. She closed her eyes and began to take deep breaths in the hopes that she could mentally close out what she was hearing. After a few seconds, there was silence, and she was left alone in the poorly lit corridor. Her only companion was the small radio she had brought. It was faintly playing a version of the Oasis song *Wonderwall*. It was her favorite band and, strangely, her favorite song. Even when the screams continued to resonate from the room, she was able to concentrate on the song and blot out everything else.

After a while, the door opened, and Devon Williams stepped out. He looked down at her with his soft, kindly eyes. It was not the look of a man who had ruthlessly tortured a man only seconds ago. Sauwa ignored him as she stayed focused on the music. He took his forefinger and slid it under her chin. With a gentle but firm amount of force, he tugged her head until she was looking up at him.

Their relationship was complicated. It often resembled more of a father-daughter relationship than a superior-subordinate one. She looked up at him. Even in the dim light, he was a polished, handsome figure, with a neatly groomed crop of wavy, raven black hair, and a heart-shaped face. In his jeans and navy P-coat, he looked like a distinguished professor or successful writer. His black eyes were like pools that consumed her. "You stepped out rather suddenly. Not getting squeamish, are you?" He looked serious.

"I don't like your methods," she replied as she removed her head from his hand and looked away defiantly.

He rested his hand on her shoulder. "Hardly anyone does, save for sadists. But these people we're fighting don't play by conventional rules or respect laws of decency when it comes to war. They're brutal and take no prisoners. We simply fight this conflict as they do and respond to their actions as necessary. Dirty wars are never easy and seldom do they yield heroes as opposed to the necessary evils everyone will remember with shame. But we are fighting for our very survival Sauwa. You and I know that better than anyone. Remember these people, or people like him, kill innocent whites who have nothing to do with the government in Pretoria, so save your tears for those who truly deserve it."

Sauwa folded her arms and dropped her head back against the wall. "I hear that speech every time. They do it, so we must do it. And, I think that is the same rationale they use when they do the same to our people. We brutalize indiscriminately, and so must they. It all just sounds like an excuse for the sadistic to justify their pleasures." She stood up and started to walk away. "I better watch outside and make sure we don't get any kids wandering in on us."

She heard William's voice behind her. "South Africa is our last hope on the continent. Don't ever forget that. These darkee bastards have chased our people out of every other country that African whites once called home including Rhodesia, our true homeland. South Africa is the last place for our kind."

"Our kind?" Sauwa turned to look back at her commander. "These rebel groups may be comprised largely of thugs and radicals. I know your own sister was just working on an aid mission when SWAPO guerrillas took her and murdered her." She knew that Williams's sister, Tara, had been in Southwest Africa (now Namibia) when she, along with several others, had been kidnapped by soldiers of the People's Liberation Army of Nambia (PLAN), the military wing of SWAPO. A few weeks later the bodies of some of the workers were discovered in a shallow grave. They had been burned alive. Williams had never been able to let it go.

"It can't be easy for you thinking that these people have any legitimacy in their cause. But let's remember the Afrikaner government in South Africa has done a great deal to fuel this. We've arrested all the legitimate black politicians for exercising legal rights, and their peaceful protests have long been met with open gunfire. The Afrikaners and their Apartheid regime have certainly gone a long way in stoking the fire and driving people into the hands of these fanatical groups."

"Careful Sauwa," Williams chided. "This sounds like

treasonous talk for a country that took us in when Mugabe and his goons were forcing us out of our own country of birth."

"Treasonous talk? The country that took me in?" She started back toward her commander. "Let's remember that Apartheid was set up for the Afrikaner rule. Their bloody Dutch Reformed Church of South Africa speaks of the Afrikaner as the master race. You and I are nothing but necessary evils to them. They let us in because they needed our expertise at covert operations and guerrilla warfare to aid them with their own burgeoning unrest. They call English the language of the oppressor and refuse to speak it when dealing with us. They allow whites of English extraction into places of authority only when necessary, otherwise, they would have us out of their country just as easily if given the chance. So, I fight for the better of two very bad evils. But don't ever tell me that I owe them when I know I'm just fodder for their war. And, what they visit on the non-whites has resulted in fostering the problem we're in right now, where we fight ruthless dirty wars with fanatics as opposed to negotiating with rational minds."

Williams said nothing. He remained stoic as he stood looking like a father realizing his daughter was becoming a young woman. Recognizing the discussion had ended, Sauwa turned. "I'm going up top to make sure we don't have any unwanted guests showing up." As she walked away, she could hear the moans of a beaten Musamba as the round of torture started again. Then the wails of pain suddenly went quiet. His usefulness at an end, he met his demise as all the others had, at the sharp end of Dove's carving knife.

17
_____

Sauwa's eyes burst open. Suddenly wide awake, she found herself staring up at the steel rails that lined the roof of the warehouse. The building was dark except for the lights from the exit signs and some random lights that remained on permanently. She lifted her head from her pillow and looked over to see if she had woken anyone. Her dreams could be quite vivid, and she felt a chill at the possibility she may have been talking in her sleep and someone might have heard her.

Across the row of cots, all the men were asleep. When she checked Tarkov and Carzona, they were asleep as well. Her watch read 0530 hours. She was wide awake and figured there was no point in trying to go back to sleep.

Sliding quietly out of her sleeping bag, her stockinged feet hit the concrete floor. She threw her jacket over her shoulders and pulled her pants up in the nipping cold. She had been wearing the same pants for the past few days, and they were starting to feel a little crusty. If she didn't get a chance to get some new clothes soon, she would need some place to wash.

Rising, she padded softly across the icy floor. She thought about putting on her boots but resisted out of courtesy to the rest of the team. Making her way to the door, she cracked it open and slipped outside.

The air was pleasant. A warm breeze coming in off the ocean cut through the early morning chill. It had a calming effect on Sauwa as she leaned against the building and looked out over the eastern horizon to the slim, orange-red lining at the base of the darkened sky. It was a pleasantly beautiful, tranquil dawn.

By 0800 everyone was up. They moved randomly through their bathroom routine, checked their personal baggage, and grabbed one of the boxes containing their breakfast. Carzona's people had gotten meals from some Greek restaurant, a tasty meal containing a salad, triangular pita chips, hummus dip, and a folded pita bread sandwich.

At 0900, the mercenaries were seated in the operations area facing Tarkov. He was holding some sheets of paper in his hand and began the briefing with an overview of the country's demographics and societal makeup, pointing out that the majority of the country's populace was ethnic Greeks with a Turkish minority. He went into the contemporary history mentioning the failed attempt of Greek nationalists in 1974 which led to the overthrow of the three-term president and religious figure Markos III. This overthrow was ultimately thwarted by the immediate invasion of Turkish military forces who seized the northeastern end of the country and divided it into a separate state with a government recognized solely by Turkey. Today the island remains partitioned with half the country under Turkish rule. Their existing border is tightly guarded and tension continues between the two sides.

The briefing went on to discuss the security forces. The military is a small national guard comprised mostly of conscripts serving twenty-four-month commitments. The police force is a national department that receives both equipment and training from a variety of different countries. Their tactical experts and investigators have attended academies such as the National Security School for the Greek Police and the national academy of the American Federal Bureau of Investigation.

After his quick background of Cyprus, Tarkov went on to discuss their mission. "There is a group that goes by the code name "The System" that seeks to undermine the government of the Philippines. A delegation of this group is here in Cyprus to make contact with an arms dealer for the purpose of procuring a sizable quantity of weapons." A black and white image flashed on the wall showing a group of four men. They were all dressed in dark, conservative business suits and looked to be the same ethnicity as their employer. At an initial glance, they appeared to be normal business executives having an informal meeting.

"The mission," Tarkov started and paused. "Our intelligence sources have identified these men as the chief representatives of "The System". They arrived in Cyprus a week ago and met with this man." Carzona flipped to a picture of another man with long hair hanging down to his shoulders and a pair of trendy horn-rimmed glasses that rode on the bridge of his nose. He was wearing a sweater and a leather jacket. He looked like some modern-day executive entrepreneur of an emerging dot.com. "This is Theo Kalopolis, an arms trafficker, who they've met with to fill their order. Our mission is to not only subvert the arms deal but ensure the weapons procured here do not make their way to their destination. In short, we are to thwart the deal in its entirety, preventing "The System" from accomplishing its goal to overthrow the Philippine government."

"Who are the primary targets?" Sauwa asked.

"Anybody who is helping them accomplish their mission," Tarkov answered. "The mission is to neutralize the problem. That means we target who and what we have to, to ensure our adversaries do not have the means to succeed." He reached for a stack of folders and began handing one to each member of the team. "These are the reports we have on the players. Read them over, so we can start discussing plans and general courses of action."

"Courses of action?" Sacchini asked in surprise. "You mean there isn't already a plan in place for us to follow?"

The Russian nodded. "Our employers found the initial means to obtain intelligence to begin making a plan. However, that's all. We don't have a concrete plan yet. We will be planning this operation from scratch right here."

The mercenaries grumbled. They were bewildered and nervous at hearing this news. They were operators, accustomed to conducting missions where the initial plan had already been established and laid out by a staff or commanding officer. The news of building not just a plan but the strategy of attack entirely from scratch in an alien country was not well received. For a moment Tarkov feared some of them might demand to be released from their contract.

Then Sauwa spoke up. "This is good." Very quickly the room went silent as all eyes fell on her. Having the floor, she continued. "Our employers don't care if we survive this or not. Since we're the ones on the ground, not them, we should have control over how we proceed. Nothing is more dangerous than following a plan from someone so far from the action."

Her words sunk in. As soldiers, they were accustomed to dealing with planners who were more closely involved with the mission. It was an alien world to deal in a clandestine environment where the higher command tended to keep an arm's length from the whole operation and the battlefield in general. They left the mission's direction and planning to their people on the ground. It was a world Sauwa was all too familiar with.

Gradually the grumbles transformed into satisfying nods. Tarkov felt a sense of relief that he didn't have to deal with a full-fledged mutiny. He looked over at Carzona who, despite not saying anything, showed a hint of relief himself. Tarkov gave a quick nod of thanks to Sauwa before resuming control of the meeting. The next hour was spent in silence as everyone began reading over the material. Carzona, having already read the information maintained a watchful eye to ensure that all papers remained in the folders or on the tables and not anywhere else.

The time was spent in utter silence as the mercenaries studied their documents. Tarkov, like Carzona, watched everyone carefully. He also had read the files prior to the briefing and wanted to make sure the information stayed in their controlled environment. He paid particular attention to Sauwa during all of this. She was the most experienced one out of all of them for this type of operation. At least that was his understanding based on his interview with her and Valikov's comments regarding her abilities in this field.

As a man who had been more soldier than spy, he

acknowledged his limitations in this field and hoped to rely on her advice to help plan and execute this mission. He watched as she scoured the dossiers and report findings intensely, annotating notes in the margins of the pages as she went along. The other mercenaries read through the documents as if it were a book they were about to discuss in class.

After a while, folders started to come down as the mercenaries finished reading. "Most of the information is on the Filipino group here in Cyprus," Sacchini said as he threw his file packet onto a neighboring table. "We only have an overview on this Theo Kalopolis person."

"The delegation is where we should be focused," De'vor spoke up for the first time. "They are the ones with the money. If we concentrate on hitting them, the rest becomes moot."

Nods and murmurs silently erupted in support of the Frenchman's idea. Then Sauwa entered the discussion. "Well maybe not. If we act against the Filipinos, what is the likelihood they'll just send someone else to continue the business? I mean they'll still have the arms trafficker available. Only next time they'll be anticipating us. Besides, can we even get to the Filipino group? From what I've read, they're holding up in penthouse apartments taking up an entire floor of one of the city's hottest hotels. They have an entire security staff guarding them around the clock. Furthermore, they only leave the penthouse when they go to conduct business. When they do leave, it's on an irregular schedule making it impossible to develop a decent timetable." She sat back in her chair feeling somewhat defeated. She looked up to see all eyes focused on her.

Apparently, everyone was waiting to hear more so she continued. "These people are no fools. They chose their location for protection well. An expensive hotel in the top tourist location in Cyprus, in a city like Limassol, where tourism is a major industry. Expect that the hotel will have its own tight security with an abundance of surveillance cameras that can capture our image with hotel detectives keeping watch for any suspicious people. It's also a good guess that the greater area will have a strong police presence. Like most tourist-heavy cities, expect to be up against the very best police officers around such expensive locations."

"Remember in an operation like this, it's not just about the successful execution of the mission. We're committing a crime, and the clock begins once we initiate until the police respond. Even after we escape, we have to worry about the inevitable investigation. In the heat of the action, the evidence is not the prime concern, and we have to worry about what we left behind for the police to trace. Professional intelligence agencies fuck this up all the time which is why so much is known about these things."

She finished speaking to hear dead silence in the room. She found she was staring back at several deadpan faces as if they had all seen a ghost. The one exception was Tarkov who was giving her a satisfied look as if she had met all his expectations. "What then do you recommend?" he asked. She eyed the rest of the group and found she was still dealing with a captive audience waiting to hear more.

With a sigh, she went on. "We should begin with understanding what we're up against by noting what's not in these files. Reviewing the dossiers, I can assume that this intelligence was compiled by a more regionally placed private network hired by our employers. My guess is that they had a good idea who this arms trafficker, Theo Kalopolis, is. He is from this region, which means they should have been able to

collect information on him more easily than a foreign businessman from halfway around the world."

"That can only mean that Kalopolis is that good at
protecting information about himself which makes him
dangerous because we don't know what we need before
going into this. Or they know who he is, but he's so
connected and dangerous that they don't want to get in his
bad graces by poking around in his affairs. If so, we can
conclude that we not only don't know what we need but
that he could prove to be an incredibly dangerous enemy for
us to have on this island."

The mercenaries remained silent. Their attention was still
entirely on her, mesmerized by her words. Even the steadfast
Carzona was clearly intrigued by what she was saying. It
had now become apparent that this was what Tarkov was
talking about back in Izmir when he mentioned her being a
key advisor. The only person who seemed to show a lack of
complete interest was De'vor, who glared at her as if what
she was saying only confirmed his disapproving image
of her.

Ignoring his condescending gaze, she pressed on. "As I
see it, the problem we have is that we have a delegation of
Filipino businessmen about to buy a massive amount of
serious weapons from a major arms trafficker. They're both
going to be incredibly hard targets to go after. They have
protective details and are anticipating a threat to themselves.
And, whoever we go after, even if successful, we are automatically going to alert the others who will take even more
precautions. We assume that taking out the Filipino delegation will end this business. But, as we have already
discussed, they represent a much larger organization that
could just send somebody else to finish where they left off.

In addition, the thought of losing a serious client might force Kalopolis to take action on his own to neutralize us just to protect this deal. Our best bet is to take Kalopolis. He's the pipeline to the arms and taking him out of the equation would be the most detrimental as it wouldn't be easy to find another arms dealer who could fill such a large order. However, as we're in his backyard here in Cyprus. We don't know what kind of security he has, or what kind of intelligence resources he has at his disposal. This means we would be flying in dangerously blind." She fell back in her chair feeling exhausted by the enormity of the task before them. She scooped up the file again and started through the series of pictures and documents as if she had possibly missed something.

When she was at an end of her dissertation, Tarkov retook control of the meeting. "Well, that's enough for right now," he said while observing the stumped expressions on the faces of the other mercenaries. "We've eaten and discussed the initial problems. Let's break for now and take care of some other pressing issues. We'll take this meeting up later tonight after we've all had a chance to think about it.

As the meeting adjourned, the attitudes amongst everyone was a dismal, collective nervousness. The soldiers walked away from the meeting feeling incredibly out of their depth. With the exception of Sacchini, who had done slightly similar work operating against Sicilian criminal groups for the Italian government, the soldiers had operated on battlefields where such considerations as police were non-existent. The missions they completed in the service of criminals put them in remote regions where they conducted business with other mercenaries, guerrillas, and warlords in the most lawless parts of the world. Sauwa, with her assessment of the situation, had opened their eyes which had been a sobering experience.

With the meeting concluded, Tarkov handed each member of the team thick white business envelopes. They were filled with Cyprus pounds. "This will be your expense money while you are here." He gave everyone a chance to examine the contents. "What you have is what you get, so spend conservatively."

The envelopes quickly disappeared into jacket pockets. Tarkov explained that their contacts would be around soon with the van to take them to one of the shopping districts, so they can pick up fresh clothes and get the lay of the land. As everyone started heading back to the sleeping area, Tarkov grabbed Sauwa by the arm. "We need to talk." She followed as he led her away from everyone else. "I'm concerned about this lack of intelligence we have regarding Kalopolis. Since it seems apparent, even by your estimation that he should be our prime target, I would like to have more detailed information to work with. What are the chances that our mutual friend could provide what we need?"

Sauwa shook her head. "I imagine Valikov knows a great deal that would aid us at this point in time. In fact, I can imagine that he knew from the beginning that Kalopolis was involved in this. He is probably hoping that killing a serious competitor would be the inevitable outcome of this operation."

Tarkov scratched his chin as he shrugged his shoulders. "Then it seems that he would be interested in helping us."

"No," Sauwa shook her head again. "He's going to keep as far from this as possible. Logically, if we succeed, the market just opened up for new business for him. If we fail, then his hands are nowhere near any of this, and he doesn't have to worry about retaliation from a powerful new enemy."

"He doesn't think supplying us with weapons and equipment will be just as incriminating?" Tarkov questioned.

Sauwa looked at the Russian as if he were an innocent child. "Selling weapons to a group is one thing. In the black-market world, no one asks what the weapons are going to be used for, and it would be easy to feign ignorance if the guns are traced back to him. Information that was used to help plan an assassination against a competitor is a lot harder to explain or deny. So, don't expect any help."

With a deep look of consternation, Tarkov scowled. He released Sauwa as he stood there pondering his next move. Sensing he was out of his element, he felt like a novice. He was used to fighting in the jungles of Central Africa or the harsh lawless grounds of the Caucasus. In a situation like this, he was inclined not to trust his own experience or judgment, and he didn't like the feeling one bit.

He looked over to see Carzona in the operations area making sure there were no loose documents lying around. All the files had been accounted for and neatly stacked in a pile that he was tucking into a metal case with a combination. He was certainly security conscious and watched all sensitive documents like a hawk. Tarkov approached, "What do you think?"

"I think that Miss Catcher was a wise choice for this operation," the Filipino replied as he scanned the area one last time. "I initially had my doubts about her. However, after seeing her in the interview and then in the meeting, I feel that she is going to prove to be a very valuable asset going forward."

"Well, you have to admit," Tarkov looked over at the

mercenaries congregating in the bedding area as they prepared themselves for their outing, "when it came to people with experience operating in this sort of environment under such restraints, we didn't have much to choose from. The Englishman claiming to have been with British intelligence was hardly impressive."

"He was burnt out and an alcoholic." Carzona shook his head. "That much was obvious during the meeting. It was clear that he was far past his prime."

A hard knock was heard at the door. Everyone stopped what they were doing and froze. The knock was followed by a voice speaking in the German-accented English they had heard spoken by the pale man the previous day. "Go ahead and open the door," Carzona called out to the mercenaries. "My people have arrived."

Carefully, De'vor and Gorzo inched over to the door. To ensure that intruders with hostile intentions would have a hard time breaching the door they had used a rubber doorstop on the inside. Kicking the wedge away, Gorzo flung open the door as De'vor stood guard. The pale man walked through the doorway and presented himself to Carzona.

"Alright let's go," Tarkov commanded.

The mercenaries finished dressing, securing their gear, and making other last-minute adjustments. Once everyone was ready, they filed out the door behind the pale man with Carzona last. They were all warned to pay close attention during the tour as this would be the only time they would have their guides. In the future, all the mercenaries would be operating entirely on their own.

18

K ennson Rhys stepped off the plane into the Larnaca International Airport in Cyprus. He was tired and wanted nothing but a warm shower and a good dinner. However, first, he was determined to meet with Lorenza's people in Limassol and gain some perspective on this vaguely explained operation.

He kept the brisk pace of a predator moving to stalk its prey as he moved through the airport. The two men accompanying him followed in his stride — one was a Nepali, Khadga Yadav, and the other was a Fijian, Iventi Mehendra. Both men had been with Rhys for a long time and were among his best men. They had been at his side through some terrible battles and campaigns in some of the worst places in the South Pacific.

Khadga Yadav had served for almost sixteen years in the British army as a soldier in the 7th Duke of Edinburgh's Own Gurkha Rifles prior to it being merged with the other Gurkha units into the Royal Gurkha Rifles. Having seen action all over the world, including time in the Falkland conflict and Brunei, he had left the service. With the Gurkha Brigade gradually shrinking, and the end of the cold war bringing a lull in missions, Yadav decided it was time to go. Instead of returning to his native Nepal, Yadav found his way to Burma, now Myanmar, where he found work in the service of the Burmese army working as part of a special unit that hunted Islamic Rohingya guerrillas hiding deep in the remote jungles. It was here he had met the New Zealand SAS soldier, Kennson Rhys, operating as part of a clandestine mission against the guerrillas. They struck up a solid friendship and a few years later when Rhys, now in the private sector, called him offering a better paying job in the Philippines, the former Gurkha didn't hesitate to say yes.

The Fijian, Iventi Mehendra, was a former soldier in the Fijian army's First Meridian Squadron. More commonly known as the Counter Revolutionary Warfare Unit — the unit was modeled after the British 22 SAS — and had worked with everyone including the U.S. Navy Seals, the Australian SASR and the NZSAS. It was on such a joint operation that he had met Rhys who he befriended. And, similar to the Nepali Yadav, he was contacted on the eve of his discharge from the Fijian armed forces, asking if he'd like to ply his trade in the Philippines. Since then both men had served with him in the service of the private army of Azio Lorenza and the Lorenza family. If the New Zealander was being honest with himself, these men were his closest family.

All three men had packed light — only carry-on luggage that made it less complicated moving through the different airports. They made their way to the doors leading outside and were instantly met with a warm, evening atmosphere. Strangely, it seemed to wake them all up. "Oh, that feels much better," Mehendra said as he rejoiced to feel the fresh, warm air all around him. "After being cooped up in that plane, I just want to walk about, stretch, and get the blood flowing in my legs again."

"I hear you," Rhys replied as he concentrated on finding some mode of transportation. "We'll get plenty of time for that just as soon as we settle things with our people here."

"We don't even know what's really going on, and that bothers me," Yadav stated in his quiet unassuming tone.

"That's why I want to get down to business before we do anything else," Rhys replied as he raised his arm to hail a cab. "I want to see these people and figure out exactly what we're dealing with." The taxi pulled up to the curb. The driver barely had time to ask the destination before the three men piled into the car. Rhys jumped in the front seat while his colleagues slid in the back.

It was fortunate that the driver spoke reasonably good English. It didn't take the New Zealander long to direct him to the hotel where Lorenza's people were staying. Giving a nod and cracking a smile to reveal a row of nicotine-stained teeth, the driver released the brake and pulled the cab onto the main road. Twenty minutes later they were in the ritzy Galatex district surrounded by expensive first-rate resort hotels. The cab was pulled up to the reception area of the Flamingo Hotel. The men left the vehicle and started up the entryway.

They were dressed casually in slacks, open-collared shirts, and jackets — the typical attire exhibited around the hotel. Making their way to the reception desk, they were greeted by a stunning young woman with piercing blue eyes and golden blond hair. She was genuinely friendly as she met them with a warm energetic smile and welcoming demeanor. "How may I help you, gentlemen?" She asked in well-spoken English.

"If you could please ring the penthouse, number 4, and tell them that Mr. Thompson from Luzon is here."

"Of course," she smiled as she picked up the phone and called to the penthouse.

She relayed the message. There was a brief exchange of words involving her describing the three men, and she finished the call with instructions that they were to wait in the lobby for someone to meet them. The men took seats in a nearby waiting area. The chairs were comfortable, and the trio relaxed. They looked like everyday guests finishing the evening with a little relaxation before retreating to their rooms. Their break was cut short when they were met by a young man wearing a white shirt and black trousers. He looked like one of the hotel's valets. The young man was polite and addressed Rhys in English. He explained that someone had asked him to deliver a message. He handed Rhys a small sealed envelope. The young man gave a bow and walked away.

Rhys looked over at his two colleagues who eyed the envelope questioningly. Slicing it open with his thumb, he unfolded a small piece of paper. The note was brief. They were to go to a bar two blocks down the street in thirty minutes and follow the instructions for how they were to identify their contact and make the connection. Rhys nodded to his men to follow as he rose from his seat and started casually toward the front door.

Outside, the three men made their way down the street until they were able to flag another cab. It was only a short distance to the meeting spot, but none of the men felt comfortable traipsing around in an unfamiliar country. The cab driver spoke little English but seemed to recognize the location when Rhys explained where they wanted to go. It was a quick ten-second drive down the street until they were parked just outside an upscale lounge at the corner of what looked like an exclusive nightclub district.

The trio exited the vehicle with Rhys following after he left a handsome tip for the driver. The street was wild with fancy clubs that advertised to the throngs of tourists cruising the street with intoxicating liquid-neon signs and trendy party music loudly blasting from inside. Like the rest of the establishments along the street, the lounge was exotically lit with inviting signs. Yet, it offered no wild music or dance floors. It was the spot for the tourist who wanted to enjoy a private drink in a quiet spot.

The men entered a dark room that contained several tables and a row of booths. The waitresses glided around in sleek tight-fitting satin dresses as they moved about filling orders. The clientele consisted primarily of expensively dressed men in their late forties and fifties. Most of them were engrossed in conversation. A few busied themselves trying to gain the attention of some of the young waitresses as they walked past. No one gave the slightest notice of the three men who had just walked in. It was a well thought out location for a clandestine meeting.

The mercenaries didn't wait to be seated. They snagged the table nearest the far corner. They didn't project the image of men who had a lot of money which may have slowed the arrival of a waitress coming to take their order. It also ensured that no one bothered to pay attention to them at all. They settled in and enjoyed some small talk with each other. The conversation revolved mostly around where to get a good meal and where to stay tonight. The long journey and the last few days of endless travel had made those their top priorities.

It wasn't too long before a short, stout Filipino gentleman with a soccer ball head and a neck as wide as his skull sauntered in. Dressed in a pair of slacks and open-collared shirt, he looked like just another tourist of only reasonable means. He was followed by two other men of shared ethnicity, dressed in a similar fashion. The three Asian men strolled across the lounge. They passed the mercenaries' table without offering them the slightest acknowledgment. The soccer-headed man let a silver medallion attached to a ribbon dangle from his pocket. Rhys recognized the engraving instantly as the image that had been drawn on the note he received. Casually, the New Zealander reached into his coat pocket to retrieve his wallet. He fished from it a Filipino peso that he placed on the table so as it would be visible to the Asian men as they passed by.

The Asians continued into the circular booth in the corner directly adjacent to mercenaries' table. For the next few minutes, both parties completely ignored each other. Then, one of the Filipinos suggested to his compatriots that they go somewhere else. The three men rose. As they did, the soccer-headed man glanced over at Rhys and his men. He reached under his shirt and let a small white package slip onto the seat. The three men started out of the lounge with as little notice from everyone as they had received coming in. The mercenaries casually rose to their feet and sauntered over to the now vacant booth. Sliding into it, Rhys scooped the package into his coat pocket. He looked up just in time to see the three Filipinos exit the front door. They had been holding off leaving to ensure that it was their contacts who received the package and not some random stranger who could compromise everything.

At long last, a striking blond waitress made her way to their booth. She looked a little exasperated as she asked if any of them would like a drink. All three of the men declined as they stepped out of the booth starting to leave. Half expecting the young woman to urge them to stay, not wanting to lose potential tipping customers, he was a little surprised to see a look of relief as she quickly darted back to a collection of well-dressed older men. Apparently, she, like the other girls, decided Rhys and his men were too poor to worry about, and they were only distracting them from the guaranteed big tippers. Neither he nor his colleagues were offended. They weren't thirsty, and they were glad they could leave with little fanfare attached.

Outside, they moved up the street until they saw a well-lit café just up the road. It was sparsely populated, catering largely to a more conservative crowd that didn't seem interested in the more exotic nightlife. Finding a small table away from everyone else, Rhys opened the package. It contained a small disposable phone and another note with instructions.

They waited until after the server had taken their orders before he called the number written on the note. He waited for three rings before someone answered.

"Mr. Rhys?" an accented voice asked. He recognized the voice instantly though he couldn't put a face or name to it.

"Mr. Sanchez," Rhys replied with the name on the note. "It is good to hear from you."

"I also recognize your voice," the voice replied in a serious manner. "You will forgive the elaborate cloak and dagger activities surrounding all of this. Our employers cannot afford to have their hands dirty in this affair. They wanted to put us in touch with each other to discuss matters."

"I understand completely," Rhys replied. "You must have been apprised of my arrival. Is there a chance we could meet sometime tonight?"

"I was about to suggest that very thing," Sanchez agreed. "There is a bar called the Mirage on the other end of town in the Karnagio district. Go inside the bar, and I will meet you there in one hour. Don't worry about any elaborate signals or codes. I know who you are, and you know me. One more thing, do not ever go to the hotel again. Our employers must be completely protected from our activities."

Rhys didn't have a chance to answer. He heard a click, and then the phone went dead. He looked at Yadav and Mehendra who were staring back at him waiting for a response. "We meet in one hour on the other side of town."

"I'm a soldier, I hate these elaborate games of intrigue these blasted spies insist on playing," Yadav groaned as he leaned back in his chair tired and exasperated.

"It's what they're paying us to put up with," Mehendra said in a poor attempt at humor.

At that moment the server returned with their meals and all three made the unanimous decision to enjoy their first real meal in two days before participating in any more adventures. It was only pita chips, hummus, and some lamb dish with small salads for each of them but it tasted like a feast.

When they arrived at the Mirage, the three men found they were looking at a quaint bar on a quiet street corner. Piling out of the cab, the three proceeded to their destination. At this late hour, there were hardly any cars on the road and the men marched across as if they were on a military parade field. Tired as they were, neither Rhys nor his associates were in any mood to banter.

They walked into the bar and made their way to the far end of the counter. The bar was a sharp contrast from the previous establishment they had been in. It was better lit inside, where one could see what was going on around them. The clientele was not the flashy spenders from the Galatex area, but a more modest working-class sort just looking to enjoy a quiet drink and some peaceful socializing.

The bartender, a bear of a man with a thick bushy mustache, towered over everyone as he made his way around the semi-circle filling glasses of old customers and taking orders from new ones. When he got to the mercenaries, it took a brief attempt at speaking to each other to realize the language barrier. He waved to a pretty, auburn-haired woman who looked to be in her early forties. She was working some of the tables when the bartender called to her. She addressed the men in English, to which they responded with requests for beers. She nodded, relayed the order to the brawny barman and quickly returned to her charges.

The barman delivered three full mugs to the mercenaries and returned to his business. Slowly, they sipped their drinks as they waited for their contact to appear. "It's been more than an hour," Mehendra whined. "What the fuck is keeping him?"

"He's probably outside, somewhere across the street, scoping out the place to verify if we are who we're supposed to be," Yadav answered.

"That's my guess," Rhys said as he sucked up a few drops from his mug. "Whatever we're dealing with, we've apparently gotten ourselves in the middle of some serious intrigues. So, I guess we'll be playing spy for a little while."

His colleagues nodded as they enjoyed their drinks. Their attention turned to the door when a small Asian man with dark, shoulder length hair and a slight mustache walked in. He was dressed casually in a blue collared shirt under a tan sports jacket and black slacks. He looked drained, almost defeated. To anyone paying attention, he looked like a guy stopping in for a drink after a long day at the office.

The man caught sight of Rhys, who was looking back at him over his beer mug. Rhys knew the man well. He had provided protection for him on a couple of occasions when the man had business dealings that took him into the jungle. His name was Jose Managua — he was a lawyer by occupation, a litigator of sorts really. He worked for many of the old money families handling dealings with underworld types that prominent citizens couldn't deal with directly. He handled assorted affairs that involved underworld factions dealing with hostile foreign powers and, when necessary, negotiating with guerrilla groups.

Managua gave the New Zealand mercenary a slight nod as he strolled over to a table in a more deserted part of the establishment. Rhys looked around to see if any attention was being drawn in their direction. The patrons in the place kept mostly to their business, not paying the slightest attention to anyone else. The barmaids seemed only concerned with filling orders and retrieving whatever gratuities awaited them at the tables they had served. Managua had chosen his location well. The mercenaries rose to their feet and sauntered slowly toward the table occupied by the Filipino. They didn't wait for an invitation, they slid into seats around him.

"I appreciate dispensing with the elaborate cloak and dagger bullshit," Rhys opened the conversation.

"I sometimes fear the people who employ us are too interested in alleviating the boredom by making things more difficult than they need to be," the Filipino replied.

"You took your time getting here," Rhys complained.

Managua exhaled a breath of air. "I wasn't given any warning of your arrival. Your benefactor dispatched you here without consulting the other parties involved. I was only told that you were being brought in for additional support. That was it. We had no timetable of your arrival. I was informed that you were in the country just a short while ago. Your decision to go straight to the hotel hosting the important people from our country sent quite a few people into a tizzy. They called me and told me to expect your phone call. I am to deal with you from here on out and see to your needs."

Rhys couldn't help noticing that Managua took great care not to reference any direct connection to the delegation of Filipino businessmen in the penthouses of the luxury hotel he had just come from. The lawyer checked his surroundings before speaking to ensure that he did not offer any information that could expose those retaining his services. "Right now, my needs are to know exactly what is going on and who it is we're dealing with that has everyone in a panic."

Managua remained guarded — hesitant to speak. It wasn't until he saw the group that was within earshot stand up and leave before he started to speak more freely. "The truth is we don't really know what we're expecting. Our benefactors had an initial meeting with the arms trafficker in Warsaw, Poland. It had been arranged by one of the prominent East European law firms that represent numerous interests and apparently facilitate such introductions for a fee. After that, I was brought in to manage our side's interests in this operation and report back to our masters on the progress. What has happened is that allies to our enemies at home have stumbled onto our operation. To what extent we don't know. And, what they plan to do is anyone's guess. Our intelligence resources for gathering information in this part of the world is limited."

"Have you informed your arms supplier," Yadav interjected. "I mean a man of his caliber must possess viable intelligence resources that could possibly help."

Managua replied. "The concern I have, and it is shared by our employers, is that we don't know this trafficker very well and if we inform him of a possible threat, we can't be sure of his reaction. He may help us find and even eliminate this problem, or he may decide to capitalize on the situation by approaching our enemies and work another deal with them and play both sides. Worse, he may reach out to them, get a far better deal and betray us outright. No, this is something we need to handle. At least, our superiors have agreed we need to enlist some additional assistance in this matter."

"That still leaves us operating in an environment with limited intelligence," Rhys reminded the lawyer.

Managua nodded as he pressed his finger to his chin. "Our masters understand this dilemma. They have recommended the services of a firm that supposedly specializes in intelligence gathering in this part of the world. In the meantime, our intelligence resources are vast, and our networks are working to figure out who we're up against from their end. When I hear from them, I'll reach out to this firm to pursue the inquiry here."

"Our own people don't know who's threatening us," Rhys said in hushed exasperation as he was again reminded of how blind they were to this looming threat. This situation could seriously jeopardize a major operation.

Managua shrugged. "Whoever is doing this is not acting at the insistence of the president but rather as an independent body acting on their own. This makes the state of affairs more difficult. We would normally have found everything out through our contacts in the military and intelligence organizations. We do know who the president's most loyal supporters are, and who would have the means and connections to be a threat. It is only a matter of time before we know who to look for."

Rhys grimaced as he looked around the table at his cohorts, who registered equally negative expressions on their faces. "It still does us little good right now. This brings us to the next question. When do we discuss the particulars of the shipments?"

Managua lifted his hand in a halting gesture. Rhys looked over in time to see the auburn-haired bar-maid approaching. She arrived asking the Filipino what he wanted — he ordered a bourbon straight. She asked the three mercenaries if any of them wanted a refill for their half-empty mugs, all three declined.

After she was out of earshot, Managua continued. "We're still in the process of working on that. It is a large order and one that is going to be loaded here in Cyprus. This breaks with the normal routine where they obtain the weapons in one of the old Soviet republics and ship from a port there to the intended location."

"Why the change?" Rhys asked.

The Filipino shrugged and shook his head. "Normally the method of moving arms shipments in this part of the world is through the air. When the cold war ended, all the

Soviet cargo planes were languishing on forgotten military bases. Former Soviet military commanders going into the black-market business bought fleets of these crafts and used them to make deliveries to their usual markets in the Middle-East and North Africa where they have established many contacts for maintenance and fuel along the route."

"Since most of the European arms business is in those areas of the world, major arms traffickers from here don't have the established connections and routes to support transportation to Southeast Asia. So, that leaves going through the next best option, cargo ships. For an order of our size, this changes the usual supply source from Russia to Bulgaria where the port city of Sophia is more amenable for our purposes. The weapons will be brought here to Limassol where they will be transferred onto another ship that will head to the Filipinos."

"And, where will this second ship come from?" Rhys inquired.

Managua raised his finger in a 'matter of fact' manner. "The ship is coming in from Thailand, captained by someone we've used from time to time for such business. He has acquired the several ships through a shell company in Bangkok that associates of ours have set up for the supply end of this operation. It set out from port three days ago. It will make good speed until it gets to the Suez Canal. Then it will reduce speed and tug as slowly as possible until we have a fixed time for it to move into port. It will get here around the same time as the ship from Sophia. The cargo will hurriedly be transferred from ship to ship, and our ship will immediately pull out and head for home."

"You aren't worried about port authorities here giving you trouble?" Rhys questioned.

Managua raised his hand in a reassuring gesture. "It is no coincidence we are here in Cyprus for this transaction. We feared that conducting this business inside a former Soviet state such as Bulgaria might prove rather complicated with the current issues and uncertain political dynamics. Both sides agreed that it would be best for all if we made the transaction here in a neutral location that has a history of being somewhat more accommodating to our sort of business than other ports in Western Europe. Here we will more easily be able to swap out the cargo manifests to show that the equipment came from some country like France or Spain — somewhere that would assume less suspicion if our craft were to be boarded by some military presence conducting random checks."

"Remember, this is not some quick operation. After this initial run, we have five other large cargo ships being dispatched to this location, one after the other, ready to pick up the cargo in the same fashion. They will then make their way home to their respective islands where the captains will make contact with our representatives who are in contact with the prominent guerrilla group of each area. The amount of weaponry and ammunition we will hand over to them should be more than enough to keep them stocked for a few months of intensive combat. They'll think that more is coming so, hopefully, they won't horde it. By the time our forces are called in because it has become too much for the military, the ammo should nearly be gone and the pipeline cut off."

The mercenaries nodded; it made sense. The barmaid returned with Managua's drink. The meeting continued with Managua now asking the questions. "As I said, I knew you had been dispatched from Manila. However, I understand you did not bring many of your own people. Instead, you were looking to recruit from the local talent to augment your team."

Rhys nodded as he took another sip of his beer. "Before arriving here, I stopped off in London and met with an old friend of mine from my military days. He's a former soldier with her majesty's 22 SAS Regiment. He retired out and drifted into the realm of private soldiering. He's worked around quite a bit and is close to the mercenary community here in Europe. He's found me about seven additional men who we've hired for this mission."

"So, you're hiring men for this operation sight unseen?" Managua was taken back.

Rhys sighed before answering. "Keep in mind, I don't know what kind of timeline I have to work with, and I'm dealing in unfamiliar territory. And, I don't have the luxury of properly vetting people to recruit for this mission. I've known my friend for years — we go back a long way. We've even worked as private soldiers together. I know him well enough to trust his judgment. The boys he's recruited are ethnic Greeks all with backgrounds in the French Foreign Legion 2eme Rep Commando Parachute Group and their foreign engineering regiments. They'll be making their individual way into this country, and I have scheduled a meeting with them in the Molos area of the city along a noted pier within the next few days."

The lawyer remained hesitant. It was obvious Rhys' explanation left him concerned. "I cannot say that I'm comfortable with the notion that a bunch of strangers you've never met or worked with before is so close to such a sensitive operation."

"I understand," Rhys explained. "This isn't ideal. But it's

a risk we have to take. If the situation requires my team to be called into action, I need people who know the area and can easily blend in with the populace. A bunch of your countrymen running about in a country like this would stick out and bring unwanted attention that would be worse than what you're concerned about."

Managua nodded nervously, but he had to concede to the mercenary. The men finished their drinks and paid their bill. Managua went on to explain "I will arrange lodgings for all of you at a beach house I know of. It should accommodate your whole team and provide a place to headquarter your activities. Until then, I have booked rooms for you and your men at the hotel where I'm currently staying."

"That will be fine," Rhys replied after looking at his two men.

The lawyer continued. "Until your headquarters is established, I would ask that we refrain from discussing any topics pertaining to our business here."

"I was wondering why we were discussing such matters in a public place like this," Yadav, interjected.

"My reasons for discussing this matter here as opposed to my hotel were deliberate," Managua answered.

"Are you concerned our mysterious enemies have gotten onto you?" Rhys asked.

"No," Managua shook his head. "It's just that Cyprus is in somewhat of a volatile state. For a long time, there has been a lot of tension between the two predominate ethnicities on the island, the Greeks and the Turks. In the mid-seventies, a military junta in Greece took control of the country with the help of Greek nationalists. This led to Turkey intervening with their own military landing forces on the island. It led to the country splitting with the Turks controlling the northeast and the Greeks controlling the southwest. Though no active fighting has occurred for a long time, there remains a lot of animosity between the two sides with antagonistic actions being undertaken by both."

"Greece and Turkey frequently involve themselves in the island's affairs which adds to the problem. On top of that, the turmoil in the Middle-East has spilled over onto these shores in the last few years. Islamic militants from Hezbollah, the PLO, and other such groups have sought refuge from the Israeli security forces here. Due to all this, I understand that the national police like to conduct random surveillance missions on hotels to see who are operating in their country and what they're doing. They like to see who they can catch discussing nefarious business."

"Are you saying we could be known to the police?" Rhys was taken aback by the sudden revelation.

"No," the lawyer responded immediately. "I don't believe so. As I've said, it's random and routine. The police are interested in threats on their shores. Not the shores of others. You must also understand that the strategic location of this country makes it a convenient Mecca for black marketers, criminals, and mercenaries. Business people here dabble in the illicit trade from other countries so, at some level, it is beneficial economically for them to allow a degree of this trade. The person I'm working with to procure weapons is a serious player in the arms business. He also owns several legitimate businesses. I could be a customer of either. The police will probably take an initial interest as part of their usual routine. So long as we're not careless or discuss anything in a hotel room that would rouse their suspicions, they'll dismiss us and move on to the next group on their list."

"It makes sense," Mehendra stated as he followed behind.

"For security reasons, we discuss business only in places like this," Managua said pointing back to the bar. "At least until I can move you out of the hotels into someplace more secure."

A cab pulled up to meet the four men. They piled into it with Rhys and his men cramming into the backseat, and Managua taking the front seat. The lawyer gave directions to the hotel and the car was off.

19

It felt great, Sauwa thought to herself as she leaned back in her chair enjoying the feeling of her new clothes. The T-shirt and blue jeans were a welcome change from the crusty attire she had been working in since being consigned to the Filipino safe house in Izmir. It was fortunate that the shopping area they were taken to hosted a series of small second-hand shops that offered a variety of cheaper clothing. Not being much of a shopper, she found a few articles that served her purpose and supplied her with enough fresh clothing to last several days. It was the softness of her clean, new socks massaging her feet that manage to almost forget where she was.

"Alright, this meeting can begin," Tarkov stated, capturing everyone's attention with his deep voice. He had a natural commanding presence about him. By now, everyone had come to accept his leadership. The Russian moved to the center of the group where all eyes focused on him. Dressed smartly now in a crisp pair of slacks and a short-sleeved blue collared shirt, he was very much the executive exuding control. "We've had time to digest the information from the meeting this morning and a chance to tour the city and get the lay of the land. Now, we need to start figuring out how we're going to proceed with this operation."

Carzona arrived with the folders from the earlier meeting. Quietly he handing them out to the group.

"Do we have any idea when the arms will be moved?" De'vor asked.

"No, we don't," Tarkov answered. "That is information we have not been able to gather." The room was silent. Everyone grimaced as they returned to reading their files.

"How old is this intelligence?" Sauwa asked. "I'm looking at the reports more closely, and some of the dates are more than a week old. Is anyone still collecting information on these guys, or is this all we have?"

Tarkov remained composed, though the look on his face suggested he was anything but comfortable with the question. "We still have assets that are keeping loose tabs on The System as much as possible. As far as the arms trafficker, your assessments from the earlier meeting were right, he's a very well-connected man. The firm contracted to fill our intelligence gap here won't go any further with him than what you're reading now. Essentially we're on our own to fill in any intelligence void when it relates to him."

"Then what you're saying is we're working blind!" Gorzo growled speaking up for the first time. "Bad enough we come into this operation with no plan, now they want us to work with limited intelligence! How the hell do they expect us to do this?"

"This is how it's done," Sauwa snapped in a tone that took command of the room. "This is how it works in the field when you're operating as part of a clandestine mission. You collect your own intel on the enemy. You develop your own plans and operations, and you work alone!" Her eyes were hard and focused as she cast her gaze on the entire room. She had everyone's full attention. "As I see it, we're wasting our time being too focused on either this Kalopolis person or the Filipino businessmen. Both are protected by professional security and are anticipating us, or someone like us. There are too many possibilities of getting caught dealing with them directly. Concentrating on them would not only be fruitless, but it is ultimately a dangerous endeavor. We need another route."

"What do you suggest?" Sacchini inquired.

Drawing a sheet from the file she had in her hand she approached the group.

"Him." She went to the board behind Tarkov and stuck it in the center next to the picture of Kalopolis.

Everyone was now looking at a picture of a man who looked to be in his late forties with a receding hairline and worn, lined face. "Yannis Prokopis." She turned to face her comrades. "Our intelligence source, whoever they are, were good enough to furnish us with a quick overview of those who work for Kalopolis. So, what we do know is that he is working on the illicit side of the business. We see him in several pictures with the arms merchant, and he looks to be someone Kalopolis takes into his confidence."

She paused as everyone returned to their file packets and began studying the succession of photographs. They also began to see the number of times the man showed up in the same surveillance shot as their target. In almost all the pictures, the two looked to be engaged in important conversations, or Prokopis was standing next to his boss while he was conducting business talks with possible clients. In either case, Sauwa was right, the man looked like he held a position of significance with the arms trafficker.

After a few minutes, and everyone had a chance to absorb the information, Sauwa continued. "When it comes to guerrilla, terrorist, and criminal groups, I have found that while the senior leadership tends to be highly concerned with their own safety and puts great emphasis toward protecting themselves, their right-hand and middle-management people tend to be less so. They're often overlooked by everyone, including professional intelligence services, who are concentrating on the top of the organization. The right-hand and middle-management people are the ones on the streets doing the dirty work and managing the mechanics of the business. I say we target Prokopis as our primary means of intelligence gathering. We probe him and maybe we might get the answers we need to plan our next move."

Tarkov was nodding as he listened. "It's worth a shot." He turned his head to check Carzona. The Filipino had his thumb pressed to his chin and tilted his head. "Yes," he said, "that definitely sounds like a good idea. We just have to figure out how we begin." The room fell as deadly silent as a cemetery. Sauwa looked up to see Tarkov looking in her direction. Behind him, she saw Carzona doing the same. By their expressions, they were waiting for her to proceed. Not wanting to misread their expressions, she waited a few seconds for someone else to speak. She saw their expressions become more obvious letting her know they were waiting for her.

"There is a multitude of ways we can collect viable intelligence," she began. "In this case, we're better off identifying where this guy lives and works. We identify his home, conduct a recce, and see where we can establish an observation post to keep an eye on his activities. Then we graduate to other measures like sifting through his garbage to see what he might have thrown away that could benefit us. Eventually, when we know enough, we break into his house and search it."

"Sift through garbage! Establish a fucking observation post! What bullshit is this? Why don't we just get some cars and follow him around?" Gorzo spoke up as if he were introducing the obvious solution. "I mean that's what cops and spies do in this situation."

"Yes, they do," Sauwa replied. "But, professional law enforcement and intelligence agencies have resources for such missions. We won't have those resources and obtaining them could be more trouble than they're worth. In the case of vehicles — where do we get them? If we steal them, we have to worry about what happens if a cop pulls us over, and we can't produce documents that prove we have the car legally. On stakeouts, it's not uncommon for surveillance teams to be compromised because they hung around in a place too long, and it roused the suspicion of the police. If we're thinking of buying or renting a car, we still have to go to someplace that would require we show identification and fill out paperwork. This means we have a paper trail linking us to vehicles we intend to use for illegal purposes. In addition, most car dealerships tend to have their lots and offices manned with video cameras in case someone swindles them or steals a car. This means that in addition to having our identities and pictures on record somewhere, we are also on camera footage."

"Even if we did have the means to obtain vehicles through fake documents, someone like Prokopis may not be walking around with professional bodyguards, but he could be using a state of the art security system. He is someone working in an extensive criminal enterprise, and he has ascended up the ranks to his current position. A guy like that certainly pays attention to details and people, because he's accustomed to being followed or having someone come after him."

"Understand that police and intelligence agencies have fleets of vehicles to work with, and they can switch them out so the same cars aren't following the same person all the time. They also have a number of agents they can alternate so the same faces don't become familiar. We won't have any of that to work with. I doubt anyone here has had any training surveilling people. He'd pick up on us after a few days at best, and then we're screwed." She looked around the room, the atmosphere was sullen as her words sank in. The mercenaries were out of their element, and they knew it.

"That's all well and good," De'vor jumped in. "But, he still is not our primary target. This doesn't change our problem of how to get at Kalopolis or his clients. They are our prime targets and are still too well guarded for us to touch."

"Which brings us to the next point," Tarkov suddenly interjected. "I have been considering our situation. I came to the realization that no matter which group we hit, even if we're successful, all that would do is delay the situation. If we hit the Filipino delegation, another would simply arrive to take over. If we managed to take out the arms trafficker, the Filipinos would simply find another supplier through the same avenue they used to find this one. Inevitably, we would just be doing a short-term fix for a large-scale problem."

"What then are you recommending?" Sacchini asked.

Tarkov turned back to Sauwa. "I believe clandestine destabilization is still your area of expertise."

Finding all eyes turned to her again, Sauwa went on. "The issue isn't the people, it's the location. Why are Filipino businessmen trying to buy weapons all the way around the world when they have access to similar markets closer to home where they have better connections and greater familiarity? The answer is that here they can operate with more secrecy. Everyone knows that Cyprus is a hub for the black market. Intelligence services and criminal organizations often run money for black operations through Cyprus banks, and Eastern Europe houses large sums here too."

"The country accommodates criminal markets in many ways. The most likely reason why this deal is being done here in Cyprus is because it is a virtual hub for every kind of black market. That said, the target is the shipment itself. We need to make enough noise that the anonymity surrounding this deal is shattered. We need to hit the shipment and draw attention to this operation. If we stop the shipment, they lose an expensive investment at the very least. If we make it loud enough, we draw a lot of attention to this operation that would make it very difficult to continue if everybody is watching."

"That is an idea," Tarkov said as he turned to Carzona looking for approval.

Sauwa returned to her seat. De'vor was glaring at her. His disdain was all too apparent.

Sacchini opened with the next question. "What are we going to do about weapons and equipment?"

"We have a contact of our own that can supply us with a wide variety of weapons for what we may need," Tarkov explained. "When we are ready and have a better idea of what we're up against, we'll submit our requests through our employer. In the meantime, I don't want to have a bunch of weapons and explosives to worry about hiding and storing until we are ready to use them."

"I don't like the idea of going out and watching this guy without some firepower," Gorzo protested.

"If we get caught by the police carrying guns, it will be a lot worse," Sauwa said. "Countries like this don't take well to people walking around with guns. Since our status here is cosmetic and wouldn't hold up to any serious check, we'd be screwed. Besides, if we get discovered doing our recce, we should consider the mission blown and our next option should be getting the hell out of the country."

The meeting adjourned with everyone handing Carzona their folders. Sauwa made her way to the workout area. She was feeling a little tense, anxious to get in a little bit of exercise. She had learned early on the dangers of neglecting her physical condition when out in the field.

Dressed in a tank top and cargo pants tucked into her black combat boots, she started with the chin up bar. She had gotten six good reps in when she was approached by De'vor, who wandered over to her as if their meeting was purely by chance. She continued her workout ignoring him. The cold shoulder and dismissive attitude had become their ritual when around each other. This time it was different.

"You really enjoy all this, don't you?" the De'vor said as he began perusing the line of dumbbells. Sauwa didn't respond. She jumped off the bar and began a regimen of pushups. She figured he was just making conversation as usual and expected him to saunter off. Instead, he stayed and looked at her as if waiting for an answer.

She continued working out saying nothing and offering not the slightest acknowledgment of his existence. "I want an answer from you," he said sternly. "I really want to know what makes a psychopath like you tick."

She leaped up to her knees and then onto her feet. "I enjoy being called such things by a person who earns his money killing people, too."

De'vor's eyes turned cold and steely as if he was deciding whether to kill her. "I'm a soldier. I kill on a battle-field, and the ones I kill are soldiers themselves. I don't murder those who are fighting dirty wars or are killed indis-criminately."

"If you say so," Sauwa replied indifferently as she went around him to the dumbbells. His piercing gaze followed her making it clear he was not finished. She reached for two twenty-pound weights and began lifting one at a time, but she kept the Frenchman in her sights. If he tried anything she was ready to throw one of the weights toward his stom-ach, the other toward his head and follow through with a violent assault. She couldn't stand self-righteous soldiers who indulged in making moral judgments. No matter what he said about the nobility of soldiering, he was here fighting the same war she was.

Still, she could understand his disdain for her. He was a soldier, a commando, who carried out missions in wars against known hostiles. Even as a mercenary, he was the kind of man who liked to think he was still fighting with rules that left some civility on the battlefield. For him, she was a soldier of a different type of war — a dirty war where there were no rules, no limits to barbaric behavior, or any definition of moral decency.

Sauwa continued lifting the weights. As if they were

having some sort of standoff, De'vor glared coldly at her for several minutes. Finally, he turned and strode off, leaving her to finish her workout in peace. She hoped that this episode would be the last, though deep down, something told her it was not over.

20

Yannis Prokopis lived in a nice, expensive townhouse off of Dasoubi beach. It was a white two-story structure that connected to a long row of similar houses. Beyond it was a neatly manicured grass lawn that covered a distance of about eighty feet before feeding into a park full of leafy trees that led to a thin strip of sandy beach and a glistening blue ocean. On the other side was a small brick walkway that led to another row of apartment buildings that towered over the townhouses. It was a clean, upscale location that catered to the professional class — lawyers, doctors, and general business types.

Following Sauwa's advice, the team started their surveillance slowly by first passing by a couple of times to get a feel for the location. Sauwa, dressed in a pair of silk running shorts and a T-shirt, had taken to going for morning jogs around the housing complex. It was a common route for many running enthusiasts, so it was an easy way to recce the area unnoticed.

The first day she ran along the beach then across the trail

that cut through the park and circled around the walkway that wound through the housing complex. She took the time to observe the layout of the area, noting what type of people frequented it. In her experience, most covert missions were thwarted not by the diligence of an elite security service as by some annoying busybody who had nothing better to do than pry into the business of everyone in their neighborhood. It was surprising how often covert operations had been blown by someone on a neighborhood watch spotting a mysterious car or van parked too long and calling the police at an inopportune time.

As she ran through the complex, she discovered the local populace were mostly younger men and women. They were generally professionals with money who focused on having a good time. They were the type that if they weren't at work or out clubbing, they were entertaining. In either case, they seemed to have an interest in what was happening outside their own world. From what she had seen of Prokopis, it was exactly his type of world.

The next day she found time to stop and stretch just outside of Prokopis's house. She came up to the small stairway leading to the door and began stretching out her leg. As she did, she took the time to look over the door. She could see that it was a hard metal barrier with a steel jamb welded tightly into a concrete housing structure. The door itself was secured with a key lock that she figured could be breached easily enough with some time and the right tools. However, they were in such a public place, getting in through the front door would be impossible.

She took time to observe the frame of the house, checking for signs of hidden cameras lining the entry points and wires leading into the house that suggested a house alarm or the possibility of cameras inside the house. Anticipating that a man in Prokopis's line of work would have some sort of security system, she had taken the precaution of wearing a baseball cap, tucking her hair up inside it, and donning a pair of dark sunglasses that covered the entire upper portion of her face. She had also worn an oversized, loose fitting long sleeved shirt that draped over her body covering her frame and hiding any other identifying features. Since women were always concerned about getting sun damage to their skin, such apparel wasn't out of place for the location.

Examining the house, she caught sight of two bird statues placed just above the door. They were positioned to observe the entire entryway and all those who approached it. She had seen similar statues and recognized them — they were custom made hidden cameras. She assumed there were similar ones over the back door. The wiring probably fed directly behind the statues into the house so they weren't visible and would not be easily accessible to cut. Not wanting to press her luck, she opted not to verify her theory by going around the back and seeing for herself. A girl simply stretching and cooling off after a run was easily dismissed. The same girl being caught on camera hanging around the back of the same house would definitely arouse suspicion. She figured Prokopis was the type to check his video feeds daily. Luckily, she knew such cameras had little memory and her image, if it was not deliberately recorded, would probably be lost within a day or two. Still, this would be the last time she would risk being so close to his house. Future runs would be conducted on the other side of the road to ensure she wasn't captured on any more footage.

The team found a spot along one of the trails that gave them a perfect observation spot. Trees and shrubs concealed them from anyone looking from the house, while the location itself made it easy to look like tourists relaxing in the shade. To Sauwa's dismay, Tarkov decided to have the observation post manned by her and Gorzo. Because they were the closest in age, the team leader insisted they should be paired to perform the surveillance mission — a young couple enjoying the day. And, if anyone should see them staring at the houses, they would just assume the young lovers were envisioning their life together.

THE BEACH WAS NEARLY DESERTED at this time of the morning. A quick swipe past the canteen showed only a small smattering of surf bums enjoying the brief privacy. Some guys, dressed in clothes that indicated they had just come straight from a wild party, appeared to be there to clear their heads after a long night of drugs and alcohol consumption. Neither group paid the slightest attention to the young couple walking past them into the park.

The two settled themselves into place, nestling up to some trees and eating out of bags of food they had picked up from an eatery a short distance away. Anyone walking by would assume they were taking the time to enjoy a nice breakfast. Sauwa laid out her bag, while Gorzo reached for one of the pita breakfast sandwiches. He cast a disapproving eye over her as she set out her equipment. He had lobbied hard to have her dress in a bikini top and cutoff shorts — attire he was sure would be more inconspicuous for their beach setting. He had not entirely won the argument, with her being allowed to enjoy a loose fitting grey T-shirt. However, despite her objections, Tarkov did agree that such a young couple should fit the part on an exotic beach, and she found herself having to strut around in a tight fitting pair of high riding cutoff jeans. "You know," he said, "a body like yours should be shown to the world. Every woman out there is wearing swimsuits. You look out of place."

"And yet, I don't feel out of place." She replied as she scanned the area one last time to see who was around and if they were paying any attention to them. The trail and surrounding area were empty of any human traffic leaving them entirely alone. She took the opportunity to break out her binoculars and notebook. Leaving Gorzo to enjoy his breakfast and stand as a lookout, she strolled into the trees. Hunkering behind a bush, she looked through her optics to see if she could get a view of the back of Prokopis' house. It was early morning, and the sun was not in the right position — the back still remained immersed in shadows. It was impossible to see anything including any security devices. She was able to see blueish-white flashing through the windows downstairs — a television was playing. It was a sign their target was home.

Reaching into her canvass bag, she pulled out a small disposable cell phone. Dialing a number, she let the phone ring a few times before she heard Tarkov answer in his gruff accent. "Yes?" He asked curtly. "We're here, and our friend appears to be home," she said. She dispensed with the usual protocol of speaking cryptically or in code because they were using disposable cell phones, not landlines or personal phones.

"Keep watching. Call us if it looks like he's getting ready to leave," Tarkov instructed and hung up.

While she and Gorzo were watching the house, Tarkov and De'vor had found a place to hang out that gave them a perfect line of sight of the garbage dumpsters that serviced the row houses. In addition to the physical observation, Sauwa also suggested that a person's garbage had often proven valuable as a means of intelligence collection — people are inclined to be oblivious to what they discard into the trash. With that suggestion, the Russian felt it wise to see what information they could snag.

With nothing happening, she retreated back to where her companion was waiting patiently. "Any luck?" He inquired as he went to hand her a sandwich rolled in some tin foil.

"No," she replied shaking her head as she accepted the sandwich. Sauwa settled close to Gorzo to give the appearance they were a couple of young lovers. Cyprus was such a romantic tourist spot, it ensured that they were left alone. Gorzo took full advantage of the situation wrapping his arm around her waist and pulling her closer and let his fingers run across the soft skin of her belly. An action she found annoying.

"I know you have a thing for older men," he quipped. "But, I should warn you, Russians make terrible lovers, and Sacchini is past his prime to satisfy a woman such as yourself." His fingers started to dip slightly into her belt line as they began to explore further. She took a quick assessment of her surroundings to ensure no one was watching before she produced a double bladed tactical knife and forcefully pressed the sharp edge toward Gorzo's inner thigh.

"If you want to remain a man, I suggest those fingers stay out of my pants," she said in a low, harsh voice.

Gorzo began to lunge in her direction but was stopped cold by the sharp metal being pressed more firmly into his leg. His hand slithered off of her belly and came up onto her shirt. His lips cracked into a sinister smile. "I like the ones that play hard to get. It gives a man the thrill of the hunt and offers the best reward in the bedroom once they have been conquered." He backed off leaning against the tree and returned his attention to his sandwich.

Having made her point, for the time being, Sauwa removed the knife before anyone came along. However, she feared she had won this battle but lengthened the war. Far from being put off, the young Italian now seemed to see her as even more of a challenge he was determined to win.

They had been in position for an hour when 0930 rolled around. Prokopis exited his sliding glass door at the back of his house. He walked to the edge of the balcony with a small glass of bourbon as he looked out over the ocean. He was dressed in a cream-colored suit with a buttoned shirt he wore without a tie and the top buttons were undone. He had a day or two of facial growth, and his hair was combed and slicked back nicely from his receding hairline. He sipped the bourbon slowly savoring every drop as he soaked up the view. He had been on his balcony no more than fifteen or twenty minutes when he returned inside and shut the door.

The sun had risen enough that Sauwa was able to get a good look at the framework of the house. Sliding under a leafy bush that shielded her from the view of the townhouse, Sauwa peered through her binoculars. As she had expected, the back door of the house was guarded by the same statues she had encountered in the front. They sat at the top corners of the door capturing images of all who stepped onto the porch.

With the downstairs clearly not an option for breaching the house, Sauwa continued to investigate for other entry points. She turned her gaze to the second floor and scanned the sliding door behind Prokopis. She took her time studying the door frame looking for any trace of a camera or alarm system. This task was rendered harder by Gorzo's antics. To provide cover from anyone passing by, he had rolled up on top of her. He had also seized the opportunity to let his hands again wander over her body. She found it difficult to concentrate on the target location while feeling a hand slowly pet and occasionally grab her bottom cheek. Due to the fact that people were now frequenting the trail behind them, Gorzo didn't receive the violent response he deserved.

Sauwa brought down her binoculars satisfied that the security features did not extend to the second floor. Prokopis apparently felt any threat to him would only come through the ground level. The couple looked too obvious and risked being noticed if any of the pedestrians on the trail decided to stop and investigate them. Taking additional advantage of the moment, Gorzo took to running his fingers across the belt line of her jeans and eventually slid them inside once more.

"What!" he exclaimed whispering into her ear. "I was hoping to enjoy the feel of satin or silk panties." He feigned disappointment as he continued to allow his fingers to explore the world under her clothes. Bringing his face close to hers, the scruff of his facial hair scratched annoyingly against her face.

She said nothing as her partner continued to molest her. To respond would have created a scene. She reached for her phone and made another call to Tarkov. By now Gorzo was kissing the back of her neck and whispering something to her in Italian. Dialing a number, she was promptly speaking to her team leader. Between the Italian's probing fingers and his aggressive actions on her neck, she struggled to maintain her bearings as she answered to the gruff Russian baritone.

"It looks like he's leaving."

"Does it look like you can get inside?" Tarkov asked.

"Not now."

"Hold your positions for another thirty, then break," Tarkov commanded.

"Alright."

She fought to tuck the phone into her pack. Thankfully, Gorzo had backed off enough to allow her that much freedom. She returned to watch the housing complex. Since she couldn't see the front to tell if their target had definitely left or not, she changed her scope of interest to the neighboring houses as she tried to get a feel for the neighbors. From her recces running through the neighborhood, she didn't see much sign that the communities were a tight-knit group. They did not appear to be neighbors who made a point of knowing everybody and everything that went on around them.

The pedestrian traffic on the trails had begun to slow to a trickle. There were only one or two people who quickly walked past paying not the slightest attention to the young couple 'romancing' in the trees. This left her free to pull out her binoculars to get a closer look at the neighboring houses. It also freed her up to respond to Gorzo's groping with a quick elbow plowing into his solar plexus. Caught off guard with a powerful jolt to his stomach, the Italian doubled over groaning in agony.

She remained on her side watching him as she waited to see what his response would be. He glared angrily back at her as he held his stomach and started to catch his breath. Was he going to attack or was he going to back down? She wasn't going to turn her back on him until she was sure which one. Gradually his bitter stare morphed into a sinister smile. He leveled an evil look at her with satisfaction.

Not knowing what to make of his behavior, she returned his look with a cold, deadly stare of her own. With a look of amusement, he eventually raised his hands gesturing his surrender. Satisfied he was no longer a threat at the moment, she rolled back onto her stomach and began to peer through her binoculars. She could feel Gorzo slowly crawl back into place over her body, this time his hands were placed more acceptably around her waist, and he was no longer kissing the back of her neck.

She continued to study the framework around the doors on the second floor and found to her delight that nothing in the form of a security system seemed to exist. What was more interesting was that one of the townhouses had the bottom door partially open, a sign that security was not a concern amongst the general community.

As instructed, the two held their position for another half hour. When nothing happened, they casually exited the trees. A few of the men walking by gave Gorzo triumphant smiles for the supposed romantic session he had instigated, while some of the older couples walked past looking at the young couple with reminiscences of their own youthful antics. Dusting herself off, Sauwa ambled down the trail with Gorzo at her side. To keep up appearances, she allowed him to keep his arm wrapped around her and tucked her body close to his. She played her part cracking a smile and leaning into his frame as they continued toward the beach.

AT THE WAREHOUSE, the team gathered in the meeting area. Everyone was present including the German they had met the first day they arrived in the country. He was accompanied by a young Greek gentleman who was dressed in a light grey suit and blue tie almost identical to his older companion. The German conversed only with Carzona and avoided speaking to any of the mercenaries. Tarkov tore open a couple of plastic bags and dropped the contents onto the floor. "When Prokopis left today, he threw these bags into the trash."

Sauwa dropped to the ground and began sifting through the debris in front of her. The rest of the team lowered themselves to the ground following suit. "Our boy is certainly the drinker," De'vor remarked as he picked through the empty bottles. There were several scraps with handwritten scribbles jotted on them, but they were all in Greek. "We need to know what these notes say," Sauwa exclaimed as she lifted a few of the scrapes and attempted to examine them.

"That is why we have him," Tarkov pointed to the young man in the grey suit. "Our employer's contact recruited him to translate any information we found."

"How are you?" The young man raised his hand to identify himself.

"We will refer to him as Nico," the Russian went on. "He speaks fluent English and knows not to say anything about what he sees here."

Rising to her feet, Sauwa walked over and handed the young man the papers she held. Nodding appreciatively, the young man perused the scraps. "Each of these notes is discussing different things — one is explaining the need to secure a pier for a ship coming out of Bulgaria in two weeks, the other one is discussing finding a different location for

233

something they were doing in Nicosia. That's the largest city on the Greek side of the country in the north."

Sauwa looked at Tarkov. He stared at Nico questioningly. She walked over to Tarkov and was about to speak when he exclaimed, "You don't think that this is happening all the way across the island, do you?" the Russian asked nervously.

"That we're in the wrong city and on the wrong coastline?" Sauwa responded. "I don't know. But this will certainly complicate things if we have to quickly move operations and familiarize ourselves with a whole new location in a short period of time."

They walked over to the table to view their map of the country. They looked for Nicosia, tracing the northern coastline. "Nico, where exactly is this place?' Sauwa inquired. Dutifully, the young man stepped over to where the two mercenaries were hunched over the map. He pointed to a large spot a good distance inland. "That is Nicosia," he said tapping the black dot.

Sauwa and Tarkov noticed that the city didn't rest on the coastline at all. Nico quickly followed up with an explanation that the city had been built along a river system and wasn't at all near the coastline. This revelation led the mercenaries to conclude that their objective was not there. Deciding to disregard the Nicosia information, everyone concentrated their focus on the first note discussing the procurement of a pier.

Nico scrutinized the document. Every so often he lifted his brow to observe the group of mercenaries that had started to crowd around him. The degree of danger these hardened killers presented was apparent, and he began to feel slightly unnerved. "This explains little more. The only other thing I can see is that the arrival of the ship is to be late at night." He continued examining the note while the mercenaries pondered the information.

"We don't know that this is talking about our objective," Sacchini commented, slightly disheartened.

"Even if it is, it hardly offers enough information to locate and recce the place," Sauwa interjected.

"You're both entirely right," Carzona spoke up. 'What we can determine though is that we seem to be monitoring the right man. He is clearly entrusted with a series of important matters for our arms broker."

"We need more intelligence that's for sure," Tarkov grumbled in exasperation.

"How do we know any of this has anything to do with the arms trafficker, Kalopolis?" De'vor asked. "I mean this guy is a criminal. He could be doing this for someone else — a completely different deal."

"No," Sauwa replied. "Men like Kalopolis don't entrust important business, such as major arms deals, to freelancers. And, securing a pier for a cargo ship is not easy. This is a trusted lieutenant in his organization. The question though is whether we're reading about business pertaining to our mission or not?"

"There is something more," Nico announced as he unwrinkled the bottom half of the note. All eyes gravitated back to him. "It says the arrangements should be made to accommodate two cargo ships. It has some words written at the bottom, *possible second cargo ship.*"

"Does it explain where this second ship is coming in from?" Tarkov asked.

Nico turned the paper around to check for any additional notes. He looked disappointed and shook his head.

Everyone walked away confused and dissatisfied. They returned to sorting through the trash on the floor. The few other arbitrary notes yielded nothing of significance. What they did find that caught Sauwa's eye were several leaflets from a club of some sort. She also noticed several disposable wristbands that had colors and a logo matching what was on the leaflets. Still sifting through the rest of the debris, they found several documents that looked like invoices.

Gathering these documents she presented them to Nico. Glossing over everything quickly, he explained that these were invoices for a club that translated into *Zeus' Kingdom*. Judging by the regularity of the paperwork, Nico realized that it was an establishment Prokopis apparently owned or partially owned.

"Really?" Sauwa pressed. "He seems to go there a lot. Anything else?"

"Based on the dates on the invoices, it looks like he goes there every night." Nico held one of the sheets up to show her.

By now, they had been joined by both Tarkov and Carzona with the rest of the team following behind as the young man explained these things to Sauwa. She looked back at her two bosses watching both of them plotting. After Nico finished his translations, he took a cue from the mercenaries' expressions and stepped away as Tarkov turned to address his team. "It's clear we need even more intel than what we have. I certainly don't think we can wait to collect it from fishing in his trash over the next week." The others nodded in agreement.

"We need more to work with — we need to get inside his house."

The mercenaries responded to this statement with agreeable murmurs.

The meeting ended with Carzona leading the German and Nico out of the warehouse. Once outside, he thanked the two men. Nico nodded and started for their car leaving Carzona and the German to speak privately. "I thank you for your help. Our mutual acquaintance, Esmeralda Morayo, said you could be relied upon for help."

The German wiped his hand across his face as he nervously looked around. "I have known Esmeralda for a long time. She needed my help to assist you in whatever you are doing. I trust her, and she offered me a great deal of money for whatever risk I'm taking. Still, I have taken a great deal of time getting you here, setting you up in this place, and now assisting in this new development. I don't want to be brought into this too deeply, and. I fear this will go much deeper."

Carzona raised his hand to the German's shoulder. "We use your services sparely, no more than is needed. We do not intend to abuse your assistance. Hopefully, we will soon have no further need of your services."

The German cracked a smile as he started toward the car. Carzona watched as he left. The German was Karl Brukman, an attorney from Munich who, like Esmeralda Morayo, specialized in international law and business. His practice gave him business all over Europe as well as connections. At age of sixty-five, he had become short of money. When young Miss Morayo approached him about helping her people get into Cyprus undetected and assisting them during their time in the country, he was hard-pressed to say no after she stacked a hundred thousand U.S. dollars on top of the polished oak table in his living room.

She explained that he didn't need to know more than his part. That she, nor any of the people involved could undertake what she was asking him to do. Her people were already in the country and couldn't afford to be recorded. That is why she was enlisting his help. He just needed to ensure that nothing he did in support of her 'friends' traced back to him. It sounded dangerous and was certainly illegal. But, staring at the fortune on his table and knowing he needed it, the risk seemed worth it. He had said yes to her and her companion, a Mr. Carzona, the man he would be meeting again at a pier on a decrepit fishing boat with a half dozen unsavory-looking people. He had arranged with a man who specialized in creating false documents to accompany him to the wharf and present each of Carzona's people with an 'official' stamp authorizing them in the country. He had, through an acquaintance, bought a warehouse that would serve the needs of Carzona and his people. He left them that day with a number to a disposable phone but hoped he would never hear from them again.

21

The Molos boardwalk was buzzing with smatterings of tourists, mostly youths enjoying a break from school, and some young couples making the most of their honeymoon or romantic getaway. Rhys strolled along the asphalt walkway as he looked out over the crystal waters of the Mediterranean. The sun was in its last stages of life as it slowly retreated from view. Halfway down the boardwalk, it widened into a large circular pattern that lengthened beyond the shoreline into the water.

It was here that Kennson Rhys stopped and took a moment to rest against the railing and enjoy the view. Not the view of the ocean, but the view of the city that was starting to brighten up with lights from the buildings and homes as the natural light began to fade. The street lamps lining the boardwalk burst to life after a few flashing jerks, cutting into the emerging darkness. He took some time to enjoy the splendor of the city before focusing on other matters.

His reason for being here this evening was to rendezvous

with the rest of his team. This was the night and the location for the meeting. His attention transitioned from the city toward the crowd walking in the immediate vicinity. By design, he was more than an hour early. He didn't like the idea of hired soldiers, men waiting around in uncertain locations, hired soldiers that he had never met or worked with before. He also didn't like the potential of an ambush or a surveillance team catching him off guard. In his experience. early arrival to a questionable meeting offered the means to assess the situation and scope out potential dangers.

The area was still awash with romantic couples taking advantage of the picturesque scenery. No one paid him the slightest attention — he was just another person out for a walk. Every so often Rhys caught sight of a local police officer on patrol. But each time the lawman walked steadily by arbitrarily looking around, not paying the slightest attention to the New Zealander resting against the railings. Rhys continued enjoying the warm breeze coming off the water as he patiently waited.

An hour later. Rhys caught sight of a man walking his way. He was Greek like most of the people here. His was dressed in jeans, tactical boots, a tank top under a tan collared shirt with the sleeves cut off, wearing a pair of dark sunglasses. The man was certainly trim and athletic looking — he had muscular biceps and a chiseled physique. What caught Rhys's attention was the tattoo depicting the bursting grenade emblem of the French Foreign Legion and the motto *Legio Patria Nostra* on his arm. *The motto* translated into *The legion is our Fatherland.*

The man also carried a black backpack with a small strip of yellow colored tape stuck along its side. It was the identifying mark the men were instructed to use for the meeting.

Rhys continued watching as the man walked up the scaffolding until he was less than a few feet from the New Zealander. The man looked around the area a few times before settling to watch the sunset. Rhys continued watching the man out of the corner of his eye as he kept his gaze on the boardwalk.

Gradually more men showed up — all with athletic builds, looking rough, and bearing small strips of yellow tape that were visible but in inconspicuous places on their bags. They joined the first man and began to congregate. It was apparent by the casual nods and gestures of polite recognition that they all knew one another. Rhys figured they were all consciously not speaking as they kept their distance and waited quietly for their soon to be employer to appear.

When all seven men were there, Rhys turned his own backpack around to reveal an X marked on it with the same yellow tape. He turned his body slightly in their direction allowing his head to twist further toward the ocean. He could see that the seven sets of eyes had noticed the yellow X and gravitated toward him. After a few minutes, he took his bag and joined the men.

"You must be Mr. Scott," one of the men said as he approached.

"I am," Rhys replied. Mr. Scott was the name he had told his friend to give the recruits to make contact. He normally didn't approve of such espionage nonsense, finding it both tedious and unnecessary. But, he understood this was not the chaotic battlefield he was accustomed to operating in where law enforcement was non-existent. In a sophisticated European country such as Cyprus, their activities were highly illegal and any one of these men could be caught by the police. He figured the less they knew about him the better.

"If you would all follow me," Rhys said as he started walking. The mercenaries trailed him moving in a loose group down the boardwalk. Little attention was paid to them as they strode past gatherings of tourists and locals. Feeling uncertain and suspicious, the mercenaries remained silent.

The journey ended at a bus stop just off the boardwalk. The group dispersed a little to not look too obvious to anyone. A few minutes later a bus pulled up. Rhys looked around at the men and gave a slight shake of his head to signal them that it was not the right one. The bus left, leaving the men waiting. This happened one more time and, finally, when the third bus arrived, Rhys' nodded subtly and pointed finger at the bus. The doors opened and the merce-naries slowly formed a line and stepped into the vehicle. Fares were dropped into a machine manned by a pudgy, smiling driver who happily thanked everyone as they entered.

The doors slid shut, and each man slipped into the closest unoccupied seat. Aside from the mercenaries, the only other occupants on board were an old man in a brown corduroy jacket and stained, collared shirt, and a young girl of about nineteen sitting way in the back. The bus began to hum as it pulled from the curb and started down the street.

Rhys liked public transportation for these types of opera-tions. Personal vehicles were too easily monitored and required paperwork and documents which made it difficult to simply discard them should they become a liability. Buses were easy to work with given they had a planned network throughout their city that made it easy to plan and offered a variety of stops that one could use to depart if they felt they were being watched. A car following a bus would be quite conspicuous trying to stay behind a bus that stopped frequently with all other traffic striving to pass it. Similarly, anyone on the bus would have difficulty following its quarry if they kept changing buses at the same time and then showing up on the same bus as their quarry. It was an easy way to travel around a city with discretion as buses went everywhere making it difficult to track someone's movements. Cars, on the other hand, could be tracked and identified through license plates and VIN numbers.

After five stops, the bus arrived at their destination. Rhys alerted his men by rising from his seat, preparing himself to move. The doors opened, and the New Zealander made his way through them. He stepped out onto the pavement and watched as the mercenaries exited the vehicle behind him.

Once they had all left the bus, Rhys led them down the dimly lit sidewalk eventually leading to a sizeable house sitting on the beach. It was a two-story structure that looked like it housed a bunch of college surf bums on vacation. The sun had set leaving the city in darkness.

From a strategic point, it was not ideal. The windows were big and provided good visibility for anyone outside looking at what was going on inside. The walkway was engulfed in plant life that had not been tended to for quite a while and was thick enough to furnish decent concealment to anyone who might want to recce the place or attack them. There was no fencing of any kind between the property and the open beach surrounding the back half of the house which was another weakness someone could exploit. On the plus side, the house was tucked deeply enough in the surrounding trees and shrubbery that the neighboring houses, a considerable distance away, could not easily observe what was going on.

They arrived at the front door. Before they could even knock, the door was flung open, and they were met by a short, shadowed figure guarding the door. Even in the darkness, it was easy to see Khadga Yadav was looking suspiciously at the group of men following his commander up the walkway. "So, we have our force, I see," the Nepali eyed the Greeks judgmentally.

"Yes, we do," Rhys replied as he gently pushed Yadav out of the way and entered the house with the others trailing behind. Yadav assessed each man as they walked past him. He had protested the hiring of unknown people for this mission from the very beginning. He was adamant that they should work with people they knew. He felt this regardless of the concern that they would be conspicuous in this country not to mention out of their element.

Inside they found Iventi Mehendra busy laying out thick reams of dark fabric over a large weathered table in the main room. Like the outside, the inside of the house looked like it had seen better days — the furniture old and beaten and the floors were slightly warped and creaky. The mercenaries filed into the room and sat down in the chairs and couches lining the walls.

Rhys walked over to Mehendra. In the better light, he got a good look at his new hires. They were all in their late twenties and early thirties, athletic, and fit. They all wore jeans or cargo pants, boots or tennis shoes, and their shirts were either cut off T-shirts or tank tops. They're less than military hairstyles looked more conducive to a wild partying scene than a military operation. Still, they sat alertly in their chairs giving their full attention to their new employer who stood at the front of the room. Yadav had followed the group and eyed them all with suspicion. His experience in the British army had left the former Gurka with a foul taste toward most European soldiers — particularly those trained by the French.

For Rhys, it was the perfect fit. A bunch of athletic young men dressed as they were provided the perfect image for the house and location. To anyone passing by, they looked like the typical summer partiers living at a beach house. They would be easily dismissed and forgotten by the local populace.

Once everyone was sitting and their attention focused on him, Rhys began his briefing. "Now that we're all here, let's get down to business."

Yadav leaned against the doorjamb, his arms folded. Mehendra leaned against the wall directly behind his superior. The Greeks were all giving their undivided attention to the New Zealander. The expression on their faces was of cold interest.

"I'll just come out and say it," Rhys started. "We're in the midst of a covert war. The people who have employed us have an important operation they intend to carry out, and Cyprus is a key hub. We have intelligence that enemies of our employers may wish to subvert said mission. This could be through military action. This team has been assembled for the express purpose of stopping any intervention that could jeopardize this operation. Now, we are flying a little blind. We don't know exactly who it is that could be our potential threat, nor do we know for sure that the threat will be something that requires our services. Our employers just wish to cover their bases. Make no mistake. This will be an alien world for most of you. We're all professional soldiers who are accustom to plying our trade in battlefield environments. We are not in that world."

"We will be operating here in Cyprus, and it will not be with the support or the blessing of the local authorities. This means if we get into a gunfight, expect the police to come after us. If you get caught, no one will come for you, and you might be looking at prison time. For this reason, each of you can expect to be paid a hundred thousand dollars American upon completion of this mission. With five thousand a week as base pay for every week you are providing your services." He watched the room, studying the faces of the Greeks carefully. If there were any of them that showed the slightest apprehension, he would have shown them the door handing them plane fare to get them back to Athens. He wasn't about to keep anyone who wasn't completely prepared for what might come.

None of the men moved or showed any hesitation —their faces were stone. They were all professionals who understood what they were getting into. It was a hazard of the life they had chosen, and everyone had decided that the reward was worth the risk. Confident that everyone was all in for the mission, Rhys continued. "In a few weeks, we will be making the maiden run for what will be an operation expected to span several weeks. A ship coming in from somewhere in the Baltic will pass on large quantities of equipment to a ship that will be heading to the prime destination. For now, we are charged with providing additional security for the transition location. If the shipments get attacked, our mission is to respond and neutralize the aggression to ensure the ships depart unmolested. Be aware our mission can change as the intelligence being provided changes. Expect our base of operation will be divulged as needed for security reasons. Are there any questions?"

"As you defined this mission, we will inevitably need weapons. What is the plan for obtaining arms?" asked one of the young men.

"Weapons will be utilized," Rhys agreed. "However, I do not wish to risk storing them here until absolutely necessary. They will be distributed prior to the mission. If the situation forces requiring them more quickly, arms can be made available within a day."

"What kind of armaments will we be using?" another Greek spoke up.

"We have access to Soviet equipment," Rhys replied. "I understand you all should be proficient with basic Soviet arms. In the short term, we will be working with AKM-74s, 5.56 caliber. We expect to be working primarily in urban environments within close quarters, making these weapons more practical than the AK or AKM-47 7.62 variety. However, we do have access to a much wider variety we can use if needed for this operation."

"I assume that Mr. Scott is not your real name," another Greek remarked. "Are we to assume that you are going to continue to be addressed by an alias?"

"Yes," Rhys countered. "For this mission, I will be referred to as Mr. Scott. My associates are Mr. Grey, he said pointing behind him to Mehendra, and Mr. Smith," he pointed across the room to Yadav. "You also may wish to give aliases for the duration of this mission. You have all been selected by trusted sources, so I have no need to follow up to verify your histories. I would point out that if anyone gets caught, the less they have to give to the police can only buy the rest of us time as we make our escape."

"Since we will be operating illegally if called into action, what will be the exfiltration protocols if we should be compromised?" the Greek continued.

"In the event any of us gets seized by the police during this operation, or if this house should be raided," Rhys responded "consider the mission terminated. The moment any one of us is seized by the police, the protocol will be to disperse and exiting the country will proceed as quickly as possible. There will be no rendezvous or coded command. The team will be dissolved, and everyone is to make their way off the island. A boat will be on standby to collect everyone and transport them to Greece. You will be briefed on the details for this procedure just before we execute the mission. The boat will be activated on my command. Once that happens the boat will wait for two hours to gather those who have not been captured. After that, you will be on your own to make your escape. Arrangements will be made at that point to ensure you receive the remainder of your pay."

As their commander spoke, both Mehendra and Yadav carefully scrutinized each of the Greeks. As professional soldiers with years of combat experience, they had both developed a good instinct for assessing people in this profession. They had seen enough of both good and bad to spot quality soldiers from flakes and blowhards. As they watched each of the Greeks, they saw nothing but solid professionals. Despite their loose attire, everyone looked fit and serious. When the briefing began all went silent and gave their full attention to the commander. No one asked foolish questions or made jokes. Indeed, they were quite impressed with what they saw. Rhys' British friend had selected his people well.

"What will be the security protocols for here?" another Greek asked.

"For now, we won't bother with that," Rhys said. "It's doubtful anyone knows of our existence, so I don't see a need to implement security measures until we go into operation. Even then, security will be subject to change based upon who we find ourselves up against. At the moment, we will always keep someone at the house while the rest of the team will focus on keeping in shape and rehearsing our mission. We all come from different military backgrounds and adhere to different tactical concepts and principles. Before we do anything else, I want to focus our downtime to emphasize training to rehearse and ensure we are all working off of the same concepts. Nothing is more dangerous in an operation than a team that is not using the same tactical book." There was a universal chorus of agreement.

"Where will we be practicing?" the same Greek asked.

"We have been allocated a warehouse along the wharf that is close to where we will be operating," Rhys explained. "In addition to housing our weapons and equipment, it will also give us a viable place to train and work out."

The meeting adjourned with Yadav leading the mercenaries upstairs to their rooms. Mehendra was tasked with masking the larger windows with thick covers while Rhys reached for his phone to brief Managua.

22

It was 2300 hours, Dasoudi Beach was moderately lively for the time of the evening. The number of beachgoers had steadily declined as the evening took over from the day. The older vacationers had retreated to the quiet of their hotels while the younger ones had taken to the club scene and the rest of the adventures the city's nightlife offered. Those remaining were sprinklings of young lovers enjoying the romantic atmosphere of a tranquil beach moonlit waters. They were hardly paying attention to anything beyond their immediate world.

Returning to the park, Sauwa walked the length of the trails for one quick recce to ensure they didn't have some unnoticed pedestrian lurking about as a potential witness or whistleblower. She had walked the park every night around the same time for the last three days as part of her preparation. She had been accompanied by Gorzo, who added to her cover. In a place like the Dasoudi beach, young lovers walking around at night were more easily dismissed and forgotten than a young woman walking alone.

They walked the entirety of the trail in the small park and were satisfied that no one was lingering nearby. The only thing they had to worry about was the police patrol. In their previous recces, they had discovered that around 2100 hours the local police kept a routine patrol pattern that had someone going through on an hourly basis. With the park generally deserted, anyone walking around was going to catch the interest of some cop. It was still a necessary risk. Having observed the housing complex, they determined that the parties seemed to be a nightly occurrence at one house or another, and generally ended or died down significantly at around midnight with the patrons drunk, tired, and or otherwise oblivious to everything around them. It was the ideal time to move on Prokopis' house.

Satisfied the park was empty, Gorzo and Sauwa slipped into the bushes where they had established their observation post. It was still shallow concealment and not what a skilled tactician would choose as grounds to launch an operation. But, under the circumstances, it was good enough to work with. Dipping into her backpack, she pulled out her operational apparel. It consisted of a long black shirt, black tactical cargo pants, and some matching tennis shoes. Gorzo stood watching her get dressed. The trees and bushes made it difficult for her as she felt around in the dark to ensure her clothing was on correctly.

She didn't dare step out on the trail to check herself. She had to make sure she could feel the distinction between her tactical clothing and the cutoffs and short sleeved shirt she had been wearing. She added a knit cap that she pulled over her head stuffing her hair up inside it. She shoved a pair of tactical gloves into the back of her belt and draped her shirt over the top.

Gorzo remained vigilant, acting as a lookout for anyone on the trail. Surprisingly he didn't take advantage of the situation and try to see the young South African in lingerie — he remained focused on the mission. Sauwa picked up her binoculars and scouted the housing complex. As predicted, one of the houses had a party going on inside. The only other signs of life were a few upstairs lights in some of the other houses. Most of the homeowners had either gone to bed or were out hitting a club or a party somewhere else.

Prokopis' house was completely dark. He had left for his usual haunt several hours ago. De'vor and Sacchini had positioned themselves on the other side for a good view of the man's house. Having watched him for the past couple of nights, they determined he kept a fairly regular schedule — leaving for his favorite club no later than 2100 hours. He kept an equally set schedule of returning around 0300 hours. The mercenaries had planned their operation around that timetable.

Sauwa waited for another half hour until the police patrolman made his routine pass through the park area. She and Gorzo laid flat, face down on the ground, their bodies hidden by the shadows of the overhanging bushes. Just like the previous walkthroughs, the patrolman had no interest in anything off the pathway. He kept his flashlight entirely on the trail in front of him, never once letting the light drift into the bush line where he might have caught the outline of the two mercenaries. Instead, he leisurely walked past as he went about his patrol.

It wasn't as if they were committing an illegal act being in the park. But, at that hour, alone as they were, they didn't look the type to be part of the upscale crowd from the townhouses across the field. They would have assuredly drawn suspicion from any halfway decent cop. He would have questioned them and possibly demanded to see some form of identification. This was attention they couldn't afford to have. Given that she was about to break into a house very close by.

The patrolman continued on down the trail. They watched as the gleam of his light steadily vanished. When Sauwa was sure he was gone, she began to move onto the trail. She walked at a steady pace — not too fast but still brisk. She continued for several meters keeping low, her movements steady. She slithered through the tree line as if she were an apparition. As she neared the housing complex, the trees and bushes more manicured and sparsely set. Still, she was able to find enough dark pockets within the foliage to keep from creating a silhouette.

She had wanted to carry out the breach during the day as this was a time when everyone was at work or somewhere else. This notion was discarded when, during the recce, they discovered that Prokopis kept a desultory schedule they could not plan around. He had stayed in his house one day until noon, another day he left a 0900 — he would leave suddenly and come home just as suddenly. They noticed several of his neighbors proved troublesome by also tending to have sporadic schedules. This made it too risky to attempt a successful break-in during such times.

At the end of the tree line, she knelt near a patch of bushes that masked her from anyone coming outside. She took some time to study the situation. A few doors down she heard the laughter of people attending a hosted evening get together. She carefully watched for signs that the back doors of any of the houses were in use by someone who could come out at any time and catch her. Her appearance lurking about at such odd hours would make it difficult for anyone in the housing complex to believe she was visiting someone or had just moved in herself. The odds were that she would be challenged and eventually escorted off the premises.

Initially, the plan had been for her to enter the house through the front door. Everyone thought she would be less conspicuous if she came from the street that ran through the neighborhood. This way she could more easily arrive at the housing complex looking like an average pedestrian, bypassing the complications presented by going through the park. However, this plan was scrapped when they saw the amount of human traffic passing by. Yet another problem were the neighbors from the apartments above — they hung out their balconies observing everything happening below.

Someone fiddling with the locks would have been quickly noticed by any one of them. The final plan was to infiltrate from the back where it was more private and contained. She had considered coming up through the street, then casually making her way around the housing complex to the back area. This would alleviate the threat of prying eyes and avoid the unnecessary complications of dealing with the trees and shrubbery. However, Tarkov had vetoed the plan, arguing that the tree line afforded better conceal-ment for the team and a more clandestine means to advance on the house. Sauwa's protests seemed to fall on deaf ears. The Russian had made up his mind.

After a few minutes of watching, she believed it was safe to move. She slipped out of the bushes onto the lawn. There were three houses between her and Prokopis' house. She reached the house just before his and quietly worked her way up the short stairwell that led onto the back porch. She quickly dusted off any dirt or brush she may have picked up that could possibly be trekked into the house. The house was owned by a middle-aged woman who was an executive for a perfume company. Like everyone else in the housing complex, she led a life of parties and social events. Searching her garbage and the neighbor's garbage on the other side of their target, they determined that she had a lover. She apparently spent many nights over at his place, leaving her house completely open. She apparently didn't have security concerns, since there were no signs of alarm systems or cameras. It was decided that the most logical means of entry would be to go through her house.

At the sliding glass door, Sauwa took a second to examine the handle. She could feel the locking mechanism when her fingers brushed across it. It was a small, one of a kind lock requiring a key. It would be slightly more difficult than the ones that had a breachable flip lock. She looked for any signs of human life in the area. Confident she was alone, she reached into her pocket and pulled out a small flashlight. She knelt down until she was eye level with the lock.

The porch was protected by a solid plastic railing providing her with concealment from prying eyes. She flipped on her flashlight, producing a red beam. She had covered the white lens with a red filter so the light wouldn't disrupt her night vision. Holding the end of the flashlight in her mouth, she reached back into her pocket to retrieve a small purse. Placing it on the ground in front of her she unzipped it, revealing a collection of small metallic picks and tension bars. From her time in the Civil Cooperation Bureau, she had learned the art of forging lock picks from heavy duty safety pins and paper clips bent into the proper shape. Such tools are less useful for door locks than locks on furniture. Happily, she found that for such an expensive home, the lock on the slider was very much like one found on an office filing cabinet — one that a makeshift lock picking tool could shimmy.

Lock-picking, a delicate art that requires not just skill but a well-practiced instinct, was a craft Sauwa hadn't used since her days in England. It had taken her several hours of practice to retrieve her abilities and the feel even remotely confident. She had practiced working on the locks of the filing cabinets and desks in the office compartment in the warehouse. Eventually, she was able to find an empty town-house with the same locking mechanism and was able to practice a few times.

She began by blowing into the lock to ensure there was no blockage that would impede her work. Next, she inserted the tension bar, a small flat strip of metal bent and twisted slightly, into the bottom of the keyway then inserted the pick — a straightened safety pin with the tip slightly bent — into the lock just above the tension bar. The pick slid all the way to the rear of the lock, and she felt it hitting the locking pins. Had this been a higher quality lock, the tools she was working with wouldn't have been adequate.

Applying a slight pressure on the tension bar to get the lock pins seated correctly, she, simultaneously jerked the pick in an outward direction — a practice in spycraft known as 'raking'. The tricky part is measuring the degree of pressure on the tension in order to turn the lock barrel once the pins are seated. The whole process required a delicate touch. Applying slightly too much pressure to the tension bar to force the pins to lock, she missed the first time. It took her another two nerve-wracking tries before she heard the click and felt the lock recede.

Before opening the door, Sauwa waited for a few

seconds. Sounds travel better at night, so she took the time to listen for any alien noises that would alert her to an impending threat. The night remained silent except for the sound of the guests at the party nearby.

Confident she was safe, she opened the door just enough for her to stand up and slide through slowly.

Slipping around the curtain, Sauwa slid the door shut behind her. A few lights had been left on removing the need to feel around for any light switches. The woman's home was immaculate — every piece of furniture was placed in a specific location as part of an obvious grand design strategy. The furniture was decorative and artsy, indicating the owner was one who wanted to impress all those who entered her home.

Sauwa checked the curtain to make sure it covered the entire door. She then looked around to make sure all other windows were covered in a similar fashion. Neighbors were apt to dismiss lights on in a house, whether they knew the owner to be home or not. They weren't so dismissive if they saw an apparent stranger walking around inside. Pressing on, she came to the edge of the dining room and peeked around to see what the next room looked like. Just as in the back, all the windows had the curtains tightly closed.

She made her way through the living room that was lit by a single lamp next to the piano off to her left. She looked for a coding pad on the wall near the main door checking for any signs of a security alarm system but saw nothing. She doubted a woman who didn't care about getting better locks for her doors would bother with an electronic security system. Making her way to the staircase, she swung around the stair post and started carefully upward.

Reaching the top of the stairs, Sauwa entered a large

open lounging area with cushioned furniture lining the walls and brass framed glass tables placed neatly in front of them. In the far corner next to a glass door was a well-stocked mini-bar offering a variety of drinks for both entertaining lady friends and gentlemen callers. She went through the lounging area to the glass doors. She opened them up and found herself on the balcony. The darkness helped to mask her and her activities if anyone downstairs should come outside. She closed the door until it was just slightly ajar so it wouldn't raise suspicion.

Slipping on her gloves, she walked toward the edge of the balcony. She looked at the grounds below and then toward the tree line nearby. Confident there was no one around, she reached the wall separating the woman's balcony from Prokopis'. Steadying herself with her other hand firmly on the ledge, she placed her feet on the ledge. Once her feet were firmly planted, she worked her way up until she was perched like a bird.

Slowly rising to a standing position, she turned carefully, edging her way toward the wall. Her tennis shoes were light, allowing her more feeling her way as she moved about in the darkness. When she was close enough, she brought her other hand to the other side of the wall. The white stone was smooth and provided very few places to grab onto. Thankfully, her gloves provided enough traction that she was able to take a firm hold as she swung her leg onto the ledge of the other house.

Repeating the exercise, she knelt down, placing her free hand on the ledge slowly lowering herself to the ground. She could feel the hard stone flooring under her feet. Now firmly planted, she proceeded to the glass door. Finding it locked, she repeated the lock-picking exercise from the previous door. And, like before, there were a few failures before she got it unlocked.

Making her way inside, she quickly shut the drape behind her and then went on to look for a light switch. She had found it was wiser when going through a home such as this at night to simply turn on the lights. It was more explainable to neighbors who would simply think the owner was home, over the more suspicious flashlight in a dark house. The lights flashed on to reveal a gaudy looking room that she surmised was the nexus for a bachelor pad. It was filled with trendy looking furniture she assumed was supposed to play into a cool hip image that the owner was clearly going for.

She walked over to a long coffee table in front of a well-used couch that she concluded was his primary place to settle when he was home. It sat across from a large television screen next to an ashtray full of cigarette butts. Beside the couch on a more elevated table was a cordless telephone with various pieces of paper littered about it. The paper looked to have writing that had been hastily scribbled on. She looked closer and found the writing to be in Greek and indecipherable to her.

Pulling a small disposable camera from her other cargo pocket she went about taking photos of the notes, spreading them out so she could take pictures of each note individually. Then she placed them back as best she could in the positions in which she found them. She went through this tedious exercise until she ran out of film. She continued about the house trying to see if there was perhaps any other place that Prokopis possibly conducted his business. A quick walk around of the upstairs showed nothing worth her time.

She ventured downstairs and came into a living room

that hosted a scene every bit as gaudy as what she had just come from. Other doors led into other rooms, but a quick glance after turning on the light was enough to tell her that there was nothing more to be found. She made her way back up the stairs and out onto the balcony having turned off the lights and re-opened the curtains behind her.

She was stopped by the sight of a couple, a man and a woman down below. They appeared to have come from a party and had stepped outside for some privacy. The woman, a middle-aged and still very pretty brunette, was angrily waving her finger and speaking to the man in an acid tone. The man, not bothering to let the woman finish, was responding with equal volatility as he growled back at her. Sauwa hunkered down in the darkness of the corner watching as the couple went on with their drama.

The show went on for several minutes until finally, someone called out from the party that forced them to both come back inside. With the coast clear, Sauwa went about climbing back over onto the balcony of the next house. She found the door as she had left from and she quickly slipped through. She walked a few paces then turned to look back and make sure that she wasn't leaving any dust or footprints that would alert that she had been in the house. Satisfied that she was leaving no trace she went back the way she had come.

At the back door, she snaked her way around the curtains and through the door which she had locked before shutting it behind her. The area was still clear, and she made her way down the stairs onto the grass. She walked slowly toward the trees line. It was only a distance of fifty meters, but it felt like she was walking for miles. She didn't turn around, it would only look suspicious. Instead, she relied on her hearing. Listening for sounds of conversation or worse the sounds of someone lurking about who might have seen her and was now taking to watching or even following behind. She heard nothing as she made it the last few steps to the trees.

Sliding into the bushes, she took to the shadows as she made her careful trek back to the observation post and Gorzo. She moved at the same careful pace she had used coming in and followed the same pathway, keeping as much to the shadows as possible. She came around the full distance and was moving up on the location of the observation post when she was suddenly met by Gorzo who emerged from the bushes to meet her.

Without any words, he grabbed her, and with a powerful pull, he brought her to the ground and into a thick leafy bush. "Our policeman is coming up this way." He whispered into her ear as he practically laid on top of her. If she had any thought that Gorzo was doing this as just another attempt to get with her, it was soon dispelled when shortly she saw the gleam of the policeman's flashlight loom overhead and the sound of his boots as they rapped against the pavement as he continued on.

The mercenaries remained as they were, motionless for a few minutes until they could no longer hear him or see his light. Gorzo slid off of her and allowed her to sit up. "I watched you through the binoculars." He said, "Quite the acrobat." He handed her backpack to her. She emptied the contents of her cargo pockets into her front pouch and then repeated her routine as she undressed and dressed back into her original attire. If anyone could have possibly seen her during any of this, they would have seen a person alone dressed in black. Not two people, dressed in light summer attire.

She finished and stood up as she ambled out of the trees onto the trail with Gorzo right in tow. Now, on the trail walking along as if they were two lovers enjoying the night, they were free to talk. "Did you find anything on your adventure?" Gorzo asked as he wrapped his arm around her waist. She found his brazen advancement irritating but resisted any direct reprisal. She had been chastised by Tarkov, who reminded her that they were paired together because they could believably play a romantic young couple and such advancements were expected from him. She didn't like it but understood her commander was right.

"I got some pictures of some notes," she said. "I hope that'll have something. Otherwise, the house had nothing, and I never want to go back there again."

They continued out of the park and onto the beach. The whole time the Italian made a point of keeping close to her. Apparently savoring the victory, he got to be more intimate and personal. They continued down the beach appearing to anyone as if they were a young couple enjoying an evening stroll.

23

Nico examined the documents as everyone waited patiently. It was a time-consuming endeavor given that the young man was having to decipher virtual scribbles. This task was further complicated by the fact that he had to view the documents through photographs taken from a cheap disposable camera. Armed with a magnifying glass, he studied the pictures closely, as if they were specimens in a lab.

The German lawyer, Karl Brukman, stayed away from the mercenaries. His refused to have any dialogue with the 'professional killers'. The only one he talked to was Carzona and, even then, only when they were alone and able to speak privately. The German had been drawn into this operation and was afraid he was going to be compromised, with the eventual police investigation leading right back to him. Anyone of these soldiers could easily finger him or provide enough information for him to be ruined.

It had been an arduous task, but Nico gradually began to make sense of the pictures he was trying to interpret and separated them into groups. He began to arrange them into series, making notes in English on the ones he considered pertinent.

"Have you found anything?" Tarkov interrupted as he walked up behind the young man and peered over his shoulder.

Lowering the magnifying glass, Nico rubbed his eyes and leaned back in his chair. He dropped his hand onto one of the stacks. "I don't know exactly what you're looking for. Most of the notes involve the club he frequents or some things that seem like personal duties. All the notes seem to pertain to issues relating to the same shipyard and pier. I placed those in this stack and transcribed what I could read into English. My notes are in this notebook."

Tarkov picked up the young man's notebook and began to read. "Remember, I was only able to write down what I could understand from everything here. It will seem a bit choppy," Nico cautioned.

The Russian patted the young man on the shoulder and gave him a sympathetic glance as he reviewed the notes. Every one of them cited the same information as the notes they had pulled from the trash. The ship was arriving at Sodap — the newest and biggest industrial port in Cyprus. The notes indicated the operation was to take place at the north pier sometime late, around 0100-0200 hours. The notes further mentioned the names of two ships: The Romanov and the Chin Wu. The sight of a ship with a Chinese name caught Tarkov's attention immediately.

Carzona walked toward him. Tarkov thrust the notebook at the Filipino pressing him to review the findings. He pointed to a page, and Carzona focused on those notes. He agreed there was a possibility this meant something.

Exploring the information further gave them a time, a location, and finally a date — four days from now.

"This has to be it," Tarkov exclaimed as he retrieved the notebook from Carzona. "These boats have to be our target."

Carzona held the expressionless, stoic pose that was becoming his signature characteristic. "It certainly could be. With what we have to work with right now, it is our most viable information. Is there any other intelligence we can use?"

The Russian shot a look at Nico checking one last time for anything else he might have discovered. Nico looked at Tarkov and said, "From all the notes available, this issue seems to be the most significant. The way they are written, many of the points emphasized the great importance of this transaction." Nico was again pointing to the collection of photographs on the table. "All these address the same issue. Whatever we are reading, it is certainly important."

Carzona's face morphed into a look of concern. "I would have liked to gather more intelligence to be sure. If we move on this, and it turns out it's not our target, we'll have blown our hand and put our enemy on alert."

Tarkov retrieved the notebook from his employer. "And, if it is, and we don't move, then we'll have missed our window, and this mission will have been for nothing. I agree this is not much to go on and if I thought we could do it, I would have Prokopis picked up and let Sauwa go to work on him. I'm sure she knows some good interrogation methods that would have him talking in no time. But, we would also be exposing ourselves if we did."

THE NEXT DAY Tarkov returned to the warehouse after walking with the team through the facilities at the Sodap port. They had spent most of the day conducting a recce of the location to gain first-hand knowledge of the area and brought a reluctant Nico along to help navigate. He took them close to where the ships came into port. Carzona opted not to go and remained at the warehouse. This recce was too close to the enemy, and he didn't want to risk being noticed and possibly compromise their plan.

The port was buzzing with activity as shipyard workers tended to facility maintenance or loading and unloading the cargo of incoming and outgoing ships. Hauling trucks of all types moved out the access roads like ants working through the caverns of their nest. Businessmen in suits were everywhere observing the movement of their goods. No one took the slightest notice of a group of foreign mercenaries as they walked about freely through the port.

When they got to their destination, the team spread out to cover more ground. The port was enormous, encompassing several miles, and was nearly a city unto itself. Tarkov went with Sauwa and De'vor while the two Italians went in the opposite direction. Nico was asking around to get a feel for the place. On one side, there was a long stretch of road over a man-made sandbar where a ship could pull up parallel to it. On the other side was a peninsula that ran along the sandbar that served to box in the port forming a single opening to enter and exit.

Once inside the port, it broke off in two directions — one side was a giant rectangular shaped pool; veering left, the other side was a more compact rectangular shape. The exterior was surrounded by a long stretch of road that led from downtown all the way to the end of the port forming a traffic loop that wrapped around the port peninsula providing multiple directions back into the city.

The team walked along the corner of the more compact rectangular area across from the sandbar. According to the notes, this was where the delivery was to take place. The surrounding area was near a set of large overhanging cranes making it perfect for accommodating the transfer of cargo from one ship to another.

"Strategically, it would be difficult to assault from this place," De'vor said disappointedly. "Only one road leads in here giving our adversary the advantage of overhead visibility if they use those cranes. They can see us coming from any direction and could meet us before we even got close to the threat."

"The problem is we don't even know what kind of opposition we'll be up against," Sauwa added. "We have to assume with something as big as this, they'll have some reasonable security we'll have to confront."

"No, a direct assault on land would be out of the question," Tarkov nodded as Sauwa looked around. "Let's keep walking and see what other options we have."

The trio continued their walk along the pier. They scrutinized the location with the eyes of professional soldiers. Sauwa could see the two commandos use their honed instincts to study the location. Their minds had become machines calculating every foreseeable situation and strategizing how best to respond to it. They took note of the strategic complications that would work against them and also made note of any factors that might work in their favor. Every one of them fretted over the fact that they had no real idea of what they would be up against.

Sauwa suddenly became aware that some other men

were walking about in the same location. She would have dismissed them as people conducting their own business, but they seemed out of place to her. What first got her attention was that they all looked fit and weren't dressed at all like the coverall clad workman around them. What was more, a couple of the men were clearly not ethnic Greeks — one was pale white and looked to be British, or possibly Scottish, while the other two appeared to be his confidants and looked like East Asians. The men didn't seem interested in either the ships moored along the pier or any of the cargo containers stacked nearby. They seemed to be looking about assessing the location itself. It was as if they were conducting a recce. She had nonchalantly alerted Tarkov to the group of men. Both he and De'vor stepped behind a set of containers as they stood watching them for a few minutes. Like Sauwa, they too figured they had just met their adversaries.

Not wanting to be noticed by the group, she and the others continued walking up and back down the length of the road. As they walked, Tarkov constantly looked over at the main road leading into the port and then at the sandbar across the way. He studied it for a long time before returning his attention to the more immediate vicinity. He also took an interest in the lighting, both on the overhead cranes and along the pier. He took some time to assess the strength of the current, the temperature of what the water would be at night, and the lighting system along the pier. His two compatriots were busy doing the same, allowing their own professional instincts to take root while they observed their surroundings imaging it as a battlefield.

The Italians, with the help of Nico, discovered that security in the facility was lax. There was only a small human contingent on the ground to keep out riff-raff and potential hijackers. Otherwise, security was minimal with only a few video cameras at the exterior of the port. It was clear that the port's clientele enjoyed a great deal of discretion when conducting their business. What they also discovered was that human traffic was constantly coming in and going out day and night. Though it did die down somewhat in the evening, sporadic groups came in for the ships that arrived during the early hours.

The team returned late that afternoon to compare notes and begin planning. "Alright!" Tarkov opened upon their arrival back at the warehouse. "We have had a chance to recce the area and gain insight into what we are dealing with." He walked the team into the planning area where a collection of long unrolled maps and blueprints their German lawyer was able to procure for them depicted the greater area of the port and surrounding land. "Now that we have had time to consider our situation, we are ready to start considering our plan."

The fluid transit situation could make it easy to sneak in without raising suspicion. The smaller numbers mean we have a better chance of moving up tactically on our adversary. This was the first idea recommended by De'vor as the mercenaries reviewed the maps.

"The lighting is dim," De'vor began. "From what we saw walking around, it looks like they keep the lampposts spaced a good distance apart so they are not in the way of the cargo system. There should be ample dead space between the stacks of steel trailers that we can use to move up on."

The Italians explained that currently most of the ships were relegated to the peninsula across the way. Kalopolis enjoyed some connections in the port administration that allowed him to be pardoned from the rules. He was allowed to conduct his business in more private settings. This meant he could cordon off his area from anyone who was not part of his group. This revelation largely prevented the idea of a ground assault.

"They can control the area if they know they are the only ones allowed out there," Sacchini spoke up. "We won't be able to feign some sort of decoy that would allow us to get close to them."

"The problem is the security," Sauwa added. "We don't know how much they'll have out there, but with both sides concerned about this deal, we must assume they will both bring their own and that adds up to a lot if we're trying to move on the ships directly. Assuming we met the very professional looking security team for one of the sides today, we can't approach this thinking we're just taking on some street gangsters. We have to expect that they'll take precautions."

"Right," Carzona suddenly interrupted. He looked at Sauwa and then around at the team. "The problem is that the end goal is destroying the cargo or the ship that will be carrying the cargo. No matter which approach we choose, it will call for using a lot of heavy explosives. Explosives we have to transport over serious dead space and set it while possibly being under fire."

"What if we don't?" Tarkov interjected. The room went silent — all eyes were on him. He continued. "Hitting the ships while they're in port is futile. We don't have enough intelligence to form a reasonable plan. We don't know if the cargo will be moved from one ship to the pier before going onto the other ship or if it will be simply moved vessel to vessel. And, as our young lady has pointed out, we will be attacking when security will be at its strongest. Any operation at this point would be both blind and stupid. We should hit the ship when it's out at sea and is more vulnerable."

"That thought has merit, Sacchini agreed.

"If we can arrange for some ocean-going craft, such as the fishing boat that brought us in," the Russian went on, "we can observe our target when it leaves port and follow it out a good distance. With the aid of smaller crafts such as rubber rafts, that we should be able to acquire, we can close the distance quickly and neutralize the ship."

"The rafts should be no problem," Carzona commented. "I have excellent contacts and access to a wide variety of equipment. On the other hand, finding a seafaring boat that meets the requirements for this mission will be difficult. If this mission is executed far out at sea, I am concerned, it may not deliver the intended results of the overall mission. Remember, you're hired to carry out an operation aimed at permanently disabling this pipeline. As it stands, we are at best only stopping a shipment. A shipment that can be hastily replaced and the threat is still with us."

"Not necessarily," Sauwa spoke up, grabbing everyone's attention. "Tarkov has a point. We can't logically take the ship or the cargo at the port with any measure of success. The ship has to be taken at sea. However, that doesn't mean we can't still attack the port itself and create some havoc that will definitely complicate things. If we can get one of our adversaries to make an appearance there, they will be more vulnerable."

"What are you saying?" Tarkov asked. "You know that this business will most likely be conducted by intermediaries. Neither Kalopolis or the buyers will be there personally."

"The buyers no," she persisted. "But this is a big deal for the arms trafficker. One he wouldn't want to lose because of a glitch. A glitch could be if a man managing all this were suddenly taken out of the equation at a most inconvenient time."

"You're talking about doing something to Prokopis?" De'vor exclaimed.

Sauwa nodded. "If we kill Prokopis just before the deal, Kalopolis won't have time to replace him, and he would likely have to make an appearance to ensure all goes smoothly. He's risking a seriously big account and can't afford to let it fall through."

"Yes, but assassinating his lieutenant could also alert him and blow the whole thing," De'vor growled revealing his disdain for the South African yet again.

"Assassination yes," Sauwa responded. "What I'm talking about is murder. Prokopis enjoys clubs in the seedier section of town. He likes to go slumming with some rough customers. If he were to get sliced up as part of a back-alley brawl that incident would be totally believable. His boss wouldn't think anything more than that. Besides, he'll be too pre-occupied with the arms deal to really stop and consider the matter. On such short notice, it should force him to be on site."

"That's wonderful," Gorzo interjected. "But how does that make it any easier to achieve our goal?"

She continued. "If we take the ship out on the water, it may or may not raise enough attention to bring the authori-ties into this. If we arrange for a high-profile assassination of a top arms trafficker at the biggest port in Cyprus, it will definitely pique serious interest from all the wrong people. Enough attention and inquiry that would bring this whole operation to an end. Especially, if the assassination is loud and audacious. With the ships in port and the weapons being transferred, they will see the cargo as the target of any threat they are expecting. Our enemies will be alert and expecting us. However, when the transfer is complete, and the ship has launched, it is perceivable that we will have a window of opportunity. The ship will have pulled out which leaves fewer people to contend with. Everyone will be focused on packing up and leaving. Their attention will be diverted enough that we can initiate an assault."

"You're making many assumptions," De'vor argued. "One of which is the time we have to spend on this assault while we are letting the ship get further away. Not to mention that we are still a small number going up against a sizable and armed detail. The idea we would get Kalopolis is a gamble at best."

Everyone waited for Sauwa's response. She took a slight breath, then went on. "You're right. This plan only works provided we conduct it at the same time we're moving against the ship. This means that we will have to split up. It also means we will need to bring on a few more men."

"That is a tall order," Carzona interrupted.

"Call Valikov," Sauwa suggested. "I think you'll find he can find you some good people on short notice. In fact, I'll bet he's kept a few people on standby just in case you called." The Filipino was taken aback, but he nodded as he let the young lady continue. "The next problem is the target. You're right. Catching him in a gunfight is an amateur consideration. What we're looking to do is not kill him in an actual assault but distract him enough to get him to walk into an ambush." She walked over to the blueprints on the table. She pointed at the target area of the pier. "They have one access road in and out. With the ship gone, they have nothing to stay and protect. Therefore, if they come under fire, their objective will be to get their charge out of there as quickly as possible. Anyone else will be looking to get away expecting that the gunfire will only attract the police. They'll be so fixated on escaping from the assaulting force that they'll be less observant of signs of a secondary attack that they could drive into on their way out."

"What kind of secondary ambush are you thinking of?' Tarkov asked, intrigued by Sauwa's thought process.

"A bomb," she replied. "The Israelis are quite adept at carrying out assassinations with the use of car bombs. One of their best tricks is to load a car with explosives, place it along the traveled route of their target, and blow it as the target goes by. We have it loaded with explosives and stage a car inside the port along the route then blow it as Kalopolis is going by."

"It is an idea," Tarkov spoke up. "Though I have to agree we're working off more assumptions than hardened intelligence. I see a lot of margin for error. We're assuming that our target will stick around long after the ship departs leaving us with far lighter security."

Sauwa nodded. "This is a big order, one of Kalopolis' biggest. We know this because he is coordinating a complex shipment to send weapons halfway around the world and far from his usual operating environment. A man with as many nearby big spending clients like him wouldn't bother unless he was being paid top dollar. And the possibility that it would be repeat business, as I'm sure is the case, he'll want to stick around until the ship carrying the cargo is out of the port. He'd want to make sure that nothing went wrong while it was in the port."

Tarkov had moved closer to examine the blueprints and photographs. He looked the location over thoroughly as he passed his hand over the paper. He used his finger to trace over the lines representing the portion of the port where the transaction was to occur. Then, he slid the same finger across the part depicting the peninsula, where he traced the road and grounds next to it. "The lighting system is focused primarily toward the land. The only lighting directed at the water are the floodlights along the pier to aid ships as they land. Otherwise, the area along the water is mostly dark at night. Even if they had someone in the high-rise cranes watching, they would only be able to see what was happening on the ground."

"You're saying we should move on them through the water," Sacchini interjected as he gazed over the blueprints following the Russian's finger movements.

"If we could find a way to get a team and equipment to the far side of the port undetected," Tarkov continued as he tapped the area of the peninsula, "we could use small craft such as rafts or canoes to move through the water using darkness as concealment and come up right alongside them where they least expect it and attack from behind."

"That still leaves the question of who will go after the ship," Gorzo asked, looking around at everyone as if the issue had been completely ignored.

Tarkov rose and stood erect to look over the room. "As Sauwa has already mentioned, we split up and attack both simultaneously. Gorzo, Sacchini and I will pursue the ship since we are all naval commandos by training and experience. De'vor, you will lead the assault with the men we are able to bring in for this mission. Sauwa, you will handle the assassination part of the mission. How do you see that playing out?"

Sauwa moved to the maps and pointed toward the road. "As I suggested earlier, we have a car moved in full of explosives. When they pass, we detonate. I and maybe two others follow up with a third team that will be staged nearby."

"Good, then we know what we have to do. We will gradually develop the plan as we work through it," Tarkov said as he ended the meeting.

Sauwa stepped outside to get some air. It had been a long day of planning and operational work, and she was feeling a bit tired. She leaned up against the wall of the warehouse and looked out at the bright blue sky. Some part of her wished this was nothing more than a vacation. She would have liked to have simply enjoyed the place and all it had to offer.

The door opened, and soon she was joined by Sacchini who walked out looking just as exhausted as she felt. He turned and spotted her right behind him. "Oh, tired of being cooped up inside yourself, huh?" He now wore a pleasant expression. He reminded her of the dopey uncle families have that always seem to be cheerful and made all the children laugh. She wondered if that was the kind of man Sacchini was when he was not being a mercenary. It was strange to think of a hardened soldier and killer as being someone different.

"I needed some air," she replied as she leaned her head back against the wall and felt the sunrays on her face.

"I felt the same way," he moved up along the wall next to her. "All this operational planning wears me out."

"Not to pry," she said, "but, you don't strike me as the action junky type."

"Action junky?" he questioned. "What type do I look like?" He smiled in a fatherly way.

She rolled her head from side to side against the wall. "I don't know. Not a professional mercenary, not someone who enjoys this type of work."

"Strange," he replied, "because you do."

Surprised she looked back at him. He didn't wait for her to speak. "I got into this because after I was out of the navy, I was hard up for work. The economy was bad; there were no jobs out there. Then I read about a conflict going on in Croatia. I had done some recces for intelligence gathering and had a fair idea of what was happening outside of what the papers were reporting. I also knew that the Croatians were hiring foreign professionals to help fight the Serb army. With nothing else happening for me, I packed some gear and headed for adventure as a soldier of fortune. I spent about a year or so there in the early nineties working operations for the Croatians.

After that, I moved around the Middle-East working personal security first then as a free-lance operative for various intelligence services. A few times I did some work for the occasional gun runner. I've been doing this for a long time, and I've gotten to see the difference between those who flirt with this life, those who are in it simply because, like me, it's the job they fell into and turned out to be pretty good at it. Then there are those people meant for this is life and were meant to lead. And, I'm sorry to say, this is who you are Sauwa. What we're doing here, this is the world you belong in."

She shot him a puzzled look. He continued, "I doubt you'll ever do anything else. It's not a bad thing, the world needs people like you and Tarkov. It just simply means that this is likely how you will meet your end, fighting in some battlefield, or on some operation such as this."

"Don't presume you know me," Sauwa replied acidly as she turned her head back toward the sun.

The Italian chuckled. "I do know you. I know you very well. I see the cold serious look in your eye when we are discussing our operation. The instinctive professionalism you employ when we're out operating. And, the utter resolve you have for carrying this whole thing out without the slightest concern for the dangers. We all see it. De'vor thinks you're a cold-blooded psychopath, Gorzo is attracted to the danger he sees in you, and me, I'm afraid of it."

"You agree with De'vor then?" she asked. "That I'm a stone-cold killer."

"No," he shook his head. "He thinks you're pure evil. I don't think you're evil. You are just very good at what you do, and you don't want to accept who you are." Sacchini lifted himself from the wall, took a deep breath and started to walk away. "Take it from an old pro who has been doing this longer than you have. Your peace only comes when it's in the shadows fighting." He didn't wait for her to reply. They both knew there was nothing more to say. He quietly walked back inside leaving her to ponder his words.

24

The door burst open and men came through it at an explosive speed one right after the other. Each man quickly vanished from the doorway to take up different positions a few feet from the wall. The first man called out in English everything he saw that could pose a threat to the team as he advanced into the warehouse. He turned smartly to the right pointing his rifle to cover the far corner as he pushed past the door jamb and approached the corner at a fast pace. He stopped a few feet from the corner before turning on the balls of his feet and heading toward the main room. The next man followed in an identical manner, but he came through the door and moved quickly to the left. The rest of the team peeled off alternating directions as they broke past the doorway. They moved to various places inside the perimeter between the first two men.

The exercise continued as the team tactically moved through the remainder of the warehouse. They covered every corner and walkway between the large wooden crates, engaging by verbal recognition the silhouettes meant to represent potential hostiles. They ended on the other side of the massive building.

Tired and sweaty the men loosened the tactical equipment they wore. This had been the third time today they had traversed the giant labyrinth conducting this exercise. The last three days had been filled with long periods of practicing this particular exercise in addition to training in a few other places. The fast pace, the lengthy maze, and the heightened tension had all taken its toll and fatigue was setting in.

Rhys looked back to where they had come from. Mehendra emerged from the stacks of crates followed by two of the Greeks. Like the rest of the team, they were decked out in tactical gear designed for an urban setting. "They were excellent this time around," Mehendra stated, not waiting for his commander to pose the question. "They hit all the targets with precision, identifying and engaging us instantly."

"Excellent," Rhys replied with a sense of deep satisfaction. During the last few days, the team had been focused on developing a uniform operating procedure for their tactical movements. With four different militaries on the team, the training and experiences of such uniform development were important. The veteran mercenary had seen firsthand how badly things went on the battlefield when the same side employed different tactics based on too many extremely different experiences. It had been a gradual effort hashing out a solid tactical procedure for everyone to work together harmoniously.

The warehouse had been reserved by Managua to give Rhys and his people a place to train. The enclosed area gave them privacy from prying eyes, while the stacks of large crates gave them an environment similar to where they would be operating when they were at the port. In between, they spent evenings practicing their tactics at their beach house when the beach was deserted. They enjoyed some privacy to practice advancing on the house and moving through the rooms and hallways. Assuming that the operation could expand beyond simple port security, Rhys wanted to cover his bases and ensure his men could operate more expansively.

Yadav wiped his brow as he walked over to join his compatriots in their meeting. He had Mehendra switch roles between playing team leader and being an evaluator throughout the training exercises. In the beginning, there had been some difficulty within the ranks accepting two Asians in leadership roles. Some of the Greeks held the old attitude of superiority, known as the *white professional*. Like many European soldiers, they saw themselves as naturally superior to those who came from the third world. They didn't take well to Yadav or Mehendra giving them orders — men like them should be learning from them how to soldier. It was a difficult hurdle to overcome.

After watching the two men in action during training, the military skills of the two Asians had gradually become apparent, impressing the Greeks who eventually allowed their racial biases to subside. It was perhaps easier for Yadav to gain acceptance from the ex-legionnaires, once they found out he had served not with some third world military but with the elite Gurkhas of the British army. It was a unit that held legendary status the world over — they had some of the fiercest and most talented fighters imaginable. Mehendra very quickly bridged the gap with a constant demonstration of his abilities.

"This was good," Rhys commented as he paced while viewing his team. He had been pleased with how fast and well the training had progressed. He had expected a week with everyone arguing tactics and experimenting with different maneuvers before establishing some cohesive doctrine for the group. It had been Rhys' experience that soldiers got set in their ways and liked to work with the familiar. He learned through his years as a mercenary that trying to impose your own tactics on those who were already seasoned fighters without regard for their own skills often resulted in unneeded conflict. In this case, the Greek and his two cohorts proved to have far better adaptability and gained everyone's respect for their abilities and experiences. With only a few experimental runs, they had developed a tactical system that everyone felt comfortable with.

Rhys continued, "We have good cohesion, and everybody performed smoothly. Now, I want to give you a thirty-minute break. Then, I am going to turn off all lights except for a few at the end, so we can practice under the actual conditions."

The men nodded showing a mixed look of self-confidence and exhaustion. Rhys walked away as the men broke and headed for the take-out food brought in by Managua from an Arabic restaurant.

"They are looking quite good, commander," Managua said as Rhys started to walk past.

"Thank you. I'm glad to have an outside opinion," Rhys replied. Managua shifted from the wall and proceeded to follow him.

"Will they be ready by the time the ship arrives?" Managua asked.

"They'll have to be," Rhys responded. "The schedule isn't going to change for us. But, they are falling in line faster than I anticipated, so they'll be worth something if they should be needed."

"That is good to hear," the lawyer spoke with a sigh of relief.

The sigh prompted Rhys to ask, "Have you got any new information on our potential threat?"

Managua shook his head. "Not yet. We are interested in a Miss Esmeralda Morayo. She's a corporate attorney who specializes in international business dealings for Filipino businesses that have interests here in Europe. She's well connected and is a known supporter of the President. She's been in contact with enemies of ours who have just returned home after a trip to this part of the world. We suspect they were here setting up this whole operation."

"That's interesting," Rhys said. "Though I don't see a corporate lawyer leading a military raid on your ship. For that matter, I can't see a corporate lawyer running a spy mission to find out about the operation."

"You're right, she wouldn't be," Managua explained. "But I have people investigating her, and I believe she'll pan out as a means to finding our enemies."

"Is that before or after I meet them in person while being attacked," Rhys said in a sarcastic tone that still got the message across.

Managua shrugged. It was all he could offer as an answer. "As I said, we're looking into her and, when we find something, we'll update you first.

The New Zealander marched off to rejoin his men — his irritation was obvious.

Zeus's Kingdom was something out of a crime noir. Situated in the less reputable part of the city, it was largely hidden amongst an assortment of like structures. The whole neighborhood was dark and looked uninviting. Messy graffiti lined almost every building and wall along the street. There were few street lamps lining the sidewalk, and the street was shrouded in eerie darkness.

Only the large electric pink neon light flashing above the entrance distinguished the club from all the twin-like structures surrounding it. Despite everything, the club seemed to draw a sizeable number of patrons with a line that extended from just outside the door to the next building. The liberal flow of human traffic entering through the doors at a steady pace rarely slowing down.

Entering the club, Sauwa found it just as ominous as the street. It was lowly lit with dark-colored neon lights providing just enough illumination for one to get around, see what they were drinking, and make sure the person they were picking up was the right gender. The rest of the place was enshrouded in a cloak of darkness that served to mask whatever nefarious activity was being conducted. She looked around and got glimpses of the customers who passed by her and saw an assortment of those she would dub criminals. There were gangsters, mercenaries, drug dealers, and others pushing different types of illicit business. The club was set up as a place for those wanting to conduct affairs privately could do so. It was probably the club's primary allure.

She meandered around slowly getting a feel for the club's setup. It had a general walkway that went above the main room full of tables and a large dance floor that was being used by the younger patrons. On the walkway, there were booths along the wall that were built in a circular fashion making it easy for the occupiers to sink deeper into the shadows for more privacy. She was sure on her journey past the booths, there were more than a few sex acts taking place, as she heard the soft feminine moans and male grunts.

The walkway took her on a path that led around the circumference of the establishment. After walking past a lengthy bar, she found her target and veered toward the stairs that led her directly to the dance floor; another walkway led her to several double doors that served as exits. She pushed open one of the doors to test how hard it would be to open it in the event she needed a fast getaway. She checked the outside terrain. A quick glimpse let her know it led to a nearly empty street in the back.

She stepped back into the bar and started moving. She was concerned that some bouncer or a lucid patron would notice her and get suspicious. Her concerns soon subsided when she saw a couple of other intoxicated ladies making the mistake of thinking it was a way to the restroom and jokingly backed away in a similar fashion. Sauwa figured she looked like just another ditzy woman with no sense of direction and proceeded to make her way back to the bar.

Prokopis was in the center of the bar sitting in a leather-covered high stool amidst a number of patrons packed together against the counter. He appeared to be sitting alone. While everyone around him was loudly talking to people in their own little groups or trying to get the attention of one of the pretty young ladies tending bar, he was nursing a small glass of some libation, eyeing the place. Every so often he would be greeted by someone passing by.

Assessing his facial expressions, Sauwa figured the man's conversations ranged from pleasantries with club regulars to more serious discussions with business contacts or potential business contacts. From a dark corner, she was able to disappear and watch what went on with Prokopis. He never left his perch and his conversations were always quick and to the point. When she gained an understanding of his pattern, Sauwa turned her attention to the bar itself.

The patrons were largely crammed into seats that ran along the counter. They were all packed in tightly, completely involved in their own little spheres. They were entirely ignorant of the world around them including the person right next to them who was not part of any immediate conversation. None were the slightest bit interested in her target. She checked carefully for any possible signs that some of them might be bodyguards or someone else was taking an interest in the same person. She saw none. The barkeeps, young women clearly working a money job, showed interest only in those patrons who were throwing money around and responding to each served drink with a sizable tip.

Confident she had an established pattern to work from, Sauwa made her move. Walking up to the bar in a slow, casual manner, she came right up to Prokopis. He ignored her completely. His attention was directed at the dance floor and the young beauties dancing in short skirts and dresses with their young male lovers. She allowed her eyes to wander as she looked around for signs of security cameras.

She didn't expect to find any in an establishment such as this. Nor did she think they would capture much in such a low lighted setting. Still, she had learned early that people were unpredictable. A quick glance showed nothing. Even if there were cameras, they would have shown only a young woman, dressed in slightly baggy party clothes and wearing a large, knit beret with all her hair sliding down covering half her face. For good measure, she had taken to wearing a large pair of dark glasses that wrapped around the upper portion of her face. They weren't so dark that she couldn't see, but dark enough that they distorted her appearance.

Having seen everything she needed to see, Sauwa slowly retreated from the bar back into the safety of darkness. She began to walk through the crowd back along the gallery of booths. She walked past the features being presented as the inebriated patrons engaged in various forms of bizarre rituals and behaviors. She continued rambling, taking her time studying the specimens, all of whom paid her not the slightest interest. It was when she came upon a table that housed about four men that she saw her opportunity.

They were all heavily intoxicated — half were passed out and the rest following closely behind. The rubbish, consisting of a small pile of bottles and vomit, told the story of their evening. It was here that she saw what she was looking for. During their wild activities, they had managed to break more than a few glass objects, and they were scattered around on the table. It was difficult to see with the limited visibility, but she was able to make out the outline of a beer bottle that had been broken and left with some sharp jagged edges. Using a paper napkin she had grabbed from the bar, she retrieved the bottle and began to walk away.

One of the first things she had been taught going through

training in the Civil Cooperation Bureau was that anything was a weapon in the hands of someone who knew how to use it. She had learned that smuggling weapons to assassinate someone was always a complicated affair, especially when the weapons proved impractical for the situation. Instead, she had been trained to assess the situation and look for normal objects within her sphere that could be used more pragmatically. These were known as *weapons of appeared innocence*. So named because no one thought of them as weapons making them easier to utilize against someone who is unsuspecting.

With the same casual pace, she made her way back to the bar. The crowd had grown making the walkway more crowded. Sauwa kept her arm at her side to keep the bottle out of sight. She found her target sitting in the same place and just as oblivious. Sweeping the area one last time with her eyes shifting from side to side she hatched the next steps of her plan.

Moving to the far end of the bar she stayed on the opposite side of the dance floor. Prokopis' attention was still focused there, and he wasn't attending to his drink. She kept her attention shifting between her target and the trail leading to the exit doors. She wanted to ensure no one would prove to be a barrier between her and her escape route when it came time to move. Aside from some small groups of people tightly clustered together, she found that the sea of human partyers was thick enough to disappear into but light enough that she wouldn't be too hindered. She also kept a continuous eye out on the people at the bar, checking to see if any had diverted their attention to her or were paying any attention to Prokopis. Confident he was of no interest to anyone she proceeded forth.

Now, less than a few meters away, she began to tighten the grip on the head of the bottle, feeling the napkin firmly in her fingers. She continued to keep the weapon at her side as she neared him. At one point, a few large men got in front of her trying to get the get the attention of one of the bartenders using exaggerated arm waves and shouts over the loud music. They provided another piece of cover shielding her from her target as she snaked around them.

With nothing in her way, she started to walk past Prokopis while his attention was still on the dance floor. Raising the bottle until it was at chest level, she drew back her elbow just enough to charge her arm. With precision and one powerful burst of force, she thrust the jagged edges of the bottle straight across the right side of the man's neck just below the angle of the jaw into the soft tissue cutting his jugular vein and the carotid artery. With a good amount of force, the long sharp edges tore into his jugular as if it were tissue paper. She let the bottle drop to the floor as she continued moving past him.

The whole operation lasted less than a half second. She barely caught sight of the man reaching for his throat as she continued walking by. Even in the darkness, she could see blood spraying wildly in all directions. She continued walking in an unassuming manner as she made for the door. She assessed the situation by watching the patrons ahead of her. They all danced happily to the music with absolutely no sign that they were the least bit aware of what had just happened. She had hit him just right and believed that in such an atmosphere, with everyone only semi-alert, it would be quite a while before anyone realized what was happening. Prokopis, himself, wouldn't have realized what had happened, and he would look like some drunk losing his balance. Even if someone had noticed, it would have taken some time for someone to get the lights on and get control of the place. Meanwhile, she had disappeared in just a few short seconds into the sea of gyrating human flesh with absolutely nothing on her person connecting her to the murder.

At the first exit, she pushed the door open and stepped out onto the open street. Aside from a few intoxicated patrons leaning up against the building, the street was deserted. She strode down the road and ducked into a side street.

Out of sight, she began to undress. Pulling off her loose party clothes, she was now in a T-shirt and a pair of black cargo pants. Her black combat boots had gone unnoticed by the bouncers at the door. Throwing off her old clothes, she removed the large beret to free up her hair. Now, she looked like a completely different person. The new image would help her be more easily dismissed by any passers-by. Taking a moist towelette packet from her pocket, she wiped her face from the forehead down to her neck. Using a small hand mirror, she quickly scanned her face to see if there were any readily identifiable blood spatters. It was hard in the limited light, but she managed. She bundled the party garb into an unobtrusive wad and continued down the road.

A few blocks away, she slipped into a small alley and walked until she came to another road. She had to assume the police would search a fairly wide area once the investigation got underway. That meant they would search garbage cans on side streets to see what may have been left. In the darkness, she couldn't tell if the clothes had any blood on them. Since it was clearly attire worn by a female, it would be enough to help the police narrow their list of suspects.

She walked a couple of miles taking care to bypass the first several bus stops. Police would likely check the nearest bus stops in the vicinity of the murder. Sauwa figured it was wise to stay on foot for a while and get a bus or cab a good distance away. After weaving through a maze of dingy streets, she finally made it to a main street that was more heavily populated. Moving out into the human traffic she continued on. She found the sea of tourists made it easier for her to vanish.

25

B erlin, Germany — Esmeralda Morayo finished her jog just short of six kilometers, the last bit of it all uphill. She was feeling the burn in her legs and stomach as she took heaving breaths through her mouth. The sweat was soaking through the upper portion of her tracksuit and running steadily down her face. All she could think about was the full pitcher of ice cold tea waiting for her at her place.

She kept an apartment in Berlin where she lived and worked when she was on the continent. It was in the building complex a team of men currently watched from their van. Strangely, the complex was rather modest for an executive level person. It wasn't one of the palatial quarters that housed the cities' corporate elite, but it was a step above the low rent housing of young newlyweds and college students. It was a modest, upscale complex reserved for professionals and middle-managers. Despite being born to vast wealth and brought up in a lavish environment, she preferred more simplistic living arrangements. Besides even if she had the inkling to go upscale while in Europe, she traveled far too much to truly appreciate the extravagant comforts of an expensive penthouse. It was enough that she had a comfortable place that she could call home and relax.

Having cooled off enough, she headed through the glass double doors of her building to the elevator. Pressing the button for the third floor, she stepped into a large, barren corridor with white stucco walls and light colored flooring. Still feeling the effects of her run, she moved down the hall at a lethargic pace. She was thankful she had no pressing issues on her schedule for the next few days and no recent messages from Carzona regarding the operation in Cyprus.

She reached the door to her apartment, her mind focused on the protein shake and vegetable juice she intended to mix up as a reward for the effort she expended. Key in hand, she stopped short noticing a series of scratch marks that she hadn't seen before. Her instincts sent a warning shiver down her spine. For someone in the Philippines coming from wealth, kidnapping or assassination was a constant concern. Those concerns had forced her to hone her survival instincts.

Pulling her arm back, she used her free hand to investigate further. A slight twist of the knob told her it was still locked. She studied the scratches more closely trying to figure out if she was being paranoid. This was a big city in Germany, not the conflict-riddled world of her homeland. She finally inserted the key into the lock and retracted the bolt guarding the door. With a turn of the knob, she pushed it open.

The unnerving feeling remained with her as she tiptoed through the doorway. Her room looked as she had left it, yet something seemed off. She stopped dead in her tracks as she explored the room. Then it hit her — the curtains in the main room were closed. She remembered leaving them open when she left. Convinced something was wrong, she slowly backed toward the door. It was then that she caught sight of it. In the hallway leading to her bedroom in a framed picture that had mirrored glass reflecting, she saw the man hiding behind the wall.

Keeping her composure, she backed outside, slamming the door behind her. With her heart pounding in fear, she sprinted down the hall. She had made it halfway toward the elevator when she heard the door behind her fly open and the sound of men shouting. She reached the end of the hall and saw three large men pursuing her out of the corner of her eye.

Forgoing the elevator, Morayo bolted for the fire escape just a short distance away. She pushed the large steel door open and raced down the concrete stairwell. She was barely down the first flight stepping onto the landing to make for the next when she heard the same door burst open with even more explosive force followed by shouts echoing loudly in the chamber as they started after her.

She could hear them gaining on her as their footsteps became louder. In an attempt to gain ground, she jumped the last portion onto the next level. Landing hard, but still on her feet, she didn't pause to feel the pain, she sprinted. Halfway down the stairs, the door behind her flew open with a man shouting at all of them in German. His shouts changed in mid-sentence from clear, coherent words to a deep gurgling choke. She looked back quickly to see that one of her pursuers had lunged at the man, driving a knife into his stomach just up under the rib cage and into his chest cutting off the man's ability to speak or scream. She didn't have time. The killer's companions rushed past him and the victim continuing their chase.

It was clear to Morayo that these men intended to harm her. She made it to the first floor and charged for the door. She barely slipped through when one of the men grabbed the door and reached his arm out nearly grabbing her by the sleeve. Racing with all her energy she made for the front door. As she did, she screamed for help as loudly as she could in the hopes that someone would respond or call the police. The hallway was empty except for her and her aggressors. With no stairs to deal with, she was able to gain some distance on the flat ground.

She was within inches of the door when she heard a loud sound of what could only have been a gunshot. She felt something whistle past her cheek. Her adrenaline was pumping harder than ever. Grabbing for the doorknob she pushed on the door with all the strength she could muster as she desperately tried to get the door to move. Behind her, she heard the loud thumping of men's boots behind her as they charged down the hall.

Frantically she pressed on the door with to no avail. Her heart was racing as was her hysteria. Then, in a moment of clarity, she remembered the door pulled open. Reversing her force, the door pulled open leaving her free to make it outside just in time to feel a hand brush past her arm. She continued on in a fast sprint, screaming as she ran down the walkway leading to the street.

People on the street were beginning to look in her direction. A few registered looks of concern as they watched the drama unfolding in front of the apartment building. A tall and rather brawny older man started across the street in her direction. He was waving his arms to get her attention.

Then she heard another cracking sound like the one she heard in the hallway. This time, it didn't culminate with a force cutting past her face, she felt something powerful hit her squarely in the back. She could feel the piercing metal digging into her spine before it tore through the tissue into her internal organs and finally exit through her lower stomach. It took a few seconds for the pain to supersede the numbness generated by her adrenaline. When it did, the gut-wrenching pain swiftly slowed her run to a weak trot. She heard more crackling sounds and more metal cut through her torso, shoulder, and thigh — each one delivering excruciating pain that dragged her to a complete halt.

Instinctively reaching down to feel the injuries, Morayo felt warm blood pouring over her hands. She started to look down but another gunshot sizzled through the air and tore through the back of her head. It was the shot that delivered the deathblow to the young woman, and her body dropped to the ground landing in a distorted heap.

Everyone who had been watching the poor girl get ripped apart by gunshots froze in their tracks. The killer had wisely taken his shots from inside the doorway of the apartment, giving him protection from being seen by the witnesses outside.

Satisfied he had eliminated his target, he retreated inside. His colleagues were guarding the halls ready to kill anyone who dared stick their heads out to witness the shooting. The halls remained empty except for the three men. They were soon joined by the rest of their team, who came through the door leading to the fire escape. Of the two, the bigger one, a man with a head and face that resembled a bulldog came up to the three. "The woman?" He barked in his native Hungarian.

The man who had served as Morayo's executioner lifted

his hand and made a cutting motion across his throat which served as the answer.

"Very well," the bulldog nodded. "If we can't get anything from her, then we have all we came for," he said turning his attention to the other man who had come with him. He dangled a black bag he had slung over his shoulder in response to the bulldog.

The men said nothing more as they proceeded to disappear into the streets behind them where the populace had not yet understood what had just occurred.

THEO KALOPOLIS WAS BURNING with anger as he paced back and forth across the wood floor of his office. "That idiot and his wild living!" He screamed to no one in particular as he lifted his gaze then lowered it, eyeing his attending operatives randomly. He walked stiffly along, his hands folded tightly behind his back as if he were a general in an army relaying plans to the troops before battle.

He was, of course, speaking of his once right-hand man, Prokopis. A man, who had inconveniently gotten himself killed in what appeared to be some idiotic bar fight. "A man in his position, holding such important information to some of my most essential dealings, and he feels the incessant need to trawl clubs that cater to the city's riff-raff. And, at this most ill-conceived moment when we're on the cusp of conducting a major deal," he ranted.

"Sir," one of his subordinates humbly spoke. "That club was a center for many business dealings and provided a place to conduct sensitive business with people whom discretion was essential."

The arms merchant glared at his subordinate who ducked his head in a submissive and apologetic way. "It still does not excuse his reckless behavior. Getting a beer bottle in the throat! That is the action of someone acting on a personal matter. Perhaps it was over a petty slight that the idiot caused when he felt up the wrong woman and her man retaliated. He was a good man for logistical work; an absolute incompetent when it came to behavior. I suppose it was only a matter of time until this happened."

"What is our next step sir?" A thin skeletal man, wearing a pair of wire-rimmed glasses and a tight-fitting grey suit, asked in a somber manner. This question seemed to feed Kalopolis' irritation. "I mean, in the next few days we still have the ships coming in, and our lead manhandling this deal is now lying in the morgue."

"I'll have to see to this one myself," the arms dealer growled as he flung back a few locks of his long golden hair that had slipped over his face. "I'm the only one who's had enough involvement and familiarity to know what's going on."

"That is taking a serious risk for a man in your position," the skeletal man reminded him in a tone that suggested that he was utterly indifferent to the decision.

"I have no choice," Kalopolis stated in a calmer tone. "Prokopis' death has forced my hand. I'll take appropriate measures and bring ample security. Right now, I am the only one who can handle this operation so late in the game." He paced the floor looking down as if expecting the answer to come from the hardwood paneling he was walking across. "As I said," he sniffed, "I will handle this affair myself."

26

"Do we know for sure he will even be there?" De'vor tried hard to contain his fury and not shout, but he was finding such a feat impossible, and his voice continued to rise. He had not been keen on killing the gun runner Prokopis. For him, the cold-blooded way Sauwa had dispatched him was grizzly, to say the least. He turned and looked at her, his eyes angry and judgmental.

"It had to be done," Tarkov reminded him as he watched the Frenchman carry on in his characteristic sanctimonious manner.

"You can tell yourself such things!" De'vor pressed the issue. "I'm a soldier, we're soldiers." He waved his finger in all directions except for Sauwa's. "When I kill, it is on a battlefield against other soldiers. Even when I worked for gangsters, I still only killed when on a mission and then they were men who carried guns and played the same game I did. I never sliced some man's throat and spilled his guts out on the floor while he was enjoying a drink at the bar." He turned to face Sauwa. "But you didn't even give it a second thought, did you. You just slaughtered him right there, and it meant nothing to you."

Sauwa casually rose from her chair and started to walk away. "Believe what you want," she replied with indifference. "He wasn't some innocent widow or orphan. The man I killed was a gangster playing in the same world as you and me. If he had been holding a gun and standing at the pier getting ready to attack you, you would have slit his throat just as easily as I did even if he was just standing around at the time. Your idea of morality based solely on locations is truly remarkable." She walked away not giving the Frenchman a chance to respond. His opinion was of no consequence to her in the slightest.

She walked past the team and went to a far table ladened with an assortment of food from a take-out joint. Surrounding the table were a number of men filling their plates. The recent additions to the team were enjoying their supper after a day spent going over the plan and conducting rehearsals. They were former members of the elite Force 17 unit, the Special Forces arm of the Palestine Liberation Organization — a unit that had been founded by the infamous Ali Hassan Salameh. They had received top-notch commando training from nearly every Middle-Eastern Special Forces group as well as most of the naval commando forces of every communist country one cared to name. It had been formed in response to the professional response to the elite commando units of the Israeli military, the Shayetet 13 and the Seyret Matkal; often conducting its own daring and complex commando operations into the Jewish state.

They had arrived shortly ahead of the break-in of the townhouse. Tarkov and Carzona had found it strange how fast Valikov had been able to assemble a group of quality warriors in such a short time and arrange their transport from Beirut, Lebanon into Cyprus within a few days. It was as if he were expecting the request the whole time. Most of the Palestinians appeared to be in their mid-twenties — a few looked even younger. They may have had ample training and some actual experience in combat but were probably limited in any leadership capacity.

Sauwa figured Carzona's organization had little intelligence on their adversary or the area they were operating in. A man as skilled and experienced in the realm of black operations as Valikov could have easily predicted that many last-minute additions were going to be needed. It was those skills that made him so successful in arms trafficking. Unfortunately, when her boss seemed to answer Carzona's requests so quickly, Sauwa suspected that the arms trafficker had a potential spy in the unit.

Tarkov was aware of his old comrade's skills and abilities when it came to running covert operations. He was inclined to believe that Valikov could have foreseen the complications that would force major alterations in their plan and prepared accordingly. Carzona, on the other hand, only accepted such an answer at face value. With his years in espionage, he was more inclined to come to a different conclusion. In either case, it didn't matter. Everyone that was now on the team was needed, and the mission superseded any concerns about Valikov having a mole in his operation. Still, the Filipino was suspicious.

After she had enjoyed a rather tasty dinner of falafel and a Greek salad, Sauwa crossed the warehouse entering through the back hallways. For their training, Carzona's German contact had obtained another warehouse in a remote, run-down part of the city. The building was a great place for them to train. Not only was it in a location that was primarily deserted — run-down structures that hadn't seen much use in years — they were located next to an old pier they could use to rehearse the assault on the port harbor. The adjoining area was a field of old rotting boats stacked high along with vacant structures and a network of forgotten roadways giving them several places to train.

She reached the back room where she found Sacchini and two of the Palestinians standing over a stack of wood pallets covered with a long plastic tarp. The tarp was flipped over on the corner closest to them revealing a series of firearms lined up across the pallets.

The three weapons that she could see were Russian made AKMS 47 assault rifles, the rifle favored by the old Soviet naval infantry. Unlike the AKM variant that had a steel framed stock that collapsed along the side of the rifle, the AKMS model collapsed underneath the weapon and could be extended when deploying the weapon. Soviet armaments were the most widely used in the hot spots around the world and the adopted weapon of the militaries of former communist client states. They were also the most easily obtainable on the black market. For this reason, it was essential that a mercenary had a working knowledge of such weapons and was comfortable in their use. It was generally what mercenaries had to work within their business.

Given the close operating range they would be in, Sauwa, like the others, hoped to get 74 models with their Kalashnikovs. They were 5.56 caliber and more practical for close quarter combat. The AK-47 models they were looking at fired the 7.62 caliber that was more practical when operating in open environments and engaging targets at a longer range.

Sacchini was handling a small PM-63 9 machine pistol, a Polish design used by the Polish airborne units and police. He handed it to her. "I imagine you'll want to work with this a bit more." She took it from his hand and examined it. It was a small pistol-like weapon that had a collapsible stock similar to the AKMS. This made it the perfect weapon for carrying it discretely. She pulled back the upper receiver to examine the chamber. Ensuring it was empty, she began practicing her drills. She aimed in a direction that didn't put anyone in her sights and began dry rehearsals pulling the weapon from its concealed position and bringing it into action. She had only worked with this sort of weapon a few times and had been reintroduced to it a few days ago when the team began rehearsing for their mission.

The weapons had been smuggled into the country through a barge welded tightly shut and dropped deep into the water and held up by a few narrow cords of strong wire. This was similar to how South American drug organizations smuggled large quantities of cocaine across the Caribbean to avoid American coastal patrol and surveillance satellites flying overhead. Just as the team had been brought into the country. A ship had come from Turkey close to the Cyprus territorial waters where it was met by the fishing boat that had met them.

A barge was dropped into the water a few nautical miles out and towed until retrieved by the fisherman who hauled it by the cords the rest of the way. Only in the safety of the secluded harbor did they bring it to the surface. The weapons were retrieved from the barge and taken to the warehouse in bundles wrapped in canvass covers. Initially, Tarkov had wanted to keep the weapons on board the ship to avoid the danger of constantly moving them to and from the warehouse. This idea was rejected when the ship's captain explained that his daily fishing schedule made such a consideration impossible. Tarkov agreed to keep the weapons at the training warehouse where it was close enough to the water for transport and easy to abandon if there was a threat of a police raid.

Not wanting to risk needless exposure, Tarkov had ordered that the weapons would not be used for practice until the last few days. The team would do their dry runs imitating using weapons until the routine and operating procedures down solid. Two days ago they took the fishing trawler far out to sea to familiarize themselves with the weapons and conducted target practice.

The small machine pistol was in good condition. By all accounts, it looked like it hadn't seen much action. When she shot it from the boat, she found it fired smoothly. Though she lamented that it was more an automatic pistol than submachine-gun. For such a mission she would have preferred a more rapid firing weapon like the Israeli Uzi or an HK-MP5k. However, in her world, one worked with what one had, not with what one wanted.

Sacchini had dismissed the two Palestinians he had been going over the weapons with. Thankfully a good number of them spoke decent English. The reputation of Force-17 had proven quite accurate in rehearsals — the men executed the operation swiftly and with precision once the routine had been established. The two men nodded politely to the young woman as they made their exit, leaving her alone with the Italian.

"You feeling good about this?" Sacchini asked as he regarded the pallets of weapons sitting at his feet.

"Whether I am or not, we're doing it," Sauwa responded

in a defeated tone. She stood by silently watching her friend. His behavior signified someone who was looking to talk.

"Well, as I see it, you'll have the dangerous part," he continued. "You'll be the one handling God knows what with little help from anyone."

"This whole project is dangerous," she said, "and, we're all handling a piece of it."

Sacchini cracked a smile and began quietly chuckling. "Maybe I'm just an old hand at my part, and so it doesn't feel as dangerous. Though I have to wonder about De'vor. Ever since he was tagged to lead the assault on the pier and command the bulk of the forces, he's been behaving as if he were the one in command of everything."

"Devor has a high opinion of himself, both as a soldier and as a self-righteous asshole," Sauwa stated.

"Yes, he does," the Italian replied still smiling.

"But, Tarkov is a good leader and keeps everyone in line," Sauwa continued.

Sacchini observed her, his face still watching the pleasant but slightly defeated look. Sauwa didn't have to ask what was wrong, she already knew. The mission was getting close, and everyone was starting to feel it. Attitudes became more somber as the mercenaries began to withdraw into their own deep thoughts and mental preparation. Even Gorzo had, in the last few days, become less cocky as reality began to set in.

She handed the weapon back to Sacchini, who placed it with the rest of the arsenal. She looked at the greater stock of weaponry that lined the room. In addition to the guns, there were several plastic containers lining the wall. She walked over to them. The containers were labeled indicating the substance had passed through East Europe. The packaging was new, signifying the substance had been recently manufactured and must have been diverted from its intended destination to their makeshift arms room.

The containers held quantities of Semtex, military-grade plastic explosive, developed and used largely by the now-defunct Czechoslovakian military. It was one of the most easily obtainable and commonly used explosives favored by terrorist groups. She had already inspected the substance and determined they were not counterfeit and in good condition. She had taken to doing daily inspections to ensure the inventory was not getting short or had been tampered with. After finding nothing wrong here, she went to another couple of boxes containing the detonation cords and blasting caps. She would be the primary user of these and had a vested interest in their condition.

Satisfied all was well, Sauwa returned to where Sacchini was sitting. She sensed he was in the mood to talk if for no other reason than to help relax. He was finishing up his own inspection and cleaning his weapon. "Strange," he began, as she walked up on him. "All this firepower for a mission that will probably last no more than a few minutes. I never seem to get over that concept."

She said nothing as she slowly joined him. He looked her up and down as if he were inspecting her, and she was no different than the rest of the equipment. "I don't care what you say," he began again. "You have the most dangerous part of this mission, and yet you're calmer about this than all the rest of us. It's so natural to you."

"It's not natural," she replied. "I just show my emotions differently than the rest of you." She dropped into a sitting position taking a place at the edge of one of the pallets staring up at him. To anyone walking in at that moment, it would have looked like a father delivering parental advice to his daughter.

"Perhaps," he said kindly. "Or, just maybe it's because you're so serious all the time that it's hard to tell."

"Maybe it is," she cracked a smile for the first time since they began speaking. She liked Sacchini. He wasn't critical and condescending like De'vor. Nor was he trying to prove his machismo by constantly trying to bed her, like Gorzo. He had been kind to her, and she appreciated it. In the time they had worked together, he had proven himself quite capable and intelligent as an operator, something she could respect.

The conversation ended with both of them leaving the supply room and heading back to the main area of the warehouse. There they found everyone decompressing after a long day of practice and planning. Tarkov and Carzona were in the planning area pouring over the maps and charts as if it were the first time they had seen them. De'vor and some of the men, who would comprise his team, were exercising. With his shirt pulled off, the Frenchman was pushing the weights hard challenging those around him. In the corner, Gorzo spoke to some of the recent arrivals. A sly smile was plastered across his face.

"He's bragging about some of his sexual conquests," Sacchini explained.

"I imagine so," Sauwa replied with a shrug of indifference. "Sex has always been a topic of discussion that men bond over."

"You're right," Sacchini agreed. "Men, both young and old, judge each other by their virility. Though, I should inform you that in his conversations, the subject of you has come up."

"I assumed that as well," she replied indifferently. She

had worked around professional soldiers for a long time. She had learned early on that in such a world a woman could not go unclaimed. "Let me guess, Gorzo is telling everyone I fell to his charms and bedded him the first or second night we met?"

Sacchini nodded, "Something like that."

"Well, I guess I should probably set everyone straight about Mr. Gorzo, and ensure I'm not fending off several more potential suitors." She looked back at Sacchini. "Care to help?"

Sacchini shot her a bemused look. It took him a few seconds to respond, "Sure."

With that Sauwa turned to face the older man. She looked at him with mischief in her eyes. Reaching up she placed her hand behind his head and pulled him down to her for a deep, passionate kiss as her hands moved to cup his cheeks. When she finally released him, he looked unsure of how to react. She turned to find the little episode had quickly caught everyone's attention, including Gorzo's — he looked slightly deflated.

"Thank you," she replied to Sacchini, who had gathered himself enough to play his part. He let his hand rise up to touch her shoulder and then, just as easily, slide down over her arm ending in holding her hand. He let her go to allow her to go back to work after sending such a clear message to all.

Sauwa walked over to join Tarkov and Carzona. Their heads were still buried in the documents in front of them.

"That was quite a display," Tarkov commented, not bothering to lift his head to acknowledge her.

"It clears up a lot of potential problems," she stated as she met his eyes.

"Actually, it does," Tarkov responded. "All the young Cossacks we have here have been paying a lot of attention to the one young lady on the team. The testosterone of so many young studs together was starting to run high. Showing all that you belong to someone has probably curtailed some potential conflicts and distractions."

"Good, then I shouldn't hear any more about it," Sauwa stated. "And, we can now focus on business."

"Yes, we can," Carzona interjected stoically.

"Are you comfortable with your part?" Tarkov asked.

"Whether I am or not, it's the plan we're going with," Sauwa replied as she gazed at the documents that occupied Tarkov's attention.

The plan relied on three components. Because Gorzo's and De'vor's backgrounds were largely based on ground operations, it was decided they should lead the assault on the piers. De'vor and his team of six Palestinians would use the fishing trawler. Gorzo, using an inflated rubber craft, would launch just outside of the port and enter through the water. Going through the mouth of the port, his team would bypass any surveillance and security measures. The darkness over the water would provide ample concealment as they made their way to their objective. The noise of cargo being moved and the sound of the ship's engines would mask the sound of their own motor as they closed the distance. Nearer to the target, they will kill their craft's motor and wait in the water until the ships start to move. Then using the interval, they will silently paddle in under darkness and pull up slightly away from the target before deploying into action.

Tarkov and Sacchini, former naval commandos, would follow in a similar raft, approaching the starboard side of the target ship, at the same time De'vor and his team were ready to initiate their assault. There, using two limpet mines, they would attach them to the ship's hull and depart. The mines would detonate, blasting two massive holes in the side of the ship that would send it to the bottom of the ocean while creating the perfect distraction for the assault team to go into action. In the event the mines had problems, or some other issue emerged that made the mines impractical, Tarkov and his team, Sacchini and two of the Palestinians, would go to the alternative plan. They would board the ship, using ropes to scale onto the main deck and commence a full attack, killing everyone they came in contact with, then destroying the ship and cargo manually using some of the Semtex. The original plan had called for his team to remain on the trawler, follow the target ship out to sea, and use an inflatable rubber craft to close the distance and commence the sabotage operation.

This plan had been altered after Tarkov found that none of the rubber craft possessed the engine speed capable of catching up to the Chin Wu once it was out to sea. Hitting it when it was in port became the only viable option. They had also understood that for De'vor and his team to effectively get on shore to initiate the attack, it would be necessary to produce some distraction that would seize the attention of the security forces on the ground. It would be a risky proposition, but given the low lighting of the port and the target ship, they figured they had a good chance to pull it off.

Sauwa, being the most skilled covert operative, would manage the assassination of Kalopolis. Once De'vor initiated the assault, the assumption was the arms broker would attempt to escape rather than stay and fight. The port road would take him out the gate. Once outside, the adjoining road presented two directions, one leading to the city and the other toward a suburb. Either route, once chosen, was a straight shot to its destination with no turns or means of getting off. With a team of three more Palestinians, Sauwa would set up an ambush point at both ends of the road. Either direction Kalopolis took, he would run into one.

Cars that would have been stolen for this mission would be armed with Semtex and a remote detonator. When the target passed either car, they would detonate the explosive. Any survivors or remaining vehicles would be met by one of the hit teams who would follow up the blast with gunfire as they shot the stunned survivors. Assuming that Kalopolis would choose the route leading directly to the city, Sauwa would be staged there with one of the Palestinians, the other two would be staged at the point leading to the suburbs. She didn't like the plan of having their forces so spread out, but it was the only logical way. The ambush was set up outside the port to avoid being seen by the security cameras or running up against any potential security patrols that might have been placed at the gate entrance.

Tarkov watched Sauwa as she studied the travel route she would be using. He was fully aware her role was more dangerous than anyones. She would be spread thin having to operate the two-man teams to cover both bases. He was also aware that while everyone else would have the benefits of larger more powerful weapons, her people would be using virtual handguns.

That she seemed to handle this with an eerie calm seemed even more unreal.

27

Kennson Rhys rubbed his brow as he listened to Managua explain the circumstances of how the young attorney, Esmeralda Morayo, had been killed in such a public and brutal display. He tried to mask his utter annoyance with the sheer clumsiness of the men sent to retrieve information from her. These specialists, a group of Hungarians operating in Germany, were supposed to have been part of an elite infiltration unit.

Managua reported that the Hungarians had broken into her home at an inopportune time and attempted to kidnap her. Their ambush failed when she ran. The response by these so-called professionals was to shoot her several times in front of her apartment with numerous witnesses watching. This was done while chasing her down several flights of stairs allowing any number of potential witnesses to view this very public display including the collateral death of a man who had the misfortune of being in the stairwell when the young lady and her pursuers ran by. It was bad enough that the man was brutally stabbed in an upscale apartment complex, but he turned out to be a well-respected veteran reporter for the noted German news publication, Der Spiegel. Morayo's death was sure to hit the headlines.

Rhys' fingers pushed harder and harder against his brow as he heard the details. If this had been Manilla or another city in the Philippines, or in Southeast Asia, it wouldn't have even been an issue. But this very public murder happened in Germany, and it happened in the very sophisticated city of Berlin where such violent acts were most uncommon and sure to arouse the interest of the police who would treat the killing of a noted corporate lawyer as a priority. This problem was on top of the fact that the young woman had been their only lead to finding out who they were pitted against.

The only saving grace Rhys could see arising from this event would be if it ended with some viable intelligence they could use. And, that nothing from this monumental cock-up traced back to them and their operation in Cyprus.

"As I was saying," Managua pressed on, "I am new to this area and am working with the only connections I have." The lawyer made this statement and repeated it at various intervals during his briefing. "These guys were supposed to be professionals. I was told they were special operators for their military during the cold war. I mean I…"

"It doesn't change anything," Rhys interrupted, cutting the lawyer off. "What is important right now is the exposure we have. Europe is a commonwealth that acts more like a single country these days. I don't want the police in Germany tracing this back to us."

"I can assure you that won't be the case," Managua said.

"The person I went through and all the coordination was done entirely in Slovakia. Nothing was done through me — it was done through a colleague of mine who specializes in the same field. He will return home as soon as he has the documents that were obtained from the lawyer's apartment. The people he hired are from Hungary. So, nothing done connects us to Cyprus."

Rhys tapped his finger irritably against the armrest. It was clear he was not satisfied with the explanation he was being given. Still, he realized there was nothing to be done about any of it. Certainly, nothing would be rectified by this conversation. He decided to move to his next concern. "How long until we receive the documents they were able to obtain?"

Managua waved his finger at the New Zealander. "That is the good news. My colleague is meeting with them as we speak. Once he has the documents, he will send them straight here via his assistant who will also have no connection to any of this. He won't even be Filipino. So, we don't have to worry about any trails leading back here. We should have our documents by tomorrow night at the earliest."

"And, we can expect that none of the documents will have been gone through by your people?" Khadga Yadav suddenly spoke up after standing quietly in the corner.

The lawyer haphazardly bobbed.

"Then, we'll have to go through all those documents ourselves to find any viable intelligence," the Nepali said acidly.

"It was too risky to have my people analyze them given the time constraints and the fact that they were too close to the crime scene to stay around after they obtained the documents," Managua feebly explained. "As your commander has made all too clear, these documents were taken in the act of committing a serious and very public crime. None of our people could afford to stay around."

Yadav shot the lawyer a disgusted look. Rhys had seen that look on his cohort only a few times, but it signaled that his friend was about to do something harmful. In an effort to defuse the situation, Rhys quickly interjected. "Perhaps it's best this way." He watched the anger in the Nepali's eyes shift in his direction.

The New Zealander continued, "Your people don't really know what we're dealing with or what to look for. It might be best if the unit on the ground looks through the documents."

Yadav's eyes darted back to the lawyer. While they still possessed a look of cold steel, they had lightened a little from what they had been. Rhys took it as a sign he had successfully calmed Yadav. At least Managua would be leaving the room with all his body parts, something that could not be said for many who angered the former Gurka to such a degree.

Managua seized the opportunity to end the meeting and take his leave. He walked out the door briskly, leaving the two mercenaries discussing the matter further. "What stupidity," Yadav growled the second he saw the door of the beach house slam shut.

"We have to forgive him this one," Rhys cautioned. "He is right that we are all in strange territory trying to work fast with few connections. The circumstances are not ideal. At some level, we have to take what we can get and hope for the best. In this case, the best is not what we got."

Yadav said nothing but stared at the door as if he were still watching Managua. Rhys continued, "We have to use what we have. It sounds like the cover-up following this shit is being well managed and, if we didn't get the information from Morayo, at least we have her documents that hopefully contain something useful."

"Hardly in time to help us," Yadav reminded him. There were only two days until the ships were due to arrive which meant the intel could still come too late to be of any real help. "That is still assuming this lawyer woman was even involved."

Rhys pressed his thumb to his lips as he leaned back in his chair. "When is Mehendra due back?"

Yadav glanced at his watch. "In about a half hour."

Mehendra had taken the Greeks out for one last rehearsal and weapons check. In actuality, it was an excuse to get them out of the house while Managua was there. Rhys had wanted to keep things compartmentalized. The team might see Managua at the dock, but they wouldn't know any more about him than that. The hired help did not need to know any more about the intricate workings of the operation than necessary.

"We'll work with what we have," the New Zealander said, as he rubbed his head. From the time he had landed until the time they were about to distribute the first of several shipments, he had been told nothing about this mysterious adversary he had been called in to neutralize. Nobody knew anything concrete, and all he had heard amounted to rumors and conspiracy theories. In the back of his mind, he began to wonder if this whole thing wasn't just some fabrication brought on by the wild imagination of a bunch of men getting paranoid over the fear of their enemies discovering their highly illegal act.

What concerned Yadav, even more, was that since their arrival the greater plausible threat would be some private investigator trying to collect evidence of the plot rather than some group of terrorists — evidence that could be presented to the government back home. If that were the case, having the top soldiers of one of the biggest private armies in the Philippines caught at some shady nighttime business at a pier in Cyprus would be playing directly into their hands. Wrestling with this very real consideration, Rhys decided that since he and Yadav were both well known for their services in Lorenza's private army, they should not be at the peer meeting. Managua, ever the negotiator of backroom deals, had agreed completely. His own presence at such a meeting brought possible exposure, but due to his long client list, he did such work throughout the South Pacific and could easily explain away his presence.

Since Mehendra was the newest member of the group and not as well known, he would be in charge of the security mission. The Fijian had spent his military career combating anti-government rebels and terrorists in his home country and defending key installations from dangerous infiltrators. During his time working with Rhys in remote jungles, Mehendra had proven himself to be highly competent as a soldier commanding troops in operations and raids against trained guerrillas.

Though it was not something the Fijian accepted easily, he had garnered a great deal of respect from the Greeks now in their employ. He had not lost sight of the fact that they were still like most European soldiers, oriented to the idea that whites were the inherently superior soldier. It had not been hard at all for Rhys to be seen and respected as the natural leader of the group while Mehendra and Yadav had had to work to earn the same level of respect. Mehendra was concerned that he would have difficulty managing the troops without Rhys around. If a situation arose that called his team into action, he could very well lose control of them if they suddenly decided that some Pacific Islander wasn't capable of doing the job. Both Rhys and Yadav understood their friend's concern, but they all agreed there was no other option. It was only after careful coaxing and reassurance, Mehendra finally capitulated and assumed control of the mission.

A short while after the lawyer left the beach house, the team returned. They had spent the last few hours going over response drills and practicing tactics and honing their skills to ensure that it was down to muscle memory. They practiced under the watchful direction of Mehendra who oversaw the day's training. That was the other reason the Fijian was now by himself with the Greek mercenaries while Rhys held his meeting. Mehendra needed time as their leader to help establish him in that capacity without Rhys around.

Filing into the house, with Mehendra leading the way, the men looked beat. The way they all flopped into the first available seats like dominoes dropping one after the other confirmed their exhaustion. Mehendra remained standing as he walked over to his two compatriots. "The training went well. They know their job and are confident with the procedures we've created."

"Good," Rhys said as he eyed the bodies sprawled out on the furniture.

"The other issues?" Yadav whispered.

Mehendra shrugged. "I'm not just some third world primitive to them at least." He turned his body slightly to eye the Greeks and then turned back to his comrades. "However, they still hold some reservations — training can rectify only so much."

"It will have to do," Rhys sighed gazing at the Fijian.

D espite the festive atmosphere dominating the city's evening, the vibes in the small Toyota pickup were tense and silent. While her male companion, a young man of about twenty-six, manned the steering wheel and avoided the sea of drunken humans occasionally pouring out of the clubs, Sauwa vigilantly tracked their surroundings from the passenger seat.

She was impressed by the casual manner James Musamba displayed as he responded to each unexpected stop with a subtle easing on the brakes that brought the truck to a halt slowly. The recently stolen truck was now packed with several kilos of Semtex explosives. She expected him to be a complete ball of nerves and drive so cautiously they would attract the attention of the police. Instead, the man drove like he was on routine business. She suspected it was from years of experience infiltrating well-guarded checkpoints run by the Israeli military. She would have preferred to have driven herself but opted not to. Both she and the man she was with agreed that a woman driving a pickup, a traditionally man's vehicle, would appear out of place to everyone watching.

At the four-way stop, the Palestinian made a right that brought them to a quieter street filled with small coffee shops and eateries for the less adventurous crowds. Sauwa had planned the route so they could weave through the streets along the beach not staying on any one street for very long but mainly on roads heavily populated with traffic. Unobtrusive vehicles, such as the low-key Toyota, would attract little attention from the police over more ostentatious modes of travel. If they traveled through the back streets at such a late hour, the towns were apt to be patrolled by bored police officers looking for something to do and would pull them over for any excuse. Sauwa wanted to keep close to the streets hosting most of the bars and clubs, while not staying on them very long. This way they could be sure the police they encountered would be too busy with bar fights, drug dealers, and out of control crowds of drunk tourists to care about petty traffic issues.

After a few blocks, Musamba pulled the truck onto the ramp that would take them to the main highway. Out of her rear-view mirror, Sauwa checked to make sure she could see the other vehicles — another grey Toyota truck and a grey Nissan van. The truck ascended the large circular ramp. A few cars behind them, she could barely see the other pickup. The van was out of view for her, but the small walkie-talkie that rested on her lap remained dormant, signaling to her that everyone behind could still see her.

She would verify their status again when they reached the highway. At that point, they would tighten their convoy and press forward. Leaving the ramp, the truck merged onto the highway. At this hour of the night, the traffic was sparse making it easy for them to move without hindrance and able to notice any other vehicle that might possibly be a tail.

She caught sight of the second pickup and soon after that the van. On her order, they all stayed in the same lane maintaining good separation so their convoy was not too obvious to the few cars traveling the road. Their trip was less than fifteen kilometers, but with all the tension, it felt like years. Finally, the road curved into a large roundabout. Musamba entered the roundabout and turned onto the left off-ramp.

Even in the darkness, the outline of the Limassol port could be seen through the rows of lighting outlining the building and harbor. From pinpricks of lights from the structures that sat along the pier, Sauwa could see the black pool of water. She could also see the outlines of two large cargo ships resting beside their area of interest. She assumed they were the Romanov and the Chin Wu. She hoped the rest of the team was in place and getting ready to move.

A short distance from the off-ramp they found themselves surrounded by an open field on both sides and a few spartan houses and buildings could be seen in the distance. Sauwa grabbed the walkie-talkie and ordered the truck behind them to drive past them. It continued down the road as Sauwa's truck drove onto the ground separating them from the oncoming traffic. The truck went across a rough area filled with wild bushes that battered the truck before they reached the opposite lane.

They continued down the road a few more meters before stopping in another open area between the port and the road. A few minutes later they were joined by the second truck that pulled behind them. It was a two-lane road, and they needed to ensure that both lanes would lead to the same destination.

The van went past them and came back passing them again until all that could be seen was the faint blink of red tail lights. The plan was to detonate both trucks and, after the assault, use the van as the escape vehicle. Sauwa had recced the road quite a few times and had found there was virtually no traffic on it, including the police, after 2100 hours. This spared her the need to plan for neutralizing any police patrols showing up at an inconvenient time. She didn't relish needless killing but a witness was a witness, and they were about to commit a serious crime. Even if she thought differently and sought a less lethal method, it was doubtful her Palestinian subordinates would feel the same way.

Removing a bundle wrapped carefully in a black cloth, she exited the vehicle with Musamba following her. Like her, he was carrying his own dark bundle under his arm. They were soon joined by their two cohorts. Together they walked back toward the van. "It won't be long," Sauwa said without a hint of emotion as she felt her operational instincts kick in. There was no reply and no need for conversation from the men as they continued walking. Everyone knew the danger they faced.

They got to the van and found their comrade waiting with a gym bag over his shoulder. Without saying anything, he reached into the bag and produced a set of night vision optics which he handed to Sauwa. Through the night optics, she had a clear view of the trucks and the road beyond.

Satisfied that they were good, she and the team walked back to the trucks. The trucks had been covered with a rubber overtop that wrapped over the entire rear of the vehicle. Removing the cover, Sauwa and Imil, the Palestinian, found themselves looking down at several bricks of the white claylike Semtex stuffed neatly in dark plastic sheathing and taped against the wall of the truck in the direction facing the road. There were five bricks weighing a kilo each tucked snugly together and held in place by thick black construction tape. Inside the truck was another small canvas bag.

The bag contained the copper blasting cartridges they stuck into the exposed back of each of the clay bricks. Next, they connected the bricks to some nickel chrome wire that they folded into a V-shape and covered with some rubber sheeting to keep the chrome ring from producing any kind of contact with the cartridge. This was a very tricky and dangerous part of setting up the explosive with only the power of a 9v battery to detonate it. Keeping the wiring from actually touching the inside charge of the cartridge, Sauwa finished it off by applying caulk to seal everything. She carefully connected the wires to a small metal box containing the battery and a disposable cellular phone that were wired together and melded into place. Placing the chrome wires into the box, she connected them to the electrical wiring of the phone. She finished by taping the box at the far edge of the Semtex.

She and Imil walked away back toward the van. She wasn't worried about the other two Palestinians working on the other truck. Like her, they had received similar explosives training from covert intelligence units and from former IRA bombers, the best urban guerrillas in the world at times, who tended to hire out their expertise to those who could afford it.

They had only just returned to the van when they heard the footsteps of the other two men following up behind them. "We're good." One of the men said as they came up to the rest of the team.

"We'll only know that when it's time." Sauwa hissed, reminding them that it only was good if the bombs detonated when they needed to.

IVENTI MEHENDRA FELT a cold shiver run down his spine. He had felt the tingle since he had arrived at the harbor. It was not from the breezy night sea air — it was the unnerving feeling he had about the situation. He didn't like conducting sensitive operations with such poor lighting. All he saw were the innumerable ways some enemy could use the shadows to get too close.

Managua, the lawyer, who was supposed to manage this affair had mentioned some rather disturbing news. It bothered him even more that he knew practically nothing about the men he was going to do business with this evening. The arms merchant and men arrived in a long convoy of sleek black vehicles.

Mehendra looked at the man stepping out from the back of the third truck. He had long, golden hair that was even visible in the scant light and was dressed in an expensive suit that had obviously been made by a very skilled tailor. As he exited the vehicle, he was flanked by two armed guards who remained at his side as he started to walk toward Mehendra.

"This is not the man I've been working with," was the disconcerting news Managua hissed into the mercenary's ear. Mehendra observed the golden-haired man and his entourage as they approached. He didn't see any behavior or action that led him to conclude this was a setup. Still, the lawyer next to him looked utterly baffled which did cause concern.

The arms merchant came up to the two Asians. Instantly, the golden-haired man extended his hand in a cordial manner that was left open for either man to take. Managua paused then gripped the man's hand with his own in a hesitant manner. "I was expecting Mr. Prokopis for this evening's business," Managua explained to the dumpy, middle-aged man they had brought along as an interpreter. The dumpy man turned in the direction of the arms merchant and began translating the lawyer's words in Greek.

Nodding politely, the golden-haired man listened. When the interpreter was done, he turned toward the Asians and began to speak. His voice was accented, but his English was clear and concise. "Mr. Prokopis will no longer be part of this affair. For this exercise, you will be dealing with me."

"What happened to him?" Mehendra asked. His tone was sharp and serious.

Theo Kalopolis observed the two Asian men coldly. He was both impressed and offended by the Asian's demand to know about his former employee. The arms merchant's first thought was to dismiss the man's abrupt request for information regarding his late employee. But, looking over the hardened figure cutting a much more intimidating figure than the Filipino lawyer, he thought better of it. "I'm afraid Mr. Prokopis has died."

The inquisitive look on the Asian's face demanded a better explanation. Kalopolis continued. "He was dispatched violently in a bar fight only a few days ago."

Mehendra felt the cold shiver in his spine intensify

hearing such news. That the key operative managing the arms shipment for the gun runners was so conveniently murdered at an inopportune time so close to the transaction occurring seemed highly suspicious. Now looking at the expensively dressed man standing before him with an entourage of tough-looking men who were obviously there for his protection and nothing more, the Fijian began to feel slightly unnerved.

Maybe he was being paranoid, and that this was all just some conspiracy theory developing in his head. But, Mehendra couldn't shake the feeling it was something more. Turning from the meeting, he walked over to his men scattered behind him in the shadows — this was to prevent them from being easy targets if this first meeting turned violent. With a wave of his hand, he gathered them in a half circle. Before issuing orders, the Fijian turned back to the arms merchant. "How many men do you have designated for exterior security?"

Kalopolis and Managua both turned back displaying looks of exasperation at being interrupted. Mehendra ignored their indignation as he walked closer and asked the question again. "What kind of security have you arranged for the outer area?"

The arms merchant exhaled irritably. "The security I have brought is for my own protection. There are armed men aboard the Romanov for protection of the cargo. I can only presume you have similar protection aboard your vessel. Otherwise, I see no reason to circulate a lot of armed men around to attract a lot of unwanted attention from whoever else is working at this hour. I've already taken more than enough risk obtaining this private location even though it goes against the port's policy."

The Fijian was aghast at hearing this response. He turned back to his men and made a quick assessment, then set about deploying them to cover the most likely means an adversary might have to infiltrate. It wasn't an easy task; he hadn't a clue what kind of threat he was guarding against. If it was a team of highly trained professionals, he figured at this hour that the enemy would come through a weak spot in the surrounding fence line under cover of darkness. They could then make their way through any number of routes through the maze of stacked cargo boxes and equipment to come through and assault them from numerous blind spots. Or, they could come through the waters of the port which gave ample concealment and a vast array of darkened places along the harbor they could come up to and launch a surprise attack. It was far too much ground to cover. The other possibility he considered, was that a lesser trained group of trigger-happy bandits might opt for the expedient way of coming in from the adjacent roadway where they could speed in on vehicles and lay into some wild cowboy attack setting onto the unprepared group.

Realizing he could not expect any help from the arms merchant, Mehendra deployed his men accordingly. He sent two up the road to the entryway to set up a vehicular assault. He dispatched two more to patrol the adjacent pier, and then he and the remaining three started patrolling the walkways between the cargo boxes.

Managua wasn't happy about finding his security detail suddenly scattered, leaving him alone, but he wasn't about to argue. His attention was focused on the ships. The captain of the Chin Wu had begun making his descent down the rickety scaffolding to the waiting group of men. He was a short and slightly frail man. His clothes looked a size or two too big for him. By comparison, the captain was followed by two brawny sailors, each armed with some unidentifiable sub-machine gun. He landed on the ground just short of his Bulgarian counterpart, who had come down from the other ship a few seconds behind him.

Both captains joined the group waiting for them on the pier. Not wanting to wait for instructions, they had both taken it upon themselves to begin transferring the cargo immediately. Being in a foreign port conducting criminal activity, both captains jointly decided it unwise to stay any longer than absolutely necessary. Managua had already met with the captain of the Chin Wu, upon his arrival and had agreed with the decision to begin. The Romanov had been given prior instructions back in Sophia as to what ship he would be meeting so it was a simple arrangement.

29

The fishing trawler appeared cold and dismal in shadowy darkness as it lay a good distance from the Limassol port with only a few red-lensed lights inverted along the bow to allow for everyone to see what they were doing. On board, everyone went about their work in silence. The crew of the trawler tended to their duties manning the ship while the mercenaries busied themselves with last-minute details. The inflatable rubber rafts had already been dropped into the water and were tied to the railing of the ship.

Dressed in dark wet-suits, the teams jumped into their respective boats with their gear and weapons. Though there was no intention of scuba diving, they had opted to wear wet gear, because their crafts were small and low to the water. During the ride over, between the speed and the waves splashing over them, they would be sopping wet when they arrived. Neither Tarkov nor any of his men relished the idea of trying to launch an attack bogged down by wet, tight, and clingy clothing when trying to run. They would have greater mobility dealing with wetsuits that wouldn't absorb water and cause problems. The wetsuits also helped them move with stealth — they wouldn't have to worry about any noise from water dripping off their clothing.

All was quiet as everyone mentally prepared for the mission. The crew of the fishing trawler was silent as they watched the mercenaries climb into their boats. De'vor took the front of the craft followed by Gorzo and then the Palestinians. The muffled sounds of metal and wood echoed up and down the craft as the mercenaries' stowed rifles that had been wrapped in thin, plastic bags to protect them against the sea water. Really, it was probably an unnecessary precaution as the AK model rifle was the most durable, small weapon in the world. But why take a chance if you don't have to.

They could see the lights outlining the target ships and the port in general. Except for two or three ships docked along the pier on the outer side of the port, the port was virtually empty. Along the peninsula that separated the inner port from the rest of the ocean, they could hear crews busily loading and unloading.

Tarkov signaled — the team in the first raft moved toward their target. De'vor waited a few minutes, then motioned his raft into operation. The two rafts traveled through the water at a moderate pace. As they moved toward the port, the outline of the trawler became smaller and smaller until it couldn't be seen. In the darkness, it felt like they had fallen into an endless void. The only reminder that they were on the ocean were the bursts of spray and the occasional gut of water coming from the waves surrounding them.

Rounding the opening leading into the port, they were guided by the meager lights attached to the concrete supports of the pier. They were no more than tiny specks in the massive body of water and the thick blanket of blackness cloaking them from sight. Even if their adversaries had the benefit of night vision optics, they would still have far too much area to cover with such a small target. The men were also aided by the use of dark rubber sheets that were pulled over them and the rafts to break up their outline. The boat motors generated only tiny humming sounds that were easily drowned out by the deep growling of the more powerful engines of the cargo ships.

Halfway across the large body of water, Tarkov's craft veered to the left and circled around toward the starboard side of the Chin Wu. De'vor and Gorzo's craft went right in the direction of the harbor. Two-hundred meters out, De'vor cut the engine. They were far enough away that they exceeded the range of the harbor lights and the moving beams of what the Frenchman determined were flashlights held by a roving patrol.

Using night vision optics, De'vor scanned the shoreline keeping his gaze on the two men walking there. Their attention and the beams from their flashlights were directed primarily at the water. The glowing flashes made it difficult to know if they were armed. He kept staring and, finally, was able to make out the rifles slung across their shoulders. By the indifference the men gave to the cargo compared to the emphasis they placed on the water, the Frenchman concluded they were there as part of the opposition and were anticipating a sea born attack. De'vor felt a slight sense of relief that they were not simple watchmen. He lamented having to kill innocents, but if they had been, he didn't have the benefit of Sauwa dispatching them for him. He was sure she would handle it without the slightest hesitation or remorse.

Studying the terrain carefully, De'vor moved his raft to the far end of the pier several hundred meters from their target and the security detail. The raft advanced through the water parallel to the shoreline. Almost reaching the far corner, he cut the motor and silently paddled the rest of the way in.

Once they were about twenty meters from the concrete pier, Gorzo and one of the Palestinians dropped into the water and quietly swam the rest of the way. Keeping their arms and legs well below water to avoid making any splashing noises, they forged their way to land. They quickly slipped onto the pier and dashed past the floodlights and into the shadows offered by the cargo boxes. The raft pulled back out into the water as fast as it had arrived. Gorzo and his cohort, now safely within the protection of the shadows, stealthily began to move. In their soft-soled rubber shoes, they were able to move silently without the distinctive clumping sound made by their normal heavy footwear.

Keeping close to the cargo boxes to avoid creating a silhouette, the two men moved with cat-like stealth, setting heels to the ground and gradually lowering the rest of the foot. They made virtually no noise against the smooth concrete surface.

They had to move a long distance at an excruciatingly slow pace which made it seem like an eternity. Thanks to the numerous rehearsals, both men could move on instinct without having to concentrate too hard on each step. This made it easier to stay focused on their targets. The guards helped shorten the distance and reduce the time by walking toward them.

They stopped several meters away and allowed the guards to close the distance. Slowly, the two men crouched down taking a predator attack position as they drew their double-edged knives from plastic sheaths and waited. As the guards neared the illumination of the floodlights, their rifles could be seen. The guards were looking out at the water with night vision optics. The few times they turned away from the water, they were either not using their optics, or they were looking too high and too quickly to notice the two crouching men.

Once they passed Gorzo, he signaled his cohort with a soft touch on the shoulder. Slowly, rising halfway to a standing position, the two men moved directly behind their quarry. Coming up behind the first guard, the Italian swung his arm around the man's head, placing his forearm against the man's mouth and, in a single motion, brought the knife up driving the sharp blade straight through the brain stem killing him instantly.

With a powerful force, Gorzo turned his whole upper body taking his victim off to the side to open up an avenue for his partner to engage the other guard. The second guard turned to see his comrade being assaulted just before the Palestinian plunged his blade deep into the guard's stomach straight up under his chest cutting into organs, neutralizing any means of speech or ability to cry out.

With the guards taken care of, Gorzo seized one of their flashlights. Slowly he raised and lowered the torch in a vertical pattern in the direction of the sea. Behind him, the Palestinian took up a position directly facing backward toward the land. He kept watching to prevent anyone from sneaking up behind them.

Out on the water, De'vor watched the progress of the two men he had sent ashore. He caught sight of light moving in a controlled vertical pattern. Using his optical vision, he saw his two men, garbed in their diving suits, signaling him as agreed. On De'vor's order, the raft was soon buzzing through the water.

It wasn't long before Gorzo could hear the hum of the raft's motor. Placing the flashlight on the cusp of the pier to serve as a guiding beacon, he and the Palestinian slid back toward the cargo box behind them. They took up security positions on either side to cover both avenues and secure a foothold that the rest of the team could use to safely infiltrate.

The raft stopped several meters short of coming within range of the floodlights. They navigated the rest of the way in using plastic oars dipped slowly and quietly into the water. De'vor stayed under the tarp to study his watch. He estimated they had less than ten minutes before the prepositioned Bangalores were set to go off and provide the diversion for his attack.

The raft nudged against the concrete pier. The mercenaries immediately began deploying onto land with their French commander leading the way. In truth, De'vor, being a commando trained from the paratrooper perspective, would have preferred a land insertion into the port. However, after the naval commandos, Sacchini and Tarkov carefully walked him through the plan and had softened to their idea. Since both his second in command, Gorzo, and the Palestinian had been trained as naval commandos, as they made their case, he agreed it would be the strongest place to assault from.

Tying off the raft to the nearest flood light, the mercenaries were now on land. Each man moved up in a well-practiced pattern. Like cards being dealt on a table, they peeled off with every other man forming into two tactical lines behind Gorzo and his Palestinian cohort. The last men from the raft joined the lines and signaled the end by patting the shoulder of the guy next to them. This pattern was copied all the way back to the beginning of the lines. Once everyone was up, De'vor gestured to Gorzo, who immediately rose to his feet and started moving to the pier. Like a chain reaction, every man rose one after the other and followed in a line pressed tightly to the cargo boxes, staying deep within the shadows.

TARKOV KEPT his eyes fixed on the bow of the ship as their rubber raft flew through the water. The cargo ship was a large fortress-like steel beast with the lowest deck still sitting high above the water. It was doubtful that anyone gazing over the side would notice them in the darkness below. At first, the Tarkov considered cutting the motor as he neared his target. But, the growling of the Chin Wu's engine was so powerful, it easily masked the sound of their approach.

The ship seemed deserted — only the engine and a smattering of lights indicated signs of life. Once in a while, they spotted the occasional sailor as they walked along the bow, oblivious to anything beyond their immediate universe. There were no signs of any security. It appeared such concerns were not a consideration for the ship's crew and captain.

Within a few meters of the ships' hull, they dropped the

raft's speed to an idle. As they got closer, Sacchini, who maintained control of one of the limpet mines strapped snuggly to his torso, moved up. He started to unfasten the metal drum. Tarkov and two of the Palestinians trained their weapons and attention on the bows, watching for any signs that someone might have taken notice.

The Italian was on his knees as he crossed the soft bottom of their raft. He felt the rubber smack gently against the steel body of the ship as he reached his destination. He leaned forward just enough to feel the mines touch the hull. He adjusted the contraption until it was firmly secured onto the ship's side. When he was sure it was properly fastened, he went to pull the pin.

He was suddenly jilted back by a powerful bump that came up under the raft. The Italian fell back into one of the Palestinians, temporarily knocking the wind out him. Everyone on the raft froze as they sought to understand what had just happened. A second later they all felt another bump, just as strong as the first. Everyone looked around in a state of confusion. What they had felt couldn't have been a wave. Then one of the Palestinians rose to his knees and nervously pointed his finger in a direction off to the side. Tarkov gaze followed the finger and realized what the man was pointing to. Just a few feet from them, he made out the outline of a large dorsal fin. No one had to guess what it was. They were being circled by a shark.

By the size of the fin, they were being accosted by a man-eater — a Tiger shark, or possibly, a Great White. The first thought on everyone's mind was to let loose with a barrage of gunfire that would rip into the shark's body and certainly end the threat. But, the professional instincts in all of them understood that the noise would alert their enemies and exchange one threat for another.

The shark's movements were getting bolder, and it was only a matter of time before it struck, sending them all into the water to be a midnight feast. Quickly, Sacchini jumped over to where the mine was and pulled the pin to arm the explosive. He grabbed hold of the mine and felt around for a second trying to find the pin in the dark. He felt the circular ring just in time to feel another bump, this time smacking against the side of the raft. Not wasting time, he slipped his finger through the ring and pulled until he could feel it slide all the way out.

"Go Now!!" He screamed, throwing tactical caution to the wind. The motor ripped into full speed as the craft started to take off. A large torpedo like silhouette exploded from the murky water missing them by just inches with a menacing set of clearly defined sharp jagged teeth. Water sprayed over the terrified mercenaries as they made their escape. Under the circumstances, they decided to forgo setting the second mine as they moved away from the ship. Their craft raced through the water and made their way to the open harbor. They had several minutes to escape and clear the distance.

DE'VOR and his team had moved up to the edge of the cargo boxes. In the darkness, it was futile to use a mirror of any sort to see around the edge. Lowering onto a knee, the Frenchman peered around the corner to see the group of men huddled at the base of the gangplank leading to the Chin Wu. He could make out only a few outlines of automatic weapons amongst the men in the crowd. It was impossible to determine how many combatants there were, and how many were just there for business. He supposed, in the long run, it wouldn't matter.

He reached his hand back to tap the arm of the nearest Palestinian. The mercenary responded by slinging his rifle behind his back reaching into the tactical pouch on the side of his hip. He produced a small, round hand grenade. Unlike their shoulder weapons, the grenades were American. They were smooth, hard metallic balls. And, different from most eastern designs, they not only possessed a lethal, explosive power but followed with a dangerous cloud of shrapnel that was guaranteed to kill or severely wound a good number of their enemies within bursting radius.

Pulling the pin and flipping the secondary lock, the grenade was now kept from exploding only through the Palestinian's hand pressed tightly against the spoon grip that ran down the side of the deadly contraption. The Palestinian moved to the Frenchman's flank to give himself throwing space.

At the same time, De'vor motioned Gorzo to move his small team around and open pathways between the cargo boxes. They would come up from behind and attack the arms dealer from the side and rear after De'vor and his team had lifted their cover fire. The Italian moved down the line of mercenaries, tapping the shoulder of the men comprising his team. Gorzo moved out, leaving De'vor with two men. One man held the grenade while the other protected their back. Gorzo and his team disappeared into the opening, leaving the three men to guard the far corner.

THE PALESTINIAN HAD GROWN concerned when he couldn't reach his team on the pier. He hadn't yet begun to suspect the worst given that the walkie-talkies they had been issued were not of the best quality. He had made several attempts before finally getting a response from his team at the gate which led him to believe the situation remained unchanged. Still, having made his rounds through the numerous structures at the far corner, he was convinced they were safe enough from any infiltration coming from the fence line, and they were now making their way back to the ships. He planned to make contact with Managua and then commence a roving patrol circulating through the openings of the cargo boxes.

He looked back to check that his men were in a well-dispersed patrol formation. In the tight confines between the cargo boxes, it would be easy to take out a whole team with a few well-trained bursts of gunfire if they were grouped too closely together. Instead, his team moved with about fifteen meters of dispersion. They were moving through the space between a row of cargo boxes when they confronted a group of armed men moving adjacent to them through another opening. Those men were wearing black diving suits and sporting Kalashnikov automatic rifles.

The Fijian needed no time to identify this group. He knew instantly they were adversaries. "Contact front!" He shouted as he brought his rifle into a firing position and sighted down the barrel at the first man in the approaching group. He let loose a burst of fire that was matched by the Greek closest to him and then another who joined them from behind.

GORZO HAD BARELY enough time to catch the sight of this encroaching group coming out of nowhere when he was met with a fearsome barrage of gunfire. He screamed for his men to take cover as he lifted his rifle to fire back. He could hear the sounds and see the muzzle flashes as his men joined him in return fire. In only a second, the small corner between the cargo boxes had erupted into a massive gun battle.

Hearing the explosive gunfire only a short distance away, De'vor didn't take long to conclude that Gorzo and his men had run into an unexpected enemy. Deciding to forgo waiting for the mine explosion, he instructed his man to toss the grenade at the body of men congregated at the docks. After a quick toss, the three men hunkered behind the thick steel of the cargo box. A few seconds later the gunfire was dwarfed by the thunderous report of the grenade exploding. The sound ruptured the air and shook the ground with a powerful vibration. It was followed by the loud blood-curdling screams of its victims who had not perished immediately. Giving an instant to allow the shrapnel to settle, the Frenchman led his troops out from behind the cargo box and started toward the remaining group, still dazed and confused from the blast. In cover behind the wall of the cargo box, he waited while his men moved to the other side. They began laying down a thick base of fire while their enemy was still grouped tightly together. More men screamed as the bullets tore into their bodies.

KALOPOLIS COULDN'T UNDERSTAND what was happening. In the darkness, he could only hear the sounds around him. First, it had been the wild gunfire in the distance, then there was a huge blast that sent him and many others falling to their feet. He felt the warm, thick liquid that could only be blood spattered from lifeless corpses. Now, there was gunfire, only it wasn't in the distance. It was close to him. He could see the flashes a few meters away, and the bullets were whizzing all around him.

He felt pairs of powerful hands grasp his biceps and lift him into the air. The arms merchant was being shuttled toward his car. The men who gripped him moved past the group of remaining bodyguards on their way to the vehicles. The man holding his left shoulder was barking orders to the men covering their escape. Kalopolis looked up and saw eruptions of gunfire all around him as his men returned fire.

Like a bag of potatoes, the arms merchant was unceremoniously tossed into the back of the last truck in his convoy. His two men barely slammed the door behind him before they were jumping into the front seat and starting the engine. The truck peeled out backward, then whirled around with a powerful force until it was facing the gate. Their tires squealed, and the smell of hot rubber permeated the truck as it raced down the road.

The gunfight was temporarily interrupted when another deep, earth-shattering sound erupted into the night. It was the limpet mine finally detonating. The sound was far more ominous as it echoed through the air and the force shaking the ship could even be felt on the docks. The Frenchman grabbed the walkie-talkie he had strapped to his side. On the other end, he could hear the gruff sound of Sergei Tarkov screaming from the other end.

"Why have you initiated early?" The Russian demanded.

"We were compromised!" Shouted De'vor as bullets flew extremely close.

"Do you need back up?" Tarkov asked, but De'vor knew he was coming whether he was needed to or not.

De'vor needed backup considering he was facing off against a continued fusillade of fire.

TARKOV HEARD the gun battle in the distance. He had seen and heard the explosion from the limpet mine. Now it was time to focus on the arms dealer and his Filipino contacts. The raft hurried into action as they navigated toward the firefight. Despite the danger, they were going in with all guns pointed to the boat on the water. If Mr. Flippers, as the shark had been nicknamed by the men, decided to rear his head, he would find the response less passive than a few minutes ago.

The raft reached the pier just as the shooting next to the ships had started to die down. The remaining members of Kalopolis' security detail had retreated to their cars and widened the distance to where the shooting became little more than sporadic shots exchanged between both parties.

Tarkov and his team jumped onto the docks and took positions behind the same cargo box De'vor and his men had occupied. Quickly assessing the situation, Tarkov led his men past the box and down the walkway where he joined De'vor and his team. With the shooting ending, they set their sights on the ship. Half expecting to be receiving fire from above, they discovered the gaping hole in the side of the ship was occupying the crew's attention.

All that remained after the explosion were the broken cargo boxes. The sound of another gunfight erupted behind them. Slipping backward, they rounded a corner to find

Gorzo and his men in an all-out gunfight. Given the awkwardness of the fighting taking place between the two sides around a corner, Tarkov and De'vor took their team to the next opening to get behind their adversaries. They moved up to the opening and were met by a hail of gunfire. Some of the men cried out in pain as they were hit by the bullets. Everyone drew back and pressed themselves against the walls of the nearest cargo box and laid down return fire. They were in such a cramped location, only two men could fire back.

Mehendra heard the gunfire behind him. He turned to see the men he had posted to protect his rear were now heavily engaged. The Fijian had anticipated the enemy trying to flank him, and he had posted his two men to guard the rear while he and the other Greek held their position. After several tries, Mehendra radioed his team at the gate, calling them back to provide backup and attempt to assault the enemy's rear. He needed them to arrive quickly.

The gunfire from behind was fierce and it quickly became apparent to the Fijian that his relief men were dealing with more than just a token force. Caught between two superior forces, he understood it was only a matter of time before he was overrun or ran out of ammunition. Taking a breath, he turned to his Greek cohort. Instructing him to grab the other two men, he planned for them to try to shoot their way through to their rear, where he figured they would be against a smaller force. Nervously, the Greek nodded. He understood they had no other option.

With the Fijian laying down a quick burst of suppressive fire, they moved back toward their two comrades. Together, they let loose a barrage of gunfire on the smaller force as all four picked up and retreated across the path to the next set of cargo boxes.

Tarkov and his men were unexpectedly hit by a larger concentration of fire than they had been dealing with. He watched as the two men they had been firing at, along with more of their comrades opened up with covering fire toward him and his men as they attempted to make an escape. The Russian and his men responded tenaciously with their own weapons as they tore into the escaping men. Muzzle flashes lit the night as both sides let loose on each other. And, like an angry swarm of bees, both sides felt the buzz of bullets flying all around them.

It ended with De'vor signaling that the enemy had escaped. Tarkov ordered everyone to cease firing and shouted the order across to Gorzo and his men. De'vor and a couple of the Palestinians darted over to where the enemy had made their escape, taking positions next to the opening to ensure they weren't still there. He could hear running feet as the enemy made their getaway.

It took everyone several minutes to regain their night vision after the brightness the gunfire flashes produced. Then they were able to get a better view of the aftermath. Where the enemy had been, there were two bodies lying motionless on the ground. With the aid of a flashlight, they found one who looked to be of Greek origin lying next to a man who looked more Asian. The Asian man had a bullet hole in his forehead.

———

IT WAS the sharp screeching of tires emanating from a gate opening that warned Sauwa and her team that their target was fast approaching. She had been on alert anticipating this moment since she heard the battle kick off with small arms fire, the ear-shattering eruptions of powerful explosions that were impossible to ignore. They had staged for the ambush sheltered within a dip in the ground a good distance from the tracks, which she watched through her night optics. Expensive looking utility vehicles were speeding wildly down the road as if trying to make a getaway. They weren't traveling in a tight tactical pattern, they were racing pell-mell, every man for himself. The leading vehicle was well ahead of the two following. It looked almost as if they were in some sort of race. It also meant that the plan of hitting everyone in one quick blast was not going to happen.

By now, she and her team had their weapons out, the metallic stocks extended from their collapsed position, and the upper receiver locked back with a round in the chamber. They were using the elongated magazines that housed twenty-five rounds of nine-millimeter ammunition. Each one of them had an additional two magazines to be able to offer as much firepower as their light weapons could provide.

Her next concern was closing the considerable distance between them and the ambush point. They had rehearsed it several times, but it still felt like they needed to come up with a more reliable solution to a complicated plan. Semtex is a powerful explosive, and they had over five kilos of it in each vehicle. It was more than enough to rip a city transit bus to shreds. On an open road, it would send a couple of those approaching trucks flying a good distance. It was also guaranteed to send a storm of lethal shrapnel through the air even farther.

This meant that Sauwa and her team had to take cover within well-fortified shelter far enough away to avoid being casualties themselves. That also meant that once the ambush was initiated, they had a lot of open ground to cover to get to their target giving an adversary time to regain their faculties and fight back or make a run for it.

The first truck was coming up on the far side of the road where her other team was parked. One of the men on her team took out a disposable cellular phone and flipped it open. A number was already programmed in, and the man held his finger just above the send button. Sauwa held her hand up, palm forward, as she watched the approaching truck, timing it instinctively, hoping she would be close enough.

She clutched her hand into a fist when she saw the target vehicle pass several yards from their truck. The Palestinian responded by pressing the send button on his phone. The signal transmitted quickly to another phone that was inside the small detonation box containing the Semtex. An electrical current passed from the phone to the blasting caps fixed to the white, gooey clay.

The explosion impacted the first utility vehicle with enough force that it shook the ground violently and tossed it through the air as if it were a child's toy. Sauwa and her team felt the explosion a good hundred meters away. The vehicle had been hit with such force that the steel frame split through the middle, tearing the vehicle into two smoking balls that smashed into the ground on either side of the road.

As anticipated, an instant later the sky was filled with flying debris. It sounded and felt like a hail storm. It lasted only a brief few seconds before the sky was clear again and the night silent with the exception of the following vehicles speeding down the road. Looking up over the berm, Sauwa and her team watched the next two trucks come to a screeching halt where the explosion had gone off. Thick clouds of smoke billowed from the explosion site casting an impenetrable fog making it extremely difficult to see what was going on.

Sauwa and her team shifted their positions and hesitated. They couldn't see or hear anything. They could easily be outgunned. She had no intention of being caught out in the open where they would no longer have the option of activating the second explosive device if the enemy was in a position to retaliate.

Abruptly, screeching sounds were heard, and Sauwa realized the vehicles were moving again. She reached for her optics as Imil held the detonator for the next truck. It was a short window of opportunity as the cloud was still hampering her vision. She could see a second truck just ahead of the cloud. Imil flipped open the cover of the cell phone and was ready to press send to trigger the detonator.

The truck blew through the smoke and sped wildly down the road. It happened so fast, Sauwa barely had time to give the signal. Like the last time, she clutched her hand, and Imil's thumb fell on the brightly lit button. Once more another wave rumbled violently through the ground with a loud thunderous boom echoing into the night. Seconds later, the sky was again filled with debris dropping on them. When it finished, the mercenaries peeked over the berm to see a fresh cloud of smoke. She could see the remains of that utility vehicle scattered on the road across from them.

There was little time for assessments when the third vehicle blasted through the cloud and proceeded to fly down the road. With no other explosives, the only option was to stop it the hard way. Bounding out of their protected position, the team sprinted toward the road just ahead of their target.

They were met by spurts of gunfire coming from the approaching vehicle. The shots were not well aimed, fired wildly in all directions. Sauwa and her team assumed the shots were coming from the occupants in the back seat, where they were not able to angle their shots well. Gradually the shots started to get closer, indicating someone from the vehicle was now sighting correctly.

When the vehicle moved into range for their nine-millimeter weapons to be effectively used, Sauwa's mercenaries delivered a controlled burst of fire aimed at the windshield. Knowing that the thick glass of the windshield deflected the direction of a bullet by about six inches, Sauwa aimed low toward the glass just short of the cab. She fired a burst of three in succession. At the same time, Imil was firing toward the passenger side in the hopes of hitting one of the shooters. The other two Palestinians were directing their fire toward the tires and the back passenger side.

Eventually, the utility truck veered off to the side of the road and headed through the ground separating the two road systems. At first, it was thought they were trying to make a getaway. But then the truck weaved about, driven like someone intoxicated. It swerved and eventually slowed to an idle, then stopped when it hit a berm that brought it to a complete halt.

Led by Sauwa, the mercenaries moved toward the vehicle. Not sure what to expect, they fanned out. Imil flanking far to her left, and the other two Palestinians fanning out to her far right to focus on the back seat. She heard the clicking sounds of magazines being locked into the weapons behind her. A couple of the team had expended their first magazines in the initial firefight and were replacing them with fresh ones.

They neared the vehicle with their weapons held in the tactical ready, aiming as well as possible in the limited light. Less than fifty meters out, the front and back door of the passenger side burst open as two men simultaneously leaped from their seats while firing a burst from their carbines in the direction of the mercenaries. Sauwa moved erratically from side to side as she approached. Tactically, the target was far more difficult to hit when it was continually moving. It did not give anyone a solid point to aim in on. Sauwa returned fire with the same short controlled bursts she had used when the vehicle was moving. She could hear the distinct crackling of fire behind her that told her the other mercenaries were firing as well.

The two men moved from the truck to the side in an attempt to escape. Magazine empty, Sauwa continued moving as she ejected the spent magazine from the gun weld and with her shooting hand retrieved one of her spares. It was all second nature to her — she didn't have to look or even think about it. She continued firing. By now, one of the escaping adversaries had stopped shooting and dropped his weapon to his side as he clutched his chest and ceased moving. He eventually sunk to his knees, fell to his side, and remained motionless. The other man managed to make it up the berm almost to the road before the same fate befell him. He dropped his weapon to the ground then rolled back down the berm onto the open ground.

Sauwa moved toward the utility truck, while the two Palestinians on her right moved to check the two corpses in the road. Reaching the rear of the vehicle, she bent down and pressed herself against the far corner to keep out of sight in case anyone was still inside training a weapon on her. Transitioning the shoulder stock to her other arm, she picked up a stone with her free hand and began to edge forward, barely moving her feet to avoid making noise.

Less than a meter from the back seat, she could hear heavy breathing. She didn't know exactly where the sound was coming from, but she thought it was coming from the other side of the vehicle. The slight sound of metallic clanking could only be a weapon being moved; it told her the quarry was preparing for battle.

It was still impossible for either of them to see; they both had to rely on their sense of sound. Sauwa stomped her foot into the ground loud enough so it was easily heard by the person inside. At that same moment, she pitched the stone at the base of the car door making it seem as though she was preparing to enter. The rock cracking against the frame was swiftly met by a burst of gunfire that tore into the ground just in front of her. She now knew her target was in the back seat. Pivoting on the balls of her feet, she swung her weapon, but not her body, directly into the back seat. Estimating her point of contact, she pulled the trigger. Her weapon bucked with a quick burst of fire, followed by another. Then she heard a man's agonized moans.

Slowly she rose to a standing a position as she carefully peeked a single eye inside just enough to glimpse at the back seat. She could make out the outline of a man's body leaning back slackly in the seat. The man remained motionless with his carbine half hanging over the seat onto the floor. For good measure she aimed her weapon and fired another burst, hitting him directly in the chest. The body jiggled against the force of the bullets penetrating his chest but, otherwise, he remained motionless.

Satisfied the man in the back seat was dead, she shot the driver the same way. Stepping back from the vehicle she kept her weapon trained on the vehicle, then maneuvered into a position to cover the greater area, occasionally looking backward to ensure no one was sneaking up on her. She caught up with the two Palestinians as they moved back in similar fashion.

They all continued moving — one watching backward while two remained fixed on the area they had just come from. They maintained their positions all the way back across the road. They discovered Imil's body sprawled out on the pavement. A pool of blood had formed across his stomach. The other two Palestinians scooped him up by his arms and feet and carried him the rest of the way.

Using a flashlight, Sauwa signaled the van driver down the road alerting him the battle was over, and they needed extraction. The van hastily sped backward in the direction of the mercenaries from where it had been hidden behind a large dirt mound. It came to a halt several meters shy of where they were. Quickly throwing open the back doors, Sauwa stood protecting the Palestinians as they loaded their dead comrade into the van. She jumped inside right after them and barely had time to shut the doors before the van was peeling off down the road.

Stripping the balaclavas from their faces, Sauwa and her team fell back breathing heavily as they all stared at Imil's body. They may have all been mercenaries and this job was done for pay but, in the end, a comrade in arms was a comrade in arms. It made it even harder knowing they would have to forgo a respectful burial over the necessity to dispose of the body quickly. In truth, they would have left his body on the street to avoid the danger of packing it. But they had to remove it because it would have been dangerous evidence to leave for the police investigation that would soon follow. Their journey back was done in complete silence.

TARKOV and his men jumped onto their rafts. Like before, Gorzo and one of the Palestinians stood rear guard while the others climbed onto the raft. It was made more complicated because the mercenaries had to load their dead and wounded first. Once the battle had subsided, and the remaining enemy had made their escape, Tarkov found they had suffered some serious casualties — three dead and two wounded.

The rafts roared into action, and the mercenaries made their escape. Behind them, the pier was littered with the dead of their adversaries, and the Chin Wu was sinking. The hole left by the limpet mine had devastated the center of the ship leaving a massive tear in the main cargo hold where water was pouring in like a river.

The fishing trawler was waiting when the mercenaries returned. The men were picked up by the ship as it idled along. The sailors quickly helped Tarkov and his men on board, then the ship began picking up speed. A plastic sheet had been laid out for the bodies of the fallen men to prevent any blood or other signs for police to find. It was a difficult action, but the trawler would head far out to sea where the bodies would be disposed of discreetly and respectfully.

30

K ennson Rhys heard about the disaster at the port when he caught the morning news on the small television playing at the corner bakery he had discovered. He had made it his usual haunt for breakfast along with his mates, Yadav and Mehendra. He had just sat down to enjoy his cup of Turkish coffee and honey covered baklava when he saw the image of the port. It was through the angle of an aerial camera shot filming from overhead depicting a large cargo ship overturned in the harbor and half submerged. The report was being given in Greek and the New Zealander wasn't able to get the details. In some cases, he didn't need to.

His men had not yet returned from their mission when he had awakened as the sun was coming up. His initial thought had been that they were held up dealing with the large shipment and that complications might have arisen between the arms broker and Managua, the lawyer. The fact that he had not received any calls on his disposable cell phone told him enough.

Paying his bill, he cut his meal short and returned to the beach house. He had just finished explaining what he had discovered to a semi-lucid Yadav when the remaining Greek mercenaries came bursting through the door. They were flushed and tired from making their escape and safe return while trying to keep from drawing attention to themselves. Rhys listened silently as they explained in greater detail the events that unfolded during the evening in greater detail.

The informal briefing ended with the Greeks withdrawing to their sleeping quarters for showers and fresh clothing, leaving Rhys and Yadav to digest the information. Yadav waited until he was sure they were alone. "With Managua missing or dead, we don't have any point of contact. You have to admit, we're on our own."

The New Zealander stared in an obscure direction and shook his head. "It won't be for long. If Managua escaped, I expect he'll be in contact with us once he has reported to his superiors and received instructions as to what they want us to do next.

"And, if he's dead or in custody?" the Nepali asked.

"Then, expect those same superiors to contact us," Rhys responded. "We'll be their chief operatives for this debacle."

Yadav dropped his head into his hands. "We should fold up our operation right now. Men we have employed for an illegal mission are dead on those docks. A ship with our people crewing it is half sunk in the Cyprus port loaded with illegal military arms. No one in their right mind would suggest we continue hanging around any longer."

"It was all the result of some enemy we still have little knowledge of," Rhys stated with irritation. "Furthermore, as complex as this project is and with the degree of importance certain people attach to it, those we report to may think differently."

The Nepali stood up and began pacing as if he were practicing drill on the parade field. "They would expect us to wait and hear from them."

"It won't be that long, I assure you," Rhys replied looking directly at his comrade. "By sometime tomorrow, we will be contacted with new instructions."

"You seem awfully sure about that," Yadav said incredulously.

"We're dealing with businessmen, not bureaucrats," Rhys explained. "This is business for them, pure and simple. And, like any business situation, they are working to mitigate the problems as quickly as possible. Right now, they're not worried about dead subordinates; they're focused on alleviating fallout and planning their next step. Once they've assessed their assets and losses, their next focus will be a new strategy. In either case, we'll be contacted quickly, because we're the guys on the ground most able to execute whatever action they wish to take."

"Then there is a team?" Yadav said suddenly. "A good portion of our team was lost in this attack. We are facing a larger force than what we've been briefed to expect, and they are certainly skilled operators. We're definitely dealing with professional soldiers — possibly commandos and trained Special Forces types."

"Oh, I'm sure we are," Rhys agreed, "which eliminates our other concerns and has made it clear what game our enemies are playing."

Yadav went on. "Then there is Mehendra. At a time like this, we lost not only a valuable soldier..."

"We lost a friend." Rhys didn't wait for the Nepali to

finish. "What's more, we can't even retrieve his body or the bodies of our other men. We can't be connected to any of this."

Yadav's eyes widened as he began to look around suspiciously. "Do you think this place is possibly compromised?"

Rhys looked back up at him. The Nepali continued. "I mean, the police are going through the clothes on the bodies of our men. Do you think they might have anything on them that will lead back to this house?"

"All the dead men scattered around are from the same ethnicity," Rhys explained. "Many of them belong to our arms trafficker. I think there would be too much confusion for the police to reach a conclusion on anything. The main problem we have would be Mehendra. If he had his passport on him, the police can trace when he entered the country. If they check surveillance footage from that timeframe, they will see him exiting the plane and going through customs with us."

Yadav sank into a nearby chair, looking utterly defeated. "We can't stay Kennson. We're sitting ducks at this point."

"We don't know that," Rhys reacted with a curt tone. "Right now, I don't want to make any hasty moves. I also would like to know who it was who attacked us last night since we might be dealing with them again if our employers decide to force some continuance of this project."

Yadav tapped his fingers anxiously on the arm of his seat. "What about our Greeks upstairs? When they come down, I imagine that after all that has happened a few of them will want to go home. Without a team, we're scrapped."

"If that's what they wish, we'll pay them what we owe them and send them away," Rhys said. "If we're ordered to continue with any of this business, we'll just have to explain the added problem of recruiting another team. I'm positive my friend back in England can furnish replacements. What we should be focused on is the information Managua's people obtained from that woman they intercepted."

"You mean clumsily murdered and made it a spectacle," Yadav quipped snidely.

Rhys ignored the interruption and continued, "They've apparently gone over some of the documents and found something that might be of benefit."

"Oh really," Yadav continued to look skeptical.

"Just before Mehendra left for the port last night, he told me they came across a name that they think may be working for her here in Cyprus. He mentioned a German lawyer by the name of Karl Brukman. He had some people investigate this lawyer and his activities here."

"Another lawyer," Yadav groaned. "Are there any who aren't conducting such business dealings as a side business?"

Rhys again ignored his comrade's remarks. "They discovered that the lawyer had documents of rentals for a couple of warehouses in the city's old port district. What is so interesting is that the rental documents are all under the name of a person who apparently hasn't been alive for several years."

The Nepali perked up, "Go on."

"He was going to go into further detail with me later when we could sit down and plot our next move." Rhys let his eyes wander as his brow furrowed. "I think, in the absence of any other option, we should check these properties out and see what's there."

Yadav took a few deep breaths as he thought the matter over. It was apparent by his facial expression that part of him wanted to pack up and go home or, at the very least, keep a low profile and do nothing that would attract attention. But, there was still the part of him, the soldier, who couldn't overlook the fact that an enemy force had gotten the better of them. In doing so, they had killed their comrades — their brothers in arms. A part of him wasn't going to let that go unanswered. "Let's do it," he replied slowly.

Casein Lorenza was not one to show emotion, at least not when it came to her professional responsibilities. Sitting quietly in the velvet chair provided for the meeting taking place in her hotel penthouse, she listened to the half-dozen well-dressed figures in the room endlessly fret over the news they had received that morning — the news of the Chin Wu's sinking, the carnage at the Soledad port, and the possible death of Theo Kalopolis. Everyone was in a nervous uproar. Casein hated the audacious displays she was witnessing. The needless posturing was nothing more than a gross waste of time. Still, she understood that for some people it couldn't be helped. They needed to engage in dramatic displays and, when it occurred, it was best to let it play out until cooler heads prevailed.

In the meantime, she scrutinized her colleagues and planned how she was going to approach matters. As the daughter of Azio Lorenza, one of the most powerful men in the Philippines, possibly all of Southeast Asia, and the patriarch of the Lorenza family holdings and interests in Europe, it was left to her to lead this group to a favorable resolution. The people arguing were the children of some of the most powerful families in their native country. Handed an important responsibility in this pipeline of weapons from Russia to the guerrillas back home, they saw nothing but a fruitful outcome and great accolades from the elder members of their clans. Everything was set to favor success and a seasoned negotiator to handle the coordination with the arms merchant and keep their hands clean from the more sordid business. One of their top soldiers had been sent in to provide protection once they were alerted about a perceived threat.

Now, they were in the midst of what was turning into a monumental disaster. After nearly an hour of hysterical antics and shouting two notches above a heated conversation, the emotion had died down leaving only two key people dominating the meeting. One was a young woman, in her late twenties looking like she had enjoyed a successful career as a fashion model before venturing into the world of business. The other, a young man who had a thick muscular frame that fit snugly into the expensive tailored suit he wore that was obviously designed to display his chiseled features. Even though neither of them was saying anything moving the group toward a viable resolution, the rest of the meeting attendees were by now too exhausted and shaken to bother interjecting.

It was then that Casein Lorenza found her opportunity. "If I may," she said in a soft but forceful tone that stopped all talking instantly. With a single motion that was both slow and majestic, she rose from her chair and started toward the center of the room. She was not a tall woman, only about four foot ten, yet everyone seemed to look at her as if she were a giant. In her black tailored pantsuit and dark red blouse, she revealed a natural stature and commanding power over everyone. All mouths were closed with no one daring to speak — to do so would be akin to heresy or treason.

"At this point, we need to focus on evaluating our situation." Her accent was deeply English with only a slight hint of her native tongue. The English was from her years abroad in exclusive boarding schools — first in New Zealand and then in England where she finished her primary education. Later, she attended the London School of Economics. Her skin was a creamy mocha color denoting the deeper ethnic lineage of her Spanish roots over the faint amount of Indian blood that occasionally made its way into the family line. Her hair was a silky raven black and was tightly drawn up in a neat roll behind her head. "As it stands, nothing traces directly back to us. We have never had any direct contact with Mr. Managua or his associates. The phone he used to contact us was a pre-paid disposable one that was carried by one of our security men not any of us. For all intents and purposes, we are here for the very reasons we have professed. We are conducting a business summit discussing our holdings in Europe."

"What about the ship?" One of the others spoke up nervously. "The captain will certainly be taken into custody if he didn't die in the attack."

"And?" Casein replied, her eyes widening with a look that questioned why the issue was worth even bringing up. "The captain and the ship are out of Thailand with papers that have them returning to Thailand. He was contacted by people from Manilla that have nothing to do with us. What else is he going to tell the police except for that story? He knows nothing about us or our connection. What we should be focused on is the next step — getting in touch with people back home and apprising them of the latest complication. We'll let them decide if they wish us to continue with this operation."

"What is there to continue?" Another member of the

meeting interrupted hysterically. "Our arms contact has been killed. The police are all over this investigation. We have no arms merchant and, even if we did, the plan was to run the weapons from Cyprus to the Philippines. That is no longer an option."

"You're right," Casein replied. "However, a few days ago, my people in Stockholm were contacted by a Mr. Andre Valikov. He was apparently offering his services as a broker of such wares. His timing was rather *convenient* actually."

"He could have had a hand in instigating this mess," the woman who previously dominated the meeting added.

"Oh, I'm positive he did." Casein's face and manner were completely devoid of any emotion as she spoke indifferently. "In fact, I'm reasonably sure he is the broker who has been supplying our enemies. He made contact with my Stockholm offices only a few short hours ago. Most likely he was anticipating this unfortunate situation."

"And you are actually entertaining the idea of doing business with him?" Another person spoke up.

"Might I remind you that this is business, not ideology? We're not dealing with moral individuals driven by a romantic philosophy, but men motivated purely for monetary gain and little else. In light of our current situation," she looked at her critic, "Mr. Valikov is a well-connected arms merchant, who supplies weapons on a very large scale. What makes him even more interesting is that he has several contacts in the far eastern reaches of the old Soviet Union. His latest message to my people was a reminder of his offer, coupled with the benefit that he has extensive connections with some of the warlords in Myanmar who can help move the weapons more easily through their usual heroin routes. This will eliminate several logistical problems, provide a faster means of transport, and look like just another black-market deal. That will meet our goal while keeping our hands clean."

The room was quiet. The rest of the participants looked at each other with disbelief and uncertainty. No one spoke, to either agree or to challenge Casein. It was exactly the response she had anticipated. Seizing the opportunity, she continued her explanation. "I am flying to Stockholm tonight to meet with Valikov. If he proves capable of meeting our requirements, I will contact Manila and see what they wish to do. In the meantime, our next order of business is to deal with this terrorist threat plaguing us."

She didn't wait to hear opinions. "Mr. Managua is currently missing; the logical answer is that he's dead. We can work with our mercenaries that are still on the ground." She turned her attention to the burly man in the corner standing like a statue. "Kennson Rhys is probably waiting for our phone call. Initiate contact and ask him if he has any leads to finding the shadow force that attacked us last night. If he knows where to find them, he is to retaliate and neutralize the problem at once. I understand that regardless of what we do next, Cyprus is no longer safe for us. Whoever attacked us is still at large and, after last night, emboldened. As long as we don't know where they are, they remain in our blind spot and can strike again wherever we locate our base. We need to retaliate if we can and disabuse them of the idea that we are impotent."

"You seem to be making a lot of decisions and taking the liberty of directing our next move." A man spoke up challenging the way Casein had taken charge. She glanced at him indifferently as she looked about the room as if no one else was there.

"For the last hour, we have been engaged in conversation. All we have been able to discuss is how this will affect the safety of everyone in this room, and how we can protect ourselves. No one has mentioned anything about how we plan to mitigate the dilemma and look after the interests of our clients — the families who have invested a considerable amount in this operation? So, if anyone has any better ideas as to how to proceed to resolve this debacle, by all means, please speak up.

The room went silent. Casein stood over them as if she were a stern headmistress ready to discipline unruly pupils. The rest of the group gradually lowered their eyes and fell back into their seats in submission signifying they would go along with her plan.

The temperament at the warehouse resembled a wake rather than the expected celebration of a successful mission. Amongst Tarkov's mercenary team, there was only silence. No one felt the need for jubilant festivities, cracking open drinks, or rehashing the finer points of the evening. The attitude was somber as everyone sat around eating their breakfast in silence. The sheer exhaustion that had caught up with them after being on such an adrenaline high for so long sent them all crashing into a zombie-like state.

Their lack of spirit was also driven by the loss of their team members. It was hardest on the Palestinians who had served together for a long time before this job and had closely shared comradary. The pain of losing men they had come to know on a very personal level over the last few weeks took a heavy toll on Sauwa and the Europeans as well. It was bad enough to lose comrades even if they were paid mercenaries and not soldiers or rebels fighting explicitly for a country or cause. It was even more painful the bodies couldn't be kept for a proper burial and had to be disposed of at sea. Harder yet was the need to cut their stomachs open and weigh the bodies down before dumping them over the side. Sauwa and her team had hated disposing of Imil's body the same way when they left it in the back of the van and ran it into the bay.

Brukman retained a doctor to patch up their wounded men. Thankfully, the wounds were not life-threatening and could be handled in the warehouse. Still, it was a grim reminder that added to the gloomy atmosphere.

The meal ended with cold bottles of beer being passed around. It was a little something extra Carzona had picked up when he went out to get breakfast for everyone. Like the meal, they too were consumed in silence. After breakfast, Tarkov stood to address everyone. An officer of the Russian navy at heart, he felt the need to deliver some sort of speech remembering those they had lost. It wasn't elegant, but it was sincere and gave everyone what was needed.

They broke to enjoy showers before going to bed. Carzona and Tarkov were left alone to talk. "It was a good operation," Carzona began, a thread of happiness was in his voice.

"Tomorrow, we'll clean any documents pertaining to this operation out the warehouse and dump the remaining weapons into the sea. Then, we'll return to our original headquarters until we can leave," Tarkov added.

The Filipino nodded. "Good. We'll make arrangements to sneak you out of the country and back to Turkey. It isn't safe to stay in this country any longer than we must. What I'm concerned about is if this operation is going to fulfill our primary objective?"

"That is my concern, too," Tarkov replied. "They certainly won't be able to operate out of Cyprus after this.

However, there are plenty of gun merchants in Eastern Europe as well as numerous cities with ports and officials who don't ask questions if the right amount of money falls into their hands. Will this mean you will be calling on my services again?"

Carzona shook his head. "It is too early to tell. Besides, that answer is out of my hands. People above me will decide what is to be done next. Right now, the emphasis should be on covering our tracks and sneaking out of here. Our bigger problem is how much they know about us right now."

Tarkov looked questioningly at the Filipino. Carzona didn't wait for him to speak. "Rita has been murdered."

"When?" The Russian could feel a slight chill run down his spine.

"A few days ago in her apartment here in Europe," Carzona replied. "And, yes, it looks like she was killed by our enemies. I don't have all the details. I was only given a brief update by the person who has replaced her as my support contact."

"If she was killed a few days ago," Tarkov paused rubbing his face and looking around as if a suspect were in the room, "They couldn't possibly have gotten anything of value from her, or they would have been on us by now. They would have been ready for us at the harbor."

Carzona remained stoic, it was a behavior Tarkov was coming to dislike. "We don't know what they were able to get or how detrimental it is to us. It happened only a few days ago in another country. Information isn't just seized and acted upon. It takes time to analyze information and draw a conclusion or find viable pieces over inconsequential documents. It's likely that they didn't have time to analyze it before the operation. Rest assured though, they'll be looking at it thoroughly. And, if they can connect any names or addresses back to Cyprus, and more importantly this city, we can expect they'll act upon it."

"In the wake of all that's going on right now?" Tarkov regarded the Filipino as if he was crazy.

"They have to," Carzona explained. "We have just violently struck at them and severely damaged their operation. If they have any thought of attempting this operation somewhere else, they have to presume we can strike at them just as easily there too. It is incumbent for them to respond to us. It won't be of any strategic value to anyone, but symbolically retaliating would send the message that they can find us just as easily and respond just as lethally. Once we know they can hit us back, people tend to lose their nerve for this sort of action."

"We don't know how many men they have here, or what kind of force we're up against." Tarkov lamented as he began to strategize the next move in his head. Carzona didn't give the Russian time to reply. "When our ship arrives in two days, we are leaving this country. That won't leave them any time to recruit fresh soldiers or operatives, so we can assume they'll likely work with who they already have."

"We're still working with a lot of assumptions based on few facts," Tarkov reminded him.

SAUWA WAITED until the men had finished showering. Though she had received several offers to join them, and modesty was not a trait she practiced, she figured a bunch of sex-starved men who had just come off a mission was not the right time to indulge in liberated behavior, especially since Gorzo had been rather candid about the promise he made to himself when the mission was over — if he survived, he was determined to sleep with her. Trying to make good on this promise would result in severe pain and agony for the Italian.

As a precaution, she asked Sacchini to accompany her. She was certain the sight of the older man following her into the shower room had some of the men speculating and arriving at the most risqué conclusions. Still, she felt comfortable that Sacchini wasn't a young buck looking to seduce her or even say he did. His presence in the room ensured that she could enjoy some degree of privacy while bathing.

He stood by while she slipped off the grimy clothes she was wearing. He was indifferent to being so close to a young naked woman though she could tell he was somewhat uncomfortable in the situation. "I won't be upset if you look at me," she said with no undertones that suggested any sorts of seductive hints. She just didn't want to make the only person who she remotely considered a friend too uncomfortable with the situation.

"Forgive me. I don't wish to appear a prude," he explained. "Being with you feels like I'm in the shower with my teenage daughter."

She slipped off the last vestiges of her clothes. Her long, black hair flowed in silky waves across her shoulders and down her back. Completely naked she walked into the large white tiled shower stall. The warm spray of the water pelted her body as she began to slather her skin with a bar of soap. It was a soothing sensation that she needed after the long night she had endured.

Behind her, Sacchini watched the door. He leaned against

a side wall leading into the locker area. By his blank facial expression and the way he fixed his attention on the door, she was sure he was deep in thought. "What are you thinking about?" She asked as she worked her hands and soap down over her legs.

"After what we just came back from," the Italian stated as if slightly shocked by the question, "what else would I be thinking about?"

Sauwa cracked a smile as her eyes looked upon him suspiciously. "A seasoned soldier such as yourself? I'm sure you have seen far worse in your career than what we encountered last night. Something else is dominating your thoughts."

Sacchini scratched his fingers across the side of his face. "I guess I'm just tired of it all. This world drains you quickly. I imagine you already know that yourself." He turned his head back in her direction. "Maybe, I've just been thinking about what else I would do if it wasn't this."

"And, you decided what?" Sauwa asked, as she stepped under the steaming shower head and allowed the water to flow over her, washing away the soap.

"That is a very good question," he replied half chuckling. "I haven't been a soldier, a commando, for a few decades now. First I was in the Italian military and then a private soldier for hire, but I'm tired of it. In this group of young energetic men, I see myself as an old man with no one even near my age. That's because mercenaries of my generation have either developed the good sense to get out and do something else, or they're dead and buried in some remote part of the world. This leaves me wondering why I am still in this business."

"Why are any of us?" Sauwa replied. "Wars we signed

up to fight in the way they must be fought eventually end. We get trained to fight a specific way, and they want us to approach the enemy. We devote ourselves to honing our skills and bettering ourselves at our particular craft. Then the war ends. When that happens, we go from being indispensable to being embarrassments. We spend time thoroughly training and developing our craft, but it becomes utterly useless to everyone except for those who are somewhere else in the world dealing with their own conflicts and need the skills and experience we have to fight their wars."

"I suppose you're right," the Italian replied with a sigh that was both deep and defeated. "How much the world can change in such a short period of time? However, it's constantly dangerous, always uncertain, and you're never sure when or where your next paycheck will come from. I've been playing against the odds for a long time now."

Sauwa stopped the water and retrieved the towel hanging nearby. "For a man so unmoved by this business, I'm surprised you even considered such a risky endeavor as this operation."

"As I said, this business is uncertain," he continued. "I needed work, and there wasn't anything better being offered at the time. Besides, the money is too good. I'm looking less at the immediate and focused on the future. I want to retire and be done with it. What they're offering to pay me is a good start in the right direction."

She was now, slipping on a fresh pair of underwear and loose fitting tank top. "I hope you enjoy it. As you've said, not many in our line of work get to have such a luxury."

"Promise me something," he turned to face her with a deadpan expression. "Don't let this consume you."

She stopped dressing in order to address his comment.

For a moment she thought he was just making conversation. It was when she stared directly at him, she realized his statement had been intended. "I have no drive to stay in this business. I'm forced to be here," she smiled as she returned to dressing.

"I know you are here for reasons somewhat outside of your control," Sacchini began. "But you, like Tarkov, are too conditioned to do this work for life. Dealing with such dangers comes naturally to both of you."

"I hardly think I'm a natural for any of this," Sauwa replied, not knowing whether to be offended or not. "But, I have seen my fair share of it all."

"No," he shook his head. "The danger doesn't seem to bother you. You seem so comfortable in this murky world of black operations. The way you plan, approach, and even execute is so easy for you. You have a natural ability."

"We all have to survive, and that means using our skills and experience when needed," she replied somewhat defensively. She finished dressing adding a pair of jeans and a fresh shirt. It wasn't the clothing she would have chosen for going to bed, however, given the fact they might have to move fast at any time, she figured expedience outweighed comfort.

She bundled her old clothing into a plastic bag. They had been the clothes she had worn during the operation and were covered with debris and residue that could link her to several murders and serious acts of terrorism. She could never put them on again. Placing them under her arm she waved the Italian toward the door.

Followed by Sacchini she walked into the main room. Outside, the men were quietly eyeing the pair as they left the showers. They said nothing as they watched the alleged couple, but the devilish smirks told her enough. For good measure and to deter any more of Gorzo's fantasies, she reached over and ran her hand gently down Sacchini's arm for all to see.

Several fists raised in a triumphant gesture toward Sacchini. Many of the men watching the action looked at the older man with admiration. She left him to face the questions and adulations he was about to receive. Hopefully, Sacchini would be a good sport and play his part to help with the ruse.

She walked out the door and toward the harbor. Along the way she took a pin and began poking holes into the plastic. Reaching the pier, she gradually looked around to ensure the area was clear. There was a large group of men who had preceded her onto the pier. They paid no attention to the surrounding warehouses when they came by. She was a little concerned they may have attracted an audience.

It being morning, the neighborhood maintained all the signs of the lifelessness she expected based on her previous walks. Satisfied she had no witnesses, she lowered the plastic bag into the water. She held it so the water could enter through the holes. Soon the bag grew heavy. She released her hands to watch it disappear into the water below. In a few days, the seawater would contaminate whatever evidence the police might hope to get from the clothes if they ever found the bag.

32

R hys stood a good distance from the gate that guarded the perimeter of the warehouse and its parking lot. He scrutinized it for a long period of time while he leaned up against the van he had obtained for this outing. By all accounts the warehouse was empty — it showed no signs of life. He looked for the slightest clue of security equipment: surveillance cameras or alarm systems for normal security. Then he checked the more subtle and unusual measures he was expecting to find like makeshift traps and systems innovative thinkers could come up with that would announce the arrival of an assault force.

Scanning carefully, he decided no such measures existed. There weren't even any good places to set them up with all the open space. His people at the port had been hit by professional commandos. The lack of security measures at this warehouse meant they were concerned with maintaining a low profile and not drawing attention to themselves. It also meant they weren't planning on staying in the country long and wanted to leave as small a footprint as possible when they departed.

Rhys was soon joined by a couple of his Greek mercenaries who had walked the surrounding area. As ethnic Greeks, they blended in better and looked more natural walking around than the white New Zealander. They met their commander next to the van parked just out of sight of the warehouse.

"It's clean of any security we can see," said one of the Greeks, a young man with a crop of bushy blond hair who looked like a school athlete. "We didn't see anybody outside, certainly no guards."

"Honestly," the other one began, "the place is wide open. We could easily make it to the door of the warehouse undetected and move on them before they even knew what was going on."

Rhys shook his head. "No, they may not have overt security outside. It's what's inside we aren't sure about. We still don't know what numbers we're up against, let alone what weaponry and internal defenses we'd be walking into. Remember, we're not dealing with street thugs. These guys are professional operators. Knowing they have no way of securing the outside only means they've probably taken more extensive protective measures inside. Based on what they've just accomplished, we have to assume that they're ready for us."

He looked back at the young men. Both looked at him with eagerness and impatience that demanded something be done. To Rhys' surprise and luck, all the Greek mercenaries had opted to stay on and continue the mission. He suspected that while they were interested in getting paid the full sum of their promised wages, their need to get even with the assailants who attacked them and killed their comrades burned deeply in their minds.

"No," Rhys went on. "If we go after these guys we need to get them when they're out in the open." His answer was vague but seemed to satisfy the anxious young men.

Earlier that day, he had received a package from a bike courier from one of the cheap shops that asked few questions and required little paperwork. Just the kind that easily forgot who they were taking from and who they were delivering to. The package contained a new disposable phone with a single number already programmed into it. When he called it, he was met with a voice familiar to him that identified himself as 'Mr. Garcia'. To which, Rhys responded with the name 'Mr. Blue', the code names that the two parties knew to identify each other by.

Mr. Garcia was brief and to the point. He explained that the loss of Mr. Managua now placed him in charge as their man on the ground. He also explained what the decision was from 'The System' leadership and his instructions in regard to what was to be done with these interlopers who had disrupted their operation. Having lost their previous means of obtaining weapons, Rhys was also given a number for a new weapons supplier as well as an account number from which to draw money.

In all honesty, the New Zealander did not like the idea of an operation to retaliate. Cyprus was not the jungles of the Philippines. In the wake of everything that had happened, and the police investigating the situation at the port, he felt now was not the time nor the place for brash actions. With the information they had recovered, his recommendation had been to alert the police to the location of their enemies' hideout and let the authorities do the rest. Mr. Garcia explained that the leadership saw a need for a response — they wanted a strong message sent.

Reluctantly, Rhys did as instructed and began his pursuit of the mysterious terrorists. In truth, his men were eager to avenge their fallen comrades. They were also highly trained professionals who wanted to strike at the enemy for the humiliation of letting them get the drop on them. It was doubtful they would have liked being told the mission was over or, worse, letting the police adjudicate on their behalf. When he told his men that the mission was now to find the enemy and deliver a powerful response, the mood amongst his ex-Legionnaires brightened.

Only Yadav was dismayed at the chosen course of action. He, like Rhys, had been inclined to cut their losses in the wake of all the attention the police were focusing on the event at the port, and the television and radio news reporting was extensive. The need for retribution for the loss of his good friend, Mehendra, did not overshadow his sense as a soldier. Men died in their line of work, and one can't look back when they must press on. For him, revenge was often costly and fruitless. Though the Nepali wanted to leave, his conditioned sense of traditional loyalty made it impossible.

Focusing his attention between the warehouse and the surrounding landscape, the New Zealander still managed to listen to everything his men briefed him on explaining all the relevant points from their recce. The conclusion was that the unknown defenses they might run into inside the fortress-like warehouse made any attempt at an assault futile. And, the wide open spaces surrounding it made trying to mount any long-term ambush impractical. The veteran soldier decided that fighting on such terrain was simply out of the question.

Rhys was now pinning his hopes on Yadav. He had dispatched the ex-Gurka, along with the rest of the men, to observe the other warehouse that was of interest. They were to conduct a recce of the area and see what they could find. He hoped this recce would yield better results than the first warehouse.

YADAV QUIETLY WATCHED from his strategically positioned vantage point. He had found a good observation post on the second floor of a nearby building. The darkness of the occupied room and the office furniture made it easy for him to remain concealed. He had spent a few hours observing the warehouse across the way and the activity around it. For the most part, the warehouse looked empty. It was only the occasional exiting from the side door by a few individuals at a time that alerted anyone that the structure was occupied.

Every so often a couple of people emerged from the drab, grey structure and walked around. Not wanting make a hasty judgment, the Nepali studied the individuals. Their clothes were largely jeans and T-shirts, not the coveralls common to workmen in such facilities. The men were all incredibly fit and athletic looking. The absence of the larger garage doors ever being opened or even the sight of equipment such as forklifts being operated stirred his interests.

He also began to notice their movements. Though appearing to be random, he began to observe a pattern. Two men would emerge from the warehouse at irregular times. They would walk about in a nonchalant manner as if they were just a couple of guys getting some air. However, they would make a complete lap around the entire the parking lot each time. While they were walking, they would make a point of stopping at every point that coincided with a good entry leading to their perimeter. It looked like it was similar to how an enemy might approach if they were intending an assault. These stops were repeated identically by every pair that came out and completed a similar rotation around the structure. He began to wonder if he was looking at a security patrol checking the area.

He also noticed that each time the men carried backpacks over their shoulders. That seemed odd to him until he realized the bags were always thrown over a single shoulder which made it easy to remove quickly for easy access. The bags were also always unzipped no less than halfway. It would be a perfect way to hide weapons from view but access them quickly in the event of trouble.

After watching this relay, Yadav became convinced he had found the ones responsible for attacking the port. He dispatched one of the Greeks back to the other warehouse to alert Rhys and link up with his team. He joined the rest of his men to conduct a more thorough recce of the area and find places they could use to stage an attack. They waited for the current security detail to retreat inside.

His attention was caught by the surprising sight of a young woman coming out the door with a coffee skinned man. Like the others he'd seen, she and the man also walked about the area in a casual manner talking to each other, but they also had their backpacks slung over a single shoulder. It bewildered him to think this young lady was performing guard duty as if she were a soldier. Not wanting to risk attracting their attention, he waited until the duo completed their round and retreated into the warehouse. Then he made his move.

Gathering his team, they made their way through the dark hallway and down the concrete stairs that echoed with every clack of their footsteps. They emerged from the back door on the opposite side of the building that allowed them to avoid their enemies. They walked a block and a half and piled inside a green van they used for transportation. One of the Greeks manned the driver's side and had the engine humming the moment the men opened the doors.

The van was soon coasting down the street. Yadav hated not leaving someone on site to keep watch, but he knew it might be dangerous. None of them were armed and if these were the people who so skillfully attacked the port, then staying too long would certainly lead to discovery. They would come back with a fully armed force.

33

Carzona and Tarkov quietly observed the mercenaries packing the remaining explosives and moving the containers toward the pier where the fishing trawler had waited. Large canvass covers were draped over the boxes of Semtex, hand grenades, and armaments to avoid attracting attention. For good measure, some pieces of fish netting were allowed to dangle from underneath the canvas to give the impression they were simply moving fishing equipment and boat parts.

They had also chosen to move the weapons at a time set to coincide with the fishing schedule to provide even more cover. Luckily, fishing was the best at sunrise which meant the boats were all casting off at the wee hours of early morning. Not only did this schedule provide darkness for the mercenaries, it also gave them a legitimate reason for being out that early. Once far out in the waters, they would dump the munitions over the side just before they lowered their netting and all traces of weaponry would be lost.

There had been heated debate over whether or not to

keep their rifles and some ammunition handy in case they were met by a hostile force. Tarkov feared being caught defenseless by a possible enemy attack. Carzona feared that with the police investigation of the port a top priority, any evidence that linked back to them was too dangerous. Holding onto illegal weapons would be the worst possible thing they could do. He didn't think it likely that the enemy would risk a direct assault and needlessly expose themselves to the danger of alerting the police. Besides, arrangements had been made for them to leave the country the following night. In such a short timeframe, he and Tarkov figured no one would have time to find them let alone plan and organize a decent assault. The subordinates were dismayed that all the weapons were to be dumped.

Moving through the gate, the mercenaries walked the short distance down to the pier to the waiting trawler. It was 0400 hours and the sky was only just beginning to show the slightest signs of brightness. The mercenaries stumbled along the wet uneven ground they had walked on several times before. In the darkness, carrying the equipment, it felt more awkward than usual.

Tarkov thought it necessary to brief them on the situation regarding Rita's death and the possibility that they might have been compromised. This left many in the ranks concerned of possible retaliation. For assurance, many of the mercenaries opted to wear their back packs containing their rifles and a few spare magazines. It was an argument neither Carzona nor Tarkov were willing to have and decided that it was a moot point for now.

Sauwa had been one of the mercenaries who had opted to hold on to her weapon. It had not been an easy choice. Normally, she would have accepted the rational consideration, that the enemy, if they were onto them, would more likely let the police do the work of neutralizing them. However, what bothered her about all of this was that she still knew practically nothing about these nameless figures they were fighting. And, what she did know amounted to how easily they were inclined to employ violence themselves. These were two factors she that did not sit well with her. Her uncle had taught her years ago that in combat rational thinking did not always dominate the decisions made.

She had kept her pack slipped over her shoulder, with the zipper partially undone. In addition, she had sneaked two hand grenades clipped to her belt and covered by the long brown leather jacket she now wore. This was the arsenal she had carried for the last day or so as they went about their cleanup of the warehouse, preparing for their next move to the next one. The team had been divided over the weapons issue with many of the Palestinians wanting to retain their weapons until they had left Cyprus altogether, and a few others, including most of the Europeans agreeing that they should be disposed of quickly.

Nearing the pier, she held the other side of the canvass covered pallet, with one of the Palestinians, a man she had come to know as Ali controlling the other end. She had only spoken to the man a few times and found him to be quite intelligent. He had been a loyal soldier of the elite Palestinian forces fighting Israel. When the Oslo accords were signed creating peace between the Palestine Liberation Organization and the Israeli government, they found no place for him. When his unit Force 17 got absorbed into Arafat's Presidential Security force, he like many others who had been highly involved in military operations against Israel found themselves out of a job. With no other prospects, he took up working as a free-lance soldier. Sauwa felt a relatable sympathy for the man and the rest of his group.

They descended the last few meters over a small mound before stepping onto the large stones and gravel that comprised the beach. As they did, Sauwa looked ahead, found her attention drawn to two men standing off to the side just a short distance away. Their bodies partially obscured by some of the old wood boats dropped up on land. It wasn't out of place to see people around coming from some of the active warehouses and buildings a few blocks over. Yet, these two men caught her attention. They were slipping on rubber raincoats which seemed to send an unnerving jolt down her spine. She didn't want to be paranoid about being concerned over such a trivial matter. However, the longer she watched them, her concern grew as they seemed intent on keeping out of sight behind the boats.

She told herself it was nothing, though she instinctively began to drop one of the straps from her pack off her shoulder. Looking over at Ali, she saw that his attentions were fixed toward the trawler. She wanted to alert him about the two men, yet she didn't want to think that she was raising concern over sheer paranoia.

It was only when he looked back in her direction that she noticed his eyes did not go toward her, but, instead cast over in the direction of the same two men she had been watching. Ali's face registered a look of concern as he looked over at them. He then looked back at her as if trying to catch her attention. As one of the straps of his own backpack slid slowly off his shoulder, their eyes met with the same concerned glance.

The rest of the team was down by the trawler and too far

away to alert. Then, suddenly the quiet exploded with the loud succession of booming sounds that thundered angrily and with enough power to be felt vibrating in the earth under Sauwa and her compatriot. The explosions were quickly followed by the loud curdling screams of men howling into the darkness. The explosions were immediately followed by a hail of loud crackling sound erupting in a wild frenzy. The sound was all too familiar to both of them as the distinct sound of AK-47 gunfire all coming from the location of the trawler.

They turned just enough to see the boat exuding a big cloud of smoke from the bow, with sparks of gunfire flashing about it. On the ship as on the pier, men were crawling about in agony from their wounds. Around them hails of gunfire erupted from a triangular position that caught them from both flanks and pinned down everyone in a terrible crossfire that was intermingled by the continued explosions of grenades being tossed onto the pier and trawler.

Sauwa and Ali dropped the pallet simultaneously and threw their bags around to their front. Dipping into her bag, she pulled the weapon out by throwing the bag off to the side. Releasing the steel shoulder stock from under the weapon she was free to engage. She caught sight of the two raincoated men as they lunged down taking cover behind the boats and lined up their rifles preparing to fire. Not giving them the chance, she raised her weapon and fired a quick burst in their direction. It went high as she saw the wood splinter in the boat just above them. However, it did enough to disrupt the two men, who in the shock of the surprise dropped their weapons as they threw their hands over their heads to shield them.

Seizing the opportunity, she sighted in as best she could

in the limited visibility and began to fire again. This time she felt a force of gunfire next to her and realized that Ali had deployed his weapon and had taken to joining her. Nodding to the Palestinian, Sauwa dropped down to one knee, as she slung her rifle across her back. She reached behind and grabbed one of the grenades. Pulling the pin and releasing the second safety, she hurdled the object in the direction of their assailants. Not waiting, she and Ali ran for the nearest cover and barely made it behind a large pile of wood planks when they heard the rupturing explosion behind them. They rose up from the pile to see a thick cloud of smoke floating from behind the now half-destroyed boats the two coated figures had taken cover. Carefully they started to walk out and saw no movement from the location.

Satisfied after a few minutes that they had killed their threats Sauwa and Ali moved to where the rest of the battle was going on. Most of the mercenaries had been on the pier when the attack was initiated. A handful, however, had been off the pier and had managed to avoid getting caught in the crossfire. She and Ali moved a short distance down the path to find Gorzo, who was taking cover along with a few of the Palestinians.

They were preparing to move up on one of the enemy's positions when they were joined by Sauwa and Ali. Taking a few seconds to analyze the situation they figured that one of the enemy positions was situated just over the berm several meters over and just overlooking the pier. The other was just off behind a large woodpile a good fifty meters away on the other side.

Deciding to split into groups, Sauwa and Ali took two of the other Palestinians to look around and take out the team behind the wood pile while Gorzo and the others circled around and hit the team at the berm. Breaking from their position, Ali took the lead as the group slid back up the pathway and past the boats. They walked by to see the mangled corpses of the two men they had fought.

RHYS LET loose with another burst of fire, while Yadav, hurdled another grenade in the direction of the embattled fishing trawler and the old wood pier next to it. He had seen the bodies of men drop like flies as explosion after explosion tore away at the vessel and the men occupying it. Likewise, the men on the pier laid motionless or crawled about with injuries unable to escape the death trap they were now in.

This was not the best plan. The New Zealander had only a day to recce the area and figure out a better plan. He knew that this area was the best chance he and his force would have for successfully hitting the enemy. To lose this opportunity would mean losing them. When they saw the fishing trawler arrive so early at the deserted location, he figured it was arranged for his enemy. Seizing the chance, he quickly separated his men into three teams. He and Yadav taking the left flank behind a large woodpile, breaking the Greeks into two other teams — one behind a berm on the right and the second behind some old beached boats. The plan was to hit the enemy's rear blocking their escape and ensuring all were trapped within the triangular gunfire.

He had wanted to wait until he had all the mercenaries on board the ship before initiating the attack, that way he had them trapped unable to escape. What few remained and tried to escape would be picked off by the rear team. Unfortunately, not having a lot of time to plan and prepare, their cover was not concealed enough and several of the mercenaries at the pier had taken notice of his men moving behind the berm. That his Greeks got anxious and initiated the attack throwing grenades, which landed on the bow of the ship. Once they went off, he and Yadav quickly followed suit lobbing their own grenades and hailing bursts of fire.

They had managed to pin the mercenaries down in the fire when they heard an explosion erupt from somewhere just behind them. Looking over they saw a huge plume of smoke emerge from the location where the other team had been staged. The half-destroyed boat frame and the lifeless bodies splayed out told the New Zealander what he needed to know. Soon, he was watching as a force of enemy mercenaries moved steadily up the hill and began circling around toward the far end of his position.

Grabbing hold of Yadav's shoulder, he pointed his friend to the encroaching threat of men moving in their direction. Without hesitation, the Nepali, lowered his muzzle as he swung around and moved up to the other side of the woodpile where he had a view to engaging them. Rhys followed up behind his comrade as they both went on to lay down continuous bursts of fire toward the flanking attackers. The enemy mercenaries moved up in a widely dispersed pattern as they took up the far flank of the wood pile. They moved up the slight hill leading from the beach and found cover amidst debris and rocks at a far angle to where Rhys and Yadav were. Though he wanted to use grenades on this aggressing force, both men knew they were in too close proximity to do so.

ALI and his men had dispersed several meters apart from each other as they began laying down controlled fire where every other man fired a quick three to four round burst that kept a continuous fire on the men behind the wood pile while conserving ammunition. They hadn't been able to circle all the way around with all the obstacles that would have bogged them down. However, they were able to apply enough force to keep the two men distracted.

Sauwa had broken off from Ali's team as they were beginning to flank the men at the wood pile. Carefully, she slipped behind an over-turned boat that provided cover until she entered a thicket of overgrown grass that concealed her as she moved slowly around to the front of the wood pile. The white sparks generated from the spray of gunfire had ceased though she could still hear the sound of AK-47 fire going off nearby. That told her that Ali and his men had done their job and diverted the attention of their attackers. Not taking any chances, she still kept her movements slow and calculated as she lowered her hand down in front of her to brush away any dried leaves or other debris that would omit noises that would alert the threat.

After each brush with her hand, she would set her foot precisely in the cleared area. She continued this pattern until she had made it all around to the far side of the wood pile. Drawing her rifle off her back, she brought it into her hands and shoulder as she slid along the last few steps. Peeking around the corner she saw the two men, one, an Asian looking man, lay prostrate on the ground seeking cover behind a thick dirt mound. The other, a white man, was knelt down pressed against the wood of the pile. Both faced with their backs to her, as they fired back at the Palestinians across the way.

Pivoting on the ball of her foot, she moved into a more stable position with one foot forward and stabilizing herself on her opposite knee. With only a small portion of her frame exposed from cover. She raised her weapon and let loose a burst of fire that exploded into the back of the Asian man tearing into his spine and muscle tissue. The man yelled out in terrible agonizing pain until another few shots from her weapon finished him off.

She transitioned to aim in on the other man and found him turned back in her direction. His weapon pointed directly at her, he fired. She barely missed the shots that whizzed past her and splintered the wood as they tore into the pile just inches over her head. Sauwa lost her footing and in a desperate effort to avoid the gunfire, rolled out into the open.

She retrieved her balance and stance just in time to catch the man pivoting in her direction and angling his rifle toward her once more. Drawing her weapon, she fired quickly. Having no time to accurately sight in the shot went off wildly. It cut close to the man, hitting the nearby ground and grazing his skin. It was enough, however, to cause him to drop his rifle and fall back slightly.

Seizing the opportunity, Sauwa raised her weapon in his direction. This time, she situated her weapon until she could look down the barrel properly. At the same time, the man had recovered his composer and regained positive control of his weapon as he turned back to face her. The two were now looking at each other with the cold steely gaze of seasoned killers. Neither moved as their fingers froze on the triggers of their guns, each anticipating the instant response of the other the second the trigger from either weapon was pulled.

The tension was interrupted by the high-pitched howling

sound of police sirens emanating from a distance and steadily growing louder. The shooting from the Palestinians maintained, but Sauwa figured it was only matter of time before they broke and retreated. Slowly the man across from her rose to his feet, his weapon still fixed in her direction he began moving past her. As he did, she kept her focus on him as she pivoted on her knee to keep him within her line of sight. He continued walking until eventually disappearing over a berm leading down toward a patch of shrubbery and into the protective shadows of a nearby building.

At the same time, Sauwa moved back toward the edge of the woodpile and carefully retreated out the way she had come. Linking up with Ali and his men they moved back toward the pier to check on the casualties. Along the way down, they were met by Gorzo and what was left of his team. Which comprised all of two men. Apparently, their adversary had a much better fighting position to defend from and Gorzo had lost quite a few men to an unfortunate storm of grenades being lobbed at them.

With no time to waste they moved down to the pier and began a quick search for survivors. It was a fairly quick search wading through the sea of lifeless corpses that lined the path as they floated onto the wooden porch. The grenades had done their job inflicting dire wounds that ensured a hasty end to most of their old comrades. Those that they did find still breathing were in a condition too bad to assume they would last much longer.

A couple of the Palestinians managed to make it onto the trawler, but the ship was completely destroyed and, like the pier, was a morbid picture of vile carnage. Whoever the grenades were unable to kill, the gunfire did. Walking along the pier, Sauwa, followed closely by Gorzo, came upon the body of Sacchini. His lifeless eyes were staring into nowhere with half his torso ripped from his body. De'vor's eye had been shot out along with the entire back of his head. Carzona, their employer, was a lifeless corpse floating face down in the water.

The sirens were getting louder, and the police would arrive shortly. Everyone dumped their weapons into the water and started to retreat. Just before their departure, Sauwa and Gorzo were caught by the sound of a low, deep moan from somewhere amongst the dead. The two moved back to quickly investigate and found Tarkov lying under a couple of bodies. His body was awash with dark red blood that was nearly black, the sign that vital organs had been hit. He would be dead soon.

"Carzona?" He managed to ask.

Sauwa and Gorzo shook their heads in response to his question.

Tarkov nodded dismally. "We can no longer take the planned route. This trawler was meant to take us out to meet our contact ship. Even so, Carzona was the point of contact for who would be meeting us for the changeup. If he's gone, then this plan is no longer an option."

"We're on our own," Sauwa stated sympathetically. "It won't be the first time."

"There is another option," the Russian said. "How much money have you got left?"

"Most of it," both mercenaries said at once.

Tarkov fought back the pain, as he reached toward the side pocket of his jacket. Unable to retrieve the contents, Sauwa did it for him. It was an envelope stuffed with the Russian's remaining expense money. "Take this," he said. "Outside of the city in the village of Zygi, I made special arrangements with a man." He pointed to a small piece of paper tucked inside the envelope. "For that amount of money, he will smuggle you and the remainder of your team out of the country."

The two mercenaries looked at each other with shock. They went to pick up their commander, but, he waved them off weakly. "I'll be dead soon. If not, then the police will offer better than what you can right now. So go, and don't look back."

Reluctantly Sauwa and Gorzo rose to their feet and started to walk away. The feeling of leaving their former leader did not sit well with either of them. Yet, the sound of the police arriving offered little time for sentimentality as the two followed the direction that the Palestinians had taken. They raced across the field and through one of the buildings where they had trained and practiced in so many times and emerged onto a road leading them away from the police.

Down the street, they caught sight of the Palestinians running well ahead of them. They watched as the tail end of the group ducked down one of the only available side streets. They followed at a quick jog hoping to eventually catch them. They were a short distance from the turn when they heard a barrage of gunfire. Sprinting to the corner, they turned just in time to see the Palestinians being mowed down by men dressed in workman's clothes and carrying sub-machine guns. In the tight confines of the narrow street, there was little room to move and no place to seek cover. That left the unarmed Palestinians at the mercy of the new assailants who moved on them with the tactical proficiency of military professionals. Moving up along both sides of the street in teams of three that ran parallel to each other. They proceeded spraying-controlled burst in a cross-fire pattern that ensured they captured all angles of the street. Those who tried to run were easily hit before they even got close to the outside road.

Sauwa and Gorzo both watched in horror as the last of their team fell to the pavement. Sauwa wanted to do something but she was unarmed and the street before them was a death trap. She watched as the last of her team fell lifeless to the pavement. She felt a hand powerfully grip her arm and yank her. She realized it was Gorzo taking her by the arm as he moved to make their escape. Understanding there was nothing to be done about their comrades now, she allowed her feet to get into the rhythm of her compatriot's as they continued down the main street.

They had only made it a few paces when a dark van approaching from the opposite direction quickly swerved across the street in front of them cutting off their escape. The side door of the vehicle flew open with men dressed like workmen emerging. The men leaped from the van and marched the last few meters toward the mercenaries. Without saying a word one of the men raised his arm in their direction. A loud cannon-like noise thundered in the air. Sauwa felt a warm moist liquid oozing all over her. She looked down and saw Gorzo lying on the street in a thick pool of blood. The back of his head was completely gone.

Realizing this was the end, Sauwa glared back at the men. She breathed deeply as she prepared for the inevitable. "Well?" she said. "I know how it works. Let's get on with it." There was no bitterness or even fear in her voice. Nor was there any sign of it her manner. She looked calmly at the man holding the gun in her direction, accepting her fate as if it were a natural law. She knew she was destined to meet her end on some lonely street. The last sound she heard was the crackling from the gun being discharged.

She felt a sharp pain in her stomach. Shortly after that, her vision became blurred and she could feel herself sinking weakly to her knees. Her last vision was of a lamppost with a black raven sitting atop it looking down on her.

She woke up to blurred vision and a head that was swimming. The feeling of velvet brushed smoothly against her face and arms. It took several minutes before her sight came back into focus. She found herself in a bedroom of some sorts with plush leather furniture, walls lined with wood paneling and a door leading to what looked like a washroom.

Sliding off of what she figured was a bed, she came to her feet and attempted to stand up. She was still groggy, and she had a hard time maintaining her balance. Eventually, she gained enough of her faculties to make for the door. She opened the door and found she was staring down a long narrow corridor. With several doors up both sides of it. She could only assume they were other bedrooms. She stumbled onto the wood flooring and started making her way down the hall.

"Stop!" cried the voice of a woman who enjoyed the ability to reach a deep octave. She turned to see a woman she recognized instantly. A tall, brawny woman with bleach blond hair tied tightly in a bun atop her head marching toward her with the commanding presence of a military general. Olga Vashvili was Valikov's personal assistant who managed his itinerary for his most important affairs.

She marched up to the South African. "I was just coming to check on you." Her voice was cold and abrupt. "Mr. Valikov wished you to join him the second you were awake." The woman towered over Sauwa and used her height to her advantage confronting the South African in a deliberately domineering way. "You can meet him as you are, let's go." She snapped while waving her hand to punctuate her order.

The large spacious room with the long black marble meeting table in the center was an all too familiar sight. Sauwa recognized it instantly. It was the meeting room on Valikov's yacht, the *Cossack*. Her dealings with the yacht were limited having only been on it when it was docked at port and then she was taken straight to the meeting room where her master conducted his work and received visitors of a business nature.

Seated at the far end, enjoying a glass of what she presumed was vodka and a cigar, Andre Valikov cast his attention down at the documents sewn in a disorderly fashion on the table in front of him. Olga wrapped at the door to announce their arrival. Valikov looked up and smiled pleasantly as if it was all an unexpected surprise.

"Aw, Sauwa," he began. "Please come and join me."

A sharp nudge from Olga sent a reluctant Sauwa pacing slowly to the other end of the room. Directed to a chair at the table that sat adjacent to her master, she sank down into the cushion.

"I must thank you for a mission well done," Valikov said as he beamed with fatherly joy. "You performed exactly as I thought you would."

Sauwa's face registered a look of confusion. "What are you talking about? Everyone is dead including our employers."

Valikov's face beamed as he leaned back in his chair and began puffing his coffee-colored Cao brand cigar. Then it came to her. "Carzona and his people were never the clients. It was the other side all along."

The Russian shook his head. "Not all along. I knew about Kalopolis' dealings with this shadowy group and of their little plan to usurp their native government by fomenting mass insurrection in their country before my old friend Tarkov and his brown employers came to me asking for my services. The problem was it was a lucrative contract I wanted, and my competitor had. I knew if I put you on the team going in that you would find a way to engineer his death leaving me free to pursue the contract as well as many others of the late Mr. Kalopolis' previous accounts. With one of the biggest arms traffickers in the region now gone, his former clients are scrambling to find a new source for weaponry. I just happen to be one of the few operations able to meet their orders. This single operation has already garnered me twice the amount of my usual business. And, the best part, my hands are entirely off of it. As far as the world knows, it was vicious Arab terrorists who killed Kalopolis and attacked the Limossal port." He smiled devilishly while he basked in the sensation of his own brilliance.

Sauwa stared at him, completely appalled at what she had just learned. "Tarkov, Sacchini, and the others all died for nothing. You sent us to be slaughtered."

"Oh, no," Valikov waved his hands innocently. "That was all you and those you were up against. I had no hand in what happened there. I just made sure you were able to complete your mission successfully and in the wake of it all, the right people got the blame."

"Right people, blame?" she looked at him puzzled.

"Why do you think I sent Palestinian mercenaries to augment you? Why do you think the mercenaries I initially recommended were those who had long histories working for Arab governments in the Middle-East? Theo Kalopolis has long supplied weaponry to Arab militaries and paramilitaries. When the police identify the bodies, the natural assumption will be that this was all retaliation for a deal gone bad between Mr. Kalopolis and some Arab terrorist group."

Sauwa's eyes suddenly widened as she stared back at the Russian in utter shock. "Then it was your people who killed Gorzo and the rest!"

"At the pier, no," Valikov leaned forward as he shook his head. That was all the work of the enemies of your Philippine employers. My understanding was that their masters wanted to present a show of strength with that retaliation."

"You said it was them at the pier." Sauwa's eyes narrowed as she looked deeply at the Russian. "Then later, those men who killed Gorzo and the Palestinians?"

Valikov smiled and allowed a slight nodding of his head. "That was me. Your activities in Cyprus garnered a lot of attention. Not just from the local police but from several countries who have taken notice of your actions. It was necessary to tie up loose ends. This way, it looks very much like the liquidation of your friends was done by an assault team the Israelis sent to eliminate known Palestinian terrorists. I had previous information about the impending attack and decided it worked in my interest to let it happen. Knowing what additional messiness it was going to create on top of what had already transpired, I couldn't allow any survivors. So, I took the precaution of having some teams on site in case it was necessary to clean up any leftovers. A man was situated in an observation post watching the whole thing. When you ran he merely directed the closest team to your route of egress to cut you off and finish what had been started at the pier."

She couldn't believe her ears. What she was being told sickened her. "Why then am I alive?" she questioned. Her eyes darted from side to side in a state of disbelief.

"Oh, that would have done me no good at all," Valikov chuckled gleefully, highly impressed with himself. "You see, many in the world's intelligence community know Sauwa Catcher. She has no history of working with Arab or Islamic governments or Arab radical groups. You are now known as the assassin of that Iranian military advisor in Bosnia a few years ago. He was also a high-ranking officer in the Qoms forces in the Iranian Revolutionary Guard. It is highly unlikely you would be employed by or would be inclined to work with any group that would have close links to Iran such as the Palestinians do. It is also known to certain intelligence services and other groups that you are frequently employed by me for such missions. If you were among the dead, it would likely spark questions and raise suspicions that might lead back to my door. I can't have that. Besides, you are still quite valuable as an operative. You have no record of actually ever having been in Cyprus so there is nothing that easily connects you to any of this. I would think your demise would be a waste when I have further use for your talents."

"What about Tarkov, your old friend? You set him up," she scowled.

Valikov allowed his face to drop from arrogant satisfaction to one of slight disappointment. "That was lamentable. I will grieve for him. However, business is business and in the end, I helped him complete his mission and he, in turn, helped me achieve my goal. So, I lived up to my end honorably and didn't betray him completely."

Sauwa was speechless, she couldn't find the words to express the anger she was feeling. She didn't have time to before she found herself being scooped up by Olga who speared her out of the room. She was directed down the hall back to her room where she was instructed to shower and dress in more appropriate attire. Olga shut the door behind her leaving the South African alone to digest what she had just learned. She sank onto her bed feeling the air in her lungs as she inhaled and exhaled. Not knowing what else to do, she dropped her face into her pillow as she screamed into it. Her feelings of anger and helplessness hitting her all at once.

I stanbul gleamed brightly under the aura of colored lights, as Valikov's limousine negotiated the narrow roadways that had carried travelers for centuries. After having zigzagged through the maze-like system, the vehicle came to a stop along the edge of the Bosporus Strait, the narrow opening of water that links the Black Sea to the Sea of Marmara and into the Mediterranean. Valikov exited the car, not waiting for his chauffeur to open the door for him.

He was out walking toward the front of the car. Sauwa had already exited the passenger side and was looking at the area. She had been brought on this trip to serve as his personal protection. As he walked past her, she fell in behind him. Though she hated the man, she was well aware of what he held over her, making her the ideal bodyguard.

They entered a neat little restaurant that was small but possessed the elegance of a high-class establishment that catered only to the wealthiest. He was dressed in a tailored grey suit, while she was clad in a pair of jeans, a blue collared shirt, that was unbuttoned at the top, and a brown leather jacket that draped down to her thighs.

By the way they entered, she figured her boss had not only been to this place before, but he had been there many times. She started to head toward the far end the bar where she would look the least out of place and have the best field of vision. She didn't understand why Valikov had not mentioned they were coming to such an upscale establishment and allow her to dress for the occasion.

He stopped her and waved for her to continue following him — a stark departure from his normal routine. Puzzled, she followed him past the main room filled with well-dressed people enjoying their meals with a view of the river outside. None of the staff stopped them as they crossed to a door leading to a back room.

Passing through the doorway, they continued down a hallway past several doors that she could only assume led to private serving rooms for guests who wished to enjoy their seclusion. Two men, who looked to be of the same ethnic lineage as Carzona guarded the door. Without a single word, one of the men opened the door, and they both moved to the side to allow passage.

Inside, they found a small dark-skinned woman, dressed in a black tailored pantsuit, sitting at a large circular table. She was elegant in the way she sat with her legs crossed while she leaned back in her chair. One hand was supporting her chin while the other held a long crystal glass containing what appeared to be Champaign. "Ah, Mr. Valikov, so good to see you." Her accent was of a posh English flavor with hints of some other country added in.

"I have looked forward to this meeting, Senora Lorenza," Valikov said, trying to sound every bit as sophisticated as she. "I would like to present my associate." He turned and waved his arms in Sauwa's direction. "This is Ms. Sauwa Catcher, one of my operatives, and formerly of the South African intelligence service."

Senora Lorenza studied Sauwa as if determining if she were an asset to eventually utilize for herself or a potential female rival. She returned her gaze to the Russian. "Might I also introduce an associate of mine, Mr. Kennson Rhys?" With that introduction, a man emerged from the curtains behind the elegant woman. Sauwa recognized him instantly as the man she had squared off with at the wood-pile on the beach in Cyprus. By the shocked and angered look on his face, he had made the same connection. Neither one moved as their eyes fixed coldly on each other in the same predatory manner as the day they had met in the gun battle.

"Mr. Rhys is formerly of the New Zealand army where he served with the elite Special Air Service unit. Now, he serves as a commander in my father's private army," Lorenza explained.

With pleasantries and introductions concluded, Valikov dropped into a chair next to Sauwa as they commenced discussing the details of their new business arrangement. The whole time, Sauwa and Rhys glared at each other from their corners. Both were ready to move on the other with the slightest provocation. The meeting concluded with both leaders paying respects to one another as Valikov rose to his feet and started out the door.

Rhys could barely contain himself or his need to walk over and strangle the young woman now following her master out the door. He was thwarted by the single raising of Casein Lorenza's arm as she halted him in his tracks.

"Leave it alone Kennson, the war is over," she said in a soft yet commanding voice he found hard to dismiss.

"We lost people in this fight!" he growled bitterly. "And, not just hired guns but our own people. That bitch is responsible. She personally killed Yadav, one of my best friends. I can't let that go."

"And yet, you will," she said with the indifference of a woman indulging a man in his childish temper tantrum. "The war is over, and there is no further need to continue a pointless conflict. Yes, men have died, men who have served my family's interests for quite some time. However, that is the nature of their profession and the risk they're paid to take. Whether they are in the military fighting for the interests of the government or a private one serving the interests of private parties, they still fight solely for the benefit of those interests. It is now no longer in our interest to fight. Let it alone."

"Why did you even have me come here tonight?" Rhys asked in utter exasperation.

Casein Lorenza smiled quaintly. "For the same reason Mr. Valikov brought his professional assassin. To send a quiet message to the other. After the grave inconvenience Valikov's actions cost us, he wanted to make it clear we should not seek retribution later in our arrangement because he has people and the means to cause further inconveniences. Just as I had you here to remind Mr. Valikov that given his propensity toward such mercenary behavior as switching loyalties for a better offer, it is best we cause him to consider that we too can deal with such difficulties and betrayals in a similar way."

Sᴀᴜᴡᴀ ᴇxɪᴛᴇᴅ ᴛʜᴇ ʟɪᴍᴏᴜsɪɴᴇ, a jubilant Valikov leading the way. She ignored his incessant bragging and self-adulation as he walked along the street basking in the success of his new business venture.

She said nothing but decided there was an unmistakable need to keep watch for signs of trouble.

She had been brought here tonight to send a message to Valikov's new client, and in doing so, came face to face with a man she knew as an enemy. A man she had seen up close, who was as cold and dangerous a killer as any she'd come across. A man who would make it his mission to finish her off one day.

Tonight, she had met, up close and personal, Kennson Rhys.

THE PLAYERS

ANDRE VALIKOV—Black market arms dealer living in Cyprus; Former Russian soldier

SAUWA CATCHER (ALIAS MARISA RAMSEY)—Manages arms deals with Valikov's most volatile clients; Former covert operator the Aparthied; betrayed by a Bosnian soldier and handed over to Andre Valikov; loaned to Sergei Tarkov

RED WOLF—Backs up Sauwa on arms deals; Works for Andre Valikov

IVAN GOREV—Works for Andre Valikov; Former diplomat with the Russian foreign ministry, now working for Andre Valikov

Filipino President's Team

COLONIAL CARZONA—Works for Filipino president

Esmeralda Morayo (Rita)—Works with Colonial Carzona; Attorney, specializing in international trade, working for a prestigious law firm in Manilla.

Thorten Ridgeway—Head of investigation firm supplying Morayo with information on, arms dealer, Theo Kalopolis; Former MI-6 as spy master heading up the SIS's office in Italy, then Greece

Sergei Tarkov—Hired by Carzona to lead a team trying to prevent an arms deal orchestrated by the powerful families against the Filipino president; Former Soviet "Special Forces" soldier now out of work due to the collapse of the Soviet Union.

Tarkov's Team

Gino Sacchini—Recruited by Tarkov; Served with the Commando Raggrupamento Subacquei ed Incursori or COMSUBIN

Jacques De'vor—Recruited by Tarkov; With the Fusiliers Commandos de 1'Air, the French Air Commandos, Escadron de Protection et d'Intervention (EPI), a crack unit of commandos with the mission of attacking airfields

Vincenzo Gorzo—Recruited by Tarkov; Formerly with the San Marco Marines

James Musamba—Agent for the Southwest African People's Organization (SWAPO)

"The System's" Team

KENNSON RHYS—Mercenary leader hired by "The System" to protect arms deal coming into Cyprus; Experienced soldier from the New Zealand Special Air Service

KHADGA YADAV—Friend and recruit of Kennson Rhys; Former Gurka soldier

IVENTI MEHENDRA—Friend and recruit of Kennson Rhys; Soldier

JOSE MANAGUA—Recruited by Kennsion Rhys; Handles tricky issues for the elites (The System) in the Philippines; former lawyer

Arms Dealers

THEO KALOPOLIS—Major arms trafficker working with the System

YANNIS PROKOPIS—Second in command to Theo Kalopolis

ACKNOWLEDGMENTS

To Rod, Gloria, Shannon, Bob, Suzi, and Arne for their time reading and editing, and to Shayne at *Wicked Good Book Covers* for the fantastic cover image.

My sincerest thanks.

ABOUT THE AUTHOR

J.E. Higgins is a former soldier who spent twelve years in the US military, first as infantryman in the Marine Corps and then in the military police with the Army. He holds a B.A. in Government and a Masters in Intelligence; intelligence operations.

Cyprus Rage is his fourth book.

You can reach J.E. Higgins at his website: www.thehigginsreport.com where he publishes monthly papers on international political trends.